"TERRY
AS A LITE
—*Toronto Star*

Praise for Terry McMillan and her novels

Disappearing Acts

...ll of momentum . . . a pleasurable, often moving novel."
—*The New York Times Book Review*

...eautiful and easy to get lost in."   —*Cosmopolitan*

"Gripping and moving . . . intensely realistic . . . Terry McMillan
demonstrates one of the fiction writer's most impressive skills:
the ability to create and inhabit very different characters with
absolute authenticity."   —*The Cleveland Plain Dealer*

"With *Disappearing Acts,* McMillan firmly places herself in
the same league with other acclaimed black female writers
such as Alice Walker, Toni Morrison, Gloria Naylor, and . . .
Zora Neale Hurston."   —*Pittsburgh Post-Gazette*

"An abundance of flash and energy . . . a gritty slice of life . . . .
an edifying experience."   —*Publishers Weekly*

"An authentic portrayal . . . with a wholesome freshness . . .
speaks not harshly of one sex, but honestly of an often-
strained bond between men and women—love."
—*The Baltimore Morning Sun*

"Wonderful. . . . The talk is frank, but the emotions underneath the story . . . strike honest chords throughout."
—*The Dallas Morning News*

"McMillan has her own voice and her own stories to tell. . . .
McMillan gives us ordinary people discovering what love is
and what it requires. . . . *Disappearing Acts* is wonderful."
—*The Seattle Times*

continued . . .

"A glorious novel. . . . A moving tapestry of familial lov
redemption, *A Day Late and a Dollar Short* transported m
Terry McMillan's fictional world and, like the best fi
helped illuminate the corners of my own heart. [It] dar
not to laugh, cry, and shout upon recognizing this glitt
complicated portrayal of African-American life."

—*The Washington*

"Reading *A Day Late and a Dollar Short*, you may . . . head
the freezer for a pint of Häagen-Dazs to complete your se
indulgent bliss. By the last pages you're weeping. You're laugh
ing. You're hooked. It's oh-so-good."   —*Chicago Tribune*

"A delicious family saga . . . poignant yet hilarious. McMillan
has an uncanny ability to render family conflict with both
humor and compassion. In *A Day Late and a Dollar Short* her
skill is honed to a razor-sharp edge. . . . An affecting and life-
affirming read . . . [which] constantly surprises as it enlightens.
A triumph."   —*Los Angeles Times*

"Moving and memorable."

—*The New York Times Book Review*

"McMillan's slam dunk of a novel should nail cheers from her
longtime fans and fill the rafters with delighted new ones. This
book is a gift."   —*Newsday*

"A touching and funny portrait."   —*People*

"A moving and true depiction of an American family, driven
apart and bound together by the real stuff of life: love, loss,
grief, infidelity, addiction, pregnancy, forgiveness, and the
IRS."   —*Publishers Weekly*

"Nobody does it better . . . sassy, inventive, humorous, and wise.
She can make me laugh out loud, but she is just as capable of moving me to tears. As in *Waiting to Exhale*, *A Day Late and a Dollar Short* embodies McMillan's belief in romantic love as the most
profound expression of one's humanity."   —*The Toronto Star*

How Stella Got Her Groove Back

"A cast of likable characters, funny lines, smart repartee, and a warm . . . ending. Irreverent, mischievous, diverting . . . will make you laugh out loud."
— *The New York Times Book Review*

"Terry McMillan is the only novelist I have ever read who makes me glad to be a woman."
— *The Washington Post Book World*

"Rich in detail . . . leaves you feeling like you've just had a gossip with your best girlfriend."   — *Mademoiselle*

"A down-and-dirty, romantic, and brave story told to you by this smart, good-hearted woman as if she were your best friend."   — *Newsday*

"A liberating love story . . . tells women it's okay to let go, follow your heart, take a chance, and fall in love."
— *The Orlando Sentinel*

Waiting to Exhale

"With relationships between African-American men and women in the spotlight as never before, here comes McMillan's report from the front . . . bawdy, vibrant, deliciously readable. A novel that hits so many exposed nerves is sure to be a conversation piece. It has heart and pizzazz and even, yes, the sweet smell of a breakthrough book."   — *Kirkus Reviews*

Also by Terry McMillan

Mama

*Breaking Ice: An Anthology of Contemporary
African-American Fiction* (editor)

Waiting to Exhale

How Stella Got Her Groove Back

A Day Late and a Dollar Short

The Interruption of Everything

Getting to Happy

Who Asked You?

I Almost Forgot About You

It's Not All Downhill From Here

DISAPPEARING
ACTS

TERRY McMILLAN

BERKLEY
New York

BERKLEY
An imprint of Penguin Random House LLC
penguinrandomhouse.com

Copyright © 1989 by Terry McMillan
Previously published in Viking, Signet, and Washington Square Press editions.
A portion of this book first appeared in *Esquire* as "Men Who Are Good with Their Hands."
Penguin Random House supports copyright. Copyright fuels creativity, encourages
diverse voices, promotes free speech, and creates a vibrant culture. Thank you for buying
an authorized edition of this book and for complying with copyright laws by not
reproducing, scanning, or distributing any part of it in any form without permission.
You are supporting writers and allowing Penguin Random House to continue to publish
books for every reader.

BERKLEY and the BERKLEY & B colophon are registered trademarks of Penguin
Random House LLC.

Grateful acknowledgment is made for permission to reprint excerpts from the following
copyrighted works: "You've Changed" by Carl Fischer and Bill Carey. Copyright © 1942,
1943, 1947 by Melody Lane Publications, Inc.; copyright renewed. International copyright
secured. All rights reserved. Used by permission, "I Try" by Angelo Bofill. Copyright ©
1974 by Purple Bull Music (BMI). All rights reserved. Used by permission.

ISBN: 9780451209139

The Library of Congress has catalogued the Viking hardcover edition of this title as follows:
McMillan, Terry.
Disappearing acts / Terry McMillan.
   p. cm.
ISBN 0-670-82461-5
   I. Title
PS3563.C3868D57 1989
813'.54—dc19 88-40412

New American Library trade paperback edition / January 2005
Berkley trade paperback edition / March 2022

Printed in the United States of America
ScoutAutomatedPrintCode

For Solomon, years from now

. . . You say it's good we love again. The acts
the houses, the abyss vary insignificantly
Only plants grow by specific will
"implacable," but without knowledge when they fail.

—The Field for Blue Corn
Mei-mei Berssenbrugge

I am grateful to the National Endowment for the Arts and the Rockland Center for the Arts for their financial assistance; Gilbert H. Banks of Harlem Fight Back, Ralph C. Thomas III of the National Association of Minority Contractors, and Myron Lampkin for their technical advice; Tilly Warnock, Marie Brown, Doris Austin, Debbie Gadlin, and Dr. William Cleveland; my sister, Vicky Zenno; my agent, Molly Friedrich; and my editor, Dawn Seferian, each of whose support helped make the writing of this book possible.

FRANKLIN

All I can say is this. I'm tired of women. Black women in particular, 'cause that's about all I ever deal with. Maybe a fine Puerto Rican here and there, but not much. They're all the same, that's for damn sure. Want all your time and energy. Want the world to revolve around them. Once you give 'em some good lovin', they go crazy. Start hearing wedding bells. Start thinking about babies. And want you to meet their damn family. They make you come and you'd swear they struck gold or somethin'. And the prettier they are, the more they want. Well, I don't play that shit no more. I try to make it clear from jump street. I ain't serious. I got enough on my mind right now without getting all hung up and twisted up with another woman.

Every time I turned around, my phone was ring-ing off the damn hook. "Hi, Franklin," one would say. And I would sit there and try to guess which one it was. "Whatcha doing?" What a stupid-ass question to call somebody up and ask. It oughta be obvious that I wasn't thinking about her, or else I'da called her, right? But naw. It don't work like that. They hedge. "You feel like some company?" And don't say, "No, I'm busy." All hell'll break loose then. "You got somebody over there?" I wanna say, "None of your fuckin' business," but that would be too cold-blooded. They wanna know what you doing every fuckin' minute of the day you ain't with them. Can't just be by yourself. They always think if you don't wanna see them, then it's gotta be another woman.

And I've been out with some of the stupidest women. I swear. Usually don't find this out until after I've fucked 'em. What was her name? Gloria. Yeah, Gloria. This chick had a ass like butter, moved like a roller coaster, but when it came to brains, she was missing about sixteen cards. Worked at the welfare department, but she shoulda been a case herself. I shoulda known better when all she talked about was getting her nails done and was forever blowdrying her fuckin' hair. She couldn't even figure out the easiest puzzle on Wheel of Fortune. I remember one night we'd had a pretty serious session, and I had to go to work in the morning, but since it was election day—Koch was running again for mayor—I got up extra early so I could go vote. I looked down at her. "You voting today?" I asked. "I ain't voted in years, Franklin," she said, just grinning and shit, like she was proud. You stupid bitch, I wanted to say, but I didn't. It wasn't worth it. "You gotta go," I said. "Now." She acted like her feelings was hurt, but I didn't care.

And all this complaining women do about men not knowing how to "make love" is a bunch of crap. A lot of 'em don't like foreplay and just wanna get fucked. Ten minutes after our clothes is off, and a few kisses later, some of 'em begged me to just go ahead and put it in. Personally, I like to take my time. If all I wanted was some pussy, I could buy some. If I like the woman, I wanna enjoy the whole experience. Coming ain't everything. Naw, I take that shit back. But it's a whole lotta women out here who don't know nothin' about passion. They do the same shit them how-to and self-help books and Cosmopolitan magazine tell 'em to do, but a man can tell when a woman's heart ain't in her moves. The shit feel rehearsed, like she do the same thing the same way with every man she ever been with. This kind of fucking is boring—which is when I usually just take the pussy and run.

One chick, I liked her a lot. Her name was Theresa, and she hated it when you called her Terri. Now, Theresa had something on the ball. Worked at a bank, and not only could she cook her ass off but she liked sports. We used to lay around all day on a Saturday or Sunday and just make love during halftime and watch every game that came on TV. She knew a call when she heard one too. And she gave the best head I ever had in my life. I don't know who taught her, but I wished he'd give lessons to a lot more of 'em. The only thing about Theresa was she wore a wig and I couldn't stand to hear her talk. She had this squeaky-ass voice that drove me nuts. It was real high like Alvin and the Chipmunks or something. Sometimes I wanted to say, Would you just shut up! And when the girl came, I swear to God, it was embarrassing. I don't remember what happened to her, to tell the truth. She just faded *out the picture, just like Karen and Maria and Sandy and Amina and all the rest of 'em. All except Pauline.*

Pauline. Now that woman. She was the last one. The one that broke my heart. Don't never fail. The one you always want is the one that always leave. Pauline was soft and sexy. She had the prettiest titties in the world. They was round and full and stood straight out. She was the only woman I ever met that could come from just me licking 'em. Pauline was a hundred percent grade-A woman. Lived in the projects with her two-year-old son. Treated me like a whole man. She was going to secretarial school so she could get off welfare. That's one thing I really liked about her. She tried. And Pauline had pride. She never called me, it was always me doing the calling, and I didn't mind. Some women you just want, ain't satisfied till you get 'em. Don't ask me what happened, but a few weeks ago when I called, she said she was busy. Busy? I let it go. The next day, I called back. She still busy. "What the fuck is going on?" I asked her. She didn't say nothin' for a minute. My chest was heaving. "Pauline, don't play with me." Then I heard her mumble something like, "I met somebody else." Met somebody else? What? Who? I heard her say some shit like she was sorry, but I just hung up the damn phone. A man don't need this kinda shit. What kinda dude could she possibly have found that could make her feel better than me? I hate this shit. I wanted to marry this woman. To tell the truth, my head was all fucked up, 'cause I kept sitting around wondering who the fuck it could be. And what he was doing for her that I wasn't doing. Didn't do. I kept drawing a blank, 'cause when I love a woman, I try to treat her like she's the only woman in the world. Sometimes, I guess, that ain't enough.

That's when I decided to take a vacation from all of 'em. They think they're the only ones who can go without sex. Well, that's a lie. A man's mind is about the strongest thing he got going for him. Let women tell it, you'd swear our brains was all in the head of our dicks. Sometimes this shit is true, but right now I'm trying to get my constitution together. I've made too many stupid mistakes, too many bad decisions. I guess dropping outta high school was the biggest one. I ain't never liked people telling me what to do. I couldn't sit still for another two years, listening to that boring shit about America and how to write a fuckin' sentence. Couldn't just learn to add, subtract, and multiply. Naw. They had to make the shit even more confusing. But woodshop. Didn't miss a class.

This was just one more reason for my Moms to despise me. She started with my Pops and worked her way down to me. But he's so damn henpecked, I still don't know how he feel about me, really. To tell the truth, I ain't never been all that crazy about them either. But when you're sixteen years old and already six foot two, ain't much they can tell you. My Moms would lay it on thick, just running her fuckin' mouth to hear herself talk. "You gon' end up with a bullet hole in you, boy. You stupid, just like that sister of yours. Y'all shoulda been twins. Can't do nothing right. Nothing. Sit up straight. Naw, just get outta my face. Make me wanna shoot

*you my damn self." Pops usually stood in the back-
ground, pretending like he was doing something
else, like he didn't hear nothin'. He always ended
up in the pantry, where he kept his scotch. But
there was only so many more stupids I was gon' be.
One day I was gon' punch her damn lights out.*

*So I did what I wanted to do anyway. Shot dope.
Played hooky. Fucked whatever was pretty and was
willing to give it up. It took me fifteen years to get
my GED. But I got it. Didn't take me that long to
give up dope. That shit got old. Had to scramble
for it. Five nights in jail once, and that was enough
for my ass. It wasn't the kind of life I pictured for
myself, that's for damn sure. Neither was marrying
Pam when I wasn't nothin' but twenty years old.
She was so fine and so sweet, I couldn't get past it.
Everybody warned me. "Leave them West Indian
women alone, man." She was from Jamaica. Two
babies later, Pam was a different woman. Fat as
hell. Never felt like making love no more; we
stopped that after Derek was born, and by the time
Miles got here, we wasn't doing nothin' but screw-
ing. I was working two jobs. Post office at night,
construction during the day. She took care the
kids, I busted my ass. And what kinda thanks did I
get? "I'm too tired." She was just too damn fat.
Pam's thighs felt like blubber, her waist looked like
a old inner tube, and what used to be firm full
breasts that I loved to suck and massage, shit, now
they fell down flat and limp on top of that gut. It
got to the point that I didn't want her, couldn't
stand the thought of touching her. The only thing
she had energy for was them damn soap operas.*

*And food. It took me three years to leave, 'cause the
kids was growing up and wasn't going nowhere no
time soon. But a man's gotta do what a man's gotta
do. This was about my sanity.*

*That was six years ago. Never did get the divorce.
I'm waiting for her to do it. She waiting for me. I
see the kids once in a while, but don't want 'em to
see me like this. Living in a rooming house with a
whole bunch of other dudes. But all I need right
now is a room. I ain't no woman. Ain't no interior
decorator neither. What I got is what I need. A bed,
a dresser, a TV, a worktable for my woodworking,
my fish tank, and my music box. I can't see spending my whole damn check on no rent, 'specially
since some weeks I don't get no work.*

*Now, the dudes that live in this rooming house is
real losers. Some of 'em been put out, some of 'em
got a habit, some of 'em just fuckin' lazy—wouldn't
work if you gave 'em a job. The rest of 'em just lost,
don't know what else the fuck to do. Grown men on
welfare. Now, that's some ridiculous shit. I ain't
nothin' like 'em. And they know it. I've got definite
plans for my life. They ain't crystal clear to me
right now, but that's why I'm working on my constitution. A man needs one. Needs to get his prior-
ities straight. Right now it don't feel like I got no
foundation. I feel more like Sheetrock. Like mor-
tar. Can't nothin' make your life work if you ain't
the architect. Took me long enough to realize this
shit.*

*My life is pretty simple. I like to get drunk on
Friday nights, but only if I worked a full week. No
pay, no play. Usually go to the bar, but I don't so-*

cialize too tough with none of these dudes in here. They ask too many damn questions, just like women. Wanna know your whole damn history. But I don't give up no information. "You got a lady, man?" I look at 'em like they faggots and say, "Why?" Nosy motherfuckers. "You got any sisters?" I got two, but I'll be damned if I'd introduce Darlene to these losers. Christine is married, which is where she should be. "Naw, I ain't got no sisters. Why?" They look like they ready to run, and then say, "I was just wondering, man. That's all."

On the weekends, I like to sit in here and watch whatever game or fights is on TV and do some woodworking. Pussy don't even cross my mind when I got a piece of wood in my hand. Get myself a bottle and stay up all night chiseling, measuring, sanding, making a scale model—don't make me no difference. You tell me what you want, and I can build it. Beds, couches, lamps, tables, wall units. And the more complicated the shit is, the more I put into it. Ain't nothin' like a challenge, especially when it turns out prettier than you expected.

But I'm slow. I like to take my time and not rush when I'm working on a piece, which is one reason I don't make big pieces for people no more. They started bugging me, wanting me to hurry up and finish it. Christmas was coming up—something. How can you hurry up when you trying to create a work of art? If the shit turned out fucked up, then I'd have to hear that shit—"I paid all that money for this?" These days, I make what I feel like making for anybody I feel like making it for. Mostly myself.

At least three days a week I work out at the gym.

Hell, working construction, I can't afford to get flabby and outta shape. Naw, it's more to it than that. I love my body and wanna keep it that way. Faggots seem to love looking at it too. A six-foot-four jet-black handsome niggah? Get the fuck outta here. I swear, I would get so much satisfaction outta whopping one of 'em in the face if they was to so much as say a word to me. But they ain't crazy. Sometimes, just to fuck with 'em, I swing my dick when I'm in the shower. But seriously, the gym is kinda like my sanctuary. I go in there and pump iron, flex, and sweat. Love to sweat. Play a few rounds of racquetball or basketball, then put on some shaving cream and sit in the steam room for about a half hour. Skin feel like satin, and the razor just slide right over it. Don't get no bumps. I feel clean inside and out when I'm done with my routine. Then I lay down and take a nap for about a hour. Shit, you can't beat it.

Only problem is afterwards I always feel like fuckin'. But just the thought of walking to the phone booth to call up some chick and talk shit for a few minutes takes most of the desire away. I got my phone turned off after Pauline, so nobody would bother me. The truth is I wish I could just stop by the corner store and say to Muhammed, "Let me have five cans of some instant pussy." Sometimes all I need is to get fucked. I don't wanna have to talk, lie, or bullshit, just come, roll over, smoke a cigarette, and watch TV. Some women fall for this shit, depending on how bad they want you, which just means it's been a long time since they had some or they just curious as hell if what they see is as good as it looks. I could just tell 'em that it is. But some of 'em wanna be more than just wham-bam-thank-you-ma'amed. So I try not to give it to 'em too good, 'cause they wouldn't never wanna go home.

Basically, I guess I'm a loner. Ain't got too many friends. Ain't too many people worth trusting. Jimmy, a dude I grew up with, stops by every now and then to borrow a few dollars. I don't never have to worry about catching up on nothin', cause all Jimmy do is deal dope. Cocaine. He's small-time, thinks he's big-time, but he ain't, 'cause if he was, he wouldn't have to borrow no money from me, would have a permanent address and drive something besides them curled-over Stacy-Adams he wears. He don't offer me none of that shit, 'cause he know, as far back as we go, I don't wanna be around nothin' that even smell like dope. Gimme the damn creeps. Make me think about jail. Me and Jimmy both almost OD'd once. We was some stupid motherfuckers. We was—what? Nineteen? At the dope house, of all fuckin' places. The shit was better than we thought it was, and in those days we was greedy as hell. We decided we was gon' get blasted and then play strip poker with some chicks we had picked up at a party. Shit. If it wasn't for them chicks, we'd both be dead. Jimmy's a stupid little fat fuck, but he's still my homeboy.

Lucky is the only dude in this building that I do associate with. He's also the only male nurse I ever met in my life, and he ain't no faggot either. Mother-fucker always in white. Work the midnight shift at some old folks' home. We play cards. Spades.

Poker. Sometimes dominoes. Lucky is smart as hell too. He reads everything, which is why we get into some heavy debates. Like the shit that's going on in the Middle East and Nicaragua, should Jesse Jackson run for President in '84 or not. That kinda shit. I like being around people who think. Who read the damn paper every day and know what's going on in the world. Lucky's biggest problem is that he lives at the track. Horses is his middle name. When he gets off work, he'll catch two buses, four trains, whatever's running, to get to the track. I hate to take his money, but hell, when you play and lose, you lose and pay. "You can suck my dick, little girl," he always say when he losing. I just laugh and say, "Put on some more music, motherfucker, go get some Kleenex, and stop crying." Lucky's got a helluva music collection too. I mean serious. That's another reason I like to sit in his room. Shit. Get us a bottle, order some Chinese food, debate about damn near anything that come on the news, and listen to Herbie Hancock or Cole Porter in the background. You can't beat it.

And I play my music loud as hell, 'cause that's how I like it. Once in a while one of these dudes'll knock on my door to complain. "Say, man, would you mind turning it down a taste?" If I'm drinking bourbon, doing some woodworking, I'll say, "Maybe," or just ignore 'em. They don't fuck with me either. Maybe it's 'cause I am six four and weigh 215. I don't know.

Shit, I'd crack up without my music. It's the best company you can have, really. It don't say "no" or "maybe," or ask no questions. Don't want nothin'

*in return except your open ears. And sometimes
the words seem like they was written for you. Side
Effect. Aretha. Gladys. Smokey, and L.T.D. If I'm
in a good mood and ain't doing nothin' in particular but, say, putting up my work clothes or just
playing with my dick and reading the paper, and
one of these dudes knock on the door, I'll usually
say, "No sweat, man." They probably think I'm a
schizoid or something.*

*I do know I can be a pain in the ass, but that's my
nature. I just like to test people, see what they made
of, where they coming from. I got discharged from
the navy because of my temper, lack of coopera-
tion. Couldn't carry out, let alone follow, orders.
And didn't give a shit. Didn't wanna go in the first
damn place. A black man got enough wars to fight
at home. When they said "draft" and they meant
army, I said, "Not me." Let me go somewhere
halfway exciting. Submarines and ships and shit.
Everybody thought it would do me some good. But
how can taking orders from the white man, killing
people that ain't never done nothing to me personally, do me some fuckin' good? It took me two
years to get out.*

*My whole family disowned me. If I was white, I
probably woulda been disinherited. My Moms said,
"You's just lost, boy, always was, always will be. Why
don't you just go somewhere far away and leave us
alone?" The bitch. And my Pops. I don't know the
right word to describe him. Weak. That's close
enough. "You could've had a future if you'd have
followed the rules, son. That's all it takes to make it
in this world, playing by the rules." Yeah, right.*

Look how far it got you, I wanted to say. A fuckin'
sanitation worker. His dream in life. Shit, I didn't
get no dishonorable, just a general discharge. I can
still get some of the fuckin' benefits. And Chris-
tine, she's a year older than me. The perfect word
for her is dumb. Just plain old dumb. How she
graduated from high school I'll never know. My
folks worship Christine, and you'd swear she was
the only child they ever had. That's 'cause she'll lick
the ground they walk on. "You got too much anger
in you, Franklin. That's your biggest problem," she
said. "You're hostile and don't know what the
words cooperate or compromise mean. Why you so
mad at everybody?" She don't even know me.
Maybe if I was high yellow like she was and didn't
never have to worry about dealing with white folks,
scarin' 'em half to death 'cause I'm so big and
black, I would be happy as a little fuckin' lark too.
That's what it boiled down to. Color.

Me and Darlene was the black sheep in the fam-
ily. Took after my Pops, and we got treated like
black sheep too. Even now, Christine live right
across the street from Moms and Pops in a Leave It
to Beaver house with her Father Knows Best hus-
band and four Brady Bunch kids. In dull-ass Staten
Island. And Darlene: "If you'da just made it
through high school, Franklin, you could be play-
ing for the Knicks. They've got hardship cases, and
you know it. You wouldn't have had to go to col-
lege. Could be making bookoo cash right now."
She pissed me off. Thinks just like everybody else in
America. Why is it that if you happen to be black
and over six feet tall, everybody thinks you sup-

posed to play basketball or football? But I let Darlene off the hook, 'cause she's as nutty as a fruitcake, thanks to my parents. She change jobs like some people change their clothes. Don't know whether she's coming or going. She ain't never got no man. Living up in the Bronx, drinking herself to death. She don't think nobody know it, but I know it.

I ain't seen none of 'em in almost a year, and that's just the way I like it, really. All except for Darlene. I worry about her. Every now and then I'll call her, just to make sure she still alive. She already tried to kill herself once. And you think my folks would go up there and see her?

All they ever wanted from us was to go along with their program, which meant don't never disagree with them about nothin'. Shit, they forgot that kids had opinions too. And it ain't no secret that they had it in for me from jump street. All they ever felt for me was disappointment. Not love. And me being their only son, you'd think they'd be more understanding. Shit. That would be too much like right. They would love to see me drive up in a brand-new car, walk in their house wearing a suit and tie, flashing credit cards and proving to them that I didn't turn out to be the fuck-up they thought I would. But even if I ever got to that point, I wouldn't give 'em the satisfaction of knowing it, since they never gave me none.

But time can do some wild shit to your mind. For one thing, it can put you in check. Make you stop and realize on your thirty-second birthday that your life is going down the fuckin' drain. That

you ain't moving. Ain't headed nowhere in particular. You're drifting, pretending like you on your
way but you don't know where. And when you sit in
a tiny-ass room, smoking one Newport after another, playing solitaire with a bottle of bourbon,
looking across the room at a piece of wood that
could turn out to be a beautiful piece of furniture—
and you know what you're doing is good but don't
know what to do about it or where to go from here—
you sorta get scared. And who you supposed to tell?
A man don't run around telling everybody that he's
scared. Especially when he don't know what the
fuck he's scared of. And for some reason, don't
nobody seem to think that Franklin Swift should be
scared of nothing.

But time scares me.

It feels like it's running out. Like I gotta go
ahead and make a move. A big move. Hell, something drastic. And if the white man would give a
black man a break, maybe I could get in the fuckin'
union once and for all. Making fourteen to seventeen dollars a hour. They tearing down and putting
up new buildings everywhere you look in Brooklyn.
Italians'll renovate anything for a dollar. But be
black and try to get in the damn union, and what do
they do? Lay your black ass off right before the cutoff date, or wanna pay you hush money or go-
home-and-don't-show-up money—anything to
stop from paying you union scale. And who can afford the fuckin' dues when they paying you six or
seven bucks a hour? So yeah, I'm still a laboror. If
I can get in a few weeks of steady work at a little
higher than slave wages, I could join. They give us

thirty days to do it. Shit, I could buy a decent car. Be outta this dingy-ass room. I could afford a one-bedroom apartment then. Send the kids more money. Let 'em spend the night. Take 'em to Coney Island. The movies. Shit, I don't need much.

And even though this is 1982, the white man still love to see black men lift that barge and tote that fuckin' bale. If I didn't do nothin' but sit around here all day like some of these dudes, then they'd call me a shiftless, lazy, no-good niggah. Almost beg the motherfuckers for a job, and they still feel so threatened they gotta send your ass home.

But a man gets tired of begging. After a while, you feel butt naked, stripped of anything that look like pride. And they love that shit. Which is why I resent every fuckin' brick I pick up, every wheelbarrow I push, all the mud I sling, every wall I've ever put up or torn down, and one day I would love to just say, "Fuck you."

But I made the bed, now I'm laying in it.

Which is why I'm looking into night school. I can't work construction for the rest of my damn life. Muscles wear out. The mind act like it wanna follow. And outta all the things I may be, stupid ain't one of 'em. One day I'd like to start my own business. Be my own man. Give the damn orders instead of taking 'em. Have some money in my pocket and money in the fuckin' bank. That's what it's all about. Ain't it?

Ask Pam. Before I got my phone turned off, she used to bug the shit outta me for money. She was worse than a bill collector. It was humiliating as hell

*to tell her I didn't never have none. Sometimes all
I had on me was enough for a pack of cigarettes and
some coffee. I'd be eating sardines and crackers.
To this day, she hates my guts. Talks about me like
a dog to the kids. When I call, I have to prepare myself for the bullshit. "You ain't been over to see the
kids in months. They always asking about you." I
guess she don't know that sometimes when I call
and Derek answers, we talk for a long time. He
starting to talk about girls and shit already. And he
just thirteen. Last time I saw him, I took him to a
closed-circuit fight and let him drink a glass of
beer. I felt good being able to do something with
him, and I know I need to spend more time with
botha my sons. Derek's the oldest, be a man before
I know it. I don't want neither one of 'em growing
up thinking of me as a dog, as some dude who
fucked their Mama and then split the scene. But
respect is something you gotta earn. Right now it
ain't much I can do for neither one of 'em, so why
should I go see 'em all the time when all they really
want is money, sneakers, designer jeans, Walkmen—
all that expensive shit I can't afford? It's embarrassing, to tell the truth. One day I'm gon' be able
to do for 'em, but it's gon' take time.*

*And that's exactly why women ain't in the picture
right now. They complicate shit. Fuck up my whole
program. All they do is throw me off track. It takes
me too damn long to swing back.*

ZORA

I've got two major weaknesses: tall black men and food. But not necessarily in that order.

When I'm lonely, I eat. When I'm bored, I eat. When I'm horny (and can't resolve it), I eat. When I get excited, I eat. When I'm depressed, I eat. When I just feel like it, I eat. When I smoked, I didn't eat as much, but smoking wasn't half as satisfying as eating, so I made a choice. I chose food. I had migrated up to a size sixteen, and that's when I looked at myself in the mirror and couldn't stand it. I said, "Just wait one damn minute here, Zora!" and, along with some of the other flabby teachers at the junior high school where I teach, joined Weight Watchers. I lasted about a year and am now down to a slender size twelve—well, it's slender enough, considering I'm almost five foot eight. Of course I've still got this damn cellulite, which drives me crazy. I can feel the ripples other people can't see. Which is precisely why I went out and bought Jane Fonda. Now, when I wake up, before I have my coffee, I work out with Jane. I've been doing it with her for a few weeks now, but so far I can't see a bit of difference.

Weight Watchers turned out to be a drag. It was just like going to the fit doctor, aka neurologist. One thing I can't stand is people telling me what to do—after all the years I'd been told what not to eat, drink, and think—so I quit when I thought I looked halfway decent in my favorite Betsey Johnson dress.

Yes, I used to have fits. And not the kind kids have when they can't get their way. Real fits. Seizures. When I was little, I fell off a sliding board and hit my head on the cement, and I guess that's what did it. But it's been almost four years since I've had one. The neurologist calls it a remission, but that's not true. I stopped taking those stupid pills is what I did, and started picturing myself fit-free. No one really believes in the power of this stuff, but I don't care, it's worked for me—so far. As a matter of fact, when I started visualizing myself less abundant, and desirable again, that's how I think I was able to get here—to 139 pounds. And no, I am not from California. I just taught myself how to say no.

I cannot lie. There are times when I have to say yes to chocolate, but I try to minimize my intake. And Lord knows I make the best peach cobbler and sweet potato pie in the world, but I've not only learned to share, but also how to freeze things that beg to be consumed in one sitting.

Except when it comes to men. I've got a history of jumping right into the fire, mistaking desire for love, lust for love, and, the records show, on occasion, a good lay for love. But those days are over. I mean it. Shit, I'm almost thirty years old, and every time I look up, I'm back at the starting gate. So yes.

I would like a man to become a permanent fixture in my life for once. But don't get me wrong. I'm not out here cruising with lasers and aiming it at hopefuls. My Daddy always said, "Sometimes you can't see for looking," so what I'm saying is that from now on, no more hunting, no more rushing to discos with Portia on a Saturday night, standing around, trying to look necessary. I made up my mind that the next time I'm "out here"—which just so happens to be right now—it'll have to start with dinner (which won't be me) and at least one or two movies and quite a few hand-holding walks before I slide under the covers and scream out his name like I've known him all my life. Some flowers wouldn't hurt either.

And just why do I feel like this? Because some of 'em don't last as long as a Duracell, no matter how much you keep recharging 'em. And I've been tricked too many times. Maybe misled would be a better word. No, maybe falsely impressed would be even more accurate. Then again, I'm really too damn gullible. I believe what I want to believe. One of my best girlfriends, Claudette, told me that my biggest problem was that I didn't do my homework. "Find out the most vital things first," she said.

"Like what?" I asked, even though I knew exactly what she meant.

"Has he been to college? Does he have a drug problem? Interested in personal hygiene? Does he believe in God, and if so, when was the last time he set foot inside a church? Does he know that respect is a verb? Does he love his mother and father? What's his family like? His friends? How

*does he feel about children and marriage? Has he
ever been married? Does he have any idea what
he'll be doing ten or twenty years from now? Is it
remotely close to what he's doing now? That kind
of shit."*

*But I'm not into interrogation. I prefer to wait
and see if the image he projects lives up to the man.
And vice versa. Let's face it: All men are not husband material. Some of 'em are only worth a few
nights of pleasure. But some of 'em make you get
on your knees at night and pray that they choose
Door Number One, which is the one you happen
to be standing behind. And it's not that I haven't
been picked before. Because I have. They turned
out to be a major disappointment. Said one thing
and did another. Couldn't back up half of what
they'd led me to believe. Then begged me to be patient. And like a fool, I tried it, until I got tired of
idling, and the needle fell on empty. Some of 'em
just weren't ready. They wanted to play house. Or
The Dating Game. Or Guess Where I'm Coming
From? or Show Me How Much You Love Me Then
I'll Show You. And then there're the ones who got
scared when they realized I wasn't playing. "You're
too intense," one said. "Too serious," said another
one. "You take them lyrics you write to heart, don't
you, Miss Z?" I told them that this wasn't high
school or college, but the grown-up edition of life.
They were still more comfortable not having a care
in the world, so I let 'em run and hide, especially
the ones that needed professional help. So now I'm
taking off the blindfolds and doing the bidding
myself. After a while, even a fool would get tired of*

bringing home the TV and finding out it only gets two or three channels.

None of this is to say I'm perfect. I just know what I've got to offer—and it's worth millions. Hell, I'm a strong, smart, sexy, good-hearted black woman, and one day I want to make some man so happy he'll think he hit the lottery. I don't care what anybody says—love is a two-way street. So yes, I want my heart oiled. I don't want to participate in any more of these transient romances—I'm interested in longevity. Let's face it: Some men take more interest in their pets than they do in their women. And even though I wish loving a man could be as easy for me as it was for Cinderella, I know it's not that simple. But it can be. And it should be. All you need is two people who are willing to expend the energy so that their hearts don't rust.

Which is one reason why I envy Claudette. She is so normal. She's a lawyer, married, has a daughter, and she's happy. She loves her husband. Her husband loves her. They are buying their house. They have lawn furniture. They ski in the winter and spend weeks in the Caribbean. He brushes her hair at night. She rubs his feet. And after seven years of marriage, they still unplug their phone.

On the other hand, Portia, who Claudette can't stand but I love, has an entirely different set of standards. "He's gotta have hair on his chest and no skinny legs. And he's gotta have some money. I don't care what color he is, but ain't no getting around no empty bank account."

"Money isn't everything," I said.

"Since when?"

Portia thinks her pussy is gold. She's not all that educated—she got as far as court reporting school— but I don't care. I refuse to discriminate when it comes to my friends. I'm more interested in the quality of their character than I am with creden- tials. Besides, I know plenty of folks with degrees that are stupid. They lack the one essential thing you need to get by in this world: common sense.

I can't lie: Sometimes I fall into that category my- self. Because I still don't know what it is about deep- black skin and long legs that turns me on, but some things aren't worth analyzing. It's taken me years to realize what I like and what I don't like. For in- stance, short men simply do not appeal to me, at least none have so far. And men who could stand a few trips to the dentist will never kiss me. Men who are afraid of deodorant knock me out. Men who roll over, stick it in, and think they've done something miraculous make me want to slap 'em instead of shudder. I can't stand vulgar men. Dumb men. Lazy men. Men who think the word respect means ex- pect. Men who are so pretty they spend more time in the mirror than I do. Men whose brains can be measured by the size of their dicks. Selfish men. Men who don't vote. Who think all the news that's fit to print is on the sports page. Liars. Men who think that the world owes them something. Men who care more about the cushion between my legs than they do about the rest of me. Men who don't stand for anything in particular. Who think passion is synonymous only with fucking. And men who don't take chances—who are too afraid to stick their damn necks out for fear that they're going to drown.

So I guess you could say that the kind of man I like is just the opposite of these. Which means I like a clean, tall, smart, honest, sensuous, spontaneous, energetic, aggressive man with white teeth who smells good and reads a good book every now and then, who votes and wants to make a contribution to the world instead of holding his hands out. A man who stands for something. Who feels passion for more than just women. And a man who appreciates that my pussy is good but also respects the fact that I have a working brain. And last but not least, a man who knows how to make love.

I have not run into him lately.

Every man I've ever loved—and there've been three and a half—or that I've cared substantially about, brought me to these conclusions in a haphazard way, but I'm grateful to all of 'em, because had I not experienced them, I wouldn't have had any.

When I was sixteen, there was Bookie Cooper, whose skin shone like india ink and whose fingernails were yellow. He had muscles. He fixed the chain on my bike when it broke, then walked me home through the woods the long way and gave me my first kiss. Bookie used to whisper in my ear. He had such a soft voice that I often had to stare at his lips in order to figure out what he was saying. He was the first boy that made me tingle. And he taught me the power of kissing—just how serious it can be. But Bookie got killed. He was crossing the street on his bicycle when an ambulance hit him. For months, I couldn't believe it. I slept with that orange elephant he'd won for me at the state fair, so I would still feel close to him. I even walked by his

house and waited for him to come out, but another
family had moved in, and this white woman with
pink sponge rollers in her hair kept peeking
through the curtains suspiciously. It took a long
time for it to register that Bookie's absence was
permanent. But I can't lie: I had to teach myself to
forget him.

There was Champagne, the college basketball
star who held my hand and stroked my hair while he
talked, and forever smelled like British Sterling.
Even though I was just a junior in high school, he
made me feel like a woman. After my senior prom,
with my very first glass of rum and Coke exaggerat-
ing everything, he talked me into giving up my vir-
ginity, and I did it because I was tired of saying no
and figured if I got pregnant at least I'd be out of
high school by the time it was born. And it hurt. I
was grateful when it was finally over, and couldn't
understand why everybody had made such a big deal
about sex if this was supposed to be the thrill of a
lifetime. I never did feel electric. But I didn't care;
I still wanted Champagne. Being wrapped inside
his strong arms was warm enough for me. As a matter of fact, I used to lie beside him and dream about
him. Play every sad, slow song by Aretha and
Smokey Robinson I could get my hands on and dig
my face in the pillow and cry. Which is how I knew
I was in love. We agreed to get married once we
both finished college and he was playing in the
pros. But what happened? I won a music scholar-
ship to Ohio State, and he went to a Big Ten university in Indiana and never wrote so much as a
word, not to mention the fact that his fingers

must've been stricken with arthritis, because he never called either.

"To hell with Champagne," is what I said when I met David, who was bowlegged, walked like Clint Eastwood, drove a Harley-Davidson, and boxed. He was so black he was purple, and I swear I could've eaten him alive. Especially after he lifted me up on top of him and let me move any way I wanted to, as long as I wanted to. And I liked it. Loved it, really. He taught me that there were no limits to passion if you didn't impose any. So every time I felt like doing it I would dial his number. Tell him I needed to see him. David's body was my very first addiction. It was so cooperative. And he would take me for long motorcyle rides—in the rain, at night, in freezing weather, it didn't matter. This was the first time I experienced real adventure and understood what freedom felt like. But we hardly ever talked. So by the time David asked me to marry him, I realized two things: that he was boring except in bed and that there was a big difference between wanting to spend the rest of your life with someone and wanting to experience continuous moments of ecstasy. I said no and told him I was moving to New York City to launch my singing career. I told him I wanted to live a bold and daring life, not a safe little cozy one in Toledo. He said he would make it exciting, but I told him I'd rather not try.

By the time I got here, I decided to take a short sabbatical from men. But not all that short. It lasted about four months. Sometimes men can be more of a distraction than anything. Marie—she's *my comedienne friend—says that I not only take them too seriously but I put too much emphasis on their worth. But I can't help it. As corny as it may sound—considering this is the eighties and everything— there's nothing better than feeling loved and needed. And until God comes up with a better sub- stitute, I'll just keep my fingers crossed that one day I'll meet someone with my name stamped on his back.*

So I met Percy, the plumber. He was a smart, handsome plumber, but he wanted a wife too badly. He had put the clamps on me in less than a month. He was from Louisiana and gave the best head I ever had in my life. As a matter of fact, he was the first man who made me come that way. All the others had always gnawed and chewed so much that it got to the point that when one offered, I refused the invitation. Percy changed all that. Of course I was already strung out by the time he asked me to quit my job, marry him, and move to some little off- the-wall town in Louisiana that I'd never even heard of and run a farm and have babies. And he was serious. I told him he was out of his mind, which is why when I found out I was carrying his baby, I rushed down to the Women's Center and did not tell him. I blacked out his name in my ad- dress book and changed my number to unlisted.

And Dillon. He was a DJ who claimed he wanted to be a record producer. I thought we had some- thing in common. Hah! He was—I later found out the correct term—a premature ejaculator. He would give me ten or twelve minutes of pleasure, and poof! it was over. He just kept telling me that I was so good I should be grateful I could make him come so fast. If he hadn't favored Billy Dee Williams so much, or listened to me sing, I'd have given up on him sooner. But Dillon had a ton of energy in other areas. He was the first black man I knew who skied. By the time I heard about a concert I wanted to see, he already had the tickets. And he talked me to death. His dreams were as loud as mine, and I liked that. As I later found out, cocaine had a whole lot to do with it. When I first met him, Dillon told me he had sinus problems, so I was used to him sniffling all the time. He also loved me fat, and actually got nervous when I started shedding the pounds. "You looked good big," he said, and swore he'd give up coke if I would just stop losing weight. Naturally, he was crazy as hell, and our goodbye was so ugly that when I missed my period again, there was no way I could bring myself to tell him. So I did it again, but swore I would never hop up on one of those tables and count backward from a hundred unless whatever came out was going home with me and my husband.

There have been others, but they're not worth mentioning because none of them made me fall from grace or feel the earth move, for lack of a better cliché.

I know I may sound fickle, but I'm not. I was taught to give all human beings a chance to prove their worth before I dismissed them. I assumed that meant men too. And even though I get so lonely sometimes it feels like I'm dying, or my heart and head get mixed up and the only thing I can do to fill the emptiness or stop the ache of nothingness is to take a Tylenol, I do not stand in front of the mirror anymore, holding these 36C's in my palms and praying that someone was there kissing them. I have learned how to satisfy myself, although I can't lie and say I make myself feel as good as a real man could. But like my Daddy always said, "Work with what you've got."

What I've got is a good set of lungs and vocal cords.

Mount Olive Baptist used to be standing room only when word got out that I was doing a solo. I used to make people cry and speak in tongues, and those fans would be swaying so fast you couldn't even see the name of the funeral parlor on 'em. There is no greater feeling than singing a song that makes people feel glad to be alive.

Marguerite—that's my stepmother—has always accused me of being too idealistic. "You always reaching for what you can't see, chile." My real Mama died in a car accident when I was three years old, which is how I got stuck with Marguerite as a replacement. Not that she hasn't been a nice stepmother, but I've never had anyone to compare her to. She did teach me how to cook, how to shave my armpits and legs, and told me when to douche. Daddy married her when I was thirteen. She's taller than him, flat-chested, with an ever-growing behind and hazel eyes. Every six weeks she dyes her gray hair black, because she says, "I ain't got no time to be looking old."

My Daddy looks old, but I guess if you'd worked for the railroad for thirty-six years and married someone who insisted you take all the overtime you *could get, then snatched your paycheck every Friday and lived at Sears, gave you an allowance, and only closed the bedroom door on Saturday nights, you'd look old too.*

When I told my Daddy I was moving to New York City to sing, he just blew a cloud of smoke out of his cigar, tapped off an inch of ashes, grinned—that gold tooth sparkling—and said, "You go 'head, baby. Life ain't nothin' to be scared of. 'Sides, the Lord'll follow you wherever you go."

I've had my doubts.

The problem is I've been influenced by so many folks that I sound like a whole lot of singers all rolled up. This has bothered me for too long, because I don't know what my real voice is. Sure, every now and then I hear myself with such clarity, with such precision, that I get surprised—even a bit scared—because what I hear sounds like someone I could envy. But it's not consistent. I can imitate just about anybody I admire. Joan Armatrading. Chaka Khan. Joni Mitchell. Laura Nyro. Aretha and Gladys too.

Sometimes I stay after school—since my piano's in layaway and I still owe three hundred dollars on it—and compose. I sit there with my eyes closed, and when my fingers press against the keys and I start to sing, the room often moves. My heart opens up and lets in light. Writing songs allows me to fix what's wrong. And when I'm singing, I'm not lonely, just overwhelmed by desire. I'm not looking for a man; I've found one. Folks aren't starving; I'm giving 'em food from my plate. I invent jobs. Get rid of torment and racism and hatred, and spin a world so rich with righteousness that usually, by the time I finish, I'm perspiring something awful, and I don't even realize how much time has passed until I walk outside and see that it's dark.

As it stands now, I do most of my singing in the shower. I get clean and let out pain at the same time—watch it go down the drain. And not just my pain but everybody else's that I've known who's ever felt or known hurt. And there are millions of us. To tell the truth, sometimes I get scared when I think of myself being in a world where I don't make a bit of difference. Where I could die and the only people who would ever know I was here would be friends, lovers, and relatives. I want to affect people in a positive way, which is one reason why I teach music. But it's not enough. I want to sing songs that'll make people float.

That's why I'm looking for a coach. I need to learn how to control my voice. Find my center. Learn to pay attention to what I feel in my heart so that it comes out of my pen, then my mouth, instead of screaming inside my head. I don't care if I'm never as famous as Diana or Aretha or Liza or Barbra. I don't have to make Billboard's Top 40 either. I'd be just as content squeezing a microphone in my hands in some smoky club, with an audience who came to hear me sing. The only way I'll ever be able to afford a voice coach is by moving out of this expensive-ass apartment, which is precisely why you can have Manhattan and its Upper West Side. I'm going to Brooklyn, where they say you can at least get your money's worth. My Daddy always said, "You gotta give up somethin' to get somethin'." I'm giving up roaches, water bugs, mice, $622 a month, and a view of a brick wall.

Right now I'm staring at the ceiling and can hear birds chirping. This is a good sign. But I can't lie: I am lonely, and it has been almost six months since I've been touched by a man. I'll live, though. Instead of wasting my time wishing and hoping, sleeping with self-pity and falling in love over and over again with ghosts, I'm going to stop concentrating so hard on what's missing in my life and be grateful for what I've got. For instance, this organ inside my chest. God gave me a gift, and I'd be a fool not to use it. And if there's a man out there who's willing to ride or walk or run or even fly with me, he'll show up. Probably out of nowhere. I'm just not going to hold my breath.

1

I stood outside the apartment I came to look at, and my first impression was that the building was beautiful. That is, until I walked inside and saw that stairwell. Talk about old. The railing looked as rickety as the ones you see in horror movies, and the stairs were so dusty that when I put my foot on the first step, a claylike powder puffed up like a cloud under my dress, and I could've sworn they were going to collapse. I was making a mistake—I knew that already. Something had told me the ad sounded too good to be true: "Large one-bedroom, fully renovated brownstone, 10-foot ceilings, all new appliances, exposed brick, southern exposure, 10 minutes to Wall Street, close to shops, subway: $500."

I heard the sound of hammering from the top of the stairs, so I took my chances and ran up. Sawdust was flying around the white room like gold snow. I looked down, saw a curved red back, then a long arm flying up, thick black fingers grasping a hammer, and when it swung back down, the sound of the impact scared me. I jumped.

He looked up, then stood. "What can I do for you?" he asked.

"Lord have mercy," was all I heard inside my head. I couldn't move, let alone speak. I really couldn't believe what I was see-ing. This man had to be six foot something, because he was towering over me. His eyes looked like black marbles set in al-monds. He wore a Yankees baseball cap, backward, and when he lifted it from his head to shake off the dust, his hair was jet black and wavy. That nose was strong and regal, and beneath it was a thick mustache. His cheeks looked chiseled; his lips succulent. And those shoulders. They were as wide as any linebacker's. His thighs were tight, and his legs went on for-ever. He was covered with dust, but when he pushed the sleeves of his red sweatshirt up to his elbows, his arms were the color of black grapes.

"Did you come to look at the apartment?" he asked.

I cleared my throat and heard a word come out of my mouth. "Yes."

Then he smiled down at me, as if he was thinking about something that had happened to him earlier. "Well, we run-ning behind schedule—as usual—and I don't know when we gon' be finished. I been trying to figure out how all these damn mice been getting in here. Ain't found it yet. And I don't know how the roaches and water bugs getting in here ei-ther. Tribes of 'em. We gon' have to fumigate this place good before anybody even *think* about moving in here."

Mice? Water bugs and roaches? This place is brand-new. Was he joking? "Are you the owner?"

"I wish I was. He's back there," he said, pointing down a long hallway. "Hey, Vinney!" he yelled. "Somebody's here to see you, man."

Before I started in that direction, I did notice that the liv-ing room was big and shaped like an L. Three tall windows ex-tended from the ceiling almost to the floor, which meant sunshine. The kitchen was over in a corner, but I could live with that. Halfway down the hall was the bathroom. I peeked in and turned on the light. I couldn't believe it. A sea-blue bathtub, toilet, and sink! And clean white tile on the floor and walls, and one of those orange lamps in the ceiling to help you dry off. So far so good. When I entered the doorway at the end of the hall, I was standing inside a sunny bedroom, with two more windows.

"Hello, Miss Banks," the owner said, then reached out to shake my hand. I shook his, even though it was filthy.

"Let me say first off that we'll be finished in a day or so. You like what you see?"

"The man up front said he didn't know when you'd be finished. He also said there were problems with bugs and mice."

"That's bullshit. First of all, like I said, we'll be finished in a day or two. And we ain't seen nothing crawling around in here except men. The place has been completely gutted— everything in here is brand-new. Frankie's known for being a jokester, but today he's pushing it."

Frankie? What a stupid name for such a striking man. "What's this little room over here?" I asked.

"Oh, that's just sort of an extra-large closet. It's too small to call it a bedroom, which is why we didn't put it in the ad. Perfect for a kid, though. But you said you didn't have kids. Use it for storage, whatever."

It was a tiny room, but I guessed I could squeeze my piano in. I walked over to the window. At least there were trees back there, even if they were in other people's yards. I looked down at the wooden planks under my feet. "What are you going to do to the floors?"

"We're laying the finest carpet available in every room except the kitchen area and bathroom. Sort of a beigy color— neutral, you know. That suit you?"

"There's no way you could put in hardwood floors?"

"You want the apartment? There's plenty of interest in it already. I coulda rented it this morning, but I knew you were coming, and I wanted to be fair, you know."

"If you can put in hardwood floors and guarantee that the stairwell won't look like it does now for too much longer, I'll take it."

"First off, when you renovate a whole building, you always save the stairs till last, or they'd be worse off with all the ripping and running the men do up and down 'em. And hardwood floors? It'll cost you a few dollars extra for the labor, and'll add a few more days to the job."

"How much extra?"

"Not much, if you get pine. Don't worry, we can work something out. You positive you want wood? They collect dust like there ain't no tomorrow."

"I'm positive." I didn't care about the dust. When I first walked in here, I had already pictured shiny wood floors, not some drab carpet. And I hate beige. It's so boring.

"Frankie," he yelled. "Come in here a minute, would you?"

He walked back into the bedroom, ducking his head under the arch. I tried not to look directly at him, because I was thinking that I wished he came with the place. I tried, instead, to look indifferent.

"What's up, boss?" he asked sarcastically.

"Why'd you tell this young lady all those lies?"

He threw his arms up in the air and grinned. And had the nerve to have dimples. "I was just kidding, boss."

"One day all your kidding is gonna cost me money, Frankie. Anyway, she wants wood floors 'steada carpet. I want you to get over to Friendly Freddy's and get a estimate today. Can you have everything finished in four or five days?"

"Maybe," he said, lighting a cigarette. He blew the smoke

upward, and my eyes watched his lips close around the filter again. I wished I was a cigarette.

"He'll have it done in five days," Vinney said. "If that's soon enough?"

"That's fine."

"Come on down the street to my office, and we can tidy up the particulars. Oh, hell, I ain't got any lease forms. I have to run to the stationery store and pick up some. You can help yourself to a cup of coffee. This won't take but a minute."

"Watch him," Frankie said to me. "He's Italian." I started to follow Vinney down the hall and had to brush past Frankie, because he acted like he didn't have any intention of moving out of my way. My breast wanted to brush against his chest, for the pure warmth alone, but I did just the opposite. When he saw this, he flung his arms up over his head and pressed himself stiffly against the wall. I ignored him and gave the place another once-over. Yep, I thought, I could definitely live here.

"Vinney just sold you a bunch of crap. You the first person to look at this place. This is a racket, they just call it business. See you in three weeks," Frankie said. He was back in the living room, driving more nails in the floor.

When the mover pulled up to my new home, Frankie was sitting out on the stoop in a tight white T-shirt, smoking a cigarette and drinking a Heineken. I swear, he looked like a black Marlboro Man without a hat and horse. Orchards of soft black hair were peeking out from the V, but I didn't want to stare. And muscles? They were everywhere. I wondered if he worked out or just worked hard. His face was drenched with sweat, and it looked like black tears were falling from his temples. I can't lie: I had to stop myself from walking over and patting them dry.

"Your bedroom floor is still wet, so you gon' have to put all this stuff in the living room."

"What? Vinney told me it was finished."

"It is *finished*; it just ain't dry."

Shit. I turned to the driver of the truck and explained the situation to him. He got out to open the back, and I put my hands on my hips and looked up at my windows. "Well, I'm here," I said, to no one in particular.

Frankie just kept on smoking.

When I'd hired the guy to help me move, he'd told me there'd be two of them, but this morning only he showed up. I'd asked some young guy who happened to be passing by if he wanted to make a quick forty dollars, and he jumped at it. Of course I didn't want him to know where I was moving, so I didn't ask him to come to Brooklyn. I had carried enough boxes myself, and now I was tired at the thought of hauling all this stuff upstairs. "Moving sure is hard labor," I sighed.

"Yes, it is," Frankie said, and took a sip from his beer. I thought maybe he'd at least offer to help, but he didn't.

"Would you mind giving me a hand?"

"I don't work for free."

Not only was he a handsome creep, I thought, but he was nasty. Even so, I couldn't carry all those heavy boxes up the stairs. "How much?"

"Not much," he said. He flicked his cigarette about three feet away and at the same time jumped off the stoop. For the next hour, I watched him lift and pull things off the truck. Those muscles kept popping up in his arms and shoulders, and he was sweating like crazy. And every time he walked past me, all I could think about was that I bet some woman loves to roll over into those arms at night.

It took close to two hours for us to get everything except the trunk upstairs. It was full of records, and I knew it was too heavy for one person to carry, so I offered to help, but Frankie refused. He slung it up in the air, balanced it on one shoulder, then walked on up the stairs like it weighed twenty pounds.

I paid the driver and ran upstairs. Frankie was busy pushing the larger things against the living room wall. Boxes were stacked everywhere, including on top of the couch. I walked back to the bedroom and stood in the doorway. Sunlight was streaming through the windows, and the floors looked like strips of gold. When I felt his presence behind me I turned around, and my nose grazed those soft black trees on his chest. My lips felt moist, and my heart was about to jump out of my chest. I inched away from him and almost stepped onto the wet floor, but Frankie grabbed my elbows and pulled me back into the hallway.

"Don't you mess up my floor," he said.

I was nervous, but I willed my mouth to talk. "You did a fantastic job on the floors, Frankie. Really. I didn't expect them to turn out this beautiful."

"Thanks," he said, turning back down the hallway and winking at me. "I try to do everything good."

I guess this was supposed to be his way of flirting. It must've been working, because all the air in the place seemed to be disappearing. I took a deep breath and prayed I could say what was necessary without sounding like I was going through any major changes. "How much do I owe you?"

"How much did you pay the white boy?"

"I gave him a hundred dollars."

Now, why did his eyes light up like that? "Was that too much? All the movers in the *Voice* asked for about the same."

"Naw, that wasn't too much."

"I've only got about thirty dollars in cash left, but if there's a cash machine in the neighborhood, I can go get more. I really appreciated your help."

"Keep your money."

"No, really. You earned it, and you said yourself you didn't work for free."

"I know what I said. A little charity every now and then won't kill me. So tell me, are you a Miss or a Mrs.?"

He sat down on a box and crossed his arms. Before I could tell him it was none of his business, I blurted out, "A Ms."

"Oh, so you one of those feminists?"

"What if I am?"

"I just asked. Does that mean you like women?"

"Give me a break, would you? Do I look like I like women?"

"Looks don't mean nothin' in this day and age. But to answer your question, no."

"Then you've got your answer." I started looking at box labels, to see which one had the dishes in it, not that I really needed a dish right then. He was making me nervous. Shit. Talk about being direct. I had to do something—anything—to keep moving, because he didn't act like he was getting ready to leave, and even though what he just asked me was tacky as hell, I didn't want him to leave yet either. "Can I ask *you* a question?"

"Only if it's personal."

"Is your real name Frankie?"

"No. It's Franklin. Why?"

"You just didn't look like a Frankie to me."

"You can call me Franklin if you want to."

Had I already given him the impression that I planned on seeing him again? Men. Not only are they presumptuous, but this one here can read minds.

"You ain't never been married?" he asked, lighting a cigarette.

"No," I said tartly, and started looking for something he could use for an ashtray.

"Don't get so touchy. I was just curious. What you gon' do with all this space?"

"Put it to good use."

"By yourself?"

He *would* have to make it sound like I'm a damn spinster or something, wouldn't he? "Yes," I said, and handed him a rusty can I found under the sink. It already had ashes in it, which meant it was probably his.

"How?"

"Why?" I asked.

"Because it seems awful funny that a single woman would pay this much rent with all this space and live here by herself, that's why."

"I sing and play the piano, and I need all the space I can get. And compared to Manhattan, this is cheap. Does that answer your question, Franklin?"

He smiled at me. "A singer, huh?"

"Yes, a singer."

I spotted a box that looked like whatever was in it would look like I needed it. As I went to lift it, Franklin jumped up to help me. Damn, even his funk smelled good.

"What's your name again?" he asked, putting the box on top of the counter.

"Zora. Zora Banks."

"That's a helluva name. Suits you. I know you heard of Zora Neale Hurston, then, right? The writer?"

As much as I hated to admit it, I was becoming more impressed by the minute. "I was named after her."

"You recorded any albums? I'm pretty up on all kinds of music, and your name don't ring no bells."

I knew one thing—his grammar was terrible, but everything else seemed to be compensating for it. "Nope. No albums yet. I'm working on it."

"Well, what kind of music do you sing?"

"All kinds," I said.

"Is that what you gon' tell a record producer? That you sing *all* kinds of music?"

"You know, you sure ask a lot of questions."

He smiled. "How else you suppose to learn things if you don't ask?"

God, his teeth were white. "Well, to be honest, that's exactly what I'm working on, developing my own style."

"I always thought it was about feeling the music. Sing me a few notes."

"Sing you a few notes? Be serious. First of all, I've just barely got inside the door of my new apartment, I don't even know your last name, I'm not in a singing mood, and I'm tired."

"My last name is Swift. I can understand you being tired and everything, but I'd like to hear you sing one day. I don't meet many singers."

Swift was putting it mildly. He stood directly in front of me. He was doing this on purpose, I just knew it. Probably just wanted to see how long it would take me to melt. He was much too good at this. "So you're assuming I'll be seeing you again after today, is that it?"

"I can guarantee it," he said, walking toward the door. "We getting ready to start on the building two doors down."

Then he was gone. I stood there looking at the door like a fool, as if I was in a trance or something. I swear I couldn't move. I felt affected. And that door kept opening and closing, and each time it opened he would just stand there, looking right through me. To snap out of it, I had to shake my head back and forth until the door stayed closed. Then I went over to the sink and dangled my fingers under the water until they could feel that it was too damn hot.

I wanted to unpack my books, but I needed toggle bolts to put the shelves up. I'm terrible when it comes to doing things like that. There are some things I really don't want to learn how to do. I couldn't put my stereo together, because there's too many wires. Which means I'll have to pay somebody to do it, just like I've always done. The phone company was supposed to have been here by now, but of course they're late, so I couldn't call anybody. And last but not least, I was starving.

I walked down the dirty stairs and noticed that the door to the first-floor apartment was cracked open, so I peaked inside. I saw a disgusting shade of yellow tweed shag carpet. I'd been told two women were moving in tomorrow. "Dykes probably," Vinney had said. "Don't bother them, and they won't bother you." I walked out the front door and locked it.

The heat was piercing and the humidity thick. I was trying to decide which way to go. When I looked far to the right, I saw lots of traffic, which meant businesses, so I went that way. At the corner was a fish market, where I bought half a pound of scallops. Right next to it was a produce stand that sold everything from vegetables to Pampers. I bought broccoli, fresh mushrooms, scallions, a large bunch of flowers, paper towels, toilet paper, and white grape juice.

I decided to walk home around the block, to get a better feel for the neighborhood. Some gay guy was standing out in front of this gorgeous little gourmet shop, trying to entice people to come in.

"Free coffee samples to celebrate our grand opening," he said. "You look like a lady with good taste. Come on in, honey. Try some. It's divine."

"Thanks. Maybe another time." I'd only taken a few steps when the rich scent of coffee lured me back. He handed me a finely printed piece of peach-colored paper that described the store's specialties. All kinds of delicacies, imported foods, breads, every kind of cheese you could think of, dried fish, and pickled everything. I went inside, and staring me in the face were samples of white Scandinavian chocolate.

"Go ahead, it's fabulous," he said.

My fingers itched with desire, but I said, "No. I can't."

"Oh, come on. One little piece won't hurt. Go on. Splurge."

The next thing I knew, not only had I eaten a piece, I'd bought a quarter pound (which I vowed to stretch out over a week or two). I also got some dilled Havarti cheese, liver pâtè, some kind of crackers I'd never heard of, and a pound of Vienna roast mixed with mocha Java.

"Come back again," he said, and I assured him I would.

Most of the neighborhood was still run-down, and even though there were scaffolds everywhere I looked, it would be years before this area was pretty. "You moved here at the right time," Vinney had said. "In a few years everybody and their mother'll be flocking to Brooklyn from Manhattan. Who can afford that rent? This is what you call a changing neighborhood. It's the pits now, but stick around a few years, you won't even recognize it. You're getting this place at a steal, you know."

By the time I got home, I was drenched. I found the box with the towels in it and took a cool shower. Afterwards, I found the box with the cleansers and scrubbed the kitchen shelves inside and out. I didn't care that they were brand-new. I didn't ever want to see another roach. Then I pulled out the pots and pans, cooked dinner, and sat down on top of a box to eat. I sure wished I had some music. I put the flowers in water in my coffeepot and set them next to my plate. Lord only knew when I'd be able to afford a dining room set. The piano comes first.

That night, I slept on the living room floor. The couch was buried in boxes, and my platform bed wouldn't do me much good because I had thrown the mattress out. I made a pallet of three blankets and flipped one of them over me like a sleeping bag. Sometime during the middle of the night, I woke up. I heard a sound, like movement, but I couldn't tell where it was coming from. I was afraid to move, so I just lay there as still as I could. This was the worst part of living alone: when you're scared and don't have anybody to turn to. The noise was coming from the refrigerator. Please, God, don't let it be a mouse. Just the thought of seeing a ball of gray fur made my stomach turn. I got up slowly and went and knocked on the refrigerator door. If it was in there, it could run out the way it came in, and I wouldn't ever have to see it. I waited a few seconds, then opened the door slowly; the only thing inside was my leftover dinner and the things I'd bought. I felt relieved, but to be sure, I opened the freezer. A plastic box was filling up with oval-shaped ice cubes. I had completely forgotten about that damn icemaker.

I lay back down and stared at the white walls, which now looked blue because of the streetlight shining through the windows. I closed my eyes, but they wouldn't stay shut. They kept seeing blue. I got up and went over to the counter and broke off a piece of chocolate and lay down again. This is how it always starts, Zora, I thought, then stomped to the bathroom and flushed the entire contents of the bag—including what was in my mouth—down the toilet.

I turned on the fan and stood in the middle of the living room, listening to it oscillate. The blankets felt cool on my bare feet, but it was hot as hell in here. I lay on top of the blankets and tried to go to sleep, but then my breasts started to throb, and I watched them rise and fall. Not tonight, I thought. I don't have the energy. My nipples hardened. This was their way of letting me know they needed to be touched, kissed—something. Without realizing it, I cupped both hands over them and started to massage them. I can't lie: I pretended they were Franklin's hands. Then a heart started beating between my legs. His hands slid down my belly, stroked the inside of my thighs until my body was electric. I couldn't help it when my legs flew open. And by the time his hands found the spot, moved in, and pressed down, I felt like a hot wet sponge being squeezed. My body jerked, and I couldn't stop shivering. I wanted him to kiss me forever, put his arms around me and hold me, keep me warm and safe. I gritted my teeth and squeezed my eyes tighter so I could keep him there. That's when I felt the tears easing out from my lids, and my hands dropped to the floor. "I'm so tired of this," I said out loud. So I wiped my eyes, got under the sheet, and pulled it up to my chin. But I could've sworn Franklin said, "Don't stop now," so I pulled the pillow inside my arms until it felt like a man.

"Come on, baby," I heard him say. "Give it all to *me*."

And that's exactly what I did.

In the morning, a knock at the door woke me up. I was lying in front of the stove; the blankets were over by a stack of boxes. I looked at my watch. It wasn't even seven o'clock. I got up from the floor, put on a cotton bathrobe, and opened the door without even thinking to ask who it was. Franklin was standing under the arch. I wiped the sleep from my eyes.

"You drink coffee?" he asked.

"Yes," I said, and let him in.

2

Don't ask me why I did some stupid shit like that. Ringing that woman's doorbell at that time of morning. And with a lame-ass line like, "You drink coffee?" I didn't have nothin' else to do all day, really. Last night, Vinney rang my buzzer and told me we wouldn't start the other building for three days. Had to wait for materials. This pissed me off, 'cause I needed the money. I promised Pam I'd bring her a hundred dollars by Friday. Once again I'ma have to look like a chump. I'm sicka this shit. Pam swears the reason I don't help her with the kids more than I do is 'cause it's my way of getting back at her. But that's bullshit. You can't give what you ain't got.

This morning I got up around six, did a few sit-ups and push-ups to get my adrenaline going, and walked to the corner coffee shop—like I do every morning—and ordered black coffee. But something told me to order two. I didn't even know if the woman was up, if she would have a heart attack and shit seeing me, but I decided to take my chances.

When she opened the door, she looked like she'd had a rough night. She was still pretty, though, even with no makeup. Her skin looked like Lipton tea. I saw them thick nipples sticking out through that pink bathrobe, and I felt Tarzan rising.

"Did I wake you up?"

"Of course you did. Is something wrong?"

"Naw. I just figured you probably didn't get a chance to unpack everything, so I thought I'd be a gentleman and bring you over a hot cup of coffee. Help you get your day started, that's all."

"Are you on drugs or something?"

"I don't do drugs, sweetheart. Outgrew it. Besides, it's a dead habit. Jack Daniel's and Heinekens I like. You looking kinda rough this morning—what kind you on?"

"Thanks a lot. I always look gorgeous when I haven't brushed my teeth or washed my face."

She turned her back to me. She definitely wasn't skinny, like most of these women running around here trying to look like fashion models. They really think they look good, but to me they look like they starving. Any man'll tell you they like a woman with some meat on her bones. Zora slid down the wall to a sitting position. Her robe was above her knees and I saw that she had skinny legs. When she realized I was looking, she squeezed 'em together and pulled the robe down to hide 'em.

"Thank you for the coffee," she said.

"No sweat." Damn, in the morning her voice is deeper than mine. I betcha she *can* sing. She ran her fingers through her short hair. Those curls looked like they was hers and not them nasty-ass Jheri-Kurls everybody's wearing. She took the lid off her coffee. I walked over to sit down next to her, and she didn't move. A lot of women are scared of me 'cause I'm so big; they don't think big men know how to be gentle.

"Don't you have to go to work today?" she asked.

"I'm laid off for a few days. Materials is late."

"Really?" she said, then took a sip of her coffee. "This stuff is really disgusting. I'll make a good pot."

She got up and walked over to the sink. She had to be

about five seven, maybe 140 pounds, and she moved as graceful as the gazelles on *Wild Kingdom*. I wish people could be more like animals. Just trust and follow our instincts without worrying about the consequences. If that was the case, I'd be getting up right now, walking up behind her, and turning her around to look me in the eye, and I would kiss her. But since we ain't animals, I just asked her, "So how was your first night?" She turned around real fast and gave me this piercing look, like I just asked her for some pussy or something. Then she put all her weight on one of them little bony legs and let out a long sigh. "I'm not trying to be nosy. I was just wondering."

"Kind of spooky, to tell you the truth. I have to get used to sleeping in a new place."

"Where'd you sleep?"

"On the floor."

"Where's your bed?"

"Over there, those boards against the wall. It's a platform bed. I threw out the old mattress and am getting a new one in a few days."

"You gon' put it together by yourself?"

"Not exactly. A friend is coming over to help me, as soon as the floor is dry. You think it's dry now?"

A friend? Why didn't she just come on out and say her man? Women. Why be so sneaky about shit. I got up to go check the floor. It was dry, all right. "It still ain't dry yet, and if you don't wanna mess it up, I'd give it one more day." When I start lying like this, it means my ass is in trouble. I shoulda went home then, but I couldn't.

"Another whole day?"

"Well, tell your man to come on over anyway."

She looked at me kinda weird. "I told you, he's a friend."

Yeah, right, and I'm running for President. Women don't

have men for friends. I don't know why I felt relieved, though. She didn't sound like she was lying, and why would she have to lie to me? I swear to God, here I go again. I'm contradicting myself like a motherfucker. I ain't got no business being here, none whatso-fuckin'-ever. But I still couldn't leave. My primal instincts always get the best of me. I watch too many damn nature shows is what it is. "What's in all these boxes? Where's your stereo? I know you got a stereo, being a singer and everything."

"Mostly books. I do have a stereo, but Eli's hooking that up too."

"He must be a good friend."

"He is."

"Look, I don't mean to get all in your business, but I'm not doing nothin' today, and I wouldn't mind helping you. You got bookshelves, I see."

"I need toggle bolts for 'em. Thanks for the offer, but I told you, Eli'll do it for *free*."

"Did I mention anything about money?"

"You're the one who said you didn't work for free."

"Yeah, and if your memory serves you correctly, I also said that sometimes I believe in charity."

"You're getting a little carried away with it, wouldn't you say?"

"Maybe. Look, you got any tools—a drill, a screwdriver, hammer—anything like that?"

"No."

"I shoulda guessed."

"Are you always this persistent?" she asked.

I just looked at her and smiled. Was I being persistent? The truth of the matter was, this wasn't even my style. Women usually come to me. But there was something kind of mysterious about this one. Ain't nothin' like a little mystery to arouse my curiosity. I wanted to know where she came from. What was she doing in Brooklyn? Did she or didn't she have a man? And if she did, where the fuck was he? Why didn't *he* help her? Naw, she didn't have no man, or she wouldn'ta spent the first night in here by herself. But why should I care? All I wanted to know was if she could really sing, or was this just a front. Some of 'em'll tell you anything to impress you. But Zora didn't sound like she was concerned one way or another about what I thought. I liked that shit. And she's the first woman I met in a long time that ain't leaning on nobody. I liked her for that alone. We *could* just turn out to be friends—if I can keep my perspective. But like I said, women don't know how to be your friend. They either wanna be your woman or they don't want to be nothin'. I'm just glad I ain't in the market.

She handed me another cup of coffee, in some fancy ceramic-type cup. I could tell she had good taste from all the shit I carried up here. She actually got real artwork, not those tacky, outdated posters most of the women I've known had on their walls—if they had anything. And she was right—this coffee was good.

"Look, I've got to get ready for work," she said.

"What kinda work? I thought you said you was a singer."

"I do sing. I just don't make my living at it yet. I teach music at J.H.S. 189."

"You mean to tell me you *teach* junior high school?"

"I do, and I also need to take a shower. So thank you very much for the coffee and offering to help, but would you mind leaving now? Please?"

"I'm not finished with my coffee yet." I wanted to mess with her, see if she really wanted me to stay. She probably did. Why would she let me in this time of morning if she didn't wanna see me? I was just testing her, and so far she was passing with flying colors. She looked like she was trying to look pissed off, which was cute. She probably just embarrassed 'cause she ain't all made up and shit. And I'm glad. "What time you get home?"

"Why?"

"I told you, all I wanna do is help you get some of these boxes outta here so you can at least move around, sit on that pretty couch."

She rolled her eyes at me, but then they softened. "I'm lying," she said.

"Finally, a woman who admits it!"

"Excuse me?"

"Nothing. What was you about to say?"

"I *do* teach, but not summer school."

"Look, I don't mean to come across like I'm macho or something. All I'm trying to do is be a nice guy. Don't women like you know how to accept help from a man?"

She looked at me all weird again. "What do you mean, 'women like me'?"

"Independent, that's *all* I meant—I swear it."

Then she started smiling—shocked the shit outta me and damn, what a sexy smile. "I've got a lot of running around to do in Manhattan, but I'll be home by six."

"I'll be here."

"So now that that's settled, would you mind leaving? I really do need to take a shower."

I laughed. "Would you be needing somebody to wash your back for you?" She rolled those pretty brown eyes at me, but I was convinced that if I hadda walked in that bathroom behind her, she wouldn'ta made me leave. And if we was both tigers, we wouldn't be playing this stupid-ass game. "Look, I didn't mean to say that. Thanks for the coffee. You have a nice day, and I'll see you later."

*   *   *

The fuckin' day dragged. I spent two hours at the gym—worked out, played some handball, steamed, took a nap—and came home and tried to do some woodworking. I looked at a tree stump I had dragged in here a few weeks ago, that I had planned on making a table out of. I had already scraped the bark off, it was good and dry, and I musta sat there for twenty minutes, just staring at the texture. How smooth it was—the same way her skin looked. I couldn't concentrate on no damn wood. She was working her way inside my mind and pressing down. Franklin, you getting it bad all over again, man. Doing the same shit you always do. Smell pussy and gotta go after it. But this feel like I'm smelling somethin' more than just pussy. There's somethin' wholesome about this woman, something right about her, and that's what scares me. This is exactly how I always end up on the damn railroad tracks. All stretched out and ready to get run over. But not this time. Besides, this woman been to college, and she probably think I ain't even in her league. And on top of everything, Zora—whatever her last name is—ain't nowhere in my constitutional plans. Period. And she live too damn close to even think I can just wham-bam-thank-you-ma'am her. So fuck her. Let Eli—or whatever his name is—help her get settled, since he's such a damn good friend.

I went downstairs to break up the monotony, get some fresh air. Lucky was sitting on the stoop, looking pitiful.

"What's up, dude?" I asked, but I already knew.

"That fucking Lady Libra—the whore—came in fourth in the fifth."

"How much?"

"I don't even wanna talk about it, man," he said, throwing his palm toward the ground. It ain't nothin' I can say to Lucky after he done lost some money. I wouldn't be surprised if he wasn't stealing from those old folks at that nursing home. I can count the days he wins. I didn't wanna watch him feel sorry for hisself, so I went back upstairs and popped open a beer. It *was* nice and cool in here. Last winter when I was working on this office building, they was getting rid of all these old air conditioners, so I brought two of 'em home. The other one is still sitting in the back of my closet. Everybody I knew cried broke when I tried to sell it.

I turned on my box, stepped out of these sweaty clothes, and dropped 'em in the middle of the floor. I grabbed my *Daily News*, pulled the box around the corner, out into the hallway, and took it in the bathroom. The dude I share it with—this motherfucker—like to hang his drawers and shit on a clothesline he put up. I keep taking it down. He used to use up all my damn toilet paper and soap and keep his false teeth in a glass overnight. I cussed the motherfucker out I don't know how many times, but since he cripple and everything, I won't hit him. Now I keep all my stuff in my room. This is the kinda shit you gotta put up with when you live in a rooming house.

Damn, sweat was dripping from underneath my arms. I took a whiff. I wasn't exactly smelling like roses. I forgot to put on deodorant at the gym, so I threw my newspaper on the floor, got in the shower, and lathered everywhere with Lifebuoy. Today I was gon' be one clean man. I heard static on the box, so I stepped out the tub to put it on the right station. One day my ass is gon' get electrocuted. Dr. Ruth came on. I like to listen to her show sometimes, but the last thing I needed to hear about right now was how to go about making love. I already know how to satisfy a woman, so I switched to WBLS and turned up the volume. They was playing a cut from Ashford & Simpson's new *Street Opera* album—"Working Man." It's a baad side. They write music that's for real, and Valerie don't look bad either.

I finished, rinsed off good, wrapped the towel around my

waist, picked up my box and paper, then walked back to my room. I fell across the bed, wet, 'cause this is how I like to dry off. I switched on the TV and turned the radio down. That's when I noticed my fingernails was still caked with dirt, so I reached over to the dresser and got my file. What time is it? The clock said one. Damn.

I know one thing—if Vinney don't pay me tomorrow, we gon' see what kind of job we'll start in three days. Fuckin' Italians. "Frankie, don't I always take care of you, man?" he ask me at least once a month. And I always say, "Yeah, just like the IRS." At least I get paid under the table. In cash. But if this Wop expect me to work on his new building, he's gon' have to come up with more money. Fifty dollars a day. Who the fuck can live off that? Shit, I got kids to pay for. I can't even afford to *buy* no pussy, which is what it's getting down to.

My beer was gone, and I felt muscle spasms in my shoulders, so I got up and rubbed some Ben-Gay on 'em, then poured myself a stiff one. I looked at the clock again and fell back down on the bed and closed my eyes. When I woke up, it was only two o'clock. I looked at the *TV Guide*. Soap operas. No more basketball games till fall. This is gon' be a long summer. I hate baseball, especially the Yankees. Ever since Reggie Jackson left, the team ain't shit. If they would get him back and keep that crazy-ass Billy Martin, they might win a game and fill up the stands like they used to.

I was bored shitless, so I decided to go to the bar. Since I was sweating again, I turned the air conditioner up, then splashed some aftershave on my face and put on a clean white shirt and some dress pants.

I was walking down the street before I even thought to see how much cash I had. I pulled out my wallet and counted seventy-three dollars. The music was coming from halfway down the block. Just One Look always got a crowd, don't make no difference what time of day it is. Shit, half of Brooklyn is unemployed. When I walked in, wasn't nothin' happening. On Friday nights, you can't hardly get in the door. They got the best DJ in Brooklyn, right here in this little off-the-wall joint. A lotta black folks think they too good to come in here—mainly the new ones moving into this neighborhood. Faggots and black yuppies. All of 'em wear Gucci this and Yves Saint Laurent that. Driving BMWs. Sporting tortoiseshell glasses. All the dudes wear identical Paul Stuart trench coats. They sickening, really. It is a fact that a few people been shot and killed in Just One Look, but I ain't seen nothin' like that go down in the two years I been comin' in here.

I sat down at the bar and ordered a Jack Daniel's. I was hoping not to run into Jimmy, but that woulda been asking for too much. He was the first person I saw after I swiveled around on the stool to check out everything—which amounted to nothing.

"Brotherman," he said, slapping me on my damn shoulder. Shit, it was still sore from putting in those floors. "What's happening?"

"Nothin', brother—you got it." I took a sip from my drink. "I'm beat, but you get that way when you work for a living." I love to fuck with Jimmy.

"I'm making a living, sucker. It's work, any way you look at it. You ain't seen Sheila in the past few days, have you?"

I shook my head no and downed the rest of my shot in one swallow. It felt good, so good that I ordered another one. Four is my limit. And when my cash is low, I drink beer, or I keep my black ass at home, buy myself a pint, get drunk, and watch TV till the static or a prayer wakes me up.

Jimmy hopped up on the stool next to me. "That broad owe me over a hundred dollars, and my shit is raggedy, man. I can't cop till I get this twenty dollars. You ain't got twenty on you till later on this weekend, do you, blood? I'm good for it, you know that."

I knew that was what Jimmy was leading up to. That's what he always led up to. But the little fat fuck been my buddy since high school. We used to tease him 'cause he had gray hair when he was fifteen. He got a whole head full of the shit now. Jimmy was always able to get older women because of that hair. Back then, I envied him. "Man, you ain't had it good till you got it from a thirty-year-old broad. Especially one that's done had a baby. They know how to grab holda your shit." I used to slap him upside the head when he bragged about it. I had just barely had a wet dream. But all that old pussy cost him. Last count, Jimmy had at least five or six kids in all five boroughs. He always have been dumb. That's one thing we didn't have in common. I didn't drop outta school 'cause I was dumb; I just didn't feel like being bothered. Shit, when I was seventeen, I started reading the dictionary so I wouldn't sound stupid when I got older, but I only got up to the *K*'s. There's a lot of fuckin' words in the dictionary. Now Jimmy's doing what everybody expected him to do: nothing. Yeah, he sell drugs, but it don't amount to shit. One thing I *can* say for him—he ain't like some of these scumbags out here. He don't sell to kids or young girls. Only to the fools that's been on the shit for years. And since heroin is outta style now, Jimmy's into coke. I hear they smoking that shit now, and from what Jimmy tell me, he don't indulge, which is obvious, 'cause the motherfucker still fat.

He leaned forward and put his little fat hands under that double chin. "Buy me a drink, Frankie."

I just looked at him. "If you got a real job, motherfucker, you wouldn't be in this position."

"Don't start, Frankie. Not today, man. I'm tired, got people waiting for me, and my shit is dragging. I'ma strangle Sheila when I find her."

I whipped out a twenty and handed it to him. "What you drinking?"

"Chivas. Thanks, brotherman."

I ordered the drink, they sat it on the bar, and Jimmy gulped it down. "You see the playoffs, man? What you think about that shit?"

"You know damn well I don't miss the playoffs, Jimmy. You still asking stupid questions, huh? The Lakers kicked Philadelphia's ass."

"Yeah, the Knicks could use a few Kareems."

"The Knicks need more than that. If Huey would get rid of that faggot-ass center, maybe they'd be able to do something besides lose. He dooflus, and scared to jump. You ain't never seen *him* doing no sneaker commercial—that should tell Gulf and Western something. They should trade him in for a 1982 model. Let some of these young dudes in the game whose dicks can stay hard all night."

"Yeah. L.A. took the money and ran, didn't they?"

I didn't answer Jimmy, 'cause I could tell he was just talking to make conversation. The playoffs was history anyway, and I wasn't in no basketball mood. That woman was on my mind, and I swear, when I looked behind the bar, she was sitting on top of a bottle of White Label. Damn. I really didn't need this shit. Not right now. I got too many other things to do. Some pussy would sure be nice. I can't lie about that.

"Catch you later, man," Jimmy said, sliding off the stool. I nodded.

By the time I finished my third shot, I decided to go ahead and take Pam some money. Wasn't nothin' jumping off in here. I stopped by the bank, withdrew my last forty dollars, and put twenty more with it. Shit, something was better than nothing. I walked all the way through the park to the projects, where her and the kids lived. I hated the projects, and the thought that she was raising my kids here always made me mad. Trash every-goddamn-where, and nobody cared. Young kids sitting around, looking like they high on everything. I used to do the same stupid shit, and look where it got me.

I pushed the steel door open and counted three bullet holes in the bulletproof glass. The hallway smelled like piss. I held my breath and got in the elevator that worked. A balled-up stinking Pamper was in one corner, a empty bottle of Thunderbird right next to it, and a old TV set was sitting in another puddle of piss. Did I really live here six years ago? It wasn't this bad then, but it seem like the place just goes down-hill year after year, and don't nobody give a shit. Pam can do better; she just too damn cheap. A hundred and ninety-eight dollars a month for this? At least my room is clean. And from what Derek told me, she still working the midnight shift at some brokerage house, running some kind of computer. What she do with all her money I don't know. And just wait. When one of the kids get in trouble, she gon' be the first one to wonder why.

She answered the door—or I should say, took up the door. "How you doing?" I asked. "Thought I'd stop by and bring you this."

She snatched the money and moved out the way. I sat down at the kitchen table. The same raggedy-ass plastic tablecloth was hiding it, dirty dishes was piled up in the sink, and the floor looked like it ain't been mopped in weeks. She'll never change, I thought. I watched her count the money.

"Is this the best you can do?"

"Look, Pam, I'm laid off for a few days, and yeah, this *is* the best I can do right now."

"How many times have I heard that? You need to get a better job, that's what you need to do."

"What you think I'm *trying* to do?"

"Try harder."

I wanted to slap her. "What about this dude I heard you supposed to be marrying?"

"Don't worry about it. When I'm ready to marry *anybody*, you'll be the first to know."

"You free-fuckin', or what?"

"That's none of your damn business, Franklin. He's doing more for the kids than you are, that's for damn sure."

"Speaking of kids, where they at anyway?"

"At camp."

"I see you still finding ways to get rid of 'em."

"For your information, they like going to camp, and it keeps 'em off the streets and out of trouble. The projects ain't changed, or can't you see that?"

What I saw was that she was up to about three hundred fuckin' pounds. I couldn't imagine what this dude must be about or what the hell he saw in her. I couldn't remember what I ever saw in her, really. And look at her now. It's a damn shame how some women just let themselves go. You'd think they'd wanna look good for themselves, not just for a damn man. Shit, I work out 'cause it makes me feel good. Women get weak over my body, but that ain't my fault.

Now Pam was sitting in front of the TV set—as usual—eating potato chips, drinking a soda, and crocheting. I was still sitting at the kitchen table, looking at the salt and pepper shakers I bought ten years ago. Damn. I got up and walked toward the door. "Tell the kids I said hi, I'll see 'em soon, and tell Derek to stop by over the weekend to shoot some hoops. I'll try to bring you some more money next week."

"I won't hold my breath," she said, and put another potato chip in her mouth. She didn't budge. I slammed the door on my way out.

*   *   *

At four o'clock, I watched *Love Connection* on TV. I was anxious, trying to figure out if I was handling this thing right. If not, at least my motives would be clear: "I was bullshitting. And I ain't interested." I watched *The People's Court* at four-thirty, and *Live at Five* with Sue Simmons—with her fine self. By twenty to seven, I figured she'd realize I wasn't coming and get the picture. My stomach was growling. I didn't have nothin' to eat, and didn't feel like cooking on that little-ass hot plate, so I put on a clean T-shirt and went to get me some Chinese food. I had barely turned the corner, and who did I run into? Shit.

"You changed your mind?" she asked.

"I got hung up," I heard myself saying.

"You could've called."

"I couldn't remember your last name."

"It's Banks. Zora Banks."

She was pissed off. Damn, she looked even prettier mad. "I was trying my hardest to get there by six, I just had some other business to take care of, and it took longer than I thought."

"You don't have to do this, you know," she said.

"I don't *have* to do nothing but die."

"Look, I'm getting bad vibes about this whole thing. You're the one who offered, Franklin."

And she was right. What the fuck. It ain't her fault that she turns me on, and I don't wanna be turned on right now, but I do wanna be turned on, but not right now and not this way. Shit. "Look, I'm sorry if I messed up your plans."

"You didn't mess up my plans, I just wasn't able to do everything I had on my list. If you want to know the truth, I rushed to get home by six so you wouldn't be standing around waiting for me."

That's right, lay the fuckin' guilt trip on me. But she was right. When I say I'm gonna do something, I usually do it.

But what the hell was I doing now? I don't like this feeling-confused shit, but I didn't want her to think I was just another unreliable blood either. "Look, can you wait till my food is ready, or better yet, I'll meet you at your place in a few minutes."

"I'm serious, Franklin—you don't have to feel obligated. I can get Eli to help me, like I told you."

"Look, just let me run home and get my tools, eat, and I'll come on over. How does that sound?"

"Sounds like you've got a guilt complex."

She smiled at me and left. Okay, so I'm a sucker. All I'm gon' do is put her stuff up and take my black ass on home. Simple as that.

When I got home, I gobbled my food, turned down the air conditioner, and left. I walked five doors to her building and rang the buzzer. Damn, she looked good running down those stairs. She was wearing some kind of Chinese-looking bathrobe. I couldn't tell if she had anything underneath it or not. Tarzan jumped at the thought.

"So how did your day go?" I asked. I couldn't think of nothin' better to say to break the ice that had formed since this morning.

"Okay, considering."

"So. You want me to start with the bed, the shelves, or the stereo? You tell me."

"You *sure* you want to do this?"

"I'm here, right?"

"Yeah, but this time I'll pay you."

"You must got a hearing problem, Zora. I'll tell you what. You can sing me a song." This was her answer: she turned the fan up full blast, then aimed it at me. "When you feel up to it," I said. "I'll start with the bed."

The phone company showed up with some outlandish excuse about why they was so late. By that time, I'd already finished the bed. Too bad she didn't have a mattress. Zora started making one phone call after another, and since I was now drilling holes in the living room wall, it was so noisy she went in the bathroom and closed the door. I was wondering who she could be talking to. I know it was none of my business, but hell, I wanted her to talk to me. When she came out, she sat down on top of a box and watched me work. Now, I dug *this* shit.

"You want a beer?" she asked.

"Sounds good to me."

"I'll run to the corner and get one."

"Wait a minute—you don't have to do that. Some ice water'll do."

"No, I don't mind, really."

She went into her bedroom and came back wearing some tight cutoff denim shorts. Her ass didn't even shake. And she had on this bright-orange T-shirt that said "It's Better in the Bahamas" on it. Her titties looked juicy underneath that sunrise. "You been to the Bahamas?" I asked.

"Yep. You been there too?"

"Nope. Puerto Rico—that's about it as far as the Caribbean goes." I was lying through my teeth. First of all, I'm scared as hell of airplanes. Even when I went in the service, I was pissy drunk when I got on. Passed out and don't even remember the ride. And second of all, I ain't never had enough money left over from a paycheck to be thinking about no vacations. Franklin, why you trying to impress this chick? My shit was crisscrossing like a motherfucker. If I was the praying type, now would be the perfect time to beg for guidance, strength, willpower, common-fuckin'-sense—all of it—I swear to God. "You trust me in your house alone?"

"Aren't you trustworthy?"

"Very much so," was all I said.

She left. I found some toggle bolts in my toolbox and finished putting up the shelves. One two three. I started on the stereo. Nice system. The woman didn't penny-pinch when it came to spending money on the music. And she knew what to buy, that's for damn sure. Akai. Bose speakers. When I get my shit together, this is the kinda system I wanna get. I was trying to find WBLS on the radio when she walked back in.

"You didn't put that together already," she said, in a genuinely surprised voice.

"I do this kind of stuff all the time. It's nothin'."

She opened a beer for me, and I took a sip, then lit a cigarette. "So you gon' join me?"

"I don't drink," she said.

Good, I thought. I been around enough lushes to last. "Well, you wanna put your books up now or later?"

"Later."

"You might as well get it over with. I know you can't reach up to the top, and I don't see no ladders around here, so why don't you use me?"

"You want me to use you, huh?" she asked.

I was trying to stop grinning. "Yeah, you hand me the books, and I'll put 'em up there for you." Shit, now that I was here, I didn't wanna leave. I felt comfortable around this woman. The next thing I knew, she was looking at me suspiciously, like she knew there was gon' be some kind of payoff, which she probably thought was between her legs. Women ain't used to men just being nice; they always think we want something in return. They usually right, but I wasn't waiting for no payoff. I was just curious.

It took us over an hour to get all them damn books on the shelves. I thought I had a lotta books, but she got me beat. She got books about everything: philosophy, foreign cookbooks, medical books, poetry, and novels—and not that Jackie Collins shit. I was impressed. Then she handed me this picture of a fat, but good-looking, woman. "Who's this?" I asked.

"My mother."

"She's almost as pretty as you are. Where is she?"

"She died when I was three."

"Sorry to hear that. Really. Where you want it?"

"Right next to this," she said, pointing to *Their Eyes Were Watching God*. That book was on part of the shelf by itself. When we finished, we sat down on her purple couch. The place was shaping up nice.

"So now what?" I asked. I still didn't wanna leave. The way I was feeling, I coulda stayed here with her forever.

"What do you mean, *now* what?"

"All I meant was, is there anything else you would like me to do since I'm here?"

"Nope. I'm wiped out. Aren't you?"

"Not really. I'm used to working much harder than this."

Then the damn telephone rang.

She got up from the couch to answer it, and I watched those juicy red lips open and close. "Hi, Portia! You finally got my message, huh? Yes indeed. I'm in here. You're in Brooklyn? I don't believe it. Sure, come on over. Boxes are everywhere, girl, but I've got some music! Okay. See you in a few minutes."

Well, just fuck me, then, I thought. I got up off the couch, put my tools back in the box, and stood in the middle of the floor like another unwanted dog at the ASPCA. I ain't used to this shit.

"Franklin," she said, after she hung up the phone, "I really appreciated your help, and when I get good and settled, I'll invite you over for dinner. How does that sound?"

"Can you cook?"

She walked over, grabbed my free hand, and pushed me out the door. I was glad. Relieved, really. Most women woulda done anything and everything to keep me there. But Zora was definitely different. She didn't act like she was starving for no man, which in and of itself was a new one on me.

When I got home, I put my tools away and looked at that tree trunk for a long time. Finally, I picked up one of my gouges and slid it in the wood. It felt soft, just like I betcha she feels. Franklin, can't you hear that train coming, man? But all I wanna do is touch her. Just once. A sliver of wood curled and fell on the floor. That's all, just once. I musta pushed that gouge through that tree at least a hundred times, 'cause the next thing I knew, my feet was swimming in chips of wood. Shit, I didn't feel no railroad tracks underneath 'em, so I kicked most of 'em off and fell across the bed.

3

"**H**oney, if he don't have at least two major credit cards, a modern car, a one-bedroom apartment, and a college degree, I say leave his ass alone—he ain't going nowhere in life. How old is he?" Portia asked.

"He looks like he's in his early thirties. And, Portia, so *what* if he doesn't have all that stuff? You've met hordes of 'em with it, and where has it gotten you?"

"Off the hook, honey," she said, which was a lie. First of all, Portia's got so many men calling her that she's afraid to answer her phone. Some people have normal hobbies. Portia's is juggling dates.

"Yeah, well, this man is nice, not to mention sexy as hell."

"That means he's over six feet tall and halfway good-lookin'. So what else is new?" she asked, and flopped down on the couch. Just looking at Portia, you'd get the impression that she's this innocent little thing. She calls it femininity. She doesn't take into account that walking down the streets of New York City in loud, tight halter dresses with bronze cleavage diminishes her demure. But she's a clothes freak. She lives at Saks and Bergdorf's. Portia flaunts everything she wears, and being a perfect size seven, she can get away with it. And even though her skin is flawless, you'll never catch her without makeup. She always looks like she's ready to party.

"He doesn't do drugs," I said.

"How do you know that?"

"He told me."

"And you believed that shit?"

"Why would he lie?"

"Most of 'em'll tell you anything to impress your ass. I swear to God, Zora. You're just as gullible as some of these twenty-year-olds out here." She got up and went over to the mirror and started brushing her hair, even though it didn't need it. She'd just gotten it done into one of those Chinese blunt cuts, and there wasn't a hair out of place.

"Well, let me put it this way," I said. "Do you know how rare it is to meet a man that makes you nervous?"

"What kinda work does he do—if any?"

"Construction."

"Construction? Pa-leeze. You know what that means?"

"No. You tell me, Miss Know-it-all."

"It means he's probably a ex-criminal and probably can't read or write."

"You make me sick sometimes, you know that, Portia? I'll tell you this much. He's a hardworking man, which is more than I can say for some of 'em I've met, and for me it means he's got potential."

"Potential is in the future, honey. We talking about right now."

"When will you realize that money isn't everything?"

"You can keep on believing that shit if you want to."

"Well, let me put it this way. I'll take happiness and love over money any day."

"Then you know what that makes you?"

"What?"

"A fool."

"Kiss my ass, Portia."

"Look, girlfriend, I'm just telling you to quit now while you're still ahead."

"Portia?"

"What?" she asked, inspecting my apartment like she was thinking about renting it herself.

"You know what your problem is?"

"No. Tell me what my problem is."

"You're too much of a skeptic, you don't have faith in anybody but yourself, and you place too much value on the wrong things."

"Oh, is that so. Well, I'll tell you something, Zora. You're too much of a fuckin' dreamer. You'd think by now you'd learn. These floors are gorgeous, girl."

"*He* did the floors."

She just raised her eyebrows and kept strolling through the place. I swear, I love Portia like a sister, but sometimes I wonder why I feel the need to get her approval for everything.

"Don't go in the bedroom—that floor's not dry yet."

She turned back. "He ain't one of these men still living at home with his Mama, is he?"

"No. He's got his own apartment," I said, even though I didn't know anything about his living situation. He hardly struck me as the type who lived with his Mama, though.

"Well, that's a relief. So many of 'em still living at home and *still* don't wanna spend no money on you. It's pitiful, really. Well, what does it look like? Old or new furniture?"

"Give me a break, would you? I haven't seen his place yet. I just met the man."

"It figures. He's probably too embarrassed. That's a sign, you know. He wants to hang out at your house but won't let you come to his. Is he married? That's probably it."

"Look, all he did was hook up my stereo, put my shelves up, and put my bed together."

"You fucked him, didn't you?"

"No, but I wish I did. I can't lie: Something magical happened between us, girl. He likes me. And even though I tried not to act like it, he knows I like him. I swear, it was this unspoken kind of thing."

"You're meditating too much, Zora. What kind of car does he drive?"

"How the hell would I know!"

"Probably travels on foot, like most of 'em that live in Brooklyn."

"Portia, most people in New York don't have cars. You don't have one, so shut up."

"What you got to drink around here? We're supposed to be celebrating, girl. Hell, this is your new apartment. Makes mine look like a dump."

I got up to get her a glass of juice.

"This is the strongest stuff you've got in the house? Not even a wine cooler?"

"We can walk to the liquor store if you just have to have a drink."

"I don't have time. I've got a date tonight. I just wanted to stop by and see the place."

"Portia, you should see him. He's so fine. Looks like he's been dipped in dark chocolate, girl."

"Here we go again with this shit. You don't even know if he can afford you, and you're already fantasizing. You're gonna get enough of this falling-in-love-with-love shit. Be out there on Gilligan's Island by your damnself. Don't I remember—and correct me if I'm wrong—but this is the same shit you were talking when you met Dillon and, lest we not forget, poor Percy!"

"That was different. They were both cases of bad judgment."

"Yeah, well, you don't know enough about this one yet to be judging him. So slow down."

"I *am* slowing down. I haven't *done* anything yet."

"You're just never gonna learn, are you?"

"If you mean pretending not to feel something when I know I feel something, then I guess I haven't. Do you know how rare it is to feel a trickle of anything when you meet a man?"

"This is true, but you ain't gotta jump ship just 'cause you think you might be sinking. You get my drift, girlfriend? Just be careful. I hope you're still coming to brunch Sunday after next. So don't go getting yourself all strung out on this—what is he? A construction worker? I swear. Didn't I tell you wasn't nothing in Brooklyn but blue-collar workers?"

"You know, Portia, you've got a lot to learn about people."

"Don't bullshit me, Zora. All kinds of lawyers, doctors, accountants, and other *professional* men'll be there. No telling who you might meet that can help you with your career. And hell, we all know it could use a lift."

"Eli just referred me to a voice coach."

"You mean that faggot you met at Bloomingdale's?"

"Why do you have to make such a big deal about him being gay?"

She started laughing. "They're probably lovers, and Eli thinks he's good because he makes him scream when he bends over!"

"Portia, stop it. For your information, he's already got a reputation and is doing me a favor by squeezing me in. He's coached some of the best." I didn't feel like telling her that I'd sent Reginald an a cappella tape, that he'd said I was a "brilliant songwriter" and that my voice was "powerful and had a host of possibilities," but he wouldn't be able to fit me in until after Labor Day.

"Yeah, yeah, yeah. I've gotta go to the bathroom something terrible. My fuckin' period is coming. I feel it." She went into the bathroom and closed the door. A few minutes later she walked out with the strangest look on her face, and she was holding a prescription bottle.

"What's this for?" she asked me.

Shit. I could've sworn I'd put all the phenobarb in the bottom of my trunk. Should I play dumb or go ahead and lie? And just what was she doing in my medicine cabinet anyway?

"What is it?"

"Phenobarbital, Zora."

"Oh. That."

"I was looking for a Tylenol, just in case these cramps hit me later, and I thought maybe this would be something for pain, but this ain't for no kind of pain—that much I do know."

"I thought I told you."

"Told me what?"

"That I've got epilepsy."

"You've got *what?*"

"You heard me."

"You mean you foam at the mouth and fall down and shit?"

"Not really. I used to have convulsions and then black out."

"Get the fuck outta here, Zora! You're putting me on, aren't you, girlfriend?"

"Yeah, I just made this up."

"Shit, I've known you more than two years now, and I ain't never seen you have no damn fits."

"Because I haven't had one in four years, that's why."

"What took you so goddamn long telling me? How would I have known what to do if we'da been sitting in a bar and you had one? This is a cheap shot, Zora. I mean really. I thought I was your damn friend."

"You are my friend. It's just that I don't go around broadcasting it."

"As much shit as we've been through, you coulda told *me*."

"Well, you know now, so just do me a favor and keep this to yourself, would you?"

"You mean you haven't told Marie and old dead-ass Claudette?"

"No."

She had a smug look on her face. "Let me ask you something. Say for instance you were about to have one—how would I know it?"

"Believe me, you'd know it."

"And just what am I supposed to do?"

"I really don't feel like talking about this."

"You know, I had a cousin who used to have fits, only back then they just said he had spells. Come to think of it, Junior never did get out the slow class. Maybe I should keep a spoon or clothespin in my purse from now on, just in case."

"Portia, I said I haven't had one in four years, damn."

"I heard you, but hell, who knows when one could just pop up again?"

"I don't anticipate having any fits anytime soon."

"This is deep, Zora. And I thought I knew you."

"You do know me; now you just know more."

"Well, all of us got some kind of bullshit we gotta deal with. This is the second period I've had this month, girl. If it ain't one thing, it's something else, ain't it? Look, I gotta run." She got up from the couch, and I walked her downstairs.

"Can I invite Marie and Claudette to this brunch?"

"Marie, yes, 'cause she's wild as hell. But Claudette, let her keep her tired ass at home with that fine-ass husband of hers and that big-headed baby. I swear, I don't know what he sees in her, and if I'da met him before she did, she'd be one single woman to this day." Before Portia closed the door she looked at me. "Zora, all joking aside. You've already had your share of losers, girl. Don't go getting yourself all hung up on another one."

We kissed each other on the cheeks, and I ran back upstairs. For the most part, Portia was right. But Franklin was different. I just knew it.

I was tired of unpacking, but I wasn't sleepy. It was only eight-thirty, and I didn't feel like watching TV, so I moved my paintings from one wall to another. The harder I tried not to, the more I kept seeing Franklin's big hands, helping me. Every time I walked past the door, I said a silent prayer. Please be downstairs, ready to push the buzzer. But there was no buzz. And please be thinking about me as hard as I'm thinking about you. My bare feet slid over the floors and tingled at the thought of him. I kept seeing sweat popping out on his forehead. Finally, I sat down on the couch, and in he walked. He sat right next to me, put my head on his shoulder, and told me I was exactly what he's been looking for—what's been missing in his life. When my head fell off the cushion, I was embarrassed at daydreaming again. I jumped up from the couch and stood in the middle of the floor. I was entirely too anxious, and wasn't about to sit in here for the rest of the night going crazy thinking about him, so I called Marie to see if she wanted to see a movie.

"What movie?" she asked.

"*My Brilliant Career.*"

"My brilliant what?"

"*Career!*" I could tell she was high.

"Where's it playing?"

"At the D. W. Griffith, on East Fifty-eighth Street."

"Shit, why isn't it playing on the West Side? Is it funny?"

"Not according to the reviews, but it sounds interesting."

"What's it about?"

"An Australian woman who writes, but no one takes her seriously."

"It sounds corny as hell. I'm not in the mood for anything heavy."

"You sound like you've been drinking."

"So what?"

"What's wrong?"

"Nothing, except I blew an audition today because the subway got stuck on Eighty-sixth Street for a half hour and I was late. My landlord's been bugging me because my rent is a month late. My check to my therapist bounced. But other than that, nothing's wrong."

"You want me to stop by?"

"For what?"

"To talk, take your mind off of things. Sounds like you need to try to relax."

"Relax? You're the one who thinks meditating solves all your problems, Zora, not me."

"I've never said meditating solves all my problems. It just calms me. It sounds like you need to do *something*."

"I am. I'm getting ready to get myself a refill."

"Well, maybe you *should* stay home, then."

"That's just what I'm planning to do."

"Call me if you need something, Marie."

"You got any money?"

"Be serious. Shit, I just moved!"

"Enjoy your movie, Zora," she said. "I'll get through this. I always do."

So I went alone. I can't stand being around Marie when

she's drunk. She gets loud and boisterous. Starts talking to people she doesn't even know. But when she's sober, she's fine. Funny as hell, which is why being a comedienne suits her. She does have a rule: She never drinks before an audition or a show. I wish she could stick to that rule all the time, but what's the point in giving people advice if they're not willing to take it?

I sat in that dark theater and was amazed. This woman had spunk, all right. She broke all the rules that applied to women during her time and did what she wanted to do anyway. Her courage paid off. By the time the credits ended, I felt reaffirmed. It was raining when I got outside. I didn't feel like getting on that nasty subway, so I hailed a cab. Hell, I had just left Australia. By the time we got over the Brooklyn Bridge, the rain had stopped. The Manhattan skyline was blinking red, blue, and yellow. When the cab pulled up in front of my building, Franklin was sitting on my stoop, smoking a cigarette.

"Hi," I said, after I paid the driver.

"Hi," he said.

"What are you doing out here?"

"Waiting for you."

"Waiting for me?"

"Waiting for you."

"Why?" But I already knew why: because you couldn't stand it. Just say it, Franklin, and we can stop this game right now.

"Because I wanted to see you."

"Why?"

"Because I wanted to see you."

"What if I hadn't come home alone?"

"Then I'da just acted like I was waiting for somebody else."

Portia can go to hell, I thought. "Would you like to come up?"

"You want me to come up?"

"Yes," I said, before I even thought about it. He followed me upstairs, and with each step, I was thinking, Lord, what am I getting myself into?

"Have a seat," I said, once we were inside. I was so nervous that I turned on the TV instead of the stereo, which is what I had intended to do. Still, I didn't want him to think I was trying to set a "mood." If there was going to be one, then we'd have to create it ourselves.

He hadn't sat down; I could feel him standing behind me. When I turned around, he was right in front of me. As if it was the only thing left to do, he bent down and kissed me on my nose, my cheeks, and then my lips. His mouth was warm and sweet. I thought maybe I should resist, but I couldn't, and then, with his lips breaking me down second by second, I asked myself, Why? I guess when my palms pressed inside the small of his back, that was his cue to go ahead and wrap those long arms around me. And that did it. I could've screamed, *"Please don't let me go!"* but I didn't. I was already falling in the black hole. He smelled so good, felt so warm and solid, that I couldn't help but think that *nothing* should feel this good. And he kissed me so slowly, so softly and deeply—the way I liked to be kissed—that my heart clicked. My eyelashes brushed his, and we rubbed noses, back and forth, back and forth, until I couldn't stand it. I swear, I tried to back up a little—just to get hold of myself—but he wouldn't let me go. Then it felt like I was floating away. Maybe because he had picked me up and was laying me down on the couch. I didn't want to open my eyes, because I knew this shit only happened in the movies. "Do you know what you're doing?" I asked, opening my eyes.

"I know exactly what I'm doing," he said. And I guess he did. He eased my T-shirt over my head and unzipped my shorts and put his big hands on my waist and rubbed. I don't know how he got my bra off, but I knew it was off when I felt him kiss my shoulder.

Then he stopped.

Here I was, aching all over, and he stopped!

"Can I just look at you?" he asked, and got up and leaned against the refrigerator. He crossed his arms and legs and smiled at me like I was a prize he'd won or something.

"You're beautiful," he said.

I smiled, because I felt beautiful. Then he moved a few inches away from the refrigerator, unzipped his jeans, and took off his shirt. He dropped everything on the floor, and just stood there. I wanted to put my hand over my mouth. I had never seen a man's body so perfect. My eyes traveled from his head on down, then stopped. Lord have mercy.

"What do you plan on doing to me?" I asked, as he started coming toward me.

"Everything," he said.

The man was no liar. He stroked my hair and my back, kissed my elbows, my belly, my thighs, even my knees and toes! I wanted to scream. To pull out every strand of his hair, my hair—somebody's hair. Finally, I thought, a man who knew that breasts had feelings too. I touched him everywhere I could reach. Brushed my lips wherever I felt skin. His body was one tight muscle after another, and so hot, so big, so strong, I wanted to beg him to never stop touching me. "Lord, Lord, Lord, Lord, Lord," I sang, as we moved like slow tornadoes. He was so considerate and smooth that by the time I heard him call out my name, I knew it was *me* he wanted.

"*Franklin!*" I sighed, and my body let itself loose.

"I'm here, baby, I'm here," he said, and kissed me on my shoulder. A river had formed in the cave of my belly, and I felt limp. He shivered. A moment passed, and he shivered again.

"You're too good to be true," he said, and lifted me up on top of him. He stared into my eyes as if he was searching for something, and after he found it we held each other like it was goodbye instead of hello. Finally, we both exhaled, and sank. We kept our arms and legs wrapped around each other like octopuses for what must have been a long time, because the next thing I knew, Johnny Carson was going off.

"Is this how you operate?" I asked.

"Is this how *you* operate?" he asked me back.

Then we both started laughing.

"So how about that song now?"

"I just finished singing. Didn't you hear me?"

"I heard you, baby, but I wanna hear you sing for real."

All of a sudden, a voice in my head told me to stop this. Just stop it. He felt too good too fast. It must have been all over my face.

"What's wrong?" he asked.

"Nothing."

"Then why you looking like somebody just died?"

"This is dangerous, you know."

"For who?"

"Me."

"I thought you didn't have a man, or did you lie?"

"No, I didn't lie. What about you? You look like you're the type that's probably got more than one woman."

"I really ain't in the market. Trying to get my life in order. Women get me all confused."

"Then what are you doing here?"

"Sometimes you have to take detours."

"Oh, so that's what I am, a detour."

"You know what I mean."

"No, I don't."

"A man knows when a woman is special. Women like you don't come along every day. I'd be a fool not to stop and check you out."

"Check me out? Is this some kind of game, Franklin?"

He kissed me on the forehead and looked me dead in the eye.

"Do this feel like a game to you?"

"No."

"So what's the problem?"

"I'm scared, I guess."

"Of what?"

"I don't know."

"That ain't no kinda answer. Talk to me."

I wanted to tell him that I was scared of him, of how he was making me feel, but when I feel so good that it makes me sad, my words get twisted up and it's hard to say what I really mean. "Well, I'm just trying to do so many things. I'm starting a new voice coach soon, school starts next month, I just moved, I'm trying to figure out—"

He cut me off. "You wanna know something? I been trying to talk myself into not thinking about you since I first met you. A month ago, I made up my mind that all I was gon' do was concentrate on how I could start my own business in a year or two, and I promised myself that I wasn't getting involved with no more women until I got my constitution together—"

Then I cut him off. "That's what I'm trying to do too, Franklin."

"So are we laying here saying we can't do both?"

"I don't know."

"How do you feel right now?" he asked.

Should I tell the truth? Yes, tell the damn truth, Zora. "I

feel like I've been hibernating and you're the sun and you just shined on me and let me know it's spring. I feel like I could levitate right up to the ceiling. What about you?"

"I feel like a man who just hit the lottery. That answer your question?"

"You sure this isn't just the sex?"

"I know the difference between good sex and a good woman, baby."

Even though I wanted to believe him, wanted to trust him, the sadness still came back. I wanted to find out up front if this man was sincere, so I decided to go ahead and tell him how I really felt. "I'm scared that if I get involved with you and it doesn't work out, then I'll be right back where I started—lonely and alone again."

"You already involved," he said. "And you ain't gotta worry about being lonely no more."

"What makes you so sure?"

"Because I'm here and I ain't going nowhere until you ask me to leave. You been thinking about me as much as I been thinking about you. So let's cut the games. That's why you went out tonight—so you wouldn't be in here suffocating with them thoughts, trying to figure out what you was feeling and if I was feeling anything close to it. Am I wrong?"

"No, you're not wrong." Why didn't I lie? Why couldn't I lie? I was opening up too fast and letting him see me. But so was he, wasn't he? Didn't he just admit that he'd been thinking about me all day?

"Relax," he said, and pressed my head back down against his chest. At first his heart was beating fast, but after a few minutes, when I put my arms around his neck and stroked it, the beats slowed down.

"Franklin, what exactly do you want from me?" Now, why'd I ask such a stupid-ass question?

"Nothin' you ain't willing to give."

"What are you willing to give?"

"As much as I need to, baby."

"Is that a little or a lot?"

"I'd say it's a lot."

"Franklin?"

"Yeah," he said, running his fingers through my hair.

I didn't want this to be just another good lay. Not this time. "I've been in this situation before. Where everything feels right, but then something goes wrong and I live through another sad ending. I'm tired of diving in headfirst, then swimming back to shore and it's empty, you know?"

"You been choosing the wrong men," he said.

"What makes you say that?"

"Because I wouldn't be here now," he said.

"How're you supposed to know who's the right one?" I asked.

"You gotta learn to trust your instincts."

"My instincts have made some bad decisions before."

"Do I feel right?"

"Right now you do. But I can't lie, Franklin: I've been here before too. This time I want something that'll be good for a long time, something that'll last."

"I hear you, baby."

I was wound up now. "And I want to be an asset to somebody—a man—but up to now it hasn't worked both ways."

"Like I said, baby, you been picking the wrong men. And since we spillin' our guts, I gotta be honest. I ain't got no money, so if you lookin' for some dude with a big bank account, I might as well leave now."

I started laughing. "I can't hug and kiss a bank account, and if I could, I'm sure it wouldn't make me feel like this."

He just kept stroking my hair and my right cheek. I swear,

he felt like an easy chair I never wanted to get out of. Then he squeezed me tighter. "You wanna know something?" he asked.

I pushed my head deeper into his chest and nodded yes.

"Sounds to me like we members of the same club."

4

"Say, Franklin?" a voice called through the door. "Could you turn it down a little, blood?"

"No problem, man. Sorry about that." I couldn't tell who it was, but it didn't matter. Shit, I felt good. Sometimes life can be sweet as hell. All that shit about being by myself until I got my constitution together went up in smoke. What I mean is, the plan is the same, the rules just changed. Hell, when you meet a woman who likes you 'cause you you, not because of how much money you bring home, or how big your dick is and how good you use it; tells you she wants to be in your corner a hundred percent and means it; asks you about your dreams. . . . I mean, she asked me what did I see myself doing five, ten years from now? Ain't no woman never asked me no shit like that. I told her the truth. Damn, it felt good being able to tell somebody. Felt good being able to talk to a woman about some real shit for a change. To tell the truth, we ended up doing more talking than fucking. Which was cool. A real nice change. She just sat there with those little bird legs of hers crossed like a Buddha and let me ramble. I told her my dreams, all right. That I was tired of working construction, never having no money. That one day in the near future I was planning on being my own boss.

And she listened. Asked questions. Didn't laugh or think I was being outrageous and shit. A man needs a woman who makes him feel like he can do anything. Shit, when you find one who can cook, knows how to make real love, is pretty and smart, knows what she wants outta life and is trying to get it, you see her as a asset, not no liability. You don't find *all* this in a woman every day. Which is why I ain't letting her get away.

I could see that she was a little scared at first. I mean, sparks was flying so fast and everything, and I was just waiting for her to tell me that her heart been broke so many times she didn't trust men no more. I was all set to tell her, "This time, baby, don't be scared. This man ain't interested in breaking your heart—he's interested in gluing it back together and keeping it for hisself." But good pussy'll make you say the first thing that comes to your mind, so I decided to keep my mouth shut on that note till I know the shit is what it is.

What time is it? Shit, I better get my ass up. Daydreaming ain't gon' get it. This place was a wreck. I ain't been home in three days, and that was only to change my clothes. I had to make myself leave, and I was glad Zora didn't want me to go. That was a good sign. I fed my fish. I really needed to clean the tank. Damn, no clean work clothes. I knew there was something I was supposed to do—go to the Laundromat. Who gives a shit? I ain't felt this good since . . . since when? Since that time when I didn't have but eight cents to my name and hit Lotto for four numbers and won $306. Naw, even that shit can't compare to this.

I did my sit-ups and push-ups, took a shower, put on some dirty jeans, and tried to wipe some of the dirt off with my washcloth. Picked up a work shirt, smelled under the arms of at least four of 'em until I found one that didn't smell so funky. I put it on. I stopped at the coffee shop and got my regular, plus a buttered roll.

"Where's Vinney?" I asked one of the crewmen. This dude was new.

"Upstairs," he said. "What's your name, man? I'm Louie, Vinney's brother-in-law."

"Franklin, man," I said, and reached out to slap his hand, but he acted like he wanted to shake, so I shook.

The building wasn't nothin' but a shell. It had already been gutted; the walls had been ripped out, and you could see all the way through to the other end. I'm just glad it's summertime. In the winter, we always bring up old trash cans and make fires. It don't help much, which is why a lot of us usually keep a half pint of somethin' in our back pockets.

I ran upstairs and stopped on each landing, but I didn't see Vinney till I got to the fourth floor. He was looking over some blueprints with another dude.

"What's up, boss?"

"Oh, Frankie," he said, like he wasn't thrilled about seeing me. I hate that tone of voice. It always mean the same damn thing. I tore part of the lid off my coffee and took a sip.

"You won't believe this, Frankie."

"Try me."

"I miscalculated. Got too many men on the job right now. Won't really be needing another man until at least next week."

"What you saying, Vinney?"

"I'm asking if you can come back next week, Frankie."

"The new guy downstairs—your 'brother-in-law.' He's taking my place? Is that how you play, Vinney?"

He threw his white hands in the air. "Frankie. Family is family. This guy's a canker sore, but I got put on the spot. He's got a drug problem, couldn't you see that?"

"I wasn't looking at him that hard."

"I give him a week, at the most. He fucks up once, I call you. Don't I always take care of you, Frankie?"

I wanted to throw Vinney down the fuckin' stairs, I swear I did. He went back to talking to that dude, and I threw the rest of my coffee on the floor, ran down the steps four at a time, and didn't see Louie nowhere in sight. I walked on outside and took a bite off my roll.

Seven-fifteen in the morning. It was already hot. Zora's probably still asleep, but I don't want her to see me now. Not with my head all fucked up like this. Feel like a million dollars for thirty-six fuckin' hours, and just like that—back to zero. The white man sure know how to bust a niggah's bubble. I can just hear Pam bitching now.

I went back to my room, got all my dirty clothes together, and went to the Laundromat. I was sitting there reading the paper, and I looked up and noticed all these blue fliers taped to the walls. I put my paper down and walked over and snatched one off the wall. Some business school in Brooklyn was trying to get minorities to enroll. Offered all kinds of classes. Computers, accounting, but what caught my eye was the one about how to be a entrepreneur. I knew what that meant. Me. The paper said they had some money and they guaranteed placement. I folded the paper up and put it inside the laundry bag. Smoked three cigarettes while I waited for my clothes to dry, and decided to clean my room and the fish tank when I got home.

Took me all damn day. Since I don't have no vacuum cleaner, the only way I can get this sawdust up is with a swish broom. I took all the dirty dishes outta the refrigerator, walked down the hall to the kitchen, put 'em in the sink, boiled a pot of water, poured it over 'em, added half a bottle of ammonia, and let 'em soak. That's the only way that hard-ass food ever comes off. I finally emptied all the clothes on top of the mattress and started folding 'em up. Not only was they wrinkled as hell, but my shorts and undershirts was pink. I keep forgetting to sort 'em out like Sandy taught me how to do. Shit. I spend more money on undershirts and shorts; rather than wear 'em all dingy—especially in the summer—I just keep buying new ones. The last time this shit happened, everything white came out dirty blue from my jeans. I poured a whole bottle of Clorox in a pail and soaked 'em for two days. When I went to scrub the shits, they just crumbled in my hands. I stay away from bleach now. I was rolling my socks together, when that piece of paper fell out. I read it twice. If I had a phone, I woulda called 'em right then and there. I put the paper on the dresser, lit a incense, turned the air conditioner up, and laid down.

Now what?

I looked over at my worktable. All of a sudden that damn wall unit I was making looked ugly as hell. Shoulda used a harder wood, and I knew it. But I'm cheap. I felt like breaking it up and throwing it in the trash but couldn't do it. I finish everything I start. But not right now. I wasn't in the mood for no woodworking. What I *was* in the mood for was a drink. I got up and poured myself a double shot of Jack Daniel's. Turned on my box, sipped some more, turned on the TV, watched *Wheel of Fortune*, won myself a car and a fuckin' sailboat while I cooked myself some liver and rice. I ate, sipped some more, then fell out. When I woke up, I heard a organ and somebody saying, "Let us give thanks to our Lord."

It was still dark outside, but I could see the sun trying to come up. I looked at the clock. Shit, it was five o'clock in the damn morning. I jumped up, did my sit-ups and push-ups, took a shower, put on my clean work clothes, and went to the corner to get my coffee. Then I caught the bus to A Dream Deferred.

I'm getting me a fuckin' job today. Even if I have to kick somebody's ass.

There was already fifteen or twenty brothers and a few Puerto Ricans standing outside A Dream. I saw a few dudes I knew. "What's happening, man?" I asked. "Nothin', man—you got it." I walked inside and put my name and stuff in the book. I was number 18. Maybe I should play that number today. The brother who ran this place, Kendricks, looked up when he saw me.

"Frankie, my man. You back?"

"Yeah, I'm back." Last fall and part of the winter, I damn near lived here. I got to shape up a lot of jobs, 'cause they know I ain't scared to work, I ain't lazy, and I'm big and strong. I usually got picked over the little dudes. I made enough money to buy my kids some decent Christmas presents, and gave Pam a couple a hundred dollars on top of that. And bought myself a suit. Just because. It's the only suit I own. I'll tell you, ain't nothin' like having some money in your pocket. I even put a few hundred in the bank. By the end of January, when the weather got real funky, everything slowed down, and I had to close my savings account. I ended up painting walls for Vinney for five dollars a hour, but it was better than nothing.

"Glad to see you," Kendricks said.

"Anything jumping off today?"

"Three or four sites, man. What happened to Vinney?"

"What always happen?"

"Anyway, sit tight, we going to Manhattan first. A hotel in midtown, man. Got your name on that one. Word is out that ain't but two bloods on the job. You interested, ain't you?"

"You damn right. I need a job, man. Yesterday."

"We leave in fifteen minutes."

I went back outside and sat down on the ground. A bottle was being passed around, but I didn't want none. I want a job, and if any weird shit go down, I damn sure don't wanna be high. Shit, I *think* I got myself a woman now, and I wanna be able to take her to dinner and shit. Zora is definitely the type that needs to be taken out. I wanna show her off—walk down the street with her hand in mine, have motherfuckers staring at us, and I be looking like, "Yeah, she mine, motherfucker. Wish you could taste it too, don't you?" And I wanna do more than just fuck her. Queens supposed to be treated like queens.

A bunch of us piled into Kendricks's station wagon, and a few carloads followed us. I was sitting next to a dude who needed more than a job. He needed to brush his damn teeth. His breath smelled like burning shit. "Could you roll that window all the way down, my man?"

"No problem, brother."

I leaned toward the back of the front seat. "Kendricks. What stage they in?"

"Excavation."

I leaned back in my seat and felt myself grinning. Shit, if we can get on, a job like this could mean not only union, but at least fourteen, fifteen, maybe even sixteen an hour. This could also mean a steady fuckin' job for a change.

"How long is it looking?" I asked.

"Man, it's a forty-storied hotel! At least a year and a half, but you know how this shit go. Something is gon' go down to drag the shit out."

By the time we got there, we saw this big-ass hole, at least forty feet deep, and it took up the whole block. They had already dynamited it. The first thing we did was a head count.

There was thirty-nine men down there driving bulldozers, cranes, and front-end loaders, and some was working with picks, axes, and shovels too—but wasn't a black or Hispanic to be seen. And once they start the foundation, they gon' need at least a hundred or more men. My palms was already itching.

Kendricks walked over to a white guy. "Say, could you tell me where the super is?"

"Who's looking for him?"

"I am."

He looked at all eighteen of us, put his hands in his pockets, and then said, "Don't know," and kept walking.

We looked at each other, as if to say, It's gon' be some shit here today 'cause these motherfuckers already playing games. Somebody musta warned 'em, told 'em we would be here. They always play this silly-ass game when they get tipped.

We walked all around the site, right down into the hole, until we spotted a white dude with papers in his hands. We knew he was the super. Kendricks got close enough to smell his breath.

"Hello, sir."

"I don't have no jobs. Got all the men I need right now."

"Did I *ask* you for a job?"

"You were getting ready to, weren't you?"

"No. My men and I here are from A Dream Deferred, and we counted thirty-nine men down here and not a single one is black or Hispanic."

"That's not true. I got two Cubans, one Hispanic, and two blacks."

"Where?"

"They just finished the demolition."

"We're talking about what we see now. Well, where's the super for the excavation?"

"He's down there," he said, pointing. "But don't tell him I sent you."

We walked down to where he was. Kendricks tapped him on the shoulder. "Excuse me, sir, but we just took a head count, and seems there's no blacks or Hispanics working on your crew."

"I've got three guys, but two of them are on another job right now, and one isn't here today."

"That's really too bad. If they're not here, they don't count. And besides, it ain't enough anyway. You need at least twelve out of forty." Kendricks looked around the site again. "The drillers are all white. You've got five rigs and you don't have a black with the driller or the helper. And you've got at least ten carpenters and six laborers."

"Look, I can't increase my work force. I don't have any room."

"Fuck all that shit, man. You know that at least thirty percent of the work force—by trade—is supposed to be black and Hispanic. If you have three men on the job, we're supposed to get one—by law. And where I live, we're hundred percent of the population and we still only get fifty percent of the jobs. And I betcha these men are probably from out of town any damn way. Where you live? Connecticut? Jersey? Philly?"

"Look, I got an OEO guy up in the shanty. Talk to him. I don't have time for this kind of shit."

"No problem," Kendricks said, and signaled us to follow him. He knocked on the shanty door, and the brother who opened it stood in the doorway like he wasn't letting nothing and nobody inside. He was wearing those tortoiseshell glasses, a sports jacket, was high yellow, had his class ring on his right hand and a wide gold band on his left. I'd put money on it that he was married to a white girl. "What do you want?" he asked.

"You know why we here, man, so let's cut the bullshit," Kendricks said.

"Say man, I just came on this job a week ago, and I don't even have all the figures yet," he said.

"You don't need no figures, I got 'em. I just made a head count."

"Well, make an appointment for the end of the week, and we'll see if we can put somebody on then."

Everybody know the OEO person is always black. He gets paid to block blacks and Hispanics from working on the site, and to make us bullshit promises so we won't stop the job. And to keep the feds off their back, the general contractor'll hire minorities all right, but they don't pay them the prevailing wage, and most of 'em don't even have green cards.

"Look, man," Kendricks said, "if you can't put some of my men on today, we gon' stop the fuckin' job now."

He closed the door.

On the way back down in the hole, we picked up some two-by-fours, pipes, and rocks. Kendricks looked at some of the white dudes and said, "Drop your tools. Turn off them engines and stop working."

The super yelled, "Don't none of you guys stop working. They aren't stopping this goddamn job."

The white dudes didn't drop or turn off nothing. They just looked at us, to see who was gon' make the first move. The super turned toward Kendricks and said, "I told you, I don't need any more men right now."

"Look around you," Kendricks said, holding a pipe right next to his thigh. "This is a hundred-and-five-million-dollar contract, and the only *black* guys around here is us. I'ma tell you this one more time. What I have here are eighteen men ready to work. You better put somebody on or else we'll stop this goddamn job for weeks."

"You want me to call the cops?"

"Call 'em," Kendricks said.

This motherfucker whipped out his walkie-talkie and we knew he was talking to Uncle Tom. This wouldn't be the first time they called the cops on us.

Then Kendricks said, "All I'm trying to do is put some men to work. You're the one breaking the law. I ain't breaking the law."

"I told you. We've got enough men. We won't even be starting the foundation for at least another three weeks. Why don't you and your men just come back then?"

"We'll come back then, too. But right now, we got excavators, concrete workers, carpenters—you name it. And we don't give a goddamn about the men you claim are coming. We got eighteen men right here who are ready to work, *today*. Take at least four or five of 'em now, or won't nobody make no fuckin' money today." Kendricks folded his arms.

"And just what am I supposed to do? Tell the sub he's got to fire the men he has in order to hire yours?"

"This is America, man. Life just ain't fair, is it?" The white boys squeezed the handles on their tools. Kendricks was talking plenty of shit, and we was all curious as to how this shit was gon' go down. We walked right past the super and back over to where the rest of 'em was working. Some of us stepped in front of anything that moved, while another man climbed up next to a driver, and made 'em turn off the ignitions. The rest of the white boys dropped their tools. It was pretty easy today, but sometimes the white boys is ready to fight. Within a few minutes, it was quiet as hell in that hole. And wasn't nothin' moving. When we spotted the cops, we still didn't budge. All three of 'em came down into the hole with their guns out.

"What seems to be the problem here?" one asked all of us.

Kendricks spoke up. "Officer, what we're doing here is

perfectly legal. I'm the director of an organization called A Dream Deferred, whose sole purpose is to assure the Office of Equal Opportunity that at any construction site where the contract exceeds fifty thousand dollars, that thirty percent of the work force is black and Hispanic. We're just trying to solve this problem here so we can put some men to work. And since there's tax abatement money on this site, the super's breaking the law. We've been trying to negotiate, but they don't want to. So he called you to get us off the site. But we ain't leaving till some of my men get put on. Simple as that."

The cops all looked at each other, then around the site.

"Look, we don't want to press charges," the super said. "But we've told these guys we'd take two men today and set up a meeting to discuss putting on more men."

All of us brothers looked at each other and tried not to laugh. This motherfucker changed his tune real quick-like. He don't want this information to get back to the wrong folks. He'd really be up shit's creek, then.

"Do you have any qualified men?" he asked, with a long sigh.

"Yeah," Kendricks said. "I've got a lot of qualified men. Carpenters and laborers."

"Then give us two," he said, "and come back next week and we'll see what we can do."

Kendricks looked at one brother, then at me. I was so happy I coulda shit.

5

I was at the beach, lying on a blanket and reading *One Hundred Years of Solitude,* while I waited for Marie, Portia, and Claudette to show up. Even though I consider them to be my best friends, we don't see each other that often; everybody's so busy. The beach wasn't crowded, because it was a weekday. During the summer, I try to come at least once a week, even though this is the nastiest water I've ever seen in my life. A far cry from the Bahamas. Last summer, I got bit by a jellyfish. The most I do now is get my feet wet.

"So was it as good as you thought it would be?" Marie asked. I turned my book facedown and looked up. She was wearing a hot-pink one-piece, and since the girl is six feet tall, has the prettiest legs in the world, and curves in all the right places, she looked fantastic. Her natural hair color was a reddish brown, but the sun had already lightened it a few shades and brought out her freckles.

"I'm not finished with it yet," I said, even though I knew what she was referring to. It seemed like I'd already told the whole world about Franklin.

"I'm not talking about the damn book."

"You mean Franklin?"

"Yeah. Now stand up and let me see you. I haven't seen your fat ass in a two-piece before."

I stood up.

"Looking good, girl. Go on with your bad self."

Claudette appeared with a big umbrella in one hand and her baby, Chanelle, in a stroller in the other. Claudette's one of the darkest, prettiest women I know. Her hair is jet black and hangs down past her shoulders, although she always pulls it back into a ponytail. She likes to swim but hates the sun. As a matter of fact, she had on shorts and a tube top. "So was the cover as good as the book?" she asked, pushing the point of the pole into the sand.

"I wanna know how many inches it is." That was Portia, of course, who was wearing a white string bikini. She could put Christie Brinkley to shame on any cover of *Sports Illustrated*.

"Wait a minute!" I yelled. "This is ridiculous. First of all, to answer your question, Marie: No. It was *better* than I thought it would be, which should answer your question too, Claudette. And, Portia, none of your *damn* business. Let me just say this: It's big enough."

"You bitch," Portia said. "Just tell me what size shoe he wears, how tall he is, and if he's got big hands. Gives it away every time."

"That shit is not true," Claudette said, shaking out her blanket, then rolling Chanelle, who was asleep, over on top of it. "Believe me, you can't go by that. I've had enough tall men with big feet and little dicks to know what I'm talking about. My husband, for one, but I'm not complaining. It's not the engine, honey, it's the engineer."

"Marie, can I have a cigarette?" I asked.

All three of them looked at me like I was crazy.

"A what?"

"You heard me—a cigarette. I don't need a lecture; just let me have one."

"Since when did you start smoking?" Claudette asked.

"I smoked when I was in college."

"So why be stupid and start again?"

"Because I'm nervous, and when I get nervous I eat, and I don't want to start gaining back what I've lost."

"You're stupider than you look," Portia said. "Would you rub some suntan lotion on my back?" I picked up the bottle, and Marie handed me the cigarette anyway. When I finished with Portia's back, I lit it up.

"You look ridiculous, girl. Turn around and let me rub some of this on your back," she said.

I shook my head no. That first puff made me dizzy as all get-out. The second one wasn't so bad. By the third one, I felt like I was high, so I pushed it underneath the sand.

"What are you so damn nervous about?" Marie asked. "We came all the way out here to hear about this Mr. Wonderful, and you haven't filled us in on a single detail, like can he eat pussy—or if he's even willing. All you have to tell us is that you're nervous?"

"All right already. I *think* I'm falling in love. He's past wonderful. And he feels like a dream come true."

"And that makes you nervous?" Claudette asked.

"I wasn't exactly honest with him about a few things."

Portia looked at me as if she was ready to ask me was it about the epilepsy, then decided against it. "So what?" she said. "Some things we're supposed to keep to ourself. That's what's wrong with women anyway. Get fucked real good, think we're in love, then we spill our fuckin' guts, give 'em our love résumés in chronological order, tell 'em all kinds of personal shit that shouldn't have no bearing or ain't got nothin' to do with them, and what kind of information do they give up? Where they were born, how old they are, and where they work and shit. We need to be more like them. And hell, what he don't know won't hurt him." She looked around the beach. "What I wanna know is where the hell are all the men today? It should be some firemen, policemen—something out here besides all these bald-headed retirees. Damn."

"They're at work, which is where you should be," Claudette said.

"For your information, I'm taking a vacation day. Why aren't you playing prosecutor?"

"Because when you work for yourself, you make your own hours. What is it you think you should've told him?" Claudette asked me, giving Portia the evil eye.

I got a lump in my throat. The baby made a noise. "That I used to be fat. You want me to check the baby?"

"She's fine, Zora. Is that all? Shoot, it looks like you've got it under control, so why bother?"

"Why don't you just get yourself some diet pills for insurance?" Marie said.

"Don't you dare," Claudette said. "You can get addicted to those things."

"That's a lie. I take one every now and then, especially when I've got a show. All they do is help me stay up, but I'm damn sure not addicted."

"You drink enough to make up for it," Portia said.

"Well, at least I don't auction my pussy just so I can go on a shopping spree. So shut the fuck up, Portia."

She had a point. And Portia was just about to say something, when Claudette cut in. "Guess who's pregnant?"

"Not me," Marie said, and started searching through her beach bag for something.

"It damn sure ain't me," Portia said.

"You again?" I asked Claudette.

"Yep. And this is it. We figured we'd go ahead and get it over with. I'm getting my tubes tied after this one."

"Good," Portia said. "There's enough retards in the world as it is."

Claudette didn't bother responding to this. We both know that Portia's just jealous, and in spite of the fact that she lives in the fast lane, she'd give anything to have what Claudette has. Steady love and security.

"I don't want nobody's kids," Marie said.

"Why not?" I asked.

" 'Cause I don't like 'em, that's why. They get on my nerves, I don't have the patience, and besides, I'm too selfish."

"They're a lot of fun," Claudette said. "Anybody'll get on your nerves when you see them three hundred and sixty-five days a year. True, kids are definitely a lot of work, but they're worth it. It does make things a helluva lot easier when you've got a husband that helps you."

"You just lucked out. They ain't all like that," Portia said.

"I didn't luck out, sweetheart. I picked the right man, something you know nothing about."

"Fuck you," Portia said.

"I've got a husband who does that, or are you deaf?"

I swear, the way they argue, you'd think they really hated each other or were sisters. "All right, let's cool it, ladies," I said. "We came out here to get some sun, relax, and have a good time."

"Okay, Zora," Portia said. "Now cut the bullshit. How much does he make?"

"Portia, you are so tacky, I swear," Claudette said, smoothing the edges of her blanket and wiping the sweat from Chanelle's forehead.

"I just asked Zora a simple question."

"How much money he makes is really none of your business," Claudette said.

"I didn't say it was my business. I just wanted to know if he's making any money, or is he as poor as a church mouse?"

"What difference does it make?"

"If I had a live-in housekeeper and was married to a doctor, I guess I could talk the same shit you're talking."

"He wasn't a doctor when I married him."

"Yeah, but you knew it wouldn't be long before he'd be raking in the dough."

"You're aggravating as hell, you know that, Portia? You think everybody in the world thinks like you do, but thank God that's not true. Women like you give the rest of us a bad reputation. But there's some of us out here who've got more than an overworked pussy to offer."

Portia jumped up, like she was getting ready to hit Claudette. "If you wasn't pregnant, I'd kick your ass, you know that?"

"I'm starving," Claudette said. "Anybody want something from the snack bar?"

"Yeah, me. I need a drink," Marie said.

"Keep an eye out on Chanelle for me, would you, Zora?"

I nodded a yes and glued my eyes toward the tiny brown body on the blue blanket. She was beautiful. One day I hoped to be so lucky. After the two of them left, Portia was eyeballing the beach again. "I can't stand Claudette, you know? She thinks she's hot shit. Well, since ain't nothing happening out here today, I might as well get wet," she said, and ran toward the water.

I put my head down and closed my eyes. All I wanted to do was think about Franklin.

After hours of gin rummy and spades, we left the beach about six. My skin looked like red clay, and I was tired. Claudette, the only one with a car, dropped Portia and Marie off at the train station when we got to Brooklyn. And since I was on the route to her house, she took me home.

"Is that him?" she asked. Franklin was sitting out on my stoop again.

"That's him."

"Damn," she said, waving, and he waved back. "I see what you mean, girl. What a hunk. I don't need any introductions right now. Some other time. Don't be a fool, Zora. Don't you listen to a word of advice Portia has to offer. You see what condition she's in, right?"

"What condition?" I asked.

"She can't keep a man. If this one treats you good and makes you feel good, give him a chance. That's what it's all about."

"So far, he does and I am." I pecked her on the cheek, blew the baby a kiss, and got out of the car. "See you soon. Tell Allen I said hello, and congratulations, girl. I hope this one's a boy."

I was glad to see Franklin, but I didn't like the idea that he was waiting for me.

"Hi, baby," he said, without moving.

"Hi," I said. "Franklin, would you not do this, please?"

"Not do what?"

"Sit out here and wait for me like this." I just didn't want him to start taking so much for granted.

"Why? You trying to hide me or something?"

"No, that's not it at all. We said we'd take this slow, give each other some space, didn't we?"

He just smiled and whipped out a bouquet of flowers from behind his back. Flowers make me weak. "I just wanted you to have these. You got so many plants up there, and the only flowers I saw was dead. A woman as beautiful as you should be surrounded by 'em."

Those dimples were showing, and I knew he knew he was flattering me to death, so I couldn't help but go along with it. "Why, thank you, sir."

"You look like you been to the beach."

"I have, with Marie, Portia, and Claudette. That was Claudette who just dropped me off. All of them want to meet you. I've told them all about you."

"What'd you tell 'em?"

"None of your business."

"Look, baby, if you're busy, I can see you tomorrow. I just wanted to give you these and tell you that I started a new job today. A hotel in Manhattan. Real money. And this one'll probably last at least a year or two. I feel good."

"That's wonderful!" I said. I was glad to hear it for his sake, because Franklin had told me about some of the problems he's had trying to get in the union and just trying to work steadily. I can't lie: As I stood there looking at him, I started to feel lucky. Lucky that someone was waiting to see me. "Well, I'm not planning anything special," I said, trying to clean up the fact that I may have given him the impression that I didn't want to see him.

"I wanted to take you out to dinner, but these white boys tried to work me to death today. There's a fight coming on tonight, and I did wanna see it."

"You can watch it here if you want to. I was going to broil some chicken, steam some zucchini, make a salad."

"You saying you wanna see me?"

"I see you now," I said, and unlocked the front door.

He chuckled. When we got upstairs, it was sweltering inside. I put the flowers in a vase. Gladiolas and baby's breath.

"You need a air conditioner, baby. I've got a extra one—let me run and get it."

Run and get it? "How far do you live from here?" I asked.

"Right up the street," he said. "Be back in a flash."

That meant he was my neighbor. Before I had a chance to think about how I felt about him living so close, he was back and carrying this gigantic thing. He set it right up, and I was just grateful that it worked. He turned on the TV, sat down on the couch, and pulled a half pint of something out of his back pocket.

"Can I get a glass of ice, baby?"

"Sure," I said. I handed him a glass, then went into the bedroom to take off my clothes.

"Can I see what you look like in your bathing suit?"

I had just slipped out of it, but I put it back on and walked out into the middle of the living room.

"That's the only bathing suit you got?"

"Why, don't you like it?"

"Yeah, I like it all right. But I don't know all about you wearing it to the beach and everything."

I put my hands on my hips and looked at him like he was crazy. "And just what are you trying to say, Franklin?"

"What I'm saying is this—No, first answer me this question: Do you consider me to be your man?"

"I'm beginning to think of you that way."

"Then if you're my woman, I don't like the idea of you prancing around no beach in no bikini."

"You can't be serious."

"Do I look serious?"

"Yes, you do, but let me tell you something so we can get this straight, right now. First of all, I'm a grown woman. I wear anything I want to wear when I want to wear it. My Daddy lives in Toledo."

"Oh, so what you're saying, then, is that it don't matter what I think, is that it?"

"What I'm saying is that you sound like you're living in the fifties or something."

"Let's drop it, okay? I feel too good to mess up my mood over some damn bathing suit."

"You're the one who brought it up."

"Yeah, well, now I'm dropping it."

I turned and started back toward the bedroom. Then I stopped and looked back at him. "Is this our first argument, Franklin?"

He started laughing. "No. This is our first disagreement."

"Oh," I said, and proceeded to the bedroom.

"You do look good in it, though, baby."

I took off the suit again and threw it on the floor. He must be nuts if he thinks he's going to start telling me what I can and can't wear. I mean, he's not dealing with one of these dingbats who can be told what to do. If it's a bathing suit today, what'll it be tomorrow? Please, Lord, don't let him turn out to be a reincarnation of Percy.

I looked into what I called my piano room. It was empty. Granted, I'm paying less rent, but it's still going to be a while before I can save up three hundred dollars to get the piano out of layaway. Once I start my voice lessons, it sure would be nice to be able to come home and practice instead of staying after school. I closed the door, then took a shower.

When I came out into the living room, Franklin was stretched out on the couch with his shoes off. I tightened the sash on my kimono and lay down on top of him. He felt better than he did the last time I was on top of him. He put his arms around me, and we watched Sugar Ray Leonard beat up somebody.

"How about a game of Scrabble?" he asked afterwards. The game was sitting on my bookshelf.

"The question is, can you play?"

He just started grinning; those deep black dimples were showing, and I had to bend over and kiss the man.

"Set it up," he said, "and cut all this mushy stuff. You getting ready to get a royal ass-kicking."

I already knew Franklin was smart; I just didn't know how smart. He came up with words I'd never even heard of. Most of them were construction terms, which I didn't think was fair. But some of them weren't. He put down the letters e-a-r-w-i-g.

"That's not a word, Franklin, so pick it up."

He leaned back on the couch, crossed his arms, showed at least fifteen of those white teeth, poked his big chest out, and said, "Challenge me."

And I did. I looked it up in the dictionary, and sure enough it was in there. I slipped in a few good ones too. Musical terms I knew he didn't know, and words that could have two c's or l's, but I still couldn't outsmart him. He was too quick. He was ahead by over a hundred points. It was embarrassing, really. But I knew I had him when he put down y-e-t-i.

"Pick it up," I said. "I know that's not a word, and I'll challenge you."

"Wait a minute, baby. Let me look it up for you, since you can't spell. I know that little pea brain of yours been working overtime, and I can see it's throbbing, so sit tight. What college was that you said you went to?"

I went to pop him upside his head, but he dodged me. An abominable snowman? A double-word score. Next came this word xu, which he dared me to challenge, but I was onto him now. I didn't dare. Triple-word score. He got up to go to the bathroom, and I grabbed the dictionary and looked it up. A Vietnamese coin? Where'd he learn all these damn words?

"You make me sick," I said when he came back.

"Don't get so upset, baby. It ain't over till the fat lady sing."

He won, of course. Next time I won't be so easy on him. I put the game away, and we ate and watched the news.

"Oh, I forgot to ask you: You want to go to a brunch with me Sunday afternoon?"

"A what?"

"A brunch."

"Is it gon' be a bunch of uppity black folks drinking white wine, eating pâté and crackers, talking about what's going on on Wall Street?"

"Is that really what you think a brunch is?"

"I don't know. I don't mean to sound so cynical, but to tell the truth, I usually work out on Sunday afternoons, plus there's another good fight coming on. For the title. I'll let you know, though, baby."

"It should be fun, Franklin, and besides, I'd like you to meet some of my friends."

"I've got a confession to make," he said. His face was somber now. I wanted him to tell me everything, because that would mean he trusted me, could talk to me. He turned away so I couldn't see his face. "I'm not the person you think I am."

"What's that supposed to mean? I know you grew up in Staten Island, you've got two sisters, you're a sports fanatic, you want to start your own carpentry business one day, you're good with your hands, smart, a fantastic lover, and you're the best thing that's ever happened to me."

"I killed my first two wives."

My throat felt like I'd just swallowed a whole cough drop. Relax, Zora, I thought. He's kidding.

"And I've been to prison for it."

Now I knew this had to be some kind of prank. I hadn't forgotten what Vinney had said about Franklin being a jokester. Besides, I couldn't possibly have fallen in love with a murderer *and* an ex-convict, could I? "You did what? Franklin, don't play these kinds of games with me."

He just looked at me, dead serious, his black eyes shining like jet. Shit, I should've listened to Portia. But no, I always have to dive in heart first. I looked over at the door and was thinking about getting the hell out of here, but I couldn't move. Here I was thinking that I'd finally found Mr. Right. How stupid could I be? And he's been married? Twice?

I was so busy tossing all this stuff back and forth in my head that it took a moment before I realized he was laughing, just like Jack Nicholson in *The Shining*. Franklin had a sinister look on his face and started coming toward me, but I jumped up from the couch and ran into the closet. "Get away from me!" I screamed through the door. This kind of shit only happened in the movies, not in real life. I started feeling light-headed, but I wasn't about to have a damn fit now. I shook my head, took a few deep breaths, and closed my eyes to regain my composure. "This is not happening," I said over and over in my head.

"Baby," he said, "I'm just playing."

I didn't believe him, and I wasn't about to come out of this closet until I could figure out what to do next.

"Come on out, baby. Can't you take a joke? I'm just jiving with you, I swear to God."

"How do I know you're joking, Franklin?" I peeked out through the crack in the door and cut my eyes at him. Then I eased the door open a little more, because he had the stupidest grin on his face. That's when I knew he was kidding. I pushed the door open, ran over to the kitchen sink, picked up a wet dishcloth, and threw it in his face. "What a low-down, dirty, rotten, coldhearted trick to play on someone who was about to tell you that she loves you."

"You what?"

"You heard me."

"Me?"

"Yes, you, Franklin Swift—*if* that's your real name. I swear, don't ever pull a stunt like that on me again, Franklin. It wasn't funny. Not one bit."

"I'm sorry. I just couldn't resist. You was really scared, though, wasn't you?"

"Of course I was scared! I was just about to get a coat hanger and beat the shit out of you! At least give it my best shot. I know one thing—I wasn't about to act like those dizzy women in the movies who fall down in the middle of nowhere or act helpless. No siree. You would've been in trouble, buster."

"I'm sorry, really," he said. He laughed some more, then put his arms around me. And for some stupid reason, I felt quite safe.

It's been three weeks since we started seeing each other, and now some of Franklin's clothes are in my closet. He only goes home to do woodworking and feed his fish. I still haven't been to his apartment, but it's to the point now where I don't care where he lives. I can't seem to do without his company. We never did make it to that brunch. Franklin's throat was sore, and I didn't want to leave him like that. I've been avoiding Portia ever since.

He just walked out of the shower, with a towel wrapped around his waist, and was dripping water all over the floor.

"Franklin, please don't do that."

"Don't do what?"

"Drip water all over the floor like that."

"Oh, I'm sorry, baby. This is just a habit. I never dry all the way off. I'm a drip-dry man. These floors can take it, believe me."

"Can I ask you something I've been kind of curious about?"

"Shoot," he said.

"Two things in particular."

"I'm listening."

"Did you have a girlfriend when you started seeing me, or what?"

"Nope. I told you I'd just started my vacation from women."

"I find that hard to believe. I mean, someone as handsome and available as you."

"Well, I ain't completely available."

"What's that supposed to mean?"

"It means that even though I've been legally separated for the past six years, I'm still married."

He didn't just say what I thought he said, but maybe I didn't hear him good, since my ears were ringing. "Franklin, did you just say you're married?"

"I don't think of myself as being married."

"Let me get this straight. But you're not divorced."

"Not yet."

Lord, not a married man, and a liar too. Right this minute, I had lockjaw. I mean, I've been tricked before, but never by a married one. So I guess I'm not supposed to care because I'm in love, is that it? I wanted to walk over and knuckle his damn ears.

"That's why I'm glad I got this new job. I can probably get in the union, and then I can afford to pay for the divorce. In the six years since I left, I just never met a woman that made me even think about going through with it, until now."

"You expect me to believe that?"

"It's the truth, Zora, I swear. I wouldn't lie about some shit like this, really. "

"You've been lying to me all this time, Franklin."

"I haven't lied to you about nothin'; I just didn't tell you the whole truth. There is a difference. I was gon' tell you when the time was right."

"Which would've been when?"

"I guess when we got to where we are right now."

"Which is where?"

"I love you, and you know it."

That much I did believe. Being *legally* separated wasn't quite the same as being really married, was it? Before I got comfortable with the idea, I wanted to find out all the details. "How long were you married?"

"Six years."

"I know you've got kids, right?"

"Two"

"Two?"

"Yeah."

"How old?"

"Thirteen and seven."

"What are they?"

"Two boys."

"Do you ever see 'em?"

"Sometimes."

"You haven't seen 'em since you've been seeing me, that much I know. That's not right, Franklin."

"I've seen 'em a few times. Whenever I said I had to make a run, that's usually where I was going."

"So why didn't you just tell me?"

"Because I didn't want to scare you away."

"Kids don't scare me, but a wife does."

"I'm telling you, she ain't been my wife in six years. I can't even stand to be in the same room with her."

Faith. That's what I needed about now. Something was telling me he wasn't lying, but the last thing I want to be is a fool.

"I want to meet your kids," I said, without even realizing I was going to say it.

"Why?"

"Because they're your kids, that's why. Why not?"

"I'm not used to this, that's all. Ain't no woman never wanted to meet my kids before. I guess you'll meet 'em one day."

"I said there were two things I was curious about. What college did you go to?"

He got the most agitated look on his face, and then he took the towel and started drying himself off, although it was clear that he was already dry.

"I didn't go to no college. I thought that was obvious."

"You've got to be kidding, Franklin. As intelligent as you are?"

"College ain't got nothin' to do with intelligence, Zora."

"But some of the words you use in Scrabble? You've got a comment about everything we listen to on the news. You beat me at Baby Boom Trivial Pursuit, *Wheel of Fortune*, *Family Feud*, and you're standing here telling me you didn't go to any college whatsoever?"

"If you wanna know the *whole* truth, I didn't graduate from high school either."

This was too much to digest for one night. Shit, I needed some air. I stood right in front of the fan, then turned it on high. "Do your homework, girl," Claudette had said. Homework. I took a deep breath and looked at him. "Why didn't you finish high school, Franklin?"

"Couldn't stand the pressure."

"Just how long *were* you able to stand the pressure?"

"Eleventh grade."

"Eleventh grade?" I immediately thought about how little I knew when I was in the eleventh grade. I couldn't believe it. I had fallen in love with a lie. If he wasn't so big, I would've kicked his ass, I swear it.

"I know what you thinking, baby. That you way outta my league, right?"

"I don't know what I'm thinking, Franklin."

"I did get my GED."

I flopped down on the couch. GED?

"I'm trying to get into this trade school, seriously. I told you about it. But now that I started this new job, I don't know when I'ma be able to check it out."

"Really?" I looked at him suspiciously. He looked sad.

"So I guess that what they say is true," he said.

"What's that?"

"That money and status and education and all that shit counts more than what people feel about each other, right?"

"Did I say that?"

"No, but you thinkin' it."

"You don't know what I'm thinking," I said. I put my hands under my chin and just looked at him. Franklin looked scared. Really scared. For some stupid reason, I started thinking about the yardstick friends like Portia and women's magazines used to measure a man's worth. They measure wrong. I mean, standing right here in front of me was a man, and a man who loves me, who just opened himself up and took a chance by telling me the truth. How many of them have told me the truth? And when was the last time I met a man this smart, this sexy, this gentle, this strong? How long has it been since any man made me feel this special, this beautiful? How many of 'em have made me laugh so much? How many of 'em have had opinions about every-thing? And how many of 'em have made my body say yes with just the touch of a hand? I looked at Franklin some more. Damn, not only was he black as midnight and my kind of handsome, but it just hit me that he's my man. I *love* him. I don't care if he never goes to college. I don't care how many kids he has. As long as he makes me happy, makes me feel glad I'm a woman, and as long as he keeps his word and gets his divorce, I'll be here forever. So far, he's been the only man I've seen beside me when I have dreams that happen twenty years from now.

He lit a cigarette and took two drags before he exhaled.

"Franklin?"

"Yeah?"

"I want you to know something. I don't love you any less now than I did fifteen minutes ago. I'm going to trust you, and hold you at your word as far as the divorce goes."

"It's in the works," he said, looking more relaxed.

"Can I tell you something?"

"I would hope so."

"To be perfectly honest, I've always wanted a man I could grow *with*, you know. I mean, we're sort of starting from scratch."

"You a few steps ahead of me, baby. Let's not kid our-selves."

"That's a matter of opinion. But tell me, is there anything else I should know?"

"No, baby," he said. "This is me, butt naked." He put out his cigarette. "Now what about you? You holding any cards under the table?"

I took a deep breath. Being married was one thing—he could get a divorce and solve that problem. But telling him about the epilepsy might just shock him. Besides, it may never come back. I'll tell him when I'm absolutely positive that it won't make any difference. And since being fat was no longer an issue, why mention it? So I said, "No," and tried my best to look sincere.

6

Zora bought me one of those Sunset Books on how to be a carpenter, plus she sent away for all kinds of information from the Small Business Association on how to start my own business. I wish she wouldn't do that shit. As soon as my constitution is stronger—when I can send Pam some money every week for the kids, pay for my divorce, get a few dollars in the bank, and be driving somethin'—I can do all this shit myself. I know she trying to be helpful and everything, but I gotta get her to understand that I gotta do things in my own way and in my own time frame. Right now the timing just ain't right. Hell, I ain't been working but a month. They paying me thirteen a hour, and since it ain't under the table, the IRS is eating my ass up in taxes. It's been a long time since I had this much money in my pocket on a Friday, and I swear, it feels good.

All I been doing is playing catch-up. I was two months behind in the rent on my room, and hell, sixty dollars a week adds up. After I cleared that up, paid a few other outstanding debts, I mailed Pam enough money to keep her off my back for a while. I didn't feel like looking at her. I still been able to put at least fifty dollars a week in a savings account. Today, though, when I cashed my check, I didn't put nothin' in but withdrew a hundred instead. I got a surprise for Zora. She been gone all day, getting her lesson plans in order. School starts next Monday, and her voice classes start the week after that.

She's nervous as all hell. Been eating like it's going out of style. Just as long as she don't start getting fat, I ain't saying nothin'.

I decided to cook dinner tonight. I can burn when it comes to broiling steaks. I made some gooey-ass Rice-A-Roni and a dynamite salad. Forgot the vegetable, but Zora didn't say nothin'. She ate everything I put on her plate. Afterwards, we watched the news, which should really be called *Showtime,* since they spend more time interviewing movie stars and rock 'n' roll stars these days. But this is New York City, and they can't help but squeeze in all the fucked-up shit that's going on before they ask some old-ass actress why she decided to put all her—and everybody else's—fuckin' business in a book.

They gave the homeless about forty seconds.

"That's a damn shame," Zora said.

"I agree," was all I said. I just knew she would be able to tell something was up, 'cause she know I always got *plenty* to say when shit like this come on the news. Hell, sometimes we miss the rest of the show 'cause we end up debating half the night about something that was just covered, when we could be fuckin'. If Zora got a position, she holds on to it. I really like that shit. Sometimes we get loud. Tonight, though, I was too excited to debate, and couldn't wait to see the look on her face when I gave her her surprise.

"Koch should be ousted," she said. "Wasting the taxpayers' money on those nasty hotels when they could probably build a damn housing complex and put those people in real apart-ments, you know. Twenty-five hundred dollars a month for a room? With rats and roaches and no heat? Give me a break. I mean, really, Franklin, does this make any sense to you?"

"Naw, but what they supposed to do when they ain't got nowhere else to go?"

"Don't they have families?"

"Probably. But shit, a lotta their families probably living in the same kind of nasty-ass, cramped-up tenements they just got burned out of. You saw them people. Did it look like they had relatives on the Upper West Side or in Westchester somewhere?"

"It still doesn't make an ounce of sense. People living on the streets, and with kids! And here I am, living like a princess or something. There's just something immoral about all of it."

"Well, ain't no sense in you feeling all guilty 'cause you taking care of yourself. Let's face it, baby: In this world, there's the haves and the have-nots. Actors and reactors. But this shit here is all about bureaucracy. Everybody know how that shit works. You pay somebody and they pay somebody and they pay somebody to keep the circle moving inside the circle. The city don't give a shit about those people. They don't wanna solve the homeless problem 'cause it's too goddamn profitable. Motherfuckers gotta keep up their mortgage payments in Sag Harbor and shit. You saw what color most of 'em was, didn't you?"

"Yeah, anybody can see that, but I swear. I'd never even heard of this kind of stuff until I moved here,"

"Well, it'll get worse before it gets better." I had already said more than I had planned to. And don't nothin' piss me off more than talking about something I can't do nothin' about. The mood was getting too heavy, and I wanted to lighten it up some. "You feel like a game of Scrabble, baby?"

"Not tonight, Franklin."

I got up from the couch and pulled her by the hands to her feet. "What are you doing?" she asked, laughing.

"Just come with me." I led her to her so-called music room, where I had still yet to hear any. "Sit down," I said.

"And just where would you like me to sit?"

"On the floor. Where else?"

She sat down like a little girl. Zora didn't know what the hell I was up to. "Close your eyes and open your hands."

"What?"

"Just do what I tell you to do, woman, and be quiet."

She closed her eyes, turned her palms up, and I put three one-hundred-dollar bills on top of 'em. Shit, I felt like *The Millionaire*. When she felt the paper touch her skin, she opened her eyes real wide. "What's this?"

"You know what it is, baby. It's three hundred dollars so you can get your piano out. Now you don't have no more excuses."

"Franklin, you can't be serious. You shouldn't be giving me all this money when you just started working. What about your kids? The piano can wait."

She went to hand it back, but I wouldn't take it. "Get the piano, Zora. Tomorrow. I been sending money over to Pam, don't worry. All I want you to do now is sit right there and sing me something. I don't care what it is." She had the nerve to start blushing. "Cut the modest act, and sing." I sat down on the floor, next to the doorway, and crossed my arms and legs. My feet touched hers.

She took one deep breath after another, like she was nervous or something. Then she closed her eyes. The first sound that came outta her mouth shocked the shit out of me. She sounded like a husky but purring cat. Zora sung this song I never heard before. Damn. I was so wrapped up in the power of her voice that I only heard the words here and there: "I flew so high over those lakes and valleys to get to you . . . You gave me juice and honey, crawled into my heart inch by inch and got struck by lightning twice . . . The phone rang, and my heart fell to the floor, broke like a piece of china . . . You promised me it wouldn't hurt, said, Baby, it never hurts, but you lied. Yes, you did, you lied."

When she finished, she opened her eyes but still wouldn't look at me. She just kept looking at the floor. My baby can sing, all right. Anybody that can sing a cappella like *that* can sing. Her voice put me in the mind of a few people I really like. Sweet Honey in the Rock, but with twists and turns like Sarah Vaughan and Nancy Wilson. She's definitely got range, 'cause she hit some notes I ain't heard nobody but Aretha reach. If she's as serious as she say she is, once she get into her lessons and everything, my baby's got the kinda voice that *could* make it to a record.

I looked at her hard and pictured her onstage with people screaming and shit 'cause she had just tore the roof off the place. Then I started wondering. Where would that leave me? Her man, the construction worker who couldn't even be sure if he was gon' get paid every week or not. Fuck it. Ain't no sense worrying about my damn ego now. "Whose song was that?" I asked.

"Mine," she said, still not looking at me.

I slid across the floor and put my knees up so I was directly in front of her. "Look at me, baby."

Finally, she met my eyes.

"That was beautiful. I mean it. I didn't know you could sing like that. And I didn't know you was no poet either."

"That was an old song, really," she said.

"I don't care if it's old or new. You wrote it. And it's your song. Damn. I didn't know you was gon' sound that good."

"You mean that, Franklin?"

"Yes, I do, baby." And I did. My instincts was telling me that she definitely got what it takes to make it—talent and drive—and I do wanna see her make it. I just don't want her to turn out to be no fuckin' overnight success.

"Really?" she asked again.

My answer to that was putting her head on my shoulder and holding her like I might lose her one day. We sat there for a while, without moving or talking. I was worrying for nothin', 'cause right now she was wrapped inside *my* arms. This was perfect, I swear it was. And during the next hour, you couldn'ta told us wasn't no carpet on that floor or no piano in that room, 'cause somebody was playing the hell out of it.

Most of my clothes was at Zora's now, but I figured I should at least go home and feed my damn fish. Clean up the place, check the mail, even though I don't hardly get none. Ain't got no bills, and don't nobody write me letters—everybody I know lives in New York. The place was a mess, as usual. I didn't clean up from the last time I was in here doing some woodworking, which felt like a long time ago. Love makes time fly, no doubt about that shit. I looked around this little dingy room. Compared to how clean and pretty Zora's place is, now this room gave me the fuckin' creeps. Painting it white still didn't help.

Since she got that piano, the woman is obsessed. She sits in that little room and pumps out some beautiful shit. I try not to bother her when she's in there, but if I'm cooking dinner and can't find something, I tap on the door. Sometime she don't even hear me. I'm the same way when I'm doing my woodworking, so I understand. We been a everyday thing since we been seeing each other, and I figured both of us could use some space, so I told her I needed to get some things done over here and that I might not see her till to-morrow—*if* I can wait that long.

I sat down on top of my bed, which wasn't nothin' but two mattresses on the floor. I noticed a envelope with my footprint on it at the door. Jimmy. I opened it, and sure enough, the twenty dollars I loaned him almost two months ago was in it. He slow, but sure. I saw mouse turds on top of some sawdust over in the corner by my fish tank. I swear to God, them motherfuckers'll eat anything. I poured myself a stiff one, turned on the box, and sat down at my worktable. This unit didn't look so bad today. I need some more sealant and box nails, but when I finish it, I'll finally have a place where I can store all my tools and books so I can see 'em.

I was sweeping up when I heard the buzzer. I hope it ain't Jimmy. Wouldn't mind a quick game of dominoes with Lucky, but I ain't seen him in weeks, which mean one of two things— either he won at the track or he in love. I ran downstairs and almost broke my damn neck on the steps 'cause the light musta just blew out. I opened the door and couldn't believe who I was seeing. My Moms and Pops was standing there like that old man and woman on that cornflake commercial. Every now and then, they do this kinda shit. Pop up and surprise me like this. What the fuck. I let 'em in.

"Franklin," my Moms said, moving her face toward mine for a kiss, which I didn't wanna give her but I gave her anyway—on the cheek. She didn't even crack a smile. I know it was Pops who talked her into driving all the way over here. Even though he ain't never came right out and admitted it, the man miss me. This is just his way of making sure I ain't dead, fuckin' up, in jail, or strung out on dope. He keeps forgetting that I ain't sixteen no more, but thirty-two years old, and don't do that silly shit no more. But since I ain't never been big on sending them no forwarding address whenever I moved, this must also be his way of making sure I can still be found.

"Hello, son," he said. He shook my hand and gave me a hug at the same time. My Pops never hugged me till I was in my mid-twenties, but I liked it; I liked it a lot. Right now he was grinning, and I knew *he* was glad to see me. After all, I am his only son. I'm about a inch or two taller than he is, look almost just like him. The only other difference between us is that my Pops is a punk and I ain't. He been going along with my Moms' program for so long, I don't think he even know if he ever had one of his own. I guess I love him, but on a scale of one to ten, my respect for him is about a four. And my Moms, I can't stand her. She shoulda been a drill sergeant, 'cause all she ever been good for is telling people what to do. My Pops obeys her, which is why, together, they make me wanna throw up.

"Why's it so dark in this hallway?" she asked.

"The light just blew out. Come on up," I said, and turned and ran up three steps at a time. Fifteen more minutes, and the damn place woulda been clean. I closed the door behind 'em.

"So what brings you two all the way to Brooklyn?" I asked, firing up a Newport.

"We were having dinner at Junior's, and since we haven't heard from you in so long, we just took our chances that you still lived here. What's it been, Jerry, a year?" he asked, turning toward my Moms, who was scrutinizing the whole damn room. I knew it was disgusting to her, and now I was glad the place was a mess.

"I don't know, Felix. I can't remember. Franklin, one of them fish is dead."

Just like her to notice.

Pops reached into his shirt pocket and pulled out a Kool. I think every shirt he owns is plaid. I was gon' light it for him, but he whipped out his matches and gave me a thanks-but-no-thanks look. He took a long, hard drag, exhaled like he had just made a decision, then looked at me. "How's life treating you these days, son? You're looking good."

"Not so hot, if you ask me," my Moms said before I could answer. "You still living in this little-ass room. When you gon' get yourself a real apartment, Franklin? Jessie and Christine just bought a new house. Four bedrooms. Brick. Right around the corner from us. It's real nice. They ask about you from time to time, but I really don't know what to tell 'em. And the boys getting just as big. All four of 'em play a instrument, you know. You used to love the drums—remember, Franklin?" She was killing a roach that was crawling up the wall, but kept on yacking. "Naw, you probably don't remember."

"Yes, I do. I remember you made me get rid of 'em because you said they made too much noise and gave you migraines. *That* much I do remember."

"You just banged on 'em to piss me off. That's why I made you get rid of 'em. If you gon' tell the truth, at least get it straight."

I didn't feel like getting into American history with her. I turned to Pops. "Anyway, I'm doing pretty good. Just started working on a hotel in Manhattan. Finally making some decent money. This one should finally get me into the union. Wanna get myself a car, you know. I even met myself a nice lady."

Pops looked interested and was getting ready to ask me something, when my Moms said, "How's your wife and the kids doing?"

"Pam ain't been my *wife* in over six years. The kids is fine. I saw 'em on Derek's birthday, last month."

Pops leaned back in his chair and crossed his arms, then his legs. The creases in his khakis was coming out, which probably meant he'd been crossing 'em all damn night. He let out a sigh, took another drag off his cigarette, and crushed it out. He still didn't say nothing, but I understood why. He's a chump.

"So do that mean you finally got your divorce?" she asked.

"I'm working on it."

"Uhn-hun, I bet you are," she said, rolling her eyes up in her head. One day I hope they get stuck up there.

I could tell Pops didn't feel like listening to her shit, 'cause he started licking his lips, then sucking his teeth the way he always did when he wanted to say something but didn't have the balls to say it. "It's good that you keep in touch with your children, son."

"You want a drink, Pops?" I didn't dare ask my Moms, 'cause she's scared of alcohol. Half her damn family is alcoholics. So is my Pops, really, but he ain't no drunk. He's one of them quiet alcoholics. Drinks while he's sitting in front of the TV or when he's cutting the grass or washing the car. He don't get rowdy and shit. Just sips all day long and keeps whatever thoughts he got to hisself.

"Naw, he don't want no drink, do you, Felix?" She wiped some sawdust off my only chair and finally sat her ass down.

"Just a taste," he said.

"You know how many people a year get killed because of drunk drivers? It's on the news every single night. If I'ma die, I damn sure don't want it to be like that."

What I wouldn'ta paid to tell her I wished she was dead now, over there floating with that fish. I poured him a tall one, and when she got up and touched the corner of my wall unit, he looked at her like she was bad news, then drunk the whole damn thing in one swallow.

"What's this thing?"

"It's gon' be a wall unit."

"You making it from scratch?"

For a minute there, she sounded like she was impressed, but I knew it was too good to be true. "Yeah. I designed it and everything."

"I saw something just like this at the flea market."

"Yeah, well, I make all kinds of things. This is just something I'm putting together to store my tools and books. It ain't supposed to be no work of art."

My Pops walked over and looked at it. "What kind of wood is this?"

"Pine. It's too soft, really, but since it's just to store my tools and stuff, it's okay. Usually, when I'm experimenting with a real piece, first I make a model of it using particleboard or plywood, 'cause they're cheap, then I fix any mistakes and make the same thing over but using better wood."

"Where'd you learn how to do this?" he asked.

He couldn't remember all the shit I used to bring home from woodshop? "I don't know," I said. "It's just something I do."

"Well, it's good, son," he said, and then looked bored.

"I'm trying to get into this trade school in January to learn how to start my own business. It *might* be in carpentry, but I gotta check it all out first."

"Really?" was all he said.

"Takes a whole lotta money to start a business, Franklin," my Moms said. She had turned on the TV but was obviously not watching it. I wished my Pops hadda came by hisself. We coulda got drunk and had a man-to-man talk—something I been wanting to do with him since I was sixteen. I don't know what I mean by "man-to-man," except maybe, with my Moms not being there listening to every fuckin' word we say, we could cut the bullshit and just be men—father and son—for once. I'd really like to ask him how he's tolerated her ass all these years. Didn't he ever just feel like leaving for work one day and never coming back? And I always wanted to know if she could fuck, or had he just got used to it? I'd like to try to explain what was happening to me when I was messing with the drugs and shit. Tell him how confused I was back then. Why I got discharged from the navy. Why I left Pam, and what I think my whole struggle is all about. Maybe we'll get that chance one day, I don't know.

I looked at my Moms and strained my voice to stop from raising it. "I know how much money it takes to start a business. You think I'm going into this blindfolded?"

"Did I say that? Where you supposed to get all this money?"

"Don't worry about it."

"Son, she's your mother, don't forget that."

He didn't even say it like he meant it. And I'm getting sick of all this "son" shit; I wish he would call me by my damn name.

"I ain't hardly worrying about it," she said, folding her arms the same way she used to do when she was cussing me out for something I did or didn't do, which was usually right before she got the extension cord and beat my ass. "You gon' be forty before you know it, and talking about starting some business. Who you think gon' lend you that kind of money, is what I wanna know."

"None of your fuckin' business."

She grabbed her purse and stood up. "Felix, let's go. Now. This boy still got a nasty mouth and no respect. One day you gon' wish you hadda listened to me. That's why you still living in a dump, like some old black widow man. You ain't gon' never have but one mother and father in your life. Remember that shit when you start your *fuckin'* business."

"All right, Jerry, that's enough. Franklin, apologize to your mother." He tried to look like he was pleading, but I knew it was just another front. His whole problem has always been trying to do the right thing.

"Not this time, Pops."

"I'm asking you to, son."

"She was out of line, and somebody need to let her know it."

"That's my job, wouldn't you say?" he asked.

I looked him straight in the eye and wanted to say, You ain't been able to do it in thirty-two years; where you think you gon' get the balls to do it now? But it wasn't my place to make him feel like less than a man, especially when she been doing a pretty good fuckin' job of it. "Yeah, Pops, that's your job," I said. "Sorry," I mumbled to the floor, which musta been good enough, 'cause he stood up. Now he looked shorter. He reached for my hand and shook it. My Moms was already standing in the doorway.

"Why don't you bring your lady friend out for one of the holidays? It'd be nice if we could count on seeing you at least two or three times a year."

Father Knows Best. I swear to God. "I'll see, Pops," I said, and he patted me on the back. He ducked when he walked through the doorway. My Moms waved her hand toward the floor to say goodbye. I pushed the door closed and hoped they didn't think I was gon' walk 'em downstairs.

I was hauling a load of bricks, when the foreman came over to me. "You can put that barrel down, son."

I dropped the grippers on the handles and took off my work gloves. "What's the problem?"

"The masoners and concrete people are haggling about some details in one of the contracts. We're not lifting another finger until this thing is worked out. It's about paperwork."

"How long do you think it'll be before we can start back?"

"I don't know. Could be today, next week, or the week after. Who knows? I'll be in touch with the guy at A Dream Deferred, one way or the other. He'll let you know when to report back. For now, go on home. Sleep late for a few days. Bang the ole lady before *Good Morning America*." Then he started laughing. This shit was a joke to him.

Sleep late. Ain't this a bitch. I walked into the shanty to change my work boots. A couple of other brothers from A Dream was in there too.

"This is bullshit, man," one said.

"Tell me about it," I said. "And they say niggahs don't wanna work. One day I'm gon' tell all of 'em to kiss my black ass."

Another dude spoke to both of us. "Y'all bloods know what the deal is, don't you?"

"No," I said.

The other dude shook his head.

"We been bought and sold."

"What's that supposed to mean, man?" I asked, even though I sorta already knew.

"Check it out, brothers. Look who's being laid off. Us. The men with the black skin. They talking that contract shit, but that ain't it. A Dream got too many of us on this site. They nervous 'cause we costing 'em too much money. Why pay us twelve or fourteen dollars a hour when they can hire some Spicks or Chinks or Polacks who just got off the boat, who most likely can't even read or write, and willing to—*happy* to—work for five or six dollars an hour? Y'all figure it out."

I couldn't say nothin'. This is the kinda shit that makes you wanna kill somebody—'cause you powerless. And you can't do nothin' about it 'cause it's the kinda shit you can't prove. I kicked off my work boots and put on my sneakers.

"A black man just can't get ahead, can he, man?" the other brother said, as he walked out and slammed the door. The

whole shanty shook. I swear, if I could do something else that
paid me this kinda money, I'd be doing it. But strength is my
biggest skill, and you don't need no college degree to sling
bricks or dig holes. All you need is muscle. And I always hear
'em thinking, That nigger looks like Paul Bunyan. Take him.

I put on my baseball cap, said, "Later," to the other dude,
and left. I caught the subway home, and it seemed like it was
full of black men who looked mad at the world. I know I musta
looked just like 'em.

Shit. Next Friday is Zora's birthday. Yeah, I gave her the
money for her piano and shit, but I still ain't paid for a
morsel of food or helped her with the rent yet. I *owed* her that
piano. She still practicing every night too. That's what I call
dedication. And I love listening to her. It's like having a live
concert in your house every night. I wish I could say we was
living together, but we ain't made it official yet. I'm gon' have
to do something, though, 'cause paying rent on a room I
hardly ever sleep in is getting to be a little fuckin' ridiculous.

I still would like to get her something nice for her birthday.
No cheap shit, 'cause she know the difference. I reached into
my pocket and counted how much money I had. Eighteen
dollars. What the fuck can a man buy his woman with this? I
ain't closing no more savings accounts, though, not this time
out. Hell, I was counting on putting money *in* the bank on
Friday. It don't pay to project, I swear to fuckin' God it don't.

Instead of going home, to Zora's—or our—house, I decided
to go on down to Free At Last, another organization like A
Dream, but I changed my mind. Hell, it was quarter to eight.
If you even halfway serious about working, they expect you to
be there by at least seven if you wanna be part of the shape-
up. Shit. Zora had already left by now, I knew that. I guess
teaching takes a lot of preparation. I know one thing—it do
feel good to have a woman that's doing something construc-

tive instead of that fleeting kinda shit. Hell, any way I look at it, her future is planted in cement.

But look at her man.

I had to do something, but what? When I got off the train, I just started walking down the side streets, smoking one Newport after another, but this wasn't getting it, so I stopped in a liquor store and bought myself a half pint of Jack Daniel's. I needed something. I took a nip every now and then and kept walking. I wish I had some alternatives. I turned the corner at my street and went up the steps. I heard music coming from Lucky's room, so I knocked on his door. He cracked it open.

"What's up, dude?" he asked, peeking out.

"Nothin', man. What's happening?"

"Got a little company," he said, grinning.

"Sorry about breaking and entering, man. I'll catch you later."

I went on upstairs and polished off the rest of the bottle. I still felt edgy and didn't wanna spend no more time thinking about my situation than I had already, so I went back to the store and bought another bottle. When I came back, I didn't feel like sitting in this room, so I went over to Zora's. I used my keys. I sat down on her purple couch, and the whole room looked like a picture in some women's magazine. Everything in here was so pretty, and nothin' was outta place. Except me. Who was I kiddin'? I didn't belong here. Wasn't nothin' in here mine. And ain't no place in here for no sawdust.

I stood in the middle of the room and felt filthy, like I shouldn't touch nothin', and I didn't. I was scared I might break something. Smudge it. Smear it. Something. It's already got to the point where I leave my work boots in the hallway when I come home. Sometimes I even drop my jeans out there too, 'cause they usually caked with dirt, dust, or mud.

I finished the rest of the bottle, took my clothes off, showered, and laid across Zora's bed. I could smell her on the pillowcases, and I pushed my nose deeper into it. I fell asleep. When I woke up, I didn't wanna be here when she got home. I couldn't tell her I was laid off, 'cause then she'd probably think that this was gon' be a regular thing. I didn't want her to think that, even if the shit was true. Hell, what woman want a man around that turns out to be a fuckin' liability instead of a asset?

I found myself standing at the top of the subway entrance. I decided to call my sister Darlene, just for the hell of it. I ain't seen her in damn near a year, so I knew she was gon' be shocked to hear from me—if she was home. She don't go nowhere but to work and school, the grocery and liquor stores. She answered on the second ring, in her usual monotone. "What's up, buttercup?" I asked.

"Franklin?"

"You know anybody else with a voice as sexy as your brother's?"

"Please," she said, in the same monotone.

"What you doing?"

"Nothing much," she said dryly. She depresses the hell out of me sometimes, and why I picked up the phone and called her, why I was about to get on the train and ride all the way up to the damn Bronx to see her, I don't know. Maybe 'cause she's all I got besides Zora.

"I wanna stop by. What you drinking?"

"The usual. Franklin, I've gained about fifteen pounds, the place is a wreck, so don't come up here criticizing me. Could you bring your drill and screwdriver? I've been waiting months for you to call, so you could put up my track lights."

"Why can't what's-his-name do it? Or is he history?"

"He's history."

"Well, I don't have access to my tools right now. I'm already at the train station. But if you got a few dollars, I'll pick up a screwdriver and a cheap drill at the hardware store." She agreed to it. Darlene usually cries broke if you wanna borrow some money, but let her want something for herself, ain't no such thing as she broke and ain't nothin' she want too expensive. She keeps a stash in the bank too. I should've known the only reason she wanted to see me was to get some work out of me. That's another reason I ain't got no phone. People used to bug the shit outta me. Everybody know I can fix or build damn near anything, and they tried to use me up. I got tired of that shit.

I forgot. I didn't have enough money on me to buy no damn tools, so I went over to my place, got the stuff, and trotted back to the train. After I bought tokens, I had exactly five dollars and some change left.

When Darlene opened the door, I was shocked. Not only had she put on weight, but a few strands in the front of her damn hair was gray. I kissed her on the cheek. "Well, they say more is better, right?"

"Fuck you, Franklin. I asked you not to say a word about how I look, so please. I'm depressed enough as it is."

"I wasn't saying nothing but hi, damn. I see you still got your sense of humor. What you depressed about now?"

"I got fired."

"So what else is new?"

"This is different, Franklin. This was a good job at an electronics company, and they were paying my tuition. I don't know what I'm gonna do now. I don't have the energy to start looking for another job, I swear I don't."

"So why'd you get fired?"

"Because of tardiness. Shit, I can't help it if the trains are always late."

"What you got to drink around here?" I asked. I knew exactly where she kept her stash, and as quiet as it's kept, I know Darlene is a closet alky. That's why she probably got fired. Couldn't wake up in the damn morning. All she do is sit up here in this overpriced apartment, watching sitcoms and re-runs all night, sipping on White Label, eating junk food, and feeling sorry for herself. Don't nobody come visit her except me. She ain't got no friends, at least I ain't never heard her mention none. In a lot of ways, she's like me. Stick to herself. But this little miserable-ass world she keep living in is getting old. The girl done had more jobs, registered and dropped out of more colleges in the last two years—I swear, I can't keep up no more. So to hear that she just got fired ain't no surprise to me.

And men? She can't keep one. She always end up finding so many things wrong with 'em that the minuses outweigh the pluses, which makes 'em "intolerable," as she put it. Darlene wouldn't know a good man if one was staring her in the face. The real deal is, she don't trust nobody, except me, and even that's questionable. To tell the truth, I wouldn't be surprised if she wasn't sleeping with women. She got all the symptoms of a lesbian. And hell, although I don't go for that kinda shit, she might be better off. I just don't want nothin' fucked up to happen to her. The girl *is* suicidal, she done proved that already. And the way she sounding, like she ain't got nothing to look forward to, and the way she looking, like walking death, maybe I need to come see her more often. What's sad about all this is that underneath all that pain, my sister is smart, and pretty as hell. This is just the end result of all my Moms' love.

Darlene sat down on the couch. "So you heard from Ma and Daddy?" I knew she knew I had. She talks to Christine all the time, who talks to my Moms every day, and Christine re-peats everything she hears, only she adds shit to it so that she ends up telling a different version from the way shit really happened.

"About a week ago, I guess. They stopped by—can you believe that shit?"

"They're good at surprises. Ma tell you about Christine's new house?"

"You know she did. The bitch. You think she could stand not rubbing that shit all in my face? Be serious, Darlene. You know Moms better than that. She ain't changed."

"I'm not going out there for Thanksgiving or Christmas. You?"

"Maybe. I want them to meet my new lady. Zora. Show 'em I'm capable of meeting a decent woman. You know Moms ain't never liked no woman I ever brought home, not even Pam, but she gon' *have* to like Zora."

"You think Ma'll care one way or another? Daddy maybe, but not Ma."

"I'm not worried about Pops. He still got half a brain. It's Moms I wanna show, really."

She shook her head. "Why waste your time?"

" 'Cause I got something to prove."

"Who is this Zora? What a helluva unusual name. I already know she's pretty. You always get the pretty ones, Franklin. And I know she's got a good body. But what else does she do, besides fuck you good? That always seemed to be your number one priority—or have you grown up?"

"Fuck you, Darlene. She's more than just pretty. She's smart. And how she makes me feel in bed," I said, laughing, "is none of your fuckin' business. She's a singer, believe it or not. We kinda living together."

"Not in that little room you don't. Unless you moved."

"I didn't move. I live with her, right up the street from my place, in a brownstone I helped renovate. We gon' have to get a bigger place pretty soon, 'cause right now she uses the extra room to practice her music, and ain't nowhere for me to do my woodworking." I lit a Newport and clinked the ice cubes in my drink. "Darlene, she ain't one of these singers who just sings. The woman writes and reads music. Went to Ohio State University and teaches music to junior high school kids."

"Get outta here, Franklin! How'd you luck out and meet somebody with so much going for her? And what are you giving her besides that ten inches of beef you've been lying about all these years?"

"Love," was all I heard myself say. The way Darlene put it, she made it sound like all I *did* have to offer a woman was my dick. I resented this shit, because part of me felt it was true, especially today, but another part of me knew that I had more to give than that. Shit, I'm a smart motherfucker myself. Me and Zora dream together. We talk about everything. Laugh, even when we making love. We tell each other what we thinking, feeling. That shit has gotta be worth something. But Darlene wouldn't understand this if I was to sit in here all night trying to break it down for her, 'cause she ain't never been there.

"What about you?" I asked. "You got anybody?" I already knew the answer, but I wanted to move the conversation away from me.

"The last thing I need right now is a man."

"Yeah, I bet."

"You hungry, Franklin?"

"Only if you ordering something, 'cause if my memory serves me correctly, you ain't never been no Julia Child, and I don't want you practicing on me tonight."

"Oh, I suppose she can cook too?"

"Like a gourmet. And she's got good eating habits too. No junk food whatsoever. The woman don't even eat sugar, don't drink no sodas and no alcohol." Darlene's eyebrows went up. "I've been eating food I can't even pronounce. I'm telling you, Darlene, I finally found her. I ain't kidding."

"I just wish I knew what she saw in you. There's the lights over there. Come on, Franklin, get your ass up before you get drunk. I'll order some Chinese food."

"I don't get drunk. I get high," I said. But that was a lie. I was pretty fucked up now, though not to the point where I couldn't function. I put the lights up.

By the time we finished eating, I was bored talking to Darlene. In some ways, she's like my Moms. Don't have nothin' good to say about nothin' or nobody. She coulda sat there all night complaining about everything, but I'll be damned if I was gon' sit there and listen to that shit. I had enough shit of my own to deal with. And I didn't mention nothin' about being laid off, 'cause I didn't come up here to cry on her shoulder. I just wanted to stop the anxiety. But I swear, Darlene didn't help none. I drank two cups of black coffee, talked her into lending me twenty dollars, and went home.

As usual, Zora was on the phone when I walked in. "Hi, baby," I whispered in her ear, then kissed her on the cheek. She acknowledged me by nodding her head.

"You're coming to New York? When?" she asked into the phone. "That's great! Of course you can stay here. I want you to meet somebody. Yes, it's a man. No, he's mine. His name is Franklin. Yes, I am. Okay. Call me. I hope to see your butt in a couple of weeks. Just let me know what you decide. Talk to you soon."

She hung up the phone and looked at me. I was trying to look sober. That coffee didn't do its job.

"Who was that?" I asked.

"A girlfriend I went to college with. She's thinking of mov-

ing to New York—she may have a job offer with some hotsy-
totsy advertising agency—and I told her she could stay with us
for a few days, since I'm the only person she knows here.
That's okay with you, isn't it, Franklin?"

"Yeah," I said, not knowing I had some say in this kind of
shit.

"So how'd your day go?" she asked.

"So-so. Went to see my sister after I got off work." I had to
lie. I didn't feel like telling her the truth, 'cause then she'd
probably start feeling sorry for me and shit. The last thing I
needed right now was pity.

"Which one?"

"Darlene. I wouldn't go see Christine if you paid me."

"Franklin, you shouldn't feel that way about your own
sister."

"You don't even know her, so how can you even say that?"

"My, are we touchy tonight. Is something wrong?"

"No. I'm sorry, baby. I just had a rough day. The white
boys had me busting my ass today. And Darlene depressed the
hell outta me. She's lonely as hell up there and won't fess up
to it or do nothin' about it. She just got fired from her latest
job, act like she ain't got the energy to look for another one,
and probably ain't had no dick in years. She's all fucked up in
the head."

"Franklin, you can be so cruel sometimes, you know that?
I mean, she's your sister, not some stranger."

"I know that, but she still dingy as hell. I wish it was something I *could* do for her, but it ain't."

"Well, I still want to meet her."

"You probably will. Maybe at Thanksgiving. We both been
invited out to my folks' house. Darlene claim she ain't going,
but she say the same shit every year and is usually the first one
to show up."

"So I'll finally get to meet the whole clan, huh?"

"I guess so. But don't go getting all excited. You'll probably wish you never had."

"What a nice thing to say about your family."

"You'll see."

"Don't you have *anything* nice to say about *any* of 'em?"

"I can't think of nothin' right now. I'm just tired, baby, really."

"Well, guess what?"

"What?"

"You know my friend Eli, who I've told you about?"

"The faggot?"

"Franklin! I swear, you've got labels for everybody, don't you?"

"Well, he is a faggot, ain't he?"

"Anyway, he called to tell me about this rhythm-and-blues band that's looking for a female vocalist. He said they were top-notch, and he told 'em about me, and they want me to come hear them play tomorrow night at Wednesday's. If I like 'em, they'll want to hear me sing. Will you go with me?"

"I don't know. Depends on how tired I am when I get home from work." In the morning, I'm going down to Free At Last. The chances of me getting on somewhere with them is good, since it's still warm outside, and as long as I get a paycheck on Friday, she ain't gotta know where it came from. Besides, they could call me back at the hotel tomorrow. I *was* excited for Zora, but I just couldn't drum up the enthusiasm. My shit was dragging like a motherfucker, and hers looked like it was about to move up the fuckin' ladder.

"Oh, here," she said, handing me a large brown envelope. "This came in the mail for you today."

I took the envelope and saw that it was from the Small Business Association. Since Zora was standing there, I felt obligated to open it, so I did. Two brochures was inside: "How to

Be an Entrepreneur" and "How to Succeed in Business." I faked excitement and pretended like I was reading 'em. Zora went to take her shower. When I heard her singing, I threw the brochures on the table. Part of 'em slid off and fell on the floor. I just stared at 'em for a few minutes, then reached inside my jacket and lit a cigarette.

7

Franklin was broke on my birthday. He called me from a phone booth and said he had to work overtime and wasn't able to cash his check. For some reason, I didn't believe him, but I didn't tell him that. He had promised to take me to a movie and dinner in the Village. I could hear how embarrassed he was, so I just told him not to worry about it, and went ahead and offered to lend him fifty dollars. He accepted my loan. Then I felt stupid, because here it was my birthday, and I was lending him money to take me out? And trying not to make him feel bad about it? Personally, I wanted to get dressed up and go dancing. I haven't heard any live music in so long, and I can't even remember the last time I rocked my hips or popped my fingers to a beat.

When he finally got home, Franklin smelled like he'd been doing more drinking than working. But I didn't say anything. "Here," he said, and handed me a small bouquet of flowers. "Happy birthday, baby—for what it's worth." He gave me a dry kiss on the cheek, then went into the bathroom. I put the flowers in water, although I felt like throwing them out the window. I sat on the couch, literally twiddling my fingers waiting for him, and after he finished showering and put his clothes on—which took forever—he walked into the living room and said, "You ready?" I simply nodded my head and got up. It felt like I was going to work instead of out to celebrate my thirtieth birthday.

"You wanna go to the racetrack next weekend, baby?" he asked, as we got on the subway.

"Why not," I said. I've never been to a horse race before. It sounded like fun. The train shook and rattled along. We were both quiet, and this was pretty unusual. Franklin almost always has something funny to say.

"You know"—he sighed—"I don't know why you wanna see this movie."

This threw me off. I've been talking about *An Officer and a Gentleman* all week long. Even Portia and Marie said it was dynamite. "Because it's a good movie, Franklin," I said. But I felt like saying, "Shit, it's my birthday, and I should be able to see any movie I want to see." But I didn't. The evening already felt like a flat note, and I didn't want to spoil the rest of it.

"I hate movies about war," he said. "War depresses me, and since it's your birthday, I don't feel like being depressed."

"It's not a *war* movie, Franklin. It's about two men who're in the service, but it's really a love story."

"Forget I even said anything," he said. "I need to stop by the liquor store first."

It figured. "Franklin, the movie's starting in a few minutes."

"They always show previews. You won't miss nothing but the credits."

He bought a bottle of something strong, and there went eight of our fifty dollars.

When we got inside the theater, the movie had already started. This pissed me off. I hate missing the beginning of a movie. We walked down the aisle, looking for two empty seats, but the place was packed. "There's two," I whispered.

Franklin knows I like to sit in the back, but he kept walking. He likes to sit close to the front. I followed him. He spotted two seats all the way in the middle, which meant a whole row of people had to stand up so we could get by. "Excuse me," I said, but Franklin didn't open his mouth. We hadn't been seated a minute when I heard the twist of the bottle cap. He put his arm around me for ten minutes, then pulled away. About forty minutes into the movie, Franklin started getting fidgety. When I looked at him, he wasn't even looking at the screen. He mumbled something under his breath.

"What's wrong?" I asked.

"This is bullshit," he said loudly. "I told you I didn't wanna see this damn movie."

"Well, I do," I said, and pushed my behind deeper in my seat.

"Then I'll wait for you outside," he said, and got up. The people in our row looked annoyed. I sat there a few more minutes, then I got up too. I was fuming now. The people I had to pass stood up again, and each of them exhaled, then gave me an irritated look. I had to trot to catch up to Franklin, who was now standing outside the lobby door, lighting a cigarette.

"It wasn't that bad," I said. He rolled his eyes at me.

"You ain't never been in the service, having some white man telling you what to do, when to get up, when to go to sleep, how many sit-ups to do, talking to you like you ain't shit, and you can't say two words back to 'em or you'll get your fuckin' teeth knocked out. So don't tell me how bad it ain't."

"Well, why didn't you tell me this before we spent ten dollars?"

"Because it's your birthday and you wanted to see the damn movie, that's why."

He started walking down the street without me. For September, it was cold and windy, so I fastened all the buttons on my jacket and caught up to him. The heels of my cowboy boots clicked. I didn't know what his problem was, but I sure wished he'd get over it. I slid my arm through his—as a sort of peace gesture, I guess.

"When were you in the service?"

"When everybody else was."

"Which was when, Franklin?"

"Look, do we have to talk about this now?"

"No," I said. I really felt like slapping the shit out of him, and if he weren't so big, I probably would have.

"Good," he said. "I hear the train. Let's go." He grabbed me by the wrist and pulled me down the stairs with much more force than was necessary. Something was obviously bothering him, but I didn't have a clue as to what it might be. Then I thought maybe it was Pam or one of his kids. But if he wanted to tell me, he'd tell me. I wasn't going to beg him for any more information. Not tonight. Hell, it's my birthday. And so far, it's the worst one I've ever spent with a man.

We got off at West Fourth Street and went into one of my favorite restaurants. There were lots of lush hanging plants and stained glass, even some lively music in the background. We sat by the window. In the summer I have sat in this same spot, but they slide the glass back so you feel like you're sitting outside. Franklin ordered a double Jack Daniel's before I could even think of what I wanted. When the waiter came with the menu, I realized Franklin didn't have enough money left for both of us to eat. I couldn't bring myself to go into my wallet one more time. Franklin ordered another double. He was puffing on a Newport and looked quite comfortable—like he could sit here all night. My left temple was jumping, fluttering, and I knew I was getting depressed. Something wasn't right about this whole night—this whole day—but I couldn't put my finger on it.

"Franklin," I said, leaning over the table to touch his hand, but he pulled it away. "What's wrong?"

"Nothin'," he said, looking out the window.

"You're acting very strange. Is something going on that I don't know about that I should know about?"

"No. And I ain't acting strange. You think I'm acting strange? Just because I didn't wanna see a stupid-ass war movie about a white boy falling in love, you think I'm acting strange? I just had a hard day, and I'm tired. The only reason I'm here is because it's your birthday. Otherwise, I'da stayed home."

"Well, why didn't you just say so? We didn't have to go out, you know."

"You been saying we don't never go nowhere, so I wanted to take you out."

"Yeah, but look what it's turned into. And if you were all that tired, why didn't you just sleep through the movie like you've done before?"

"Look. Why don't you order something to eat, to keep this celebration going before it goes all the way downhill?"

"I'm not hungry," I said, and leaned back in my chair.

"It figures."

"Why'd you say that?"

"You ain't hungry because you don't think I got paid today, do you? Tell the truth, Zora."

Earlier, the thought had crossed my mind, but then I thought about it. Maybe he didn't have time to cash his check. But why would he bring something like this up if there wasn't any truth to it? "*Shouldn't* I believe you, Franklin?"

His jawbone started twitching. What the hell is going on? I wondered. He's drunk. That's it. I've never seen him drink like this before, and I don't like it. And he just keeps picking at me. But why tonight?

"Look, let's skip the subject, okay. I'm under a lot of pressure at work and just got a lotta things on my mind. I don't wanna take it out on you or spoil your birthday no more than I already have, so why don't you go ahead and order something so we can get outta here?"

"We can leave now," I said, and got up and started putting my jacket back on. I really didn't need this—really I didn't.

"Good," he said, and gulped down the rest of his drink. He paid the waiter and didn't leave a tip.

When we got outside, we sort of stood on the corner, not moving, and neither of us said anything. The wind whipped around us, and dust flew in my eyes.

"Well," he said, digging his hands inside his pockets.

I didn't feel like going underground, didn't feel like sitting or standing next to him, didn't want our shoulders to touch—and I especially didn't feel like talking to him. He had ruined my damn birthday, and I still had no idea why. "Franklin, let's take a cab home."

Without saying a word, he walked over to the curb and held his arm out. Three empty cabs in a row pulled over toward him, then kept going.

"You motherfuckers!" he yelled. He held his arm out again—halfway—and stuck his index finger up to hail another one. It passed him by too. He had the most humiliated look on his face—one I've never seen before—and after five or six more minutes of the same thing, he looked like he was ready to explode. Finally, he walked over to me. "You try it."

I stepped down off the curb into the street, held my hand out, and within a few seconds a cab stopped. I opened the door and turned back to Franklin. He looked up into the black sky, then walked over to the cab and got in.

"If you big and black in America, that's two strikes against you—did you know that, Zora? They think all black men is killers and robbers and that we gon' cut their throats, then take all their fuckin' money. Ain't that right, sir?"

The cabdriver turned around. "I don't want any trouble, man."

Franklin slammed the door and leaned back in his seat. A silver sign posted on the plastic partition said, "Thank you for not smoking." Franklin whipped out a Newport and lit it. The driver looked at him through the rearview mirror but didn't say a word. I just shook my head and pressed my cheek against the glass.

We didn't say a single solitary word all the way home.

Once we were inside the apartment, Franklin turned on the TV and flopped down on the couch. I went into the bedroom, took my clothes off, and put on some ugly pajamas—the ones I knew he hated. I was starving, but I was too mad to eat. I just brushed my teeth and got in the bed. I heard him come into the bedroom, and I could feel him standing over me, but I refused to acknowledge him. My face faced the wall.

"Look, I'm sorry, Zora. Really I am."

I didn't say anything, but I was thinking, Fuck you, awfully hard.

I don't know how long he stood there, but when I woke up the next morning, I didn't feel his body next to me. I sprang up, and his side of the bed was empty. My heart raced, and I was wondering if he had left. I can't lie: I felt a sense of relief, really, in the thought. When I rolled over to get up, my foot hit something big. I looked down at the floor and saw Franklin curled up inside a nest of blankets. I stepped right over him.

* * *

Franklin didn't cash his check on Monday either. And now I know why. His friend Jimmy stopped by on Tuesday morning as I was about to lock the front door on my way to work. Franklin had left about quarter to seven, like he always does.

"Mornin', sweetness. Is Franklin still upstairs?"

I turned down the volume of my Walkman and slid the earphones off. "No. He's at work, Jimmy."

"Good. They called him back. Cool. I hate to be around that dude when he's laid off, don't you? He's like a big baby, ain't he?"

"Sort of," was all I could say. Laid off? Why didn't he just tell me? Then I figured I would play along with Jimmy to find out exactly how much he knew. "Well, it's been—how many days has it been now, Jimmy?"

"Over a week, ain't it? When I saw him last Tuesday at the bar, his head was all fucked up. Excuse my language, sweetness. All he was worried about was you and your rent. What you was gon' think—that he wasn't shit. That you was gon' realize you was too good for him. A man shouldn't love *no* woman as much as he love you, but then again, you ain't all that bad-looking." Jimmy let out a wail, and the fat on his forehead wrinkled up and formed rows and creases. His belt hung below his belly. I smiled. I know what he does for a living; Franklin told me. But he's never brought any drugs to our house, and I've never heard him mention any. I guess I just thought of Jimmy as one of those people who hadn't found his place in the world yet.

After I said goodbye, I caught the bus to work. Kids were swarming around McDonald's doorway, which was right across the street, and I decided to get one of those breakfast specials. Why couldn't Franklin have been honest and told me the truth? Why'd he have to lie? He could've given me some credit for wanting to understand. I mean really. By now I thought he knew we were in this thing together.

The hallways looked even longer today. Sterile. Even with hundreds of students moving along the tiled floors, leaning against gray lockers, I felt as if I were in a movie that was running in slow motion. I did not want to be here today, but I walked into my homeroom and sat down. My eighth graders all said the customary good morning. When I went to reach for my attaché case, it wasn't there. Shit. Where did I leave it? I thought back to the bus. No, I had walked off with it; that much I remembered. McDonald's. That was it. This is not a good sign, Zora, when you start forgetting simple things. Why does he *work* construction if he's constantly getting laid off? Can't he think of something else to do to earn a living? At least until he goes back to school? I know one thing—I can *not* handle him taking his frustrations out on me, and I don't even want to think about popping phenobarb again, just so I can cope with him being all stressed out. No way. And the lying. There's nothing I hate more than a liar. I'll just tell him—simple as that. I don't need this kind of shit, and if we're going to get through this—through everything—he's going to have to find a better way of dealing with disappointment. Period.

"Would someone like to do me a big favor?" At least six arms went up, and I pointed to a boy I'd had in seventh grade. Lance.

"I forgot my attaché case over at McDonald's. Just tell them I'm your homeroom teacher. Here's a note and a pass."

"You got it," he said, and walked out of the classroom, bopping.

"So how is everybody?" I was trying to sound enthusiastic.

"Tired," they said in unison.

"Whipped," a few more said.

"I feel great," a Hispanic girl said. "You look pretty tired, Miss Banks. What were you doing all night, huh?"

Half the class started laughing. I tried to crack a smile, but it wasn't all that funny. For the past three nights, I haven't had any reason to stay up.

I took roll, and to my surprise, Lance came back with my attaché right before the bell rang for first period. I dragged myself to class. Finally, I had the room I've been waiting for. The acoustics in here were excellent. The floors and walls were cement, and the windows were gigantic. A perfect listening room. Beethoven, Brahms, and Schubert sounded magnificent in here. And Leontyne Price? My God, I could sit in here and listen to all of 'em forever. Of course, most of my eighth graders could take or leave this kind of music. But let me play some Bruce Springsteen, they'd go crazy. I liked Springsteen myself, and before this semester was over, I was going to surprise them by bringing in one of his tapes.

"Okay," I said, sitting on top of my desk. "I'm Miss Banks."

"We already know that," someone said.

"Good. Then tell me something I don't know. Why are you here?" I wondered where Franklin was, and where he'd been disappearing to all last week when he acted like he was on his way to work.

"Because we're being punished!"

"Because we have to be!"

"That's not true, and you know it. Anyway, let me just tell you how I run my class. First of all, if you ever get bored, let me know immediately, is that clear?"

"I'm bored," someone said.

"But not today," I said, and tried to smile. "I'm going to introduce you to some of the best music in the world." I just wished it didn't have to be today.

At least fifteen of the thirty-six kids let out a long sigh.

"Who's ever heard of Tchaikovsky or Brahms or Schubert or Beethoven?"

About five hands went up.

"Who's heard of Gladys Knight, Bruce Springsteen, the Doobie Brothers, and—"

Every hand in the room went up, accompanied by screams.

"Okay, okay. This is what we're going to do. You're going to hear *all* this kind of music, and more. I want to teach you guys how to listen. We'll learn the fundamentals of music reading, so you'll be able to understand basic notes, and you'll even get to write and record your own song. Music has a history, and I'm going to try to make it as interesting as possible."

"We've heard that before!" someone yelled out.

"Do I look like a boring teacher?" I asked. I had deliberately worn a straight denim skirt with a hot-pink blouse and sandals and big earrings. I don't like to look threatening.

"No. You look pretty hip to us. How old are you anyway, Miss Banks?"

"Why?"

"None of our teachers tell us how old they are. You know how old we are. What's the big secret?"

They had a point. "I'm thirty years old."

"You don't look that old."

I was flattered. I can't lie: Sometimes these kids help me take my mind off things I've been thinking too hard about. Thank God.

I looked down at my notes, so I wouldn't forget what I was supposed to ask next.

"What kind of music do you normally listen to, or should I even ask?"

"Rock!" was what I heard the loudest.

"Rap!"

"Soul music!"

"How many of you like to sing?"

Only a few hands went up.

"How many of you play a musical instrument?"

Not a single hand went up.

"How many of you would like to learn to play an instrument?"

About half the class raised their hands.

"That's good," I said. "Now, does anyone know what a concerto is?"

No one said anything.

"How about an overture?"

There was more silence.

"A symphony?" A few lazy arms went up. I exhaled. My level of enthusiasm was dropping. "Well, today let's just start by listening to a few strings." I looked at them, then down at my lesson plan. I swear, I didn't feel like being a teacher today, so instead of listening to fifteen minutes of Beethoven and delivering my speech about music as a living art, I took George Benson out of my Walkman and pushed him into the big recorder. They looked surprised, then grateful. The next thing I knew, they were leaning forward in their seats, rocking their shoulders and popping their fingers to the beat.

I had already rehearsed my speech, and when I heard Franklin's key turning in the door, my heart started pounding real fast.

"Hello," I said. I was hoping my formality would give him a clue that something was wrong, but he was grinning.

"Guess what, baby?"

"What," I said. It was a statement, not a question.

"I'll probably be starting a new job in a day or two. One

that's gon' put me where I should be. No shit. The city's already been given the go-ahead for a office building—right in downtown Brooklyn. We shaping it up in the morning. The money looks good. Real good. Let me make your birthday up to you, baby. Name anything you want. Anything. Go ahead, baby, name it!"

I didn't realize it at first, but I was grinning too. Franklin looked so happy, like the man I had fallen in love with. His dimples were even more pronounced, and I hadn't seen them in over a week. The longer I looked at him, the clearer it was that it wouldn't do either of us any good for me to let on that I knew about him being laid off, so I kept my mouth shut.

"What about the racetrack?" I said. Franklin walked over and put my arms around his waist. Then he wrapped his arms around me and pulled me up against him.

"No problem," he said. "You tired?"

"No. Are you?"

"Come on, baby, be tired. Don't you feel like taking a little nap with me?"

I yawned. "Now that you mention it, I guess I could stand to lay down for a few minutes."

Our bodies fell apart, and he held my hand as we walked back toward the bedroom. I was almost happy, but my head still felt thick. Franklin did a fine job of thinning it out.

On Wednesday, I coughed all day long. My students kept telling me I should go home. But I wouldn't, even when I started getting hot and cold chills and could hardly pick up the chalk to write. When I finally got home, I flopped down on the bed and listened to the phone machine. Judy was postponing her trip. She didn't say why.

By five o'clock, I couldn't breathe. When Franklin came home and saw me like this, he played doctor. Made me hot tea with honey and wanted to put some of his Jack Daniel's in it, but I told him no. It wasn't until I woke up, about nine-something, that I remembered I was supposed to go listen to that band. Shit. I had Franklin call and explain. I rubbed more Vicks under my nose, he rubbed it on my chest and back, and I figured maybe I got sick for a reason. Maybe it wasn't time for me to be auditioning for a band. After all, I start my voice class next week.

For the next two days, I stayed in bed. I couldn't have gone to school if I wanted to. Franklin gave me hot baths with Epsom salt, kept me filled with chicken noodle soup and enough tea and juice to last the rest of my life. He even brushed my hair. It was precisely at times like this that I was grateful I had a man who loved me.

"So you're a friend of Eli's," Reginald said.

"Yes, I am, even though I haven't seen him in ages."

"He just moved to San Francisco."

"What? Since when?"

"Last week. He's touring with a dance company for a year."

"He could've told me. My goodness."

"Well, anyway, tell me a little more about yourself, Zora."

"What do you want to know?"

"Where you're from. How long you've been singing. Where you've sung. Why you want or feel you need lessons. What kind of singing you're interested in. What your long-range goals are. That sort of thing."

"Well, to start, I was raised in Toledo, Ohio, and grew up singing in a Baptist church."

"Any solos?"

"At least one Sunday a month."

Reginald was nodding his head.

"I guess I've been singing since I was about ten or eleven.

One day I'd like to sing professionally. I'm partial to rhythm and blues, but I also like to sing my own version of jazz and folk. That's one reason why I'm here, to figure out if I can fuse them all together. And also to learn how to control my voice."

"Have you ever had any training before?"

"Just high school choir."

"Any talent shows?"

"Two, but that was when I was in high school. I did win first place both times."

"So tell me who some of your favorite singers are."

"That's a loaded question, but I respect quite a few of them. But to name a few, I love Joan Armatrading and Nancy Wilson. Chaka Khan, Laura Nyro, Aretha, Sarah Vaughan, Joni Mitchell. Is that enough?"

"I'm getting the picture. Let me tell you how I work. I like to meet once a week, and for the first three weeks or so, we'll start off by concentrating totally on breathing. In your letter you said you teach music—do you have a piano?"

"Yes." I had to smile just thinking about how I was able to get it. Franklin. God, do I love that man.

"Good. Because you'll have exercises to do at home. Anyway, we'll work on breathing techniques for about twenty minutes each session. Then we'll do the scales for about fifteen, and the remaining time you'll sing. Now. The first thing I want you to do is imagine that you're a balloon being filled up with air."

"Right now?"

"Can you think of a better time?"

"I just didn't know I was going to do anything like this today."

"Well, what did you think we were going to do?"

"Talk."

"I teach voice, not talk."

"Okay. What do you want me to do, again?" I was nervous as hell. I wasn't prepared for this.

He pointed to my stomach. "I want all of it to go in your diaphragm, right there, so you feel like a pregnant woman. Then I want you to exhale, so everything springs back. We're going to practice doing this fast and slow. The whole idea is to help you to control those abdominal muscles correctly. Once you learn how to do this—and it won't be overnight—you'll notice how much easier it is for you when you sing. Do you get tired easily when you're singing?"

"I don't know. I've never sung for any extended period of time."

"Well, we'll watch and see what happens."

I tried to concentrate, but I wasn't used to breathing like this. Reginald kept correcting me, and finally I felt so frustrated I said, "I'll practice this some more at home."

"I told you this takes time."

But I was pissed off because I wanted to do it right. Today.

"Well, pick a song," he said.

"To sing?"

He looked frustrated now, like I'd just asked a stupid question.

"Okay," I said, and cleared my throat. When I opened my mouth, nothing came out. I wasn't used to this.

"Take a deep breath, and try to relax," he said.

That was easy for him to say. I must've started Laura Nyro's version of "Gonna Take a Miracle" four times before it felt right and I was able to get through it. I was perspiring like it was going out of style.

"I'm impressed," Reginald said, after I'd finally finished. "As we go along, particularly when we're working on a specific song, we're going to concentrate on posture, the position of your head, and all the things that have to do with stage presence. Try to remember to bring a cassette to class so we can record each session. I want you to hear what you're doing, and in a few months you'll be able to hear your progress. And let me warn you now, if you're not serious, miss classes, don't do the work, and that kind of thing, I'll drop you. Is that clear?"

I nodded. He sounded like a teacher all right. But all the way home, it felt like I'd acquired Franklin's dimples, because the lining of my cheeks tickled. All I kept thinking was that I had taken the first step, and I was on my way.

8

"This is where you live now, Daddy?" Derek asked, walking around the apartment.

"Yeah, this is where I live," I said. I betcha he was thinking that it damn sure was a improvement over that room. I didn't know if he could tell that none of the shit in here was mine, but at least it looked like I was living right. I heard Miles banging on Zora's piano. "Miles, what you doing back there, boy? Don't be messing with that piano. It ain't no toy. Now get your little bird butt outta there and close the door."

Miles came walking down the hallway, looking like E.T. The boy ain't but seven years old and already got long, wiry legs and not a drop of meat on him. He looks like his Mama, but if he lucky, he'll grow out of it. Derek looks like me, except he's a few shades lighter.

"What size shoe you wearing now, Derek?"

"Elevens."

"Damn, I don't wear but thirteens myself. Your feet gon' be bigger than mine. You gon' have to get a job, man."

He started grinning. "So where's your girlfriend, Daddy?"

"She's still at school."

"She go to school? Is she that young?"

"Naw, naw, naw. She *teaches* junior high, but she usually stays a little later to get ready for the next day."

"You gon' marry her?" Miles asked.

"What you know about getting married, chump?" I grabbed his little round head and knuckled it. He started squirming, and then Derek jumped on top of me and tried to help him. We was tussling something terrible, when I heard a crash. Aw, shit. "Hey, hold it, fellas. Hold it." I looked over and saw one of Zora's lamps had fell over and broke. Damn.

"I'm sorry, Daddy," Derek said.

"Me too," said Miles.

"It's okay, dudes. It wasn't nobody's fault." Just then I heard Zora's key turn in the door. The boys ran over to the couch and sat down like they was waiting for a beating. "Relax, fellas. She ain't gon' bite you." They just looked at each other, then back at the door.

When Zora saw 'em sitting on her couch, at first she looked surprised, and then she just smiled this stupid smile and said, "Hi."

Derek and Miles both blushed and mumbled a "Hi" back. Miles was hiding his face behind Derek's back, and Derek kept trying to push him away.

"Hi, baby," I said, and walked over and kissed her on the cheek.

"And just who are these handsome young men?" she asked.

"I'm Derek."

"I'm Miles."

"Well, I'm Zora. Glad to meet you guys. Your Daddy's told me a lot about you."

They started laughing.

Zora looked at me like she couldn't understand what she said that was so funny. "Well, Derek, Franklin tells me you're quite a basketball player, and Miles, what grade are you in?"

"Second," Miles said, then dived behind Derek again.

"What happened to the lamp?" she asked casually.

"I'm sorry, baby. I'll replace it. We was wrestling on the floor, and I guess we knocked it over."

"Don't worry about it," she said. "So are you guys staying for dinner?"

Both of 'em hunched their shoulders and started laughing again. "I was about to take 'em out for pizza and a movie."

"But how many opportunities do I get to cook dinner for your sons, Franklin?"

"They'll come back again," I said.

"You love my Daddy?" Miles blurted out.

"Give me a break, Miles, would you?" I asked.

"Well, Mama said that's why people live together, 'cause they in love. Do you?"

Now Zora looked like she was blushing. "Yes, I love your Daddy," she said.

"You gon' marry him?"

"I don't know. You have to ask your Daddy that."

"Daddy, you wanna marry her?"

"One day, Miles. You dudes about ready?"

"I like your piano, Miss Zora," Miles said.

"You do?"

"Uhn-hun. You know how to play it for real?"

"I sure do. Do you know how to play a piano?"

"Nope."

"Well, I'll tell you what. If you promise me you'll come back, I'll show you how to play a few songs. Would you like that?"

"Yeah!" he said, and got up.

"I'll see you later, baby." I kissed her on the lips, and she said her goodbyes to all of us.

When we got downstairs, Derek was awfully quiet. "What's wrong with you, dude?" I asked him.

"Nothin'."

"Then why ain't you talking?"

" 'Cause I ain't got nothing to say."

"Didn't you like Zora?"

"I didn't say that, did I?"

"Well, what's wrong, then?" I asked, even though I knew what the deal was. This is the first woman he's ever seen me with since me and his Mama split up. I didn't know I was ever gon' be in a position where I was gon' have to explain this stuff or defend my feelings. Shit. How you supposed to tell your kid this kinda shit without hurting their feelings?

"It's just funny knowing you live with another woman that ain't Mama, that's all."

"I know, man. But look. You know how long it's been since me and your Mama been together, right?"

"Yeah, but it just don't seem right."

"Can I explain something to you?"

"What?"

"You like girls, don't you?"

"Yeah, but what's that got to do with this?"

"Well, when you grow up to be a man, you might find yourself doing more than just liking 'em. You might fall in love, the same way I did when I met your Mama. Only sometimes things happen, and people find it hard to live with each other, and they go their separate ways. After that happens, sometimes you meet somebody else you love, and you kinda start all over again. Your Mama met somebody else, didn't she?"

"Yeah, but he don't live with us."

"But he might one day, you know."

He looked at me like the thought had never crossed his mind.

"Do you like him?"

"He's all right."

"Well, as long as I know he ain't mistreating y'all, I want your Mama to be happy with him. You know what I'm saying?"

"I guess."

"What you mean, you guess?"

"Yeah."

"It ain't no fun being by yourself all the time. A man likes having a woman to keep him company. But it don't mean I'ma forget about y'all or ain't gon' wanna see y'all. You get my drift?"

"But what'll happen if you was to marry her and then have some more kids? What about me and Miles?"

"First of all, you and Miles gon' always be my sons, and I'm gon' always love you, so don't forget that shit. But if this'll make you feel any better, I don't plan on having no more kids."

"Yeah, but say if you did—then that would make them our half brother or sister, right?"

"I want a sister," Miles said.

"Yeah. But ain't no sense in worrying about something that most likely ain't gon' happen, now is it?"

"You gon' marry her, ain't you?" Derek asked.

"I might."

"Well, if you do, don't look for me at your wedding."

"Come on now, man. Would you wanna see me miserable for the rest of my life?"

"No."

"I'll come," said Miles. "I like that lady. She talk like white people, but I could come live with y'all and then I'd have two Mamas, huh, Daddy?"

I popped him upside the head as we walked into the pizza place.

"Derek?"

"What?" he asked, flopping down in the chair.

"Regardless of if I marry Zora or not, and regardless if I did happen to have another kid, I'm your Daddy and always will be. I wouldn't never do nothin' deliberately to hurt you, and if you ever need me for anything, all you gotta do is pick up the phone. You understand what I'm saying, man?"

"Yeah," he said. "You mind if we get pepperoni?"

I shook my head. He was jealous. I could see that. But I didn't know what else to say that would put him at ease. In a way, it made me feel kinda good, 'cause it showed me that he still loved me.

Zora was trembling. It was so good for her. I didn't come, but it was okay. I still felt satisfied.

"What's wrong, Franklin?" she asked. Why do women always think something is wrong when a man don't come? Sometimes I just like feeling her body. Coming ain't everything.

"Nothing, baby," I said. "The little spermazoids was all ready to run out and play. They had their beer in their hands, little picnic baskets, their swimming trunks on, but then they heard a voice that said, 'It's getting ready to rain, so we better stay in and play today.' They on punishment, so I'm making 'em sit this one out."

Zora cracked up. Right now I need to keep her laughing, 'cause that job didn't come through. Everything is always put on hold for some stupid-ass reason. So all I been doing is working a day here, two days there. But things is getting too tight. Here it is November, it's getting cold outside, and work is starting to slow up. I been to every organization in town, and it's the same story. A man can only wait so long for shit to happen.

The phone rang, and Zora was getting ready to jump up to get it. "Let it ring," I said, and she did. Something told me it was probably Pam. Derek gave her this phone number, and she been calling on a weekly basis, bugging the shit outta me, but at least she ain't been nasty when Zora answer the phone. Zora even act like she wanna meet the bitch—which is some sick shit, if you ask me. I told her they didn't have nothin' in common, and what was the fuckin' point. "Because she was an important part of your life," was what she said. So the fuck what? "You think I wanna meet any of your old boyfriends? To look at 'em and know you used to fuck 'em? Hell, no," I said. "Franklin, all I know is that she's the mother of your children. Why should I hate her?" Women.

She rolled over and collapsed on her side of the bed. "Why you move?" I asked.

"What?"

"Why you move? You felt good, baby. Come back over on top of Daddy."

"I've gotta go to the bathroom," she said, and got up.

I was looking out the window, at the wind blowing all the leaves and shit off the trees, and thinking that if I was bringing in some money, this could be just another nice lazy-ass Saturday. We been watching kung fu movies all morning, which Zora hates because the words don't match the dudes' mouth when they talk. But it was either this or wrestling, and she think wrestling is phony. We've made love twice this morning, and even though my dick keeps getting hard, I'm just fuckin' to get some of my frustrations out. The shit still ain't worked yet.

Zora came back and picked up this book she was reading: *Nobody Knows My Name*, by James Baldwin. When I first saw her reading it, I told her that I read that book a long time ago. It was the truth too. I've read all kinda books. Shit, if you ain't in school, it's up to you to educate yourself. That's the way I figured the shit supposed to go down.

But for somebody that's been to college, Zora is one slow-ass reader. It's been over two weeks now, and she still only halfway through it. I can read a whole book in a night—if I like it. Get me a pack of Newports and a cup of coffee, and I'll hang till it's over. Most writers, I give fifty pages to get the shit moving. If they beat around the bush and shit, I'll put the motherfucker down. They don't get no second chances neither. You snooze, you lose, in my book.

I looked over at Zora. She seemed tired. And it's probably my fault. She been dealing with my bullshit like a champ. "Don't worry about it, Franklin," she said. "Things'll pick up." But how much more can she take? I know she gotta be tired of me not helping her. She's paid the rent for the past three months. Bought all the food and insisted on paying for the bets when we went to the track. I don't think she really know how this shit makes me feel. Which is why I couldn't come.

"You think I should move back to my room?" I asked. I didn't plan on saying nothing like this; it just came out.

She looked up from her book, then let it drop in her lap. "What?"

"Let's face it, baby. My shit is raggedy. I ain't paid no rent over here in ages. I can't help you out, and you don't really need me here." Then I thought about what I had just said. I mighta been speaking too soon, 'cause I'ma get thrown outta my room soon. Ain't paid no rent over there in almost three months either.

"Franklin, we just made love, and we've already talked about this before, so why'd you have to bring it up again now?"

" 'Cause it's fuckin' with me, that's why."

"Do you want to leave?"

"You know I don't wanna leave, baby."

"So what'll going back over there prove?"

"It'll take some of this guilt offa me. I feel like I'm pimping or mooching offa you, baby. I'm used to paying my own way."

"I *know* you're not mooching, and you better not even think you're pimping anybody but yourself. Things may be a little lopsided right now, but it comes with the territory, doesn't it?"

"I don't know. You tell me."

"Well, I'm hoping things'll change soon."

"What if they don't?"

"I've got faith in you, Franklin."

"I just can't stand feeling like this—helpless and shit."

"Look, Franklin," she said, putting her book down. "As long as I know you're trying, I can be patient. I love you, and I'll hang in here as long as you don't give up. Can we leave it at that?"

She reached over and put her arms around me. Damn, she felt good. It's nice as hell when your woman holds *you,* and sometimes Zora do it just when I need it. My dick started getting hard, and this time I knew I could come, but I didn't wanna burden her.

"How about a grilled cheese sandwich?" I asked.

"With tomatoes?"

"If that's how you like it, baby."

"You know how I like it," she said, and winked at me. Damn, do I love that woman. One day, I swear to God, she gon' be proud that I'm her man.

I went to get outta bed, but she put her hands around Tarzan. She knows how to squeeze him just right, stroke him just right, and suck him just right, but right now, if she knew what was good for her, she'd better let him go. "Don't do that, baby. Tarzan is tired. He been swinging all day."

She kissed him on his head. "I hope he's got one more dance left in him," she said, and leaned back into the pillow.

Zora thinks she slick. Either she's one helluva actress, or she really ain't feeling as miserable about this shit as I am. I know she cleaned out her savings account, and that was the money she was saving up for her studio rental—among other things. True, it's a ways down the road, but between the rental and her maybe having to pay musicians to get a demo tape together, we talking about some real cash here. And now that money is gone—because of me. She over the limit on two of her credit cards, 'cause I heard the messages on her answering machine. Some nights, when we both couldn't stand being in here, she said, "To hell with this, Franklin, let's go out to dinner." And she'd whip out one of those cards. I ain't never had no kind of credit cards, and it's embarrassing that every time you go somewhere, your woman is paying for it.

She got two checking accounts too, and this month's rent check was gon' bounce, so she wrote a check to herself and deposited it in the other account to stall for time. Yesterday morning, when she thought I was still sleep, I heard her asking her Daddy for a loan. And she had called him, 'cause I didn't hear the phone ring.

I laid in bed and felt like a chump. Laying up in my woman's apartment, and she gotta call her Pops to ask for money. This shit didn't make no kinda sense.

I kinda burned the sandwiches, but what the fuck. I took 'em in to her anyway. She put her book down, looked at the sandwiches, then started laughing.

"They taste better burnt," I said, and sat down on the edge of the bed.

"You know, Franklin, I've been thinking."

"Oh, hell. When you start thinking, that's dangerous," I said.

"Seriously."

"I'm listening." I lit a cigarette. I already knew I didn't wanna hear this. I hate anybody doing my thinking for me, and something told me that was gon' be the case now.

"Have you ever thought about doing some other kind of work?"

"Like what?"

"I don't know. There's lots of things you're good at. I mean, aren't there other things you can think of to do to earn a living, while you're waiting for school or something else to happen?"

"Like what?"

"I don't know." She got up and stood by the window.

I hate this shit.

"All I know how to do is construction, baby."

"That's not true, and you know it, Franklin. You can fix anything, build anything. Why don't you put an ad in some of the local papers and put up some flyers."

"Why don't I do what?"

"You heard me. It doesn't sound so far-fetched to me. Who knows what might happen?"

"Why don't you just go ahead and tell me to leave, Zora?"

"Because I don't want you to leave, Franklin. I'm just asking you to look at your alternatives."

"Right. Okay. If it'll make you feel better, I'll take out some ads and get some flyers printed up on Monday." I dropped the rest of my sandwich on the saucer, then lit another cigarette. "Who's gon' pay for all this shit?" I asked, looking at her hard.

"Me."

I knew she meant well, but Zora just don't understand nothing about timing. Three whole weeks went by, and not a single person called. Not only had my constitution not even gotten off the ground yet, but as I walked up and down the streets of Brooklyn ripping down them flyers, it felt like what little foundation I thought I had had just fuckin' disappeared.

9

My period is late.

It was due two weeks ago. I wanted to tell Franklin, but I couldn't. The last thing we need right now is a baby. And besides, I'm not even his wife. I just imagined what he would say if I told him, "Franklin, guess what? We're having a baby." He'd probably look at me and say, "A what?" It wouldn't be like it is on TV, that's for damn sure. He probably wouldn't throw his arms up in the air and say, "I'm gonna be a Daddy? Hot damn!" No. He probably wouldn't be all that thrilled.

He's been going through a lot of changes as it is, trying to keep Pam at bay, and last month, when Derek turned fourteen, Franklin didn't have any money to buy him a birthday present. I asked him what did he think Derek would want? "Nikes," he said. "What size?" I asked. He told me elevens. I spent thirty-nine dollars on a pair of high-tops—since Derek plays basketball—and gave them to Franklin. "Take these over to him," I said. "Baby, you didn't have to do this. He ain't even your kid." My kid. "I know he's not *my* kid," I said, "but he's *your* kid, and I want him to know that his father didn't forget his birthday. Can't you forget your stupid pride for once? Don't disappoint him, Franklin." Derek never has had too much to say to me, but the last time he came over, he was smiling and wearing those sneakers. I felt like we were finally making progress. All I wanted to do was get to know Franklin's kids.

My Daddy would have a fit if he found out about *this*—him being in the church and all. And Marguerite is so old-fashioned, she'd probably persuade Daddy into talking me into coming home and having it anyway. I'd have to listen to them condemning me for getting involved with a married man—which is what it boils down to—so I can't tell them either.

I swear, I don't want to have another abortion—really I don't. But what other choice do I have? Franklin's job situation is so iffy, I'd probably end up taking care of all three of us. I couldn't handle that. Lots of women are having babies these days without being married, but I never imagined myself giving birth without having a husband to go along with it. I can take feminism only so far. We've never even talked about having kids. What if he *doesn't* want any more? But what if he does?

Any way I look at it, I'm still scared.

I'm also starting to feel like shit. When I wake up, Franklin's cigarette smoke—especially those disgusting ashes—makes me feel like I want to throw up. The other day, I was cleaning out the bathtub, and the Comet made me feel the same way. It seems like I smell everything twice as much now, and the scents pass through my nostrils, land in the pit of my stomach, then work their way back up inside my throat and stay there. I should've known something was up—the way I've been eating these past few weeks—but with all the other things I've got on my mind, I haven't slowed down long enough to think about it. This morning, the scale told the truth—I'd gained six pounds. I looked at the calendar on the bathroom wall, then stuck my finger between my legs. I was hoping to see red. My fingers came back the same color, and I panicked. I knew it wasn't coming, because every twenty-eight days it arrives like clockwork. Shit.

Ironically enough, Claudette's on her way over here with the baby. Why does she have to be six months pregnant? I know it was stupid of me to invite Portia and Marie too, but I wanted them all here. I had to tell *somebody*. And I can't keep this to myself. Not this time.

Franklin was at the gym and was spending the day with his kids. His kids. When I heard the buzzer, I started to run down the stairs like I always do, but something rushed to my head and made me feel dizzy, so I walked. Portia and Claudette were standing there together.

"Hurry up, girl. It's cold as hell out here," Portia said through the door.

"Where's Chanelle?" I asked Claudette.

"Home with her father. She's got a little cold, but I felt like getting out of the house. So can we come in, or what?"

I unlocked the door, and we went upstairs.

"So, girlfriend, what you gon' do?" Portia asked.

I walked over to the sink and got out the coffee cups. I took the croissants from the refrigerator and slid 'em into the oven. For some reason, I wasn't hungry. "I really don't know," I said.

I heard the door buzz. "Claudette, would you let Marie in, please?"

When Claudette got up, the only thing I noticed was her big belly. I put my hands over mine and rubbed it. Why now, God? I wondered. And why me? It wasn't as if I didn't use anything. Should I be reading this differently—that I'm *supposed* to go through with it? That things happen for a reason? This would make three abortions. Three times that I stopped a life. But having it would be stupid. Where would it sleep? We'd have to get a bigger place, which would mean more rent; pay a baby-sitter—*everything* would change. I'd probably have to stop my voice lessons, and how would I learn to juggle my time so I wouldn't have to give up singing altogether? What if my seizures flared back up and I'd have to get back on phenobarb? I'd be taking a chance that my baby could be born with something besides ten fingers and ten toes. I don't want to take that chance. Not right now. Not until I can trust science more. You're just being selfish, Zora. All you're thinking about is yourself. No, I'm not. Yes, you are. If *I* don't, *who* will? Of course I've read about women whose seizures had long since stopped, and they had perfectly normal pregnancies and healthy babies. But it'd be just my luck to have fits for the next nine months. And Franklin would find out before I had a chance to tell him. Maybe he'd feel deceived and leave me. I do not want to be a single mother, that much I do know.

"Hi, girl," Marie said, as she kissed me on the cheek. "Are you okay?"

"I'm trying to be," I said. "The cups are right here; half-and-half, sugar; the croissants should be warm enough. Help yourselves."

"Let me ask you a question, Zora," Claudette said. "What exactly were you using? You *were* using something, I hope?"

"The jelly that goes into my diaphragm."

"And that shit didn't work?" Marie asked.

"Obviously not," I said.

"Why didn't you use the damn diaphragm too?" Portia asked.

"Because Franklin's too big. In the beginning we tried it that way, but it felt like it was moving up into my damn chest."

"Niggahs and their big dicks, I swear," Portia said, and took a sip from her coffee. "Why don't you just take the pill?"

"Because I can't," I said.

"What do you mean, you can't?" Marie asked.

"I've tried about five different kinds, and each one gave me a different side effect. I got white splotches all over my face. My breasts got even bigger and were so tender I couldn't stand to touch 'em myself. I never wanted to make love—"

"Well, that ain't the end of the world, you know," Marie said.

"Well, maybe not. I was on one kind for about two months, and I put on fifteen pounds. I just gave up." The truth of the matter was, back then the phenobarb screwed up my metabolism so much that it broke down the hormone in the pill. I'd have gotten pregnant anyway.

"You should get yourself an IUD," Claudette said. "They work—believe me. Before Chanelle was born, I had one for five years, and it never gave me any trouble."

"You don't want no IUD, girl," Portia said. "Those things are gonna be taken off the damn market. Hell, ain't you heard about those women who been hemorrhaging and dying from them things? Some of 'em are sterile, and some have gotten pregnant with them things still up inside 'em. You don't even wanna think about getting one of those."

"Right now I'm not worrying about what to use in the future. I'm worried about what I'm going to do about this." I had put my hand over my stomach, which was throbbing. It felt like my period was coming, but I didn't feel a thing sliding out.

"Have you told Franklin?" Marie asked.

"No."

"Why not?"

"Because he'd probably want me to go through with it."

"How do you know that?" Claudette asked.

"It's just a feeling, but the bottom line is that I want this decision to be mine. Franklin has a way of talking me into things that I sometimes regret later. I don't want this to be one of 'em."

"Well, I don't know what the big deal is, really. Why don't you just go on and have it? You love the man, don't you?"

"Yes, I love him. But it's more complicated than that, Claudette. We're not in any position to get married right now."

"What exactly do you mean by 'not in any position'?" Marie asked. "This guy isn't married, is he?"

All three of them turned their eyes toward me. They wouldn't understand if I told them that Franklin's been separated for over six years. They wouldn't understand that the reason he hasn't gotten his divorce yet is because he hasn't been able to afford it. They just wouldn't understand.

"No. He's not married," I said. "But he's laid off work right now. We've got bills coming out of our asses, and my voice lessons aren't exactly free. I don't know what I would do with a baby right now."

"Zora, it's nine whole months away," Claudette said.

"I wouldn't have nobody's baby without a diamond on my finger," Portia said.

"Would you marry him if he asked you?" Claudette asked.

"I don't know, to tell you the truth. I love him, but we've got our share of problems."

"Who doesn't?" she said.

"We're constantly broke. Franklin wants to go back to school this winter. He wants to learn how to start his own business."

"What's his B.A. in?" Marie asked.

Damn. Why do they have to ask so many questions? "He doesn't have a B.A.," I said.

"Well, where'd he go to college?" Claudette asked.

"He didn't finish," was all I said. I had to defend him. They wouldn't understand if I told him he never finished high school. They wouldn't understand that Franklin's brilliant on his own terms, that college doesn't automatically make you smart. They just wouldn't understand. "By trade, he's a carpenter. You see that cabinet my stereo's on?"

They all turned to look at it.

"Franklin made that," I said.

Marie and Claudette looked impressed, but Portia said, "Right now the question is, Is the man really trying to find work, or is he just laying up on his black ass, daydreaming?"

"He's trying, believe me, and the saddest thing in the world is to see your man out of work."

"Well," Claudette said, "if he can build furniture like this and he's trying to get back into school, I'd hang in there. It'd be different if he wasn't trying."

"I'm not thinking about giving up—yet. But how do you know when you've hung too long?"

"When you get tired," she said, eating her third croissant. "Or when you feel you're running in place."

"Personally, I wouldn't wait that long," Portia said.

"Hell, when Allen and I got married, I was in law school and he was only in his third year of medical school. Talk about hard times. Sometimes I was ready to fly out the door. After I passed the bar, I was making all the money, paying all the bills—while he studied. But he had asked me if I really thought I could handle it, and I said yes. It's called commitment, honey.

"And don't be so naive as to think that Allen and I are always lovey-dovey. Honey, we argue, scream, slam doors. Once in a while I break a dish. I even pulled the phone out of the wall once. But this is all par for the course. You've got to take the bitter with the sweet. Just as long as you're not the only one doing all the struggling, I'd stick with the man."

"I plan to, Claudette," I said, "unless I run out of gas."

"All this Ann Landers shit sounds good," Portia said, "but we supposed to be trying to help the girl decide what's best for *her* right now—not *him*."

"I say get rid of it," Marie said.

"How late are you?" Claudette asked.

"Two weeks."

"Well, that's good," Portia said. "There's lots of places in Manhattan where you can get it done early. Have you ever had one before, Zora?"

At first I thought about lying, but then I realized we were all women, so why should I? "I've had two."

"Shit, I've had three or four of 'em myself. It ain't no picnic, is it? I swear, if men only knew what we had to go through just to get a damn nut—this kind of bullshit," she said.

"Well," Marie said, "when they finally come up with birth control for *their* asses, I bet they won't be so quick to unzip their pants. The burden of responsibility's been on us for too damn long, if you ask me."

"What kind of birth control do you use?" Portia asked her.

Marie got the strangest look on her face, then blurted out, "Foam." Something, I don't know why, told me she was lying. I've never heard her mention any particular man before, but I've never had the impression that she was gay either.

"Well, the last one I had was a bitch," Portia said. "They gave me a damn Valium, and that shit didn't do nothing, girl. It felt like somebody was pulling dry, brittle branches out my pussy."

"All right, Portia, spare us the details," Claudette said.

"I was knocked out both times," I said. "How much does it cost now?"

"Your insurance should cover it, won't it?" Marie asked.

"I can't let the school find out about this."

"Well, fuck it," Marie said. "You got any money?"

"Not really," I said, embarrassed.

"Well, all you gotta do is look in the *Voice*—there's a whole page of ads for 'em," Portia said. "They compete with each other, girl. You wanna get knocked out again, don't you?"

"I have to. I couldn't take being awake, watching it, knowing what they're doing. I swear I couldn't."

"Then it's probably gonna cost you about three hundred."

"Three hundred?"

"Look, I can lend you about a hundred," Marie said.

"Where are you getting money from?" I asked.

"I got a gig."

"Well, why didn't you tell me?"

"Shit, since you've been in love, you've been so busy. Who can catch up with you? Whenever I call, you're either playing the piano and singing, or wrapped up in Franklin's arms, or some shit like that."

"I can lend you a hundred too," Claudette said. "More if you need it."

"I'm good for fifty," Portia said.

"Thanks, you guys. I don't know what I'd do without you—really I don't."

"Well, I'll go with you, 'cause you're gon' need somebody," Portia said. "It don't matter if you're wide awake or knocked out. When it's over, you damn sure ain't gon' wanna be alone."

I heard the key in the door, and saw Franklin and Derek.

"Hi," I said. "What are you doing back so soon?"

"I didn't mean to interrupt anything," he said.

"You're not interrupting anything," I said. "I just didn't expect you, that's all."

"Hello, ladies," he said.

Everybody blushed, then said hello. Boy, did the room get quiet all of a sudden.

"Hi, Derek," I said. I introduced everybody, and then the silence grew even more obvious.

"Where's Miles?" I asked.

"He's got the chicken pox," Derek said.

"Oh," was all I said. I knew Franklin could tell we'd been talking girl talk, and I prayed that he wouldn't suspect anything other than that.

"Well, I'd better be getting back to check on Chanelle," Claudette said, getting up.

"Can I get a ride to the train station?" Portia asked.

"Look, ladies, you don't have to leave on my account. I just came to get my racquetballs, that's all."

"We were about to leave anyway," Marie said. "Let me just get my coat."

Franklin looked at me apologetically, then went to get the balls. He gave me a kiss on the cheek, and everybody left at the same time.

I sat down on the couch and felt so light-headed that the room started to spin. "No," I said out loud, and got up. I walked up and down the hallway until I felt stationary. I forced the room to stop turning.

Portia met me in front of the place. I'd been throwing up all morning, until I'd gotten the dry heaves. Now there was nothing left in my belly but the baby. I kept getting hot and cold chills, and felt so weak that I had to take a cab. Franklin had left at his usual time and wouldn't be back until after three. I'd been told that I'd be home in less than three hours and feeling pretty much back to normal by afternoon.

"How you feeling?" Portia asked. She didn't give me a chance to answer. "You don't look so hot. But don't worry, girlfriend. It'll be over before you know it."

When we got inside, the large white room was full of

women. Some of them looked miserable, some just looked scared. I knew I felt both. I signed in and walked back over to Portia.

"Just try to relax a minute, Zora. Now sit down," she said.

"Portia, God is going to punish me one day for doing this, I know it. Just watch: When and if I ever decide to have a baby, it'll probably come out retarded or deformed or an epileptic. I can't keep doing this, I just can't."

"Don't even talk no stupid shit like that around me. This is damn near nineteen-fuckin'-eighty-three, girl. Women got a right to decide whether or not they wanna have a goddamn baby. Shit, just because the fucking birth control didn't work, why should we have to suffer? You know how many of our lives are fucked up 'cause we got kids we can't afford, didn't plan, or didn't want? And with no help? You don't wanna be one of those statistics, honey, so sit your ass down and be quiet."

I waited for them to call my name, and when I finally heard it, I was scared to move. The room suddenly felt like it was full of women who weren't moving.

"It'll be okay," Portia said, and ushered me to the door. I couldn't even turn back to look at her.

My head is falling off my shoulders as they wheel me into a light-blue room. They stick a plastic needle into my vein. I feel the walls of my mouth expanding. It tastes like gasoline. But I don't have a car. Someone in a white mask tells me to start counting backward from a hundred. Why one hundred? One hundred. Baby number three. Gone. Down the drain. Make it quick, would you? I've got a voice class. What voice? You've taken my voice? It's gone? I can't sing, anything, ever again? Is this how much a baby cost? Ninety-nine. I promised Dillon or Percy or Franklin—one of them—something. What was it? Dinner. Oh, shit. All we've got in the house is

baby food. Ninety-eight. *No. There's steak in the freezer.
But it's frozen. Stiff as a stick.* Ninety-seven. *Steak. Stick.
Who, me? No, I didn't. Go ahead, stick me. I dare you to
stick me.* Ninety-six. *Go ahead, step across that line. I'll hit
you back, I swear it. I warned your ass!* Ninety-five. *Cheater.*

When I woke up, I was lying on a table in a different room.
There was a beautiful dark-skinned girl in a burgundy recliner. She couldn't have been more than eighteen. She
looked African—Senegalese, maybe? What was *she* doing
here? Another woman, who looked about my age, was in a
black recliner. Both of their legs were propped up.

"How do you feel?" the doctor asked me.

"Okay, I guess." I didn't feel any pain, anywhere.

"Then why don't you sit up and come over and rest like
these young ladies over here," he said. I got up with relative
ease and sat down beside the dark-skinned girl. There was a
square white pad on the empty seat. I eased into the chair, and
the doctor pushed on the back of it. My feet went up into the
air. They were on the same level as the girl's. The doctor left
the room.

I couldn't think of anything to say to her, so I just stared at
my feet. I put my hands on my belly. It was empty now. Tears
started rolling down my cheeks, but I didn't feel like wiping
them. The girl handed me a Kleenex, and I nodded thank
you. Why couldn't Franklin and I have just fallen in love and
gotten married? Why couldn't he have a regular job? Why
couldn't I have a recording contract? Why . . . "Where are you
from?" I asked her.

"Senegal," she said.

Why I felt relieved, I don't know.

"What were you using?" I asked her.

"Nothing," she said.

"Oh."

The doctor came back into the room, and without even realizing it, I heard myself ask him, "What was it?"

He just looked at me. "I'm not at liberty to say. Don't you worry yourself about that now," he said, and walked over to another woman, who was now on the recovery table. She was lying on her stomach. Her hair was thick, black, and matted. She looked around the room until she spotted the three of us.

"Where am I?" she asked.

None of us said a word.

"This is so silly," she said. Then she turned her head sideways and closed her eyes.

Portia was reading *Cosmopolitan* when I came out. She threw it on an empty chair and rushed over to me.

"So you feeling okay?"

"Yeah. Just a little tired is all."

"I told you it was nothin' to it, didn't I?"

After convincing Portia that I'd be fine, I took a cab home. Franklin wasn't there yet—thank God—so I lay down. When I heard the door slam, I sprang up in bed. He came into the bedroom and stood in the doorway.

"What's wrong with you?" he asked.

"I've got a yeast infection, that's all."

"Oh, yeah?"

"Yeah."

"How'd you get it?"

"Women just get 'em every now and then. It's a buildup of bacteria, and I have to use these suppositories to get rid of the infection."

"But I need some pussy, baby."

"You'll just have to wait, Franklin."

"You mean you can't make love?"

"No."

"Why not?"

"Because I could give this to you, and you'd be itching and everything, and then you'd have to take antibiotics. You wouldn't want to go through that, would you?"

"I can use a rubber."

"No, you can't. I'm not supposed to have anything inside me until the infection's gone."

"Well, just how long will that be?"

"Two weeks."

"Women," he said. "I'm glad I ain't one. Y'all get more shit wrong with your bodies than any other species on earth."

"Yeah, but what would you do without us?"

"What's that supposed to mean?"

"Just what I said: What would you do without us?"

"Action speaks louder than words," he said, and walked back out the front door.

What did I say?

Three days went by, and I still hadn't seen or heard from him. I didn't know who to call or where he might be. But more than anything, I couldn't understand what I'd said or done to cause him to leave. I was going crazy. I mean, really crazy. I couldn't eat, couldn't sleep, and I even stayed home from school for two days. I couldn't face those kids. I wanted to call my Daddy, but what could I say to him? Claudette, Marie, and Portia had already given me so many pep talks to help me get over the guilt that I didn't have the nerve to call them and tell 'em about this. So I kept it all tucked neatly inside me. I stared at the walls, at my plants, then back at the walls again. Maybe this was for the best, him leaving. It would mean I could get my life back to normal. But what was normal now? The phone rang and scared the shit out of me. I ran over and answered it on the first ring.

"Baby, I'm sorry. I just want you to know that," he said. He was breathing awfully hard. "But why couldn't you tell me?"

"Tell you what?" I asked.

"Come on, baby, I ain't that stupid. I know when your period is due. Who rubs your stomach and back every month when you get it, huh? But you didn't get it this month, and all of a sudden you got a yeast infection? Why couldn't you just tell me?"

"I was too scared."

"Scared of what, baby? Scared of what?"

"That you might want me to keep it."

"Oh, so you wouldn't want my baby?"

"Of course I would, Franklin, but look at us. Are we in any position to think about having a baby?"

"That ain't the point. We supposed to talk about this kinda shit, ain't we?"

"Yeah."

There was a long silence, but it sounded like somebody was speaking over a loudspeaker in the background. "Franklin, where are you?"

"I'm at Brooklyn Hospital. I had a accident on the job today and cut my chin open. I'm getting stitches, if these motherfuckers would hurry up. I could bleed to death standing here waiting for them. If I was white, I'd be fixed up and home by now. I love you, baby."

"Are you okay? I love you too, and I swear I didn't do this to hurt you. I didn't really want to do it, but it didn't feel like I had a choice. I'm sorry, Franklin. Don't move. Please. Stay right there. I'm on my way."

I couldn't find my purse fast enough. But I locked the front door in slow motion and walked down the dark street, putting one foot in front of the other as if I were walking inside someone else's dream. When I got to the emergency room, I saw Franklin sitting with his head back against the wall. He looked like he hadn't slept in ages. There was a growth of beard on his face. Blood was all over the front of his shirt, and he held a stained handkerchief up to his chin. I could smell the liquor before I even got close to him.

"Are you okay?" I asked, looking down at him.

"I'm all right. Don't worry about me. What about you—how you feeling?"

"I'm feeling okay. Let me see it, Franklin."

"It ain't nothin' but a little cut, really." He didn't move the handkerchief but sat up straight.

I walked over to the nurses' station.

"Can you tell me what's taking the doctors so long, miss? My husband's bleeding like crazy over there. This *is* supposed to be an emergency room, you know." I couldn't believe I had called Franklin my husband, but how else was I to refer to him?

"We were about to call him in now. Did you say you're his wife?"

"Sort of," I said.

"What's that supposed to mean? Either you are or you aren't."

"I'm not," I said.

"Then you'll have to wait out here."

"Take it easy, baby," he said. "Everything's gon' be okay." Then he disappeared through a white door. I sat there for what felt like hours, wondering what he was going to say to me when we got home. I dreaded the thought. I wished we could pretend this never happened and just get on with our lives. When he finally came out, I could see even around the bandage that his chin was swollen.

"Franklin, how many stitches did you have to get?"

"Just a few," he said.

"Come on," I said. "Let's go home."

"You mean I still got one?" he asked.

I just looked at him. I lifted his long arm up and pulled it around my neck, then I slid my arm around his waist. As we started walking down the street, I could feel his weight falling on my shoulders. I let him lean on me.

10

Zora was singing this Billie Holiday song when I turned the key and cracked open the door.

. . . Wish I'd forget you
But you're here to stay.
It seems I met you when my love went away.
Now every day I start by saying to you
Good mornin', heartache, what's new?

I can take a hint.

For five days I busted my nuts, tearing down a old hospital. Then I spent three days hauling rotted wood, bricks, and garbage where a park is supposed to be built. And I'm stinking like hell now, 'cause I just finished digging up a sewer, down in a cold-ass hole with rats—and I come in here and gotta hear her singing some shit like this? What I felt like doing was taking off these nasty clothes, holding 'em up under her nose, and telling her to "heartache" this. Just smell what love can make you do. Yeah, you can sing about disappointment, baby, but I'm the one standing knee-deep in it, and I'm sinking by the day. I wish I could tell you that, but all I got left is my pride.

I tried to pull off my boots, but the insides was packed with cold dirt and wasn't budging, so I took off my gloves to get a better grip. My fingertips was stinging like a motherfucker, and I could feel the ice from my mustache melting and dripping on my top lip. And she singing about heartache? Gimme a fuckin' break.

By the time I got all the shit off, Zora had stopped singing. When she came out to the living room, the first thing I noticed was that her hair was cornrowed. But I didn't say nothing. I just looked at her. It ain't that I don't like cornrows, but damn, she didn't even tell me she was gon' do it.

"You like it?" she asked, spinning around so I could see all of 'em.

"I didn't know you was getting your hair braided."

"It was supposed to be a surprise, Franklin."

"Well, I'm surprised."

"Don't you like it?"

"Yeah. It's all right."

"All right? I spend eighty dollars, sit for seven hours, and all you can say is 'all right'?"

When I heard her say eighty dollars, it felt like somebody had stuck me in the head with 1,000 volts of electricity. I don't make but fifty-six dollars a day, and she just spent eighty on some goddamn braids? "Didn't you go to school today?"

"It's Veterans Day," she said.

It didn't make sense for me to say nothing else. And she had the nerve to get those extensions put in, so her hair looked longer. Women. It musta been at least two hundred braids crisscrossing all over her head, and dangling at the end of every last one of 'em was some kind of bead. It *was* pretty, but I didn't feel like telling her, so I just went to take my shower. When I came out, she was singing that fuckin' song again.

"What you so sad about?"

"What makes you think I'm sad?"

" 'Cause you singing a sad song."

"It's not really a sad song, Franklin. It's just a blue one."

"What's for dinner?"

"Leftover lasagna."

The phone rang, and as usual, she answered it. I knew it was for her 'cause don't nobody call me, and whenever I do answer it, I feel like her damn answering service. It's always one of her silly girlfriends, and since I ain't got too much to say to none of 'em, I usually let the phone ring till she get it.

"Hi, girl. No. I'm getting ready to leave in a few minutes. For my voice class. Eight o'clock? Where? Portia, I can only stay for about an hour, really. I've gotta get up early. Because my students are rehearsing for their Christmas performance. Why do you think? Okay, okay! Let me go—I can't stand to be late. I'll see you later."

She hung up the phone and put her coat on.

"Franklin, I'll probably be a little late tonight."

"Why? Where you going?" I heard every word she just said, but I didn't want her to think I was listening. That damn Portia ain't nothing but a dickhound. Why Zora gotta hang out with her is what I wanna know.

"After class, Portia wants me to meet her at some new club. I'll be back about ten."

"You know, if your girlfriends had a man of their own, they wouldn't be trying so hard to drag you out in the streets all the time."

"Now, what's that supposed to mean?"

"Just what I said. You got a man, and all of 'em—except for Claudette—don't. Every time I look around, one of 'em is calling here, trying to get you to go somewhere."

"So? What's wrong with that? They're my friends, Franklin, and I don't see any of 'em that much anymore."

"If they had a man, you think they'd be calling so much? It's 'cause they lonely as hell—and everybody know misery loves company. I betcha they drill you. Wanna know if I'm finally making any money, or how good I'm fucking you, don't they?"

"Franklin!"

"Don't give me that Franklin shit. I know women. I'd bet you a hundred dollars right now that Portia probably know how big my dick is. Don't she?"

"No, she doesn't."

"Tell me something, baby. Are you as lonely as she is—is that it?"

"Franklin, please. I'm just meeting her for a drink."

"That's what you want me to believe."

"You know something—you're changing, Franklin. I'm starting to notice that every time I get ready to go somewhere without you, you start pouting. Why make such a big deal out of nothing? Now relax, and I'll see you later."

"You're the one who's changing. In the beginning, you didn't hardly wanna leave my damn sight. Now it seem like whenever you get a invitation to do *anything*—and *especially* without me—you jump at the fuckin' opportunity."

"Half the time you never want to go when I do ask, and besides, there's some things I like doing by myself or with my friends. You just don't like 'em—why don't you go ahead and say it?"

"It ain't that I don't like your girlfriends—I don't hardly know 'em—but one thing I do know is that when one woman ain't got no man, and their girlfriend do, they can't stand it. You just too blind to see what they trying to do."

"Which is what?"

"Pull you away from me."

"Your imagination is running too wild," she said, and gave me a empty kiss, like it was just a habit instead of a feeling. She didn't even say bye.

And fuck you too, I thought.

How high was I supposed to turn up the oven to heat up this shit? Who knows? I put it on 500. I watched *Wheel of Fortune* and won a trip to Hawaii, some patio furniture, and a new stereo. When I smelled the food burning, I jumped up to get it. By the time I scraped out all the burnt noodles, I had missed the damn bonus round. I wanted to try for that car, even though it was a Oldsmobile.

I needed a drink. But I didn't want one. I been drinking too damn much the past six months, and I know it. I don't want alcoholism to sneak up on my ass. I done put on five or ten pounds since the summer, and on top of that, Zora's cooking is hard to turn down. Two twenty-five is as big as I ever wanna get. Alcohol blows you up. I poured a glass of this weird juice she gets at the health food store, and to my surprise, the shit was good.

Wasn't nothing on TV worth watching, and since I ain't read a decent book in a while, I looked over the shelves until I spotted one called *Tragic Magic.* I took it down and opened it, read a few pages, and knew I was gon' like it. There was a beat to each sentence that I ain't never read before. And the author, who I knew was a brother—Wesley Brown—can write. I took the book in the bedroom and laid across the bed. Twenty more pages, and I was into it. This dude went to prison instead of going to Vietnam. Now, this was my kinda man. I swear, Zora got some good books around here. I wondered if she had read this one, or was it just collecting dust?

Hell, I was up to page 106 when I looked over at the clock. It was quarter to eleven. Where the hell was she? She said she'd be back by ten, didn't she? I hope ain't nothing happened to her. But then again, she's with that wild-ass Portia, so ain't no telling. I read a few more pages but couldn't hang. Around eleven-thirty, I guess I fell asleep.

When I felt her easing in the bed, I pretended like I was just turning over, but what I did was glance at the clock. It was almost one o'clock! "So you finally decided to come home, huh? What happened? You got lost, or you met somebody?"

"Franklin, please. The music was good, and I danced like a madwoman. I just wasn't paying any attention to the time."

"Well, next time pay attention to it."

"Look, I didn't know I was going to get the third degree when I got home—I mean really. Being a little jealous is one thing, but expecting me to punch in and out is another."

"Ain't nobody said nothing about punching in. And I ain't *jealous* of nobody."

"Well, what are you saying? That you're giving me a curfew?"

"Did you hear me say that? You the one who said you'd be back by ten, and it don't look like ten o'clock to me."

"Look, Franklin, I'm a big girl."

"Yeah, but I was worried as hell about you. I didn't know if something had happened to you or not."

"All right, already. Nothing happened, okay? Next time, if it looks like I'll be later than I said, I'll call. So let's drop it. I'm tired."

"I bet you are," I said, and rolled over as close to the wall as I could get. She stayed on her side of the bed and didn't put her arms around me the way she usually do. I betcha she met some-fuckin'-body.

*   *   *

Darlene called the day before Thanksgiving. She musta got Zora's number from directory assistance, 'cause I didn't give it to her.

"You going?" she asked.

"You?" I asked her back.

"I will if you go, but I'm not going out there by myself. No way."

"What the fuck," I said.

"You're bringing Zora, right?"

"Yeah."

"Then I'll see you tomorrow. Be prepared for some kind of drama, Franklin."

"Yeah, right. I'll check you later."

Zora was excited as all hell about going to my folks' house. We took the ferry over there, and I warned her, "Don't expect to have no fun, and just give me a wink or something when you can't stand it, and we can leave."

"You know, Franklin," she said, "you really should give your parents more credit. So you don't agree with every little thing about 'em—big deal. You're not the first person who wasn't thrilled about the way they were brought up. You're thirty-two years old—I mean really. Can't you find it in your heart to forgive 'em for whatever it is you think they did wrong?"

"Skip it," I said. She just don't understand what it feels like to know your own Moms never loved you, treated you like shit, and your Pops was so damn weak, he was too much of a chump to do anything about it.

"Franklin?"

"What?"

"Will you do me a big favor?"

"What's that?"

"Be nice?"

"You look beautiful," I said.

"Thank you, Franklin. Do I look nervous?"

"Naw, and you ain't got no reason to be."

I need to check myself. Today *is* a holiday, and I'ma try to make the most of it. Zora looked dynamite. Sexy as hell. Times like now is when I'd like to just take a bite outta her. Those braids looked pretty, dangling around her face. She was wearing this fuzzy orange sweater, cut to a V in the front, but not so low it'll give my Moms reason to whisper in Christine's ear. Her lipstick even matched it. And since I'm always complaining that I don't never see her legs—except in bed— she wore a skirt for me. I felt proud as hell bringing her home.

My other sister, Christine, and her nitwit husband, Jessie or Jesus—whatever it was—beat us there. Their station wagon was parked in the driveway behind my Pop's Oldsmobile. Zora was squeezing the hell outta my hand as I knocked on the door. Since nobody answered, I let myself in. Christine's boys was sitting on the sun porch, watching the end of the Macy's parade, and the TV was turned up so loud I don't think they heard me when I said hi. Then I saw Darlene sitting at the dining room table, and it was obvious that she been here all damn day, 'cause she already looked lit up.

Pops walked out of the pantry with a glass in his hand. He had on his uniform: plaid shirt and khakis. My Moms and Christine was back in the kitchen. The house smelled like Thanksgiving, and one thing I *can* give my Moms credit for is that she can cook her ass off.

"Happy Thanksgiving, everybody," I said, but didn't nobody respond.

"So you're the mysterious Zora I've heard so much about, huh?" Darlene asked.

"Hello," Zora said to her. "You must be Darlene."

"How'd you guess?" Then Darlene started laughing.

"I'm Felix, sugar. So nice to meet you—have a seat," Pops said, and held out his hand.

"Nice to meet you too, Mr. Swift." Zora shook his hand, giving me this I-thought-*your*-hands-were-big look.

"Call me Felix, baby. We're not that formal around here. Come on and make yourself comfortable."

Zora sat down at the table, and Moms and Christine came out the kitchen. Both of 'em was wearing aprons. My Moms was wiping her hands on hers, and looked at Zora like she couldn't see outta her glasses. She don't wear glasses.

"Well," she said, with a sigh.

"Hello, Mrs. Swift," Zora said. I could tell she was nervous.

"Call me Jerry if you call me anything," she said.

"I'm Christine, Zora. Nice to meet you." Christine gave her a Stepford Wife smile. If I had brought home a prostitute, she'd act the same damn way.

"You want a drink?" my Moms asked. Her eyebrows went up, 'cause she wanted to find out up front if Zora was a alky like she thinks everybody who takes a drink is.

"A glass of water or soda would be fine."

"Darlene, what you sitting there for—get this girl a drink." She turned back to Zora. "So I hear you some kinda singer and music teacher. That true?"

"I do teach, but I'm working with a voice coach, so I don't actually sing yet."

"Uhn-hun," she said.

"Well, I've heard a lot about you, Mrs. Swift. It's nice to finally meet you."

"I can just about imagine what Franklin done told you," she said, and started walking back to the kitchen. "And I said to call me Jerry."

Pops called me out to the sun porch, since the parade was over and the football game was starting. What's-his-name was sitting out there too now. He didn't say hi like normal people, he grunted.

"She's a fine-looking young woman," Pops said to me.

"Thanks. That she is."

By the middle of the first quarter, I was sweating like hell, 'cause this damn plastic on the couch was sticking to my back through my shirt. My Moms got this shit on everything—it's been like this as long as I can remember—but ain't nobody in here now to tear nothing up but her and Pops. Even the damn flowers and plants was plastic.

"Get yourself a drink, son."

"I will, in a minute."

From where I was sitting, I could see Christine and Moms in the kitchen, busy as little bees. Darlene was leaning on the table, and Zora was sitting across from her. They was talking, and I heard 'em both laugh. I looked over at what's-his-name, and the fool was out cold. He just as dooflus as Christine, I swear to God he is. They make the perfect couple. He works his ass off—two jobs, one in some factory on Long Island and as a mechanic or something. He'll do damn near anything to please my sister. Christine wanted a new house— Christine got a new house. Christine wanted a new car—she got a new car, a fuckin' station wagon, no less. But she always did get everything she wanted, even when she was living at home, so marrying this high-yellow chump just kept up the momentum. I turned my eyes back to the game, then toward the dining room again. My Moms and Christine was both sitting down now.

"You know," I heard Zora say, "you guys make a handsome family."

"Well, thank you, honey," I heard my Moms say. She always

start out on the right foot, but I didn't know how long this front she was putting on was gon' last. It would be a miracle if we could get through this day without some kinda bullshit going down.

"Watch him!" Pops yelled. "Run that ball, boy!"

I switched my attention back to the game. What's-his-name's mouth was hanging wide open, and he was snoring and drooling like a damn pig. "Pops, shake him, would you?"

"Aw, he's just tired. He came here straight from work. He ain't been to sleep yet."

I walked over and shook him. He snorted, then closed his mouth and was quiet. I went and poured myself some scotch and came back on the sun porch. The boys was outside in the front yard, playing with a rubber football.

"You and Franklin could make some pretty babies," Darlene was saying. I looked at Zora, but she didn't flinch.

"We've got too many other plans before we start thinking about having babies."

"Like what?" Darlene asked, leaning on both elbows.

"Well, he's going back to school in January."

"Franklin? In school? I gotta see that to believe it," my Moms said.

"He is," she said, defending me. "Franklin wants to start his own business one day, and I'm hoping to get a record contract, so it'll be some time before we start thinking about babies. Besides, marriage comes first."

"I would think so," Moms said.

"What about you, Darlene?"

Darlene looked down at the plastic tablecloth. "I don't want any kids."

"You don't?"

"Nope."

"Why not, if I'm not being too personal?"

My Moms cut her eyes at Darlene.

"Because I just never wanted any. I can't picture myself being a mother. I've got a million things I want to do in my life, but having babies is not one of them."

That was only part of the truth. Darlene can't have no kids. Somebody fucked her up in high school. The whole family found out about it by accident. She comes home, complaining that she's in pain, and it turns out that she couldn't stop bleeding. When my Moms found out the truth, all she said was, "Serve your dumb ass right."

"But, Ma, what would you'da done if I had come home pregnant?"

"I don't know. But you didn't have to go to no butcher and damn near get yourself killed."

They had to rush Darlene to the hospital. And a few days later, I heard that they took her insides out. My Moms still didn't show her no sympathy. "Now I guess you satisfied," is what she said when they got home.

"Hey, Zora," Pops yelled. "Come on out here and have a Thanksgiving drink with us."

"She don't drink liquor, Pops."

"Okay," I heard Zora say, and she appeared in the doorway.

Was I hearing things, or what? She must be bored as hell already—that's gotta be it. I ain't never seen her drink nothing stronger than a soda. I wanna see this shit myself.

"I'll have another one too," Darlene said.

"You look like you've had enough," I said.

"Nobody's talking to you, buffalo head, so be quiet."

Darlene got up and poured them both two tall ones. Zora brought hers out on the sun porch. I looked at her, but she wouldn't look at me. She took a sip. Her nose turned up and she squinched her eyes, but she didn't put it down. What was she trying to prove?

"You know, I'll be happy to drive you two home later on, or you can spend the night here—plenty of room," Pops said.

"We both gotta get up early, but you can give us a ride to the ferry," I said.

Just then he shouted at a tackle being made on the third down, and what's-his-name still didn't budge. The kids was running around the house, and after a while I looked at the fake fireplace. There was pictures of all four of Christine's boys, from the time they was babies till now. Where was my kids' pictures?

"Jerry, how's the food coming?" Pops yelled. It was almost halftime, and what's-his-name finally woke up.

"We putting the food on the table now, Felix."

Zora got up and went back into the dining room, carrying her now half-empty glass, and offered to help. My Moms told her she didn't need any. The game was getting heated, but I sat down at the dining room table because Christine and Zora was now in some kinda conversation that I felt like getting in on. Darlene was just sitting there like a zombie, not saying nothing, and you couldn't tell if she was even listening. Zora was running her mouth faster than I'd ever heard since I've known her.

"I just wish that black people wouldn't harp so much on the past and stop blaming white folks for everything." Zora gulped down another slug. "I mean, we've got more opportunities now than we've ever had before. Some of us are just too lackadaisical."

I knew Christine didn't know what the fuck that word meant. I did. And why I wasn't taking this shit personally, I don't know. Maybe 'cause there was some truth to it. And since I ain't never really heard Zora's real feelings about this kinda stuff, I decided to just kick back and listen. One thing

I did notice was that every time my Moms brought something to the table, she looked at Zora and rolled her eyes.

"I don't know *nobody* with a college degree," Christine said.

"Well," Zora said, and polished off the rest of her drink. "I just wish some of us had more courage to make our dreams come true. Too many of us are hung up on what we don't have, can't have, or won't ever have. We spend too much energy being down, when we could use that same energy—if not less of it—doing, or at least trying to do, some of the things we really want to do. You know what I mean?"

Christine just nodded her head, like she was trying to put all this together.

"We all need a master plan in order to get ahead."

My Moms, her lips curled down, plopped a bowl of mashed potatoes on the table. She shook her head as she walked back to the kitchen. Christine and Darlene tried to act like they didn't see her.

"What exactly do you mean by 'master plan'?" Darlene asked. I guess she musta reentered the real world.

"You know, sort of like a blueprint, a plan. Thinking and planning how you want to get something accomplished, then setting out and doing it. I think too many of us give up when we don't see instant results. But like Confucius said, 'Everything takes longer than you think.' "

"Who?" Christine asked.

My Moms was standing by the table with her hands on her hips and looked like she was pissed off about something. She let out a long sigh and then said, "Can we eat now?" The table was packed with big bowls and platters of food.

What Zora said made perfect sense, and I had a few questions of my own I felt like asking. But I didn't wanna come across like me and my woman don't talk about this kinda shit, so I kept my thoughts to myself.

Everybody sat down, and Pops said grace. Afterwards, he insisted on refilling everybody's drink. I looked at Zora, but it seemed like she didn't even know I was there. "I'll just have half of one this time, and that'll be it for me."

"So are you saying you think the situation of black people today ain't got nothing to do with racism?" I asked. I smiled when I said this shit, and Zora gave me one of those sexy grins. I wanted to swallow them orange lips whole.

"I didn't say that, Franklin. All I'm saying is that we can't keep blaming white folks for *everything*. I mean, a lot of us are definitely victims, but I also think the reason some of us fail in life goes back to our parents."

My Moms jabbed her fork against her plate, and it made a scraping noise. She just looked at Zora, then shoved some food in her mouth. She looked like she was getting ready to say something but was too damn mad to say it. The real deal was that Zora just struck a damn chord.

"Meaning what?" I asked.

"Meaning if they instilled more confidence in us, maybe we'd grow up feeling more secure about who we are and what we're capable of doing, that's all."

Just then my Moms threw her fork down on the table, jumped up, and said, "Why don't you just shut up!" She dug her fingers in her plate and threw some mashed potatoes in Zora's face.

Everybody—including me—lunged up, then stood around the table staring at my Moms like she was crazy. I swear I saw silver stars dancing in fronta my eyes, so I blinked hard a few times, then realized this shit was happening for real. Zora was backing her chair away from the table, looking like she was in shock. I didn't even realize I

was walking in my Moms' direction, with my fist balled up.
But Pops grabbed my arm.

"Son, please," he said. Then he turned to Moms. "Jerry!
You just had to do something ignorant, didn't you? You just
couldn't be satisfied until you spoiled everything, could you?
Who in the hell do you think you are, pulling some stupid-ass
shit like this? Damn." He threw his napkin on the table. Pops
was fuming—his nostrils was flared—and he was licking his lips
like he was getting ready to spit on her or something. I ain't
seen him this mad in years. He was looking down at her like
she was a dog that just bit him and he was trying to decide if
he should kick it.

I couldn't believe he had just talked to her like that, even
though this ain't the first time she done pulled some rank shit
like this.

"The girl talks too damn much. Just like the rest of them
sluts Franklin done brought home, trying to get my approval.
They all the same, except this one done been to college and
think she know everything. Well, not in my book. And I ain't
gotta sit in my own house listening to what she thinks is wrong
with black folks 'cause she think she so damn high-and-
mighty."

"Jerry, just shut up," Pops said. He was still standing there
like he was waiting to do something.

The boys was covering their mouths and laughing, and what's-
his-name just kept on eating like nothing had went down.

"Mama!" Christine yelled. "She didn't say nothing
wrong, and so what if she did. She's got a right to her own
opinion, and who the hell are you to be throwing food in
somebody's face 'cause you don't agree with 'em? This is
embarrassing as hell."

I couldn't believe this shit. Christine was talking back to
her too?

My Moms turned to her. "Be quiet, Christine. You the one who started this mess."

"All of you need to just shut up!" Darlene screamed out. She was crying, and she threw her empty glass against the wall, turned, and ran downstairs to the basement. I heard the door slam.

"Apologize to Zora, Jerry," Pops said. He was still standing over her, like he was building up to an explosion. I couldn't wait.

Zora was just sitting there, not moving.

"I don't *owe* her no apology. I said exactly what I felt like saying," Moms said, and picked up her fork and went back to eating her dinner.

"I said apologize, Jerry, and I mean it."

She rolled her eyes up at him and put a forkful of stuffing in her mouth and started chewing. When Pops grabbed her by the arm so that her fork fell out her hand, she gave him one of them are-you-crazy? looks. I wished he woulda kicked her ass in front of all of us. I woulda got so much satisfaction out of that, but I knew that was wishful thinking. Moms snatched her arm away from him, and he just backed away the way he always end up doing. But as far as I was concerned, he had accomplished a whole lot today.

"Forget it, Pops," I said. "She ain't gotta apologize for being a bitch. She can't help it." Then I looked her dead in the eye. "Mashed potatoes in my baby's face? You better be glad he's here—you know that, don't you?"

She picked her fork back up and kept on chewing, like she was the only person in the room. How can he stand her?

"I'm sorry, Zora," he said, and lit a cigarette, then drank the rest of his drink.

Zora was still in a daze, so I led her upstairs, and I could hear everybody jumping all over my Moms' case. Something is wrong with that woman, and why she ain't never been checked out before, I don't know. I ain't never seen nobody get so much pleasure outta causing other people pain, especially their own damn kids.

"I'm sorry, baby," I said to Zora, once I got her inside my old bedroom. "I told you it would be fucked up, didn't I?"

She flopped down on my twin bed. "I feel sick, Franklin."

"You need to go to the bathroom?"

"No. I just feel like I need to lay down for a little while." Then she fell back on the bed, and I figured I'd let her sleep it off.

"Franklin?"

"Yeah, baby?"

"What did I say to make your mother do something like that?"

"Nothing, baby. It ain't got nothing to do with you. I'm sorry about this, but you lay down for a little while, then we getting the fuck outta here."

On the way downstairs, all I kept thinking was how much longer I was gon' be able to stand being in this house. "Just ignore her," Pops said, and we went back out on the sun porch to watch another game, or the same game, I didn't know no more. My Moms was still eating. And now Darlene was sitting in a corner, by the china closet, looking like she was completely in orbit or something.

"Anybody want dessert?" my Moms asked, just like June on *Leave It to* fuckin' *Beaver*.

When didn't nobody say nothing, she sat her ass down at the table by herself and ate a big piece of sweet potato pie. Christine was washing up the dishes, the boys was in the basement and what's-his-name was down there with 'em.

A hour passed.

I decided to go see if Zora was feeling better, and when I

opened the bedroom door, I couldn't believe my fuckin' eyes. She had her skirt pulled up and was pissing in my old toy chest.

"What you doing?" I asked, yanking her by the arm, and piss started running down her legs and on the floor.

"Using the bathroom," she said. Her eyes seemed like they was looking at something—but it definitely wasn't me. If this little bit of alcohol fucks her up like this, she won't be doing no more drinking around me. I cleaned her up, sat her down on the edge of the bed, then led her downstairs and got our coats.

"We ready," I said to Pops. He downed the rest of his drink and went to warm up the car. Everybody except my Moms said goodbye. And on the way to the ferry, Zora fell back to sleep.

"How can you stand her, Pops—I mean, for real?"

"She wasn't always like this, you know."

"Coulda fooled me. It's the only way I ever remember her. Don't you ever hate her fuckin' guts?"

"When you've been with a person this long, you take them in stride. Your mother has her good and bad points, but she really don't mean any harm. I think she's just lonely since all of you've grown up and gone your separate ways. You children don't call or visit anymore, except for Christine. And whether you believe it or not, she does love all of you—in her own way. I think she just doesn't know how to show it."

"Well, she could stand a refresher course."

By the time we pulled into the station, Zora was waking up.

"She's a nice girl, son. Lord knows she can't hold her liquor," he said, laughing. "But I like her. And she's a smart one."

"Thanks, Pops. And don't bother asking when you'll see us out here again. If you wanna see us, come to our house, and don't bring *her*."

"Goodbye, Mr. Swift," Zora managed to say, and even waved. I shook his hand, then slammed the car door. By the time we got on the ferry, he was still sitting in the parking lot. I know he didn't wanna go home. I led Zora out on the deck, thinking the cold air might sober her all the way up.

"How you feeling?"

"Better. It's cold out here, Franklin. Can we sit inside?"

"No, you staying right out here. I'm going to get us some coffee. Some fresh air'll do you good. You sure you okay?"

"I'm freezing, and my head is killing me."

"Serves you right," I said, and went to get the coffee.

By the time we finally got home, Zora was back to normal.

"I'm sorry, Franklin, really I am."

"I told you. You didn't do nothing wrong."

"I had to have said something pretty insulting, or why would your mother have done what she did?"

"Because she's not playing with a full deck."

"Franklin, please."

"I'm serious. The woman's got problems, Zora, and I'm just sorry that you had to be the victim. I know one thing—now I know why you don't drink." I started laughing. "Pissing in my toy chest!"

"What?"

"I busted you pissing in my toy chest—thought you was in the bathroom and shit." She put her hand over her mouth and held her head down. "It's okay, baby. Don't even worry about it." I lit up a cigarette. "Tell me something. How come you don't drink?"

"Because it gives me migraines."

"So why'd you drink some today?"

" 'Cause I was nervous."

"Well, look. Let's just go to bed and try to forget this whole day, okay?"

"I feel like taking a shower first. That'll make me feel much better."

I took off my clothes and laid across the bed. Some kinda way, I wanted to make this up to her. This whole day was a mistake. My dick started getting hard, and my body felt like it needed her, and right now. I turned on the TV, but my mind wasn't on it. I fell back down on the bed. I wish she would hurry up. By now I had slid my hand around Tarzan and was stroking him, pretending it was Zora's hands keeping him warm. When she finally came in the bedroom, she opened the drawer with her pajamas in 'em.

"You won't be needing them."

She turned and looked at me. "Good," she said, closing the drawer. "Because right now, Franklin, I need you to hold me—plus some."

"Come on over to Daddy, then," I said. She pressed that luscious body down on top of mine, and I swear to God, I coulda came right then and there, but I didn't. I wanted to feel her for a while, just like this. But Zora knows how to get what she wants when she wants it. She placed my lips on her breasts and whispered, "Pretend they're peaches." Damn, they was juicy and sweet. Everything she gave me was juicy and sweet. So we apologized to each other half the night. Just like that.

I thought I heard a loud thud.

I turned over to put my arms around Zora, but she wasn't there. Then I heard shit falling, and I sat up and opened my eyes. She was on the damn floor, jerking and carrying on, like she couldn't help it. "What the fuck is going on?" I asked, but when she didn't answer me, I jumped up to see if maybe she was just having a bad dream.

But this wasn't no damn dream. I went to grab her but couldn't hold her still. She was stronger than me. What the fuck is going on? *"Zora! Zora!"* But now she was drooling, and her body was flipping back and forth like a fish that just been caught. I didn't wanna step on her, and I didn't want her to hurt herself, so I started pushing some of this shit out the way— these goddamn plants and the dresser. When I turned around, this time I mustered up every drop of strength I had and tried to pin her hands and arms to the floor. Then she just collapsed—stopped moving altogether—and I felt her body go limp. *"Zora?"* But she didn't make a sound. Her eyes was closed, and I shook her real hard, when it occurred to me that maybe that was a stupid thing to do. Then she started breathing real hard, and that's when I saw the blood on the floor. I let go of her arms, and she curled up like a snail. *"Zora baby?"* But she still didn't answer me. I searched her whole body, until I saw that the blood was coming from her fingers. My poor baby. I picked her up and put her in the bed and pulled the covers up over her. Then I ran to the bathroom and got a cold, wet washcloth. "Zora?" But she was still out cold. I put my hand on her heart to make sure she was still alive. Shit, I was scared. I didn't want nothing to happen to my baby. Nothing. When I felt her heart beating, I ain't never felt so relieved in my life. I wiped the sweat from her face and cleaned off her mouth. Then I threw the rag on the floor and sat there just looking at her, waiting for something to happen. Just when I had decided to call a ambulance, she moved. "Zora? Baby?" But her eyes still didn't open. I pulled her body up against mine anyway, and put my arms around her and squeezed that woman so tight I had to loosen my hold so she could get some air. I started rocking her and couldn't stop—I mean, I really couldn't stop. The next thing I knew, the sun was coming up, and I was still rocking. Finally, I felt her head, and her temperature felt normal. I laid her back down and put my arms around her. "It's okay, baby," I said, and kissed all two hundred of them braids on her head, and kept rocking. "Don't worry, baby," I whispered in her ear. "Whatever this is, Daddy's here."

11

I didn't want to wake up.

I was aching all over and afraid to move. I know I hit the floor last night, but that's all I remember. I wanted to move my hand to see if Franklin was still there, but I was afraid to do that too. What if he wasn't? I scared him to death, I just know it. If I hadn't drunk that disgusting scotch, this probably never would've happened. But since I hadn't been on any medication, I figured one little drink wouldn't hurt. Now I know that shit doesn't make a bit of difference. And just when I thought they were gone. It's been four whole years. Shit. And I blew it because of a few ounces of damn scotch? How stupid can I be?

I decided to take my chances. So I slid my left hand across the sheet, and sure enough, it was cold and empty. I should've told you a long time ago, Franklin. It never would've gotten to this point. If you knew how I felt right now—the way a light-skinned person who's been passing for years and has finally been found out might feel: exposed, and terrified of what I stand to lose. I can't even lie my way out of this.

"How you feeling this morning?" he asked.

My heart started thumping so hard it hurt. I looked up anyway, and Franklin was standing over me in front of the bed. His eyes were bloodshot, which meant he'd probably been up all night, worrying about me. I swear, I wanted to fly over his head and out of the room—or just disappear altogether. I didn't know what to say, really, but he was waiting for a response, and I had to give him one. "Fine," I mumbled.

He sat down on the edge of the bed, and I had to scoot over to make room. My fingers were sore and swollen, but I felt like sticking 'em in my mouth and chewing.

"How long this been going on, Zora?"

I bit my lip until it stung. "It started when I was twelve."

"So why didn't you just tell me?"

"Why do you think, Franklin?" Tears started forming in my eyes, and I couldn't stop 'em.

"Look, baby," he said, and started wiping my face dry with a corner of the sheet. "In the beginning, I told you about all my bullshit, and I asked if you was holding any cards under the table, and what did you say?"

"I said no." My voice cracked between the n and the o.

"Don't cry, baby. It ain't that bad."

"Yes, it is."

"Why couldn't you just tell me the truth?"

"*Because.* A lot of people act differently toward you once they know."

"We ain't talking about 'a lot of people' here."

"Okay. So I was afraid I might lose you if I told you so soon."

"You mean you didn't think I cared about you enough to be able to handle this?"

"At the time, I wasn't sure, Franklin." I looked up at him. His eyes were a warm black. "And I'm not sure how you're taking it now."

"Well, let me put it this way: Where am I?"

"Sitting on the bed next to me."

"Then that should tell you something, baby. You had me scared to death, and if I'da known what the deal was, I'da known exactly what to do. Besides," he said, and started rubbing his hands up and down my braids, "there's a whole lotta worse things that could be wrong with you."

"This is plenty," I said.

"All you got is epilepsy, right?"

"All?"

"Well, having it ain't the end of the world, is it?"

"No," I said, and hearing him say that meant a lot. Now my damn lip was throbbing. Why'd I have to be so stupid and bite it? And why haven't I had more faith in you, Franklin? Why have I always assumed that my love for you was much stronger than yours was for me?

"Tell me something, Zora. Did this have anything to do with you not having the baby?"

"It had something to do with it."

"Plus the fact that we ain't married, right?"

"That too."

"Well, I'll tell you something. By the time spring get here, I'ma be divorced—and that's a promise."

"You mean you still want to marry me?"

"Don't ask such a stupid question. One damn seizure ain't enough to scare me away, baby. It'll take a whole lot more than this to get rid of me."

I put my hand on his thigh and rubbed it. My fingers didn't feel all that bad now. One of the things I've loved about Franklin from the start is how safe he makes me feel. Protected. I'm not even talking about his job situation. I'm talking about my heart. When he puts his arms around me, if the wind was blowing a hundred miles an hour, I wouldn't know it. No man has ever made me feel like this. And no man has ever set me on fire when he touches me—not the way he can.

One thing I'm sure of—when God made him, He should've had him cloned. More women need to feel like this.

"Can I ask you something else?"

"Yeah."

"How come you ain't had no seizures since I been here?"

"Because they stopped four years ago."

"Why?"

"I don't know. But I also stopped taking my medication."

"Why?"

"Because it didn't stop the seizures the way neurologists claimed it was supposed to. A lot of people like me don't take their medication for that very reason. All most of it does is dope you up. Sometimes seizures just stop for no apparent reason. And some of us have learned how to manage 'em without the pills."

"So why you think it happened now?"

"I probably shouldn't have drunk that scotch. I don't know, really. But I didn't think a drink would hurt."

"Correction. You had two big ones."

"Anyway, what probably triggered it was coming down from it. It screws up my metabolism."

"You think you should start taking your medicine again?"

"No."

"Why not? Don't it help *some*?"

"I was on phenobarbital, Franklin. All it did was make me tired. I never had any energy, and it slurred my speech. You'd swear I was drunk if you saw me on that stuff."

"So why'd they put you on the shit if it didn't stop the seizures and did all this other shit?"

"Because they don't really know how to stop seizures; all they do is try to control 'em by prescribing pills. They've never found anything wrong with my brain. And if you want to know the truth, I've always resented taking those damn things. Every time I took one, it was a constant reminder of what I had. I didn't need any reminders."

"Well, you know better than me. So I take it you won't be doing no more drinking, then, huh?"

"No way."

"Good." He bent over and kissed me on my lips. "I love you," he said.

"I love you too—more than you realize."

"I'ma fool—tell me anything," he said, grinning.

Seeing his dimples again made me feel even better. I sat up and put my arms around his back and squeezed him as tight as I could. I buried my face against his chest and never wanted to move. He felt so good, so warm, so solid, that I kept inhaling the scent of his body until it filled up my heart.

"Baby, I can't breathe!" he yelled.

"Good," I said, and pulled him down on top of me.

"Let me move over," he said, and rolled off of me. He got under the covers with his clothes still on. "Now come here." I slid over to him until I fit inside the mold he always creates that prevents even air from coming between us. He wrapped his arms around me and held me until my body felt soft. I felt like a woman. I lay there, feeling his heartbeat against my spine. He was warmer than a good sleeping bag. He didn't try to undress me and didn't take his clothes off. He just kept caressing me until it not only felt like I didn't have clothes on, but if I could've opened my eyes—or moved, for that matter—I would've blown on every single one of those flames.

Franklin was gone when I woke up. I decided to take these damn braids out. With my fingers bandaged, it took nine hours to do it, but my head felt like it was breathing again. I looked wild. My hair had grown about an inch, and was crinkly and sticking straight out.

"Hey, wild child," he said, when he walked in. Then he just shook his head. "Couldn't stand it, huh?"

"She put 'em in entirely too tight. I was starting to see double."

"Well, next time, baby, before you run out and spend all that money, let me braid it."

"Rub it in, why don't you. Just rub it in."

"How you feeling?"

"Fine." I started walking across the room. I didn't know if he understood that once you have a seizure, you're fine afterwards. "Franklin?"

"Yeah?"

"Will you do me a favor?"

"What's that, baby?"

"Please don't start asking me how I'm feeling all the time, okay?"

"I just wanna make sure you okay, that's all."

"I know. But I'm not sick. And constantly being asked doesn't help, you know what I mean?"

"I get you."

"I'm going to the Laundromat."

"You sure you should be doing that?"

"Franklin?"

"I just wanna make sure you all right, baby. Them clothes can wait."

"Let me say this and be done with it. You saw how long a seizure lasts, right?"

"Yeah."

"Well, afterwards . . . I hate to use this term, but I'm back to normal. It's over. Gone. So are all your dirty clothes in the laundry bag?"

"Did you look under the bed, inside your piano, and in all the closets?"

"Franklin!"

He was still laughing when I left. My orange angora sweater was sticking out through the pile. I could see where the fuzz was stuck together from those mashed potatoes. If I had it in me to hate, his mother would be on the top of my list. I've just always assumed that people who hurt other people have usually been hurt so badly themselves that all they know how to do is hurt back. I think she's in pain. But I wasn't going to bring her or that incident up again. And like Franklin always says, "It's history now."

It started snowing. Everywhere you looked it was white. The air was crisp and clean, and Christmas decorations were being put up all over the city. Franklin was moving all of his stuff into the apartment. He didn't have that much, but what he did have was so masculine, and so ugly, I had a hard time trying to find places for him to put things. That worktable was one of them. He'd put it in the living room, right next to the dining room table, and pushed it up against the wall.

"Not there," I said. "Please, not there, Franklin."

"Then where?"

I looked around the room. When you first come in the door, you can't see around the corner, where there's a walk-in closet. So I moved a few plants and said, "Here."

"What about my tools and all my wood? You got a hiding place for that too?"

"Franklin, please."

We took my summer clothes from that closet and put 'em into boxes, which we sat against the wall in my music room. There was no way this would feel like my sanctuary now. Franklin put everything else in the front closet. Then there was his stereo—which not only was old but didn't even work. We had to put that in my music room too, since he didn't want to throw it away and there wasn't any room left in the closets. The fish tank was pretty and didn't bother me at all.

So now it was official. We lived together.

I can't lie: I'm getting tired. Tired of asking Franklin about jobs that were supposed to come through but didn't. So now I've decided to just wait for him to come home and tell me if he's working or not. I don't inquire about how long it'll last either, because they never seem to last as long as they're supposed to. For the past two weeks, he's been up and out the door before five-thirty in the morning. The doors to A Dream Deferred don't even open until seven, and it's only a ten-minute bus ride or a twenty-minute walk from here. Franklin walks. Some mornings, the moon is still in the sky when he leaves.

I've heard him searching through the sock bag until he found just the right ones. I've watched him pull out all his thermals until he found the color he wanted. Then he'd try on two or three different pairs of work pants. Sometimes he'd wear all three. And shirts. He vacillated. Should he wear the one with the split elbow or the one with the missing button? I watched him think. The decisions seemed so difficult for him to make.

To keep him company, I'd often stand in the bathroom doorway and watch him dry off after he showered, without saying a word. He shaved in slow motion. The razor grazed his face, and he took such care in trimming his mustache that while I stood there looking at him, naked from head to toe, I'd think, In so many ways he's perfect. He was so handsome, his long body so black and strong, that sometimes I had to touch him to make sure he was real.

I'd make him Wheatena, which he loved, and he'd usually eat two bowlfuls before he left. I'd fill his thermos with steaming black coffee, and his lunchbox with three thick sandwiches full of real meat. He never wanted anything sweet.

By the time I'd get home from school, he'd be sitting on the couch with his wool hat still on, his boots free of mud, sipping his umpteenth cup of coffee and reading the sports section. I could always tell how long he'd been there, because he reads the paper from back to front. Franklin says he likes to know the good news first.

Today, when I walked in, he was doing the same thing. I said hi and he just grunted. I sat down next to him on the couch and put my arms around him.

"I don't want no pity from you, baby. So please, spare me the sympathy, would you?"

I lifted my arm up and put it in my lap. I don't know when *is* a good time to touch him anymore. I'm used to hugging him whenever I feel like it, and now it's turned into a guessing game. I have to keep asking myself, Is it okay to kiss him now? All I've been getting is rejection. He doesn't kiss me when I get home the way he used to, and even in bed, he hugs the wall instead of me. I hate this not being able to talk to each other, but I wanted to cheer him up some kind of way. "Well, why don't you go to the gym? You always feel better after you work out," I said.

"For what? I ain't done nothing. So what's the point in working up a sweat?"

It's getting to the point now that I don't know what to say to him. I think he's dying a little bit every day, but I swear, I don't know what to do to make him feel better. I've tried to let him know that I've got faith in him, that I know we'll get through this—but he doesn't buy it.

"Franklin, I think I understand how humiliated you must feel," I've said.

"You couldn't possibly understand, baby," he said.

"Why not?"

"Because you ain't a black man."

I couldn't argue with that, but what has often irked me is that he thinks I have absolutely no concept of what he might be feeling. And on the other hand, he seems to think that this problem is his alone. But it's not. It's ours.

He puffed through five or six Newports, while I sat there pretending to be interested in the news. Eventually, he pulled out a pint of rum from under the couch. I got up and edged my way over to the sink to start dinner. A million words and thoughts were running through my mind, but I couldn't say 'em because I knew he didn't feel like hearing 'em. I was grateful when the phone rang.

"Hi, Daddy! Fine. Yep, I got it. Of course it helped. No. I don't need any more. I want to, Daddy, but we can't afford it right now. Really? But you've already done so much. He's right here. Just a minute."

I put my hand over the mouthpiece. "Franklin, Daddy wants to talk to you."

He just shrugged his shoulders.

"Come on, don't be such a drag. He just wants to say hello."

He got up from the couch and took the phone from me.

"Hello, Mr. Banks. I'm fine." I couldn't believe it, but the whole tone of his voice changed. It went up one octave. "Just going through a rough period here. Yes, sir. Construction work slows down in the winter if you're not in the union. No, not yet. The Mafia runs it. Yeah, I'm serious. I'm trying to treat her the best I can, considering." He actually started laughing. "Yes, I do. Yes, I do. I try. As soon as I get on my feet. Christmas? That's two weeks from now, isn't it?" "Isn't it?" he said, not "Ain't it?" "Yes, sir. I'd love to. I can't let you do that. Pride, sir, pride." He laughed again! "Then can we consider it a loan? Yes, I do. I'm looking forward to meeting you. Very nice talking to you too, sir."

He handed me the phone. I was grinning. He was grinning. My Daddy always did know how to work magic. "Okay, Daddy. Yep. Tell Marguerite I said hello. We'll see you in a couple of weeks. Love you too."

I hung up, then turned to look at Franklin. "What did he say to you?"

"He asked me if I loved you, and I told him yes. He asked me if I wanted to marry you, and I told him yes. Then he asked if I was giving it to you every night—"

"Franklin, he did not!"

"I ain't kidding, Zora. That's what he asked me!" He started laughing so hard he kicked over his glass of rum. I threw him a dish towel and he cleaned it up, then he went to put the bottle under the sink.

"So what did you tell him?"

"I told him I was trying like hell! Not really. Your Pops thought the shit was funny. Now I see where you get your spunk, baby. But he talked me into something I ain't so sure about."

"What?"

"Sending us round-trip airplane tickets to come for Christmas. I told him it would be a loan. You know I ain't about charity, baby, but I couldn't tell him that."

"Do you want to go home with me for Christmas?"

"Why not? As long as don't nobody throw mashed potatoes in my face. Seriously, he sounded like a decent man, and besides, he asked me if I played poker."

"Do you?"

"Yeah, I play poker."

"How about teaching me?"

"There's only one kind I know how to play."

"What kind is that?"

"Strip. Get the cards."

I didn't like this game, but we ended up taking our clothes off anyway. And after a week of nothing, tonight we discovered something all over again: that we still need each other. Now I know how Liz Taylor must've felt when she met Richard.

Franklin got a job painting walls in a brand-new apartment complex. We were both grateful it was inside, because I can't stand to see him when he comes home cold. He often looks broken, and I wonder where he gets the strength to get up in the morning. But he keeps doing it. This job was supposed to last through January—maybe even longer—and so far it's been a whole week. He beat me home today, and the first thing he did when I walked in was kiss me and hand me his paycheck.

"You don't have to give me this," I said. It had been so long since he had had his own money, I didn't want to take it.

"I won't feel right unless I do. You give me twenty dollars, that's all I need. Enough for cigarettes and maybe a half pint on Friday."

"Franklin, this is the first check you've had in ages. Keep it."

"Look. You been paying for everything for so damn long, lending me—giving me—money, and this little chump change wouldn't even put a dent in what you done spent. You gotta be about tired of this shit by now, but I give you all the credit in the world, 'cause you ain't never complained once. Besides, things is looking up. Vinney called and told me they was starting another brownstone, and wants me to be on his crew. He said it should last through the summer."

Here we go again with the promises, but I wasn't about to say anything about it. "What about your kids?"

"What you mean, what about the kids?"

"Christmas. I know you plan on giving those kids something."

"Baby, I been so broke I forgot all about that."

"Well, I haven't. So that's what we'll do with this money."

He looked at me and smiled. "You're a good person, Zora, you know that? I swear, I'm one lucky man."

"Well, since we're both in a good mood, how about we do two things?" I asked.

"What's that?"

"You feel like laughing tonight?"

"You know I love to laugh, baby. Every morning when I wake up and look at you . . ."

"Fuck you, Franklin!"

"Is that a promise?"

"Anyway, my girlfriend Marie—you remember Marie, don't you?"

"I don't remember what she looks like, but she's the comedienne, right?"

"Yep, and she's opening at the Improv tonight. I told her I'd come to see her. Will you come with me?" I crossed my fingers. Please say yes, for once. We need to get out of this house. We need to do something. We haven't been anywhere in so long, I've almost forgotten what it feels like.

"Is she really funny?"

"Last time I saw her she was."

"Okay. What's the other thing?"

"Let's go get our Christmas tree."

"You mean to tell me you want a Christmas tree, Zora?"

"Why not? I get one every year. What's Christmas without a Christmas tree?"

"But we won't even be here."

"There's before and after, you know."

"You mean I fell in love with a big baby?"

"You've got that right, and I want to sit on your lap right now, Santa."

He slapped his thighs, and I went over and sat down between them. "So have you been a good little girl all year?"

"Yes, Santa."

"Well, then, tell Santa what you want him to bring you for Christmas, sweetheart."

"I'm sitting on it," I said.

Franklin looked so handsome. He was wearing my favorite red and black sweater that shows how broad his shoulders are and even those muscles. And blue jeans that made me want to grab his ass. We got a good table, and this felt so good, being out with him and both of us were in such a great mood. We laughed all the way here. He ordered a drink and asked me if I was hungry. I wasn't. I got a club soda and looked around at all the people. The place was packed. Franklin's legs were between mine under the table and his hand was on top of mine. This was just great. He even agreed, while we were sitting there, that we were going to get out more often. That's when this guy came out on stage and we turned our attention toward him.

"Ladies and gentlemen. Boys and girls. Boys and boys. Girls and girls. Whatever. Tonight, the Improv is proud and pleased and blah-blah-blah to bring you, straight from the streets of our very own lower Manhattan, the funniest lady to hit this stage since my sister fell off of it last week: Miss Marie Swan. Give her a big hand. No—two hands. No—three hands."

The crowd was laughing and clapping as Marie walked out on stage. I didn't even recognize her. Marie—who is fairly attractive, six feet tall, and as thin as I'd like to be, and has specks of freckles and natural red hair—was disguised. Her hair was white. Pure white. She was dressed up like an old lady in a housedress, turned-over shoes, and support hose. She even had a cane.

"Howdy, folks," she said.

The audience said howdy back. Then she sat down in this old armchair and tried to cross her legs but pretended like she couldn't.

"This always have been a problem," she said. "Jake used to love it when I couldn't cross 'em. That's probably one of the reasons he stayed with me for so long, bless his heart. He's dead and long gone now. And only the Lord knows how grateful I am. Y'all wanna know why I've been trying to cross my legs all these years?" The audience yelled out yes. " 'Cause when that poor man pried 'em open, he went on a treasure hunt, but he always went crazy once he found the treasure. Of course he didn't have but three or four inches to work with, but the way Jake went to work, you'd swear he had a ten-inch jackhammer at his disposal. Poor thing. Poor me, really. I always felt like I'd been galloping on wild horses by the time he finished. Hell, to get through it all those years, I just pretended he was Clark Gable. I remember one night I got carried away and even yelled out, 'Clark, Clark, Clark!' And Jake said, 'Who?' And I had to clean it up real fast, so I yelled out, 'I meant, Jake, Jake, Jake!' I'll tell ya, be thankful times have changed, 'cause if I'da knowed how little he had to work with, and how hard he tried to make up for it, I never woulda married him. Now I can't even give this shit away. Tell me, which one of you young fellas out there want some seventy-year-old pussy? I know I wouldn't, and I don't want no seventy-year-old pecker neither. That's why God gave us the gift to dream, and let me tell you, Clark ain't aged a bit."

The audience laughed. Even Franklin was laughing. Marie

went from one funny routine to another, and we laughed so hard my stomach was hurting. Franklin never finished his first drink.

"So?" I asked Franklin, afterwards.

"She *was* funny," he said. "She was definitely funny."

When Marie saw us sitting at the table, she came over and joined us. "I didn't think you'd really come, girl," she said. But she was looking at Franklin. "You sure are one helluva hunk of a good-looking man. How'd you like to come home with me tonight, sugar? I can give you something Zora ain't never even thought of. What you say?" She leaned over the table, then licked her lips. She was trying hard not to laugh. Her breasts were jutting out over the edge of her leotard, and Franklin was trying not to stare, but he was staring.

He laughed. Even looked like he was blushing—as black as he is. We talked for a while, and Marie said she'd stop by and have a New Year's drink with us. On the way home, Franklin said, "I *like* her."

And for the first time since we'd been together, I was actually jealous. Now, ain't *that* some shit?

We were at the airport, about to board, and I was thoroughly pissed off. Franklin had been drinking all day. I didn't want him to be drunk or smelling like liquor when he met Daddy. I wasn't so much worried about Marguerite.

"Could you ease up some?" I asked.

"I'm scared, baby."

"Scared of what? My Daddy won't bite you."

"Of flying."

"You're what? Franklin, be serious."

"I am serious. I only been on a airplane once in my life, and they scare the shit outta me."

"Well, what'd you do when you went to Puerto Rico?"

"I ain't never been to no Puerto Rico. I was just trying to impress you. When I went in the service I had to get on one, but I was so fucked up I don't even remember it."

"I swear," was all I said. In a way, this was funny. By the time the plane took off, Franklin had passed out. His head had dropped to my shoulder, and he had put his arms around me. Eventually, I had to go to the bathroom, but I couldn't wake him up. "Franklin," I said, shaking him as hard as I could. "Wake up!" But he was dead weight, and I couldn't move. By the time we landed, my bladder was about to break. He had drooled all over my shoulder, and when he finally sat up, his eyes were as red as his sweatshirt, and his breath was reeking. "Get yourself together," I said, and handed him some Tic Tacs.

"We here already?"

"No, we're there," I said, and worked my way back to the bathroom.

Daddy and Marguerite were waiting for us at the gate. Daddy looked older. Maybe because he was. His hair was entirely gray, but there was hardly a wrinkle on his face. Marguerite's hair was blacker now. She looked good. Still hefty, and I never realized just how much taller she was than Daddy. At least four inches.

Daddy grabbed me, pushed me away to look at me, then kissed me on the cheek. "Just look at you!" he said.

Marguerite gave me a peck too. "Chile, you need to start eating again 'fore you disappear," she said.

"Hello, son," Daddy said to Franklin, and shook his hand. "Damn, you got some big hands, son. Well, look at this man, Margie. What are you, seven or eight feet?"

Franklin laughed. "Six four," he said. "Nice to meet you, Mr. and Mrs. Banks."

"You can call me Daddy or Harvey, whatever you feel the

most comfortable saying. This is Marguerite, but you can call her Margie."

"Well, one thing I can say, Zora," Marguerite said. "You sho know how to pick 'em."

"I picked her," Franklin said, and smiled again. He almost looked sober.

The house looked bigger to me this time. It was an old wood-framed house, but well kept up. Years ago, Daddy had had it painted white, with blue trim, at Marguerite's insistence. The front yard was long and wide, and in the summer had the prettiest, greenest grass I've ever seen. Now it was white.

Uncle Jake was sitting in the living room, but when we walked in, he jumped up.

"Uncle Jake!" I screamed. "What are you doing here?" He was my favorite uncle, Daddy's only brother. He was smoking his usual cigar, just like when he used to sit me on the couch and tell me all about the blues.

"Just taking it easy, baby. You looking like a thoroughbred woman now. Ain't that something? Skinny as a bean pole, but he must be eating what's left on your plate. Who is this? One of the New York Giants?" He gave out a howl, and his bowlegs swayed.

"Uncle Jake, this is Franklin."

"How do, son. Cigar?"

"Fine, sir. Sure, why not?" Franklin took the cigar, and I walked through the house, then up to my old bedroom. Marguerite still hadn't changed the eyelet bedspread and matching curtains. The walls were the same pale yellow, and my bed was stuffed with animals. The first one that caught my eye was that elephant Bookie had won for me at the state fair when I was a teenager. God, does time fly. And on my dresser were the awards I'd won in talent shows. There wasn't a speck of dust on anything. I went back downstairs, and Daddy was bringing the luggage in. Marguerite was in the kitchen. Franklin was sitting on the couch next to Uncle Jake.

"You like the blues, don't you, son?"

"Yes, I do, sir."

"Who in particular?"

"Muddy Waters for one. B.B. King, Bobby 'Blue' Bland . . . most of 'em, really."

"Good to hear it. Listen to this one. Tell me if you know who this is."

Uncle Jake put on Slim Greer and leaned back on the sofa. Daddy walked in.

"What you drinking, son?"

"Nothing, Pops. I mean Daddy."

"You can call me Pops—don't make me no never mind. So you ain't drinking nothin'? Hell, it's Christmas."

"I had a little too much on the way here."

"Your head bad?"

"That's putting it mildly. A cup of hot coffee would sure be nice."

"Margie!" he yelled. "Put on a pot of coffee, honey!"

"You ever hearda Blind Lemon Jefferson or Mississippi John Hurt?" Uncle Jake asked.

"Afraid not."

"What about Sun House or Albert King?"

"No, sir."

"Well, boy, I'ma give you a education while you here. Colored folks should know all about the blues, you know."

Franklin laughed. I plugged in the fake Christmas tree, and boy, it felt good being home.

"Zora?" Marguerite yelled from the kitchen, so I went in. She must've cooked earlier, because all kinds of pots and pans and roasters were on the stove.

"So how've you been, Marguerite?"

"So-so. You hungry?"

"A little. What've you got here?"

"Some collard greens, ham, corn bread, macaroni and cheese, candied yams, and some potato salad in the refrigerator. It's your Daddy I'm worried about. His arthritis acting up something terrible. Always in pain, but he won't admit it. You need to tell him something about hisself, honey."

"What can I say?"

"He's *your* Daddy. Think of something."

"Has he been to the doctor?"

"Yeah, but the wrong one. All he do is give him these pain pills that don't do nothin' but make him sleepy."

"I'll talk to him. You mind if I have a slice of ham?"

"That's what it's here for, chile. So. How's the singing coming? Anything exciting?"

"Well, not really. My voice classes are coming along, and by April, my coach is helping me get a demo tape together."

"What's a demo tape?"

"It's a tape of me singing a few popular songs and some of my own that I'd send to record producers, and if they like what they hear, I might be able to get a record contract."

"Really? Well, it sounds like something *is* happening. Just take it like you find it, baby."

"You sound like Daddy," I said.

"I'm his better half, chile."

"Where's Aunt Lucille?"

"Home. She done caught Jake with another one of them floozies at some motel, and you know when she put him out, where do he come?"

"He's still doing that?"

"He's here, ain't he?" She took a tray with the coffee on it into the living room. We sat there for over an hour, listening to Uncle Jake talk about the blues. Finally, we ate dinner. By eleven o'clock, Franklin and I were both exhausted and went upstairs to sleep. Marguerite followed us.

"Your room is down here, Franklin."

Marguerite pushed open the extra-bedroom door, and Franklin looked back at me and winked. "Good night, baby," he said. Then he turned to Marguerite. "Is it all right if I give her a good night kiss?"

"It ain't my business. If y'all was married, I'd put you in the same room. Maybe next time when you come, it'll be like that. What you think?"

"We're working on it," he said. Marguerite said good night and went into her and Daddy's room and closed the door. Daddy came upstairs and watched Franklin press his lips against mine. Then Franklin turned and started walking toward his room. He didn't see Daddy.

"Where you going, son?"

"To sleep, Pops."

"Why ain't you sleeping in Zora's room—with her?"

"Miss Margie told me to sleep in here."

"I swear, she's behind the times, ain't she? Where you sleep when you at home, son?"

"With Zora, Pops."

"Then that's who you gon' sleep with here. Hell, this is the eighties, and both of y'all damn near middle age," he said, slapping his thigh. That's his favorite thing to do, slap his thigh. "I don't know where Margie's brain is sometimes. Now, y'all go on, and sleep tight."

Franklin hunched up his shoulders and walked toward my room with me. "Good night, Pops."

"Looks like it might be one now, huh?" Daddy winked at Franklin, then closed his door.

Franklin wanted to do it, but I couldn't. My Daddy was only

two doors away, and we—or I should say I—have a tendency to get loud. Franklin does more shivering and shaking than anything. I would've been embarrassed as all hell or felt so restrained that I probably wouldn't have enjoyed it. So instead I considered another alternative—one that always makes him make promises he could never keep.

When I woke up, Franklin was gone. I went downstairs and saw him standing on a ladder on the front porch.

"What are you doing?" I asked. It was colder in Toledo than it was in New York, but he didn't have anything on but a T-shirt and his jeans.

"Fixing this light."

"Why?"

" 'Cause it's broken, that's why."

"Did Daddy put you up to this?"

"Naw. It just look like he ain't able to do some of the things that need to be done around here, so I'ma make myself useful. When I'm through doing this, I'ma build him some shelves in the garage, and that toolshed in the back is gon' look like brand-new when I finish with it. I feel good, baby," he said.

I just smiled.

For the next few days, Franklin fixed everything around the house he could find. He and Daddy laughed, drank, and played poker with Marguerite and Uncle Jake, while I watched. Aunt Lucille finally came over when she heard I was here, and I guess she felt sorry for Uncle Jake, because she let him go home with her. I even went to church, but Franklin hadn't brought the one suit he owned, so he stayed home. Daddy insisted on staying home to keep him company. They were both drunk when we got back, and laughing like two friends reminiscing about old times.

On Christmas morning, we exchanged gifts, and there were two envelopes under the tree, for me and Franklin. Daddy had given us each five hundred dollars. Daddy definitely liked Franklin.

"You didn't have to do this," I said.

"I feel the same way, Pops. You've been too generous already," Franklin said.

Daddy just took a puff off his brand-new pipe I'd bought him, and blew out a big cloud of smoke. At one minute after midnight last night, he had convinced me that it was officially Christmas and opened his boxes. Marguerite, who was a copycat, had opened hers too. She was wearing her new kimono now.

"Looka here, son," Daddy said. "It's my money, and if I wanna spend it on you and my baby, that's what I do. Understand?"

Franklin grinned at Daddy, and Daddy smiled back—that gold tooth just shining.

"What'd you get Zora for Christmas, Franklin?" Marguerite asked.

"That's none of your business, Margie," Daddy said.

"She'll get it when we get home," Franklin answered.

Daddy slapped his thigh and blew out more smoke.

Marguerite didn't go to the airport with us, because she was waiting for her new washer and dryer to be delivered from Sears. Once we got inside the terminal, Daddy looked Franklin in the eye. "You take care of my daughter, son. I mean that. You've got the best there is, and don't ever forget it."

"I won't, Pops. Believe me, I won't."

"And you remember what we talked about, you hear?"

"I will."

"And you keep singing, baby. Something gon' happen.

Good things always come to people who work at it. You take care of him," he said, pointing at Franklin. "He's a good man, and I want some grandbabies what look just like him."

"I will, Daddy. And what did you promise me?"

"That I'll go to the doctor. Margie got the biggest mouth in Toledo, don't she? Happy New Year, you two." Daddy kissed me on the forehead and shook Franklin's hand hard.

We said the same to him and boarded the plane. By the time we were airborne, it occurred to me that Franklin hadn't had a drop to drink before we left, hadn't stopped at the bar like he'd done on the way here, and when the hostess came by, he didn't even order one.

"So did you have a decent time?" I asked.

"It was the best Christmas I've had in a long time," he said. "In a long, long time. Thank you, baby."

"Well, I'm glad to hear it. And thank you for coming with me, Franklin."

"Your Pops is all right. A wise man," he said, then leaned back in his seat and looked out at the clouds.

"What makes you say that?"

"A lotta things. We had a real good man-to-man talk, something I been hoping to do with my own Pops, but this was the next-best thing."

I pushed my seat back so that it was even with his.

"What'd he say?"

"He just told me to go ahead and be a man. That just because I get laid off from time to time, that that ain't no reason to feel like less than one. I needed somebody to tell me that, baby—another man. He told me about how hard it was for him when he was just getting started, and he told me to believe in myself first and don't never give up. Don't even think about it, no matter how bad things get. I like your Pops, Zora, and wish like hell mine could be more like him. You tired?"

"Sort of."

"Then put your head here, baby," he said, tapping his shoulder. He lifted his arm up so it went behind my neck, and his hand landed on my arm. He stroked it, the way you would a crying baby.

"Aren't you scared, Franklin?"

"Of what?"

"Nothing," I said, and pressed my head against his shoulder.

12

"So what you wanna do?" I asked.

"Anything but stay home, Franklin."

"Well, all the best shows and concerts is already sold out, and I ain't spending no seventy-five dollars to go nowhere and dance—I'm telling you that right now."

"Why not? We can afford to splurge at least one day out of the year. Where's the newspaper?"

"Call some of your girlfriends. One of 'em should know where a decent party is. Try Portia—she's like Rona Barrett when it comes to what's happening, ain't she?"

"You don't like Portia, do you?"

"Did I say I didn't like her?"

"No, but you always make such sarcastic remarks about her."

"Well, I didn't mean to sound sarcastic. Call her."

"I will, in a minute. Let me look through the paper first."

"Ain't Marie supposed to be stopping by on New Year's?"

"That's what she said, but you never can tell about Marie. She might have forgotten."

"Call her up to remind her."

"Why? Do you want to see her that bad?"

"I just thought she was an all right lady, and I dug her

style. Besides, she's funny as hell, and she *is* a friend of yours, ain't she?"

"Don't think I didn't see the way you were staring at her boobs that night."

My face felt hot. Shit, who wouldn't stare at 'em when they looking you dead in the face? I ain't used to seeing Zora act jealous. I love it. Every once in a while, when we're walking down the street and she notice my eyes on some young girl's ass, she'll say, "Like what you see?" "What's that?" I ask, and the whole time I'm trying to keep the grin off my face. "If you want it, why don't you go on over there and try to get it?" I play dumb. "I don't know what you talking about, baby." This is when she usually hiss and start walking faster than me. Hell, I ain't thinking about no young girls. Any man in his right mind'll look at a eighteen-year-old ass when it's squeezed into something tight. It's called lust, and why women always think just 'cause we looking means we want it, I don't know. The woman I want is walking on my side. All this shit is a test. If she loves you, she'll get pissed off, which almost always guarantee you gon' get some super-deluxe loving that night— 'cause she'll fuck you like she got something to prove. But if she don't act concerned one way or another, a man gets to wondering what the real deal is.

"I wasn't staring at Marie's breasts, Zora. They was begging everybody in the whole damn place to look!" I started laughing, and to my surprise, she thought the shit was funny too.

She was leaning over the kitchen counter, flipping through the paper, and I walked up behind her and pushed Tarzan against that sweet round ass of hers. "Franklin, get away from me. I'm not kidding."

"I just wanna feel you, baby. But if you want me to wait till Marie gets over here, fine with me."

She turned around and slapped me. Not hard, but hard enough.

"Okay! I'm sorry, I'm sorry. How about a game of Scrabble when you finish?"

"Then get the board ready. Look, here's something at the Savoy, and it's only fifty dollars."

"Apiece?"

"Yeah. And the Savoy is *really* nice, Franklin. Let's go there."

"Zora, fifty fuckin' dollars? Gimme a break. Call Claudette, too, and anybody else you can think of. At least *try* to find out if something free is happening."

She picked up the phone and dialed. I guess it was Claudette who she called first, 'cause I heard her congratulate her on her new baby. How could anybody name a kid George in this day and age is what I wanna know. Zora told her all about her voice classes and that demo tape she supposed to start working on, and she just kept running her mouth, while I'm sitting there listening if she was really trying to find out if something was happening on New Year's or not. Finally, I cleared my throat a few times. "Girl, I've gotta go, but I'll be out to see you and the baby within the next few weeks. Promise. *Or* you can bring him and Chanelle over here. I bet she's big now. She is! Well, kiss little George for me, and Happy New Year's to you and Allen both, honey."

"You forgot to mention the First Amendment, you know. Now, after all that, I betcha ain't no happenings, right?"

"Be quiet, Franklin," she said, and started dialing again.

"Marie, this is Zora."

She musta got one of them damn machines, "Get your ass over here for your New Year's drink and call to let me know if anything free and exciting is going on tomorrow night. Bye."

"Step on it, would you, baby? I'm ready to kick some ass over here."

"Take it easy, Franklin. You wanted me to find out what's going on, and that's what I'm trying to do. You'll be crying in a few minutes anyway, so go get some tissue."

She stealing my lines. I watched her dial again, and I knew she was calling Portia, who, to my surprise, was at home. From what I overheard, Portia was going to the Savoy. "What do you mean, house parties are out of style, girl? That's true. Okay, point made. You do? Great. Then we'll definitely see you there. What's his name? Well, if you guys get there before us, try to get a good table. Don't worry, we'll be there. Bye."

"Why'd you tell her that lie?"

"What lie?"

"That we'd see her there."

"Look, Portia's got two extra tickets. Another couple she knows had to cancel, so at least we can get in. And besides, it's a swank place, and we don't have anything else to do, and at this point I don't care how much it costs. All I know is that I don't want to be sitting in this apartment on New Year's Eve playing Scrabble. Roll 'em."

"I ain't in the mood now. I feel like doing some wood-working."

"Fine. And just what am I supposed to do?"

"Go sing something." I got up and went over to my little corner and sat down in front of my worktable. I heard her stomping toward the back, and then her door slammed shut.

I bought myself a bottle. It was New Year's Eve, so I said fuck it. I had stayed up all night sanding and shaving a piece of wood and didn't even know what I was making. I left sawdust everywhere, and didn't crash until late this morning—after I had polished off the whole pint. When I finally woke up, I went to make a pot of coffee and watched Zora dust, polish, wipe, and swish that broom across the floor until I was bored shitless. She still wasn't speaking to me and spent most of the afternoon cleaning the place inside out. I went and laid back across the bed and started watching a football game. By the time she made it back here, she finally said something to me. "Get up."

"Look," I said. "I think I'm going down to the bar. I'll be back later on." I'll be damned if I was gon' sit in here the rest of the night getting the silent treatment. Women. They worse than kids when they can't get their way.

"Take your time," she said.

That's exactly what I planned on doing. First, I took a shower, shaved extra close, and then got *clean*. I put on the only suit I owned, her favorite cologne, and my best pair of Stacy-Adams. Zora rolled her eyes at me when she saw me. She ain't never seen me in no suit before. It wasn't that I was pissed off. I just didn't like her attitude: Because Zora wanna spend fifty dollars to go dancing, Zora thinks we should spend fifty dollars to go dancing.

New Year's ain't that big a fuckin' deal to me, really. All the crazy motherfuckers in New York City is out on the streets; you can't never get a cab, and if you go to a public place, you don't know no-fuckin'-body, so you stand around looking stupid or pretend like you having the time of your life. You dance a few sides, drink up forty or fifty dollars' worth of liquor—'cause they always up the price of 'em for the occasion— and then you go home, either too tired or too fucked up to even think about fucking.

Zora was in the bathroom on her knees, scrubbing out the tub, when I left. I didn't bother to say bye.

I thought I heard something hit the other side of the door

after I closed it, but I wasn't sure. I had a pocketful of money, I was looking good, smelling good, and feeling like a million dollars. So I got a evil-ass woman at home—I ain't letting her spoil my mood.

I stopped in Just One Look, but everybody musta been home getting their act together for tonight, 'cause wasn't too much going down. The music was live, even though it was only six-thirty. I sat down at the bar and ordered a double Jack Daniel's. Then I felt a hand on my shoulder, then some lips on my right cheek. They definitely wasn't Zora's, 'cause I'd know them lips anywhere. These belonged to Terri.

"Long time no see," I said.

"You're telling me, Frankie. How've you been? *You* sure looking good."

"You ain't looking too bad yourself, sweetheart. What you doing in here?"

"Looking for you."

"Yeah, right. What you drinking?"

"Rum and Coke."

I flagged the bartender and ordered her a drink. It felt good being able to buy a lady a drink for a change. Terri looked as good as always. Not only is she pretty and look like a black Chinese, but she got these Donna Summer lips. While I watched 'em slip over the rim of the glass, I couldn't help but thinking about how good they used to suck Tarzan. She also got the longest legs I ever had wrap around me. Damn. My dick started getting hard just thinking about it. But she was still wearing that damn wig.

"So tell me, Frankie. Where'd you run off to? I mean, damn, you just upped and disappeared off the face of the earth. What's her name?"

"Zora."

"Well, where is she?"

"At home."

"What's she doing at home on New Year's Eve?"

I was looking at her ass hugging the edge of the barstool. That squeaky-ass voice of hers didn't sound so squeaky now— unless it was just my imagination, I don't know. "Cleaning."

"Frankie! How sexist," she said, running her fingers through her wig.

"Well, you asked, so I told you. I ain't *making* her clean; it was her bright idea."

"So what else have you been doing for yourself?"

"Working. What about you?"

"Same old thing. Still at the bank. I got a promotion, though—I'm a head teller now." She was swirling the mixing straw around and around in her glass, locking them slanted eyes on mine like she had already made up her mind what she was gon' do next.

"That's nice," I said.

"So tell me, Frankie, how you spending your New Year's Eve?"

"With you," I heard myself say. The words just slipped outta my mouth, and I swear to God I wasn't even thinking no shit like this. I ain't one for fuckin' around on my woman— even if she ain't speaking to me. But I couldn't renege now. And Terri always was a hot one—besides, let's face it, all women like to get fucked on New Year's. They don't forget you after you done fucked 'em good either. I know that's what Terri was thinking when she saw me.

"Let's get outta here, then," she said, and jumped off the seat.

"I can't stay long," I said. I wanted that clear up front.

"Don't worry. I'll have you home in time for the countdown."

"You still in the same place?"

"Nope, I moved, but it's only ten minutes by cab. Come on, Frankie. You know it'll be worth the ride."

She opened the door to her apartment. What a tacky-ass place. Compared to me and Zora's, this looked like the set of a old B movie. What a dump. Not that Terri ain't clean, but you could tell she didn't buy nothing but cheap shit. Everything in here was crushed velvet. And why she have to pick burgundy? She musta got one of them furnish-a-whole-apartment-for-under-three-hundred-dollars deals. Old rock 'n' roll posters was Scotch-taped to the wall, and her stereo wasn't even a name brand.

"Make yourself comfortable, while I get outta all of these heavy clothes."

I sat down on the couch. Women sure have changed. Used to be a man had to scheme or beg for the pussy. Now if one wants your ass, she'll just come on out and tell you not only how she want you but when and where she want you. I don't know how I feel about this liberated shit. It takes some of the challenge out of it. But fuck it. How often do a man just get offered some hassle-free pussy?

She came back out wearing this lacy shit, and Tarzan didn't move. Something was wrong here. For one thing, I really didn't feel like fucking now—at least not her—but I got myself into this shit, and I'ma have to fuck my way out. I wondered what Zora was doing.

"Drink?" she asked.

"Why not."

She turned on the radio, of all the tacky-ass things to do, and all I heard was static. "Ain't you got no albums?"

"My turntable is broke," she said. "Just a minute, I can get it on the right station; sometimes the antenna just needs to be moved."

She got up and started juggling it, and her ass shook while she did it. It didn't look as good as Zora's. Would she really go out without me?

"Here," Terri said, handing me a drink.

"Thanks." Then I couldn't think of nothing to say. "Your place is real nice."

"So are you, Frankie," she said, and started toward my neck.

"Wait a minute, baby. Let me get a sip of my drink first. We got time." I drank the shit down in one swallow. The next thing I knew, that black wig was all in my face. "Terri, ease up a minute, baby. Can't you take off that wig?"

"No," she said, and grabbed on to it.

"Well, let me get another drink, and I'll be right."

She backed off and took the glass from my hand, like she was in some old Hollywood movie. "I definitely want you to feel right, Frankie," she said, and winked at me. When she came back, I polished off this rum and Coke too, and it felt like everything I'd drunk since this afternoon rushed up to my head. Fuck it. Take the pussy and run, man. When she sat back down next to me, I just dug my middle finger in her pussy. I woulda never done this kinda shit to Zora.

Terri started kissing me every-damn-where and slid her hand down inside my suit pants. Tarzan was still limp. Obviously, she wasn't worried about it, 'cause the next thing I knew, she had took my suit off and had them juicy lips around him. He felt like rubber. If I'm lucky, I can get outta here without having to stick it in her. Shit, I forgot. Terri likes to blow till she come, then sit on your dick and work until she come again. Shit. This could take all damn night.

She was working Tarzan steady, but wasn't nothing happening. What time was it? In between watching her head bobbing up and down, I was looking around the room for the clock. But I didn't see one. I put my hand on her wig and rubbed it. "Sweetheart," I whispered, but she musta not felt the shit or heard me. "Hey," I said louder, and then she looked up. The girl looked deranged, and for a minute, I swear, I forgot who she was. "Where's your clock?"

"My what?"

"I need to know what time it is."

She let out a long sigh, checked her watch, and said, "It's only quarter after eight. Why?"

"I was just wondering."

"You gotta be home at a certain time, is that it?"

"I'ma grown man, baby. Don't nobody give me no curfews."

"Glad to hear it," she said, and dived back down.

This shit was boring. Tarzan was still dead, and after what felt like hours, she started squirming and jerking, and I finally heard that damn squeal. Now I remember how it used to drive me crazy. "Frankie, ooooh, *Frankie!!!* I've missed you, baby. *God*, have I *missed* you." She jumped up and pushed me down on the couch and tried to sit on Tarzan, but he fell over. She picked him up anyway, but he still didn't wanna cooperate. All I wanted to do was get the hell outta here. And knowing how Zora likes to be on time, she'd probably leave by nine if she was going without me.

Terri managed to get him in, and was pumping her ass off, when it occurred to me that *I* wasn't doing the fucking—she was fucking me.

"Hold it, baby," I said, and lifted her up by the waist.

"What's wrong, Frankie? It's not good. Let me make it good."

"It ain't that. It's just been a long time," I said.

"So what?"

"So people change." I sat up.

"You wait until I'm ready to explode and got the nerve to push me away and then tell me that people change? What kinda shit is this?"

"You see this?" I grabbed my dick and flipped it back and forth. "He ain't felt nothing, and I don't want you to take it personally, baby, but I gotta go. Really." I started putting my clothes back on, and I swear I wanted to take a shower, but not here. She crossed her arms like she woulda kicked my ass if she coulda, and after I got my coat I couldn't bring myself to kiss her.

"I'm sorry, Terri."

"Fuck you," she said.

I let myself out.

Why she had to move way the hell over here where you can't hail a cab, I don't know. I ended up walking eight cold blocks to the subway station, only to find out that the train was outta service. I couldn't believe this shit. It's 'cause I didn't have no fuckin' business over here, that's why.

I stood outside for a few minutes, trying to figure out what to do. It couldn't ta been no more than ten degrees. I took my leather gloves—which Zora had gave me for Christmas, and I still ain't got her nothin'—outta my pocket and put 'em on. I looked up and down the street. At first it was just dark and deserted—lined with beat-up-looking brownstones—but then folks started coming outta doorways, all dressed up and heading for the subway. "It ain't in service," I said, I don't know how many times. I wanted to call Zora, but I didn't see no phones. Somebody told me the closest train station was six blocks away. I started walking. By the time I got there, my lips and fingertips was numb. All I wanted to do was get home, take a shower, and put my arms around my woman. I damn sure didn't feel like dancing, didn't feel like dealing with no mob of people, and didn't wanna have to wait on another train to do it.

By the time I turned the key in the door, it was after nine. I smelled perfume. Luther Vandross was singing "A House Is Not a Home." Why she have to play that? I closed the door. "Zora?"

"I'm in here," she said from the bathroom. I was kinda scared of what I was about to see, and my feet stopped in their own tracks once they got inside the doorway. She was dressed up, all right. Wearing a tight purple leather dress that showed off everything she had to show off. Her legs was covered with black crisscrossed stockings. Her high heels was the same color as the dress. Damn, even her ankles was sexy. She was leaning close to the mirror, putting on some pink lipstick.

"You look nice," I said.

"Thank you." She creased her lips, then stood back to look at herself.

"Where you going?" I asked. All of a sudden, my head was killing me. I shouldn'ta mixed bourbon and rum, and I knew it.

"Out."

"What you mean, 'out'?"

"Just what I said."

"What would you do if I said I didn't wanna go out?"

"I'm going anyway."

"Without me?"

"Without you."

"So it's like that, then, huh?"

"Franklin, look. You're the one who got all duded up,

boozed it up all day, then left, and now you come strolling back in here three hours before midnight and expect what?"

"I don't expect nothing but a little consideration."

"Consider—what?"

"You don't even try to understand what I'm feeling, baby—and today ain't no different."

"Explain what you mean by that, would you?"

"Let's face it, baby. The only reason you all geeked up and wanna run out on New Year's Eve is 'cause the white man says that's what we supposed to do. Most of the people going out tonight is only going 'cause they ain't got nobody at home to be with. You got me. And on top of that, you wanna spend a couple hundred dollars that we don't have to do it. For the first time in months, I got a few dollars in my pocket, and I don't wanna give it all to the white man in one night 'cause they say it's a fuckin' cause to celebrate."

"That's how you see this?"

"Yeah, that's how I see it."

"Well, let me tell you how *I* see it. I think you're just being cheap. If my Daddy hadn't given you this money, you wouldn't have had any. Before I met you, Franklin, I *always* had it, and didn't spend half my time worrying about it either. I never go out anymore, because *we* never have any money. All we do is fuck and play Scrabble. Well, I'm sick of it—to use your favorite phrase, really fuckin' sick of it. And whether you like it or not, I enjoy putting on a dress and high heels and perfume and makeup and going out for dinner and dancing. If I can't do this with you, who can I do it with?"

The phone rang, and she snatched it off the hook. "Hello. I'm on my way," she said, and slammed the phone back in the cradle. Damn, she's so pretty when she's mad.

"I can understand your feeling this way, baby. But you ain't asked me *why* I'm trying to hold on to this five hundred dollars, have you?"

"Go ahead, tell me. I'm just dying to know."

"You can cut the sarcasm, baby."

She made her fingers clip the air so it looked like she was cutting something. I'ma let this go. For one thing, what she said was too true, but I still didn't feel like being chumped off. "I wanna buy us a car."

"You wanna buy a what?"

"You heard me. A car."

"What kind of car do you think you can buy in 1983 for five hundred dollars, Franklin? Tell me that."

"I was hoping you'd put your five hundred with mine."

"Oh, is that what you were hoping?"

"Yeah."

"Well, my five hundred is gone."

"Gone?"

"I had credit cards that were past due, remember? And a phone bill and a gas bill, and—"

"Look, if we had a car, it would make finding and getting to work all that much easier. We could go anywhere we wanted to when we wanted to. I'm working now, baby, so I can save a few extra dollars in a couple of months and get us a decent ride."

"Knock yourself out."

She went over to the closet and got her coat. Shit, she was serious. She *was* going without me. "Tell me something, baby. How you getting to your destination?"

"By cab."

"And you gon' walk down this dark street at ten o'clock at night on New Year's Eve by yourself with all these dope fiends and shit on the loose?"

"Franklin, please, that one won't work."

"I hope you ain't planning on doing no drinking."

She cut her eyes at me.

"Well, you know what they say, don't you, baby?"

"About what?" she said.

"That whoever you spend New Year's Eve with is who you gon' spend the rest of the year with?"

"Who said that?"

"I don't know who said it, but what difference do it make? Just think back over the past few years. Who'd you spend yours with last year?"

"I'll ponder over it while I'm dancing."

"Then you have a good time, baby."

"I will."

"We got any popcorn?"

"I don't know. Go look."

She went to get her purse and keys, and was just about to put her coat on. I walked over and stood right in front of her. "I'm not trying to mess up your New Year's, baby, I swear I ain't. All I wanna do is be with you, that's all. We got the rest of our lives to dance and party. And we gon' do that, I promise. You know how many more New Years I wanna spend with you? All I'm trying to do now is get our constitution down, build us a solid foundation, so in the future when we *do* go out and party, we ain't gon' have to worry about how much it's costing us. Can't you understand that?"

She opened her eyes as wide as she could get 'em, and I saw the tears working their way inside the rims.

"Can I at least give you a New Year's kiss before you go?"

Zora wiped her eyes, and that black stuff smeared underneath both of 'em. Then she leaned back on one of them high heels and started biting her bottom lip. She looked up at the ceiling and back down at the floor. Then she looked up at me. Her eyes looked sad. She let out a long sigh, then walked toward me and stood on her tiptoes. Her breasts pressed against my chest and collapsed. By the time her lips found mine, I felt her coat drop to the floor.

13

"**B**itch! You said you and Franklin was coming, and me and Arthur sat there and sat there, and waited and waited, and your asses never showed up! I shoulda known he wasn't gon' let you out the house. What are you, his prisoner or something?"

Portia leaned forward on both elbows and put her face inside her palms. Something told me she had taken our not coming too easily over the phone. She's been holding it all in, just waiting for the right moment, so she could throw it directly in my face.

"No, I am not his *prisoner*. Franklin got sick, and I didn't want to leave him. By the time I called you back, you'd already left." Now, why'd I just tell that barefaced lie? And to Portia, of all people? If I told her the truth, all she'd do is accuse me of being too gullible—I know how she thinks. But why should I have to defend how I feel about my man?

"What was wrong with him?"

"Why?"

"You're lying, Zora. I can see it all over your face. He talked you outta coming, didn't he? Tell the truth."

"No, he didn't *talk* me out of anything, and I wish we could skip the subject. Are you ordering or not?"

"Since I got stuck with a hundred dollars' worth of fuckin' tickets, you're paying for this. It's a good thing Arthur ain't cheap, or I'da had to fork up the cash myself."

Portia looked up and down the menu, and I stared out the window at people trudging through the snow. All of a sudden, I felt like getting up from this table and walking and walking until I ended up in a place that was totally peaceful. It's so hard trying to please everybody. They just keep pulling at me. Franklin expects this. Portia expects this. Reginald expects me to practice more. Breathe harder. Then lighter. Make a record. Sing. And school: Miss Banks? Miss Banks? Miss Banks? Can you be on this committee? That committee? No, not this week. Next week? Yes. Remember your responsibility to the children. To the school.

Up to now, I've done a pretty good job of dealing with things. Faking it is what I've really been doing. Pretending that nothing is wrong. That Franklin's being married hasn't bothered me. That his being out of work hasn't bothered me. That his not having a formal education hasn't bothered me. But it's getting too hard, this acting. I'm scared of what the outcome of everything will be. Me and him. My friendships. Teaching. Singing. Me. And now the thought of these damn fits. Right this very minute, my head feels like a hot-air balloon. I'm beginning not to trust myself.

I put my purse in my lap and searched inside until I found the bottle. I've been carrying it for months, thought of it as insurance. I twisted the top off and took one tiny pill out and popped it into my mouth. Portia didn't even notice.

"I'll have the shrimp scampi and a glass of white wine," she said.

I took a sip of water. "So. Will this Arthur last until Valentine's Day, or what?"

"Maybe, maybe not. He's nice as hell, and he ain't stingy, so that's two things working in his favor."

"What's working against him?"

"He's married."

"Oh, is that *all*."

"You know, Zora, why you so damn sarcastic today? What's going on?"

"Nothing, girl," I said, and started fidgeting with my water glass.

"Are you pregnant again?"

"Pregnant? Be serious. What would make you ask that?"

"Well, something is on your mind. And you just ate four pieces of French bread. Come on, spill it."

"I'm just getting nervous. Next week Reginald wants to start working on songs for the demo. I've got a few originals, but I don't know how good they really are. This whole process is kind of scary, if you want to know the truth."

"He thinks you're ready, right?"

"Yeah. He's almost more excited about it than I am."

"You can't sit here and tell me that you ain't excited about this shit."

"Of course I am. It's just that *I* don't know if I'm as ready as I thought. It feels like it was only yesterday that I had my first lesson. I'm really just getting used to singing on a regular basis. And now we're getting ready to go into the studio."

"Ain't you the one who been saying how tired you are of teaching?"

"Yeah."

"So I don't get it. The time is now, and you getting cold feet, girlfriend?"

"It's not that. I've just got so many other things on my mind, I don't feel focused enough, like I'm not in a position to give this my all."

"Meditate more, girl. You the one who said that shit gets you 'clear'—correct me if I'm wrong."

"You're right. But I haven't meditated in ages. Since Franklin moved in, it's felt weird sitting in the middle of the room chanting, knowing he's in the bathroom shaving. And lately it's been hard enough trying to drag myself out of bed to get to school on time."

"Not Miss Guru herself?"

"Go to hell, Portia."

"Come on, Zora, cut the bullshit. Don't tell me you gon' turn out to be one of these women they write about in *New Woman, Today's Woman, Tomorrow's Woman, Anybody's Woman.* . . ." She started laughing. "Seriously, girlfriend. You heard what they been saying about women who want success so bad they can taste it?"

"What?"

"When it's finally staring 'em in the face, they get scared. All of a sudden, they don't feel worthy and shit, start fuckin' everything up or doubting themselves so much that they don't get what they started out to get. Please don't turn out to be one of them, Zora. Hell, when I first met you, all I heard was, 'I know I can sing. And one day I'm going to sing to a roomful of people, and folks'll push me into their cassettes while they're laying on the beach and driving down the highway.' Didn't you used to tell me that shit like it was going outta style?"

"I guess." The waitress came to take our order. I was starving, so I ordered a spinach salad and linguini with clam sauce. Portia changed her mind about the scampi and ordered a steak. "It'll still be a while before we actually go into the studio. It's just so damn expensive."

"So what! You're worth it, ain't you?"

"Of course I am."

"All right, then. Anyway, back to Arthur. It ain't nothing, girl. I just feel like being kept for a little while. The man is only five foot six, so you know I ain't serious. He's got some nice friends, though."

"Where was his wife on New Year's?"

"In South Carolina with her family. Her Mama got high blood pressure or something. But who gives a shit."

"What a terrible thing to say, Portia."

"You always got to be Miss Goody Two-shoes, don't you?"

I didn't answer her. Franklin should be getting home soon, and I'm praying that he'll have good news. Not about a job. He went to that trade school to talk to a counselor, and I'm hoping it went well.

"Zora, snap out of it, girl. You seen Marie?"

"No. She was supposed to stop by for a drink on New Year's, but I haven't heard from her."

"She's probably in a gutter somewhere. Maybe I'll stop by to check on her. We need to do something to get that girl in AA, I swear."

"She won't go. Marie swears up and down that she doesn't have a problem."

"Problem ain't the word for it! Shit, some nights I've talked to her and she made perfect sense. But the next day? She can't remember shit. I'll let you know what I find out. What about Claudette—you talk to that bitch?"

"She had a baby boy."

"La-di-ta-ta."

All during dinner, I kept looking at the clock. It was almost seven, and rush hour should've been over by now. I wanted to call Franklin, to let him know I was on my way. "I've gotta go to the bathroom," I said. "Be back in a minute."

"The phone is right outside the door, girlfriend."

Portia makes me sick.

Franklin answered on the second ring.

"Hi," I said.

"Hi," he said.

"Everything okay?"

"Yeah, fine. Where you at?"

"In the Village, having dinner with Portia."

"What time you gon' be home?"

"In about an hour. How did it go?"

"How did what go?"

"The consultation at school."

"Can we talk about it when you get home?"

"Sure."

"What am I supposed to eat while you eating out?"

"Franklin, there's plenty of stuff to eat around there. Did you look?"

"I thought that was your job."

"My job?"

"Yeah. The way you laid it out to me, you said you'd always do the cooking, or did the rules change?"

"Look, Franklin, I just called to see how things went and to let you know I was on my way."

"Well, consider getting here soon, would you?"

"Goodbye, Franklin," I said, and hung up. Why'd I even bother? I went back to sit down, and Portia was eating her salad, which she always saves until last. She looked up at me with disgust. "Well, did he tell you to get your ass home 'cause he was hungry and you his woman and he can't eat unless you cook, or what?"

"Go to hell, Portia."

"You need to check yourself, girlfriend. Your whole world is starting to revolve around this man. Don't nobody see you no more, and I'm surprised you was able to sneak out the house today. But hell, you can't even have dinner in peace without running to the phone to check in."

"It's not like that at all. All I was doing was trying to find out how things went for him at school today."

"Sure, Zora. You even starting to fool yourself. You better be careful, or you gon' start disappearing a little bit at a time, and before you know it, you gon' be just like them damn Stepford Wives. Won't even remember who Zora Banks was."

"How can you be so presumptuous? You don't know what my relationship is about with Franklin."

"That's the whole point. You used to share shit with me, Marie, and Claudette. Now everything you do is such a big fuckin' secret."

My temples were throbbing. I hadn't planned on telling her, but all of a sudden I wanted her to know. "I had a seizure a few months ago."

Portia dropped her fork. "You did?"

"Yeah."

"What happened, girl? Where?"

"At home, and yes, Franklin knows."

"Well, I'll be damned. What did he do?"

"He took care of me, that's what. He was a little upset that I hadn't told him I had it."

"And?"

"And he said he could handle it."

"No shit."

"He still wants to marry me."

"When?"

"Soon."

Portia leaned back in her chair and crossed her arms. "How soon?"

Now my entire face was burning. Portia was right. I did use to share everything with her, because she was my friend, but since I've been with Franklin, I've kept things pretty much to myself. And I know why. Sometimes your friends judge you harsher than anybody else, and I didn't want her, Marie, or Claudette to get the wrong impression: that I was a fool for falling in love with a man who never finished high school, who worked sporadically, and who was still married. "When he gets his divorce," I blurted out.

"His what?"

"You heard me. Divorce. Franklin's been separated from his first wife for almost seven years now, but they've just never bothered with the paperwork."

"You're bullshitting me, Zora. You mean he's married?"

"I don't look at it like that."

"I guess the fuck you don't. But I ain't gon' rub this in your face, girlfriend. At least now I know you ain't Little Miss Muffet after all."

"He is getting it, Portia. He just hasn't had the money."

"That's the best one I've heard yet. Is he working?"

"Yes, he's working. What made you ask that?"

"Don't lie to me, Zora. If you supporting this mother-fucker and busting your ass trying to please him too, this probably ain't gon' be the last seizure you gon' have."

"I'm not supporting him and never have."

"Sure. Anyway, so it didn't scare him off, huh?"

"No, it didn't. The man loves me, Portia."

"Shit, you're a good catch. You're pretty, got a college de-gree, a steady job, and on the verge of getting rich and fa-mous. So you have a little seizure every four years. Gain a few too many pounds once in a while. Big deal. If I was a man, I'd probably be in love with your black ass too. Now the question is, can you fuck?"

She started chuckling, but I didn't think it was funny.

"You've got tunnel vision, you know that, Portia?"

"Well, maybe if I got to know the man, I wouldn't be so

prejudiced. But you ain't doing too bad a job of hiding him either."

"Look. I'll tell you what: Are you free next weekend?"

"I can be. Why?"

"Because I feel like inviting a few people over. We can have dinner, play Scrabble, and just sit around and talk."

"Sounds good to me. I can bring a date, can't I?"

"Don't you always?"

"It ain't too many places I like going unescorted."

"You want to know something, Portia?"

"I'm listening."

"If you had a man that was a permanent fixture in your life, you'd understand that when you love someone, it takes a certain amount of compromise and compassion. That was *compassion*, not passion, which is the only part of the word you seem to be familiar with. And I'm not disappearing, as you put it; I'm just giving what I have to offer."

"And what's that?"

I stood up and put my coat on, then dropped money on the table. "Love," I said. "I've gotta go."

"I'm sure you do," she said. "I'm sure you do."

Franklin was eating ravioli out of the can when I walked in, and listening to Stephanie Mills's "I Can't Give Back the Love I Feel for You." I tried not to take it personally.

"Hi," he said.

"Hi," I said back. I prayed that this wouldn't turn into yet another deep conversation. I need a break. What I wouldn't pay to come home for a change to a happy man who had had a great day. Who maybe had dinner ready, a bouquet of flowers, some soft music.

"Before this turn into a long discussion, baby, all I gotta say is, I didn't go talk to nobody, 'cause I can't prove I got my GED."

"What do you mean, you can't prove it?"

"I don't know where the fuck I put it."

"Don't you keep important papers like that in a safe place?"

"If I did, I wouldn't have to look for it, would I?"

"Well, you can call the place where you got it, and they could send you a copy."

"That's the problem. I can't even remember the name of the damn place. It was some correspondence school in Jersey, and we talking about a few years ago. Look, I'm sorry for taking this out on you over the phone." He set the empty can on the counter. "But I'ma be honest, Zora. Sometimes when you with your girlfriends and I feel like I need you here with me, I do get a little jealous. But just take it with a grain of salt, baby, would you?"

"Okay," I said, relieved. "Would you mind if I invited a few friends over for dinner this weekend?"

"No. I don't mind."

"Really?"

"Why you acting so surprised? Damn, you'd think I told you I didn't want your friends over here. Did I ever give you that impression?"

"No."

"So invite 'em. You know, I been meaning to ask you. What ever happened to that white girl that was supposed to be moving here?"

"Judy? She's living in Manhattan."

"Well, how come she ain't been over?"

"Our schedules just never coincide, that's all, and with her new job, she works long hours."

"Invite her over too. What the hell."

"Okay. Why don't you invite your friends too?"

"I don't know how to get in touch with Jimmy, and Lucky moved in with some chick. I don't know where he lives now."

"What about Darlene?"

"I'll call her."

"Good," I said. "You feel like a game of Scrabble?" I really didn't feel like playing, but I thought it might take his mind off things, cheer him up.

"Not tonight, baby. I need to look through some of my old boxes. One of my biggest problems in life is being too fuckin' unorganized. If I find it, I can probably start school this summer." He walked over to the closet. "Ow!" he said, while he pulled a box out into the living room.

"What's wrong?"

"My knee."

"What's wrong with it?"

"It's swollen, like I got arthritis in it or something. I don't know. Feel."

I went over to touch it through his jeans, but it didn't feel any different than the other one. "Does it hurt?"

"Yeah, but it comes and goes. Right now it feels like somebody's sticking needles in it. I just need to get some of my weight off of it, that's all."

"Why don't you lie down for a while?"

"Will you lay down with me?"

"I really should work on my song for a while. Reginald'll be mad as I don't know what if I'm not ready on Thursday."

"All I been hearing is you singing from behind closed doors. You mind if I listen while I go through one of these boxes?"

"No, I don't mind. Come on."

I went and sat down at the piano, and Franklin sat on the

floor. I was wondering if his knee really hurt all that bad, considering the way he folded his legs. Then I remembered the first time I sang for him. It was in this room. God, does time fly. I was scared to death of what his reaction would be, but now I'm just glad he's still in my audience. I sang a ballad I'd written, "Take It or Leave It"—sort of a cross between Joni Mitchell, Patti LaBelle, and me. When I finished, I was drenched with perspiration and tingling. It felt great. Cleansing. If only I could feel like this all the time. I slid the stool away from the piano and looked down at Franklin. He was stacking up piles of paper.

"Well?"

"You definitely star material, baby," he said.

"You liked it?"

"Who wouldn't like it? Those classes is paying off."

"Well, I just hope I can get a record contract."

I wanted him to say something, but he didn't. He was too busy sifting through papers.

"Franklin?"

"Yeah, baby."

"Did you hear what I said?"

"No, I didn't hear you. My knee is really killing me."

"Well, take a Tylenol."

"Good idea," he said. "Now, what'd you just say?"

"I said, I just hope I can get a record contract."

"Yeah, baby, I hope you do too. Maybe I *should* lay down for a few minutes. You coming?"

"In a few minutes," I said, and reluctantly started folding up my sheet music. Franklin stood up with ease. There's nothing wrong with your knee, I thought. What's really killing you is me.

The next evening, Franklin's wife phoned. It had been a while since Pam called, and I knew he'd be pissed, because the only time she calls is when she needs money. As usual, I was cordial.

"Franklin!" I called out for the second time. He was in the bathroom, reading the paper.

"I'm coming, baby."

I handed him the phone. "It's Pam."

"Yeah," he said, and I walked away to give him some privacy, even though this apartment isn't that big, so voices carry. "Your insurance won't cover it? I ain't got that much," he said. Then I smelled cigarette smoke. Franklin always has to smoke when he talks to her. "I'll drop it off tomorrow. Yeah. Later." When I heard the phone being placed in the cradle, I walked back out into the living room.

"Is everything okay?"

"Derek ran into some little boy on his bike, and the boy broke his damn arm, and Pam's gotta fork up some cash if she don't wanna get sued, so you know who's gotta pay, right?"

"Is Derek okay?"

"Yeah, he's all right."

"How much?"

"Enough so we won't be getting no car no time soon."

"Don't worry about a car, Franklin. We've done without one all this time; a few more months won't hurt."

"That's easy for you to say, baby. Every time I get a dollar, somebody got their fuckin' hand out. A black man just can't get ahead, can he?"

"Are you still going over to the school to talk to a counselor?"

"I said I was, didn't I?"

"And you'll tell 'em you can't find your certificate?"

"Yeah."

"Good."

"What's so good about it?"

"Everything. I'm sure they'll be willing to make some kind of exception, Franklin. I mean, who would lie about something like this? There has to be a way they can verify it through the Department of Education. I mean, really."

He reached under the kitchen cabinet and poured himself a stiff one. I wanted to ask if he thought that was a good idea, but I didn't want to start an argument. Sometimes Franklin does things ass-backward, but I have to be careful about how I criticize him. He's so sensitive and takes everything as a personal attack. I've learned that the best way to avoid confrontation is by keeping my mouth shut.

I was hungry, even though I'd finished dinner less than an hour ago. I opened the freezer, took out a pint of vanilla Häagen-Dazs, and scooped out two big humps.

"Still a little hungry, are we?" he asked.

"A little," I said.

"See you in a little while, baby," he said, and gave me a peck on the cheek. I sat there and ate the ice cream without tasting it. When I finished, my stomach still felt empty. I walked back to the freezer and pulled the pint out again, but this time I didn't bother putting any into the bowl. I ate from the carton. The next thing I knew, I was throwing the empty container into the trash. At that very moment, it dawned on me what I'd just done. I ran to the bathroom and stood on the scale. One forty-nine. How did I gain ten pounds?

I felt antsy. I should read something, to relax. But not the newspaper, not *Essence* and not *People* and not *Rolling Stone*. I needed a sustained form of escape. I needed to stop thinking about myself for a while. To simply unplug all the wires that were beginning to short-circuit inside my head. I mean, things had started out so simple between me and Franklin. We fell in love. And it felt so good. But he's married. And I have fits. He's got employment troubles. And I would really like to be able to quit my job. There's a chance I could be a successful singer. And he's not sure what he really wants to do or just how he's going to do it. He drinks too much. And I'm starting with the food again. Our lives have gotten so thick that my head is beginning to feel like it's full of cotton. I just wish I knew how all of this was going to turn out.

I put on my Patti Austin tape, turned it down low, lay down on the bed, and opened the yellow book that was lying on the table next to the bed. I started reading. There were cigarette ashes between pages ten and eleven. Franklin must've read it already. How ironic. He reads more than I do.

My own snoring woke me up. The last thing I remember was that the guy who'd just gotten out of prison for refusing to go to Vietnam was trying to get to his parents' house, but he got sidetracked by—what else?—a woman. I closed the book and looked at the clock. It was almost midnight. Where was Franklin? He should've been back hours ago. I knew I shouldn't worry. What I needed to do was go back to sleep. There's nothing worse than facing thirty-six fourteen-year-olds at eight o'clock in the morning when your eyes are burning.

I heard the front door close softly.

"Franklin?"

"Yeah, it's me, baby."

His voice was heavy, which meant he was drunk. When he came into the bedroom, he smelled like a bar. He didn't say anything, just fell down on me and kissed me. It was disgusting. I tried to push him away.

"Not tonight, baby, please don't push me away tonight. I need you."

"What's wrong?"

"All I wanna do is go to school so I can start my own business and take care of you so you can quit teaching and sing so you can be a star!"

"What did they say?"

"Who?"

"The counselor at school."

"I didn't make it."

"What do you mean, you didn't make it?"

"I got sidetracked. I'll go tomorrow."

"Franklin?" All two hundred and twenty-three pounds of him were on me, and I could barely move. I tried to sit up, which caused him to roll down to my thighs. "What do you mean, you got sidetracked?"

"I'm scared, baby. Scared. Can't you understand that?"

"Scared of what?"

"I don't know," he said, slurring.

I wanted to strangle him. "All you were supposed to do was get some information and tell them about your GED. What's so scary about that?"

"If I can't find it, I can't prove it. To them I'm still a dropout."

"So you can just take the test over again."

"You know how long it's been since I been to school?"

"All you have to do is study and then take a simple test. You're no dummy, Franklin. And it can't be that hard."

"That's easy for you to say. You got a college education, baby. I can't even write a decent sentence."

"Then we'll work on it together."

"You're sweet, you know that? And that's why I love you. Put your arms around me, baby, please?"

He was so pitiful that I was completely turned off. I put my arms around him anyway, but I didn't hug him. I could feel him getting hard as a rock.

"I need you tonight, baby," he slurred. Then his whole face fell on mine. His lips were wet and foul-tasting.

"Franklin, I don't want to."

"Come on, baby. It won't take but a minute."

He always says that when he's drunk, and there's no way I can talk him out of it.

"Can I at least take my clothes off?"

"Let me take 'em off for you." He started yanking on my slacks until he got them off. Then he pulled up my T-shirt, but it got stuck around my neck and I couldn't breathe. When he finally yanked it over my head, my chin snapped and I bit my tongue. Instead of taking my bra off, he lifted it up so that my breasts flopped out. Then he pushed them together until they felt like one. He started sucking my nipples as if he was really hoping to get milk.

"Franklin, take it easy, would you?"

He didn't say anything. I don't think he heard me.

When he got tired of my breasts, he dropped them. Then he dug his middle finger inside me. I was as dry as a desert, but he jabbed his penis inside me anyway. That's when I screamed. "Franklin, please! You're hurting me."

"I'm sorry, baby."

And off he went to the races. At first it felt like I was in a tractor going over a bumpy road. Then I guess he decided to be a bulldozer. I looked at the clock. His minute was long since up, but of course I wouldn't dare say that. I still hadn't moved a muscle, and I decided to help, just to get it over with. Now, when he pushed, I pushed back.

"Thank you, baby," he muttered.

I pretended my body was a roller coaster and moved accordingly—that is, until the combination of his weight, his sweat, his funk, and that breath was unbearable. Finally, I put both hands on his ass and pushed him in as far as he could go and squeezed. This usually works, but I should've known better. He moaned but didn't shiver. Then he fell off of me and rolled over to his side of the bed.

"Maybe I'm too high," he said.

"Maybe?"

He flopped both arms over me, and within a minute he was snoring. I twisted myself out of his grasp, went to the bathroom, scrubbed his scent off; then I walked into the kitchen, ate six Oreo cookies, standing up, and washed them down with a glass of milk.

"So what'd you think?" I asked Reginald.

"I've heard you sound much better."

"I know." I walked over by his piano and looked down six flights at the traffic.

"What's wrong with you today, Z?"

"Tired, maybe."

"Bullshit. You haven't been practicing, have you?"

"Yes, I have."

"Your posture is for shit, you're missing notes—flat from one key to the next—you're breathing from everywhere except your diaphragm, and you're straining like hell. Come on, where's your concentration? This is no time to start slacking off. What's going on?"

"What if I don't have all the money for the studio when it's time?"

"There are ways to cut a few corners and still be able to get a good production sound."

"How?"

He explained that we didn't have to hire musicians for every song. That he'd do the keyboards, lay all the parts for each instrument, and we could use a computerized drum machine, rent a synthesizer to reproduce the bass, horn, and string sounds.

I started walking around his loft and sat down on his white leather sofa. It was soft.

"Didn't you say you've already put away five hundred?"

"Yeah."

"Well, I know where we can get a good studio for about fifty an hour."

"Fifty dollars?"

"Some go as high as two hundred, so don't complain. It shouldn't take us more than about thirty hours."

"Thirty hours?"

"Well, it's almost income tax return time. Aren't you getting a refund?"

"Yeah, but I hadn't thought about that."

"We're not under any deadlines, so don't worry about it."

"Have any of your other students gotten nervous once they get to this point?"

"Of course. But it's only natural. I mean, you sing your heart out for years in the church choir and then you decide to pursue it on a professional level. It's different. It's competitive, and you start having your doubts about your talent. But, Miss Z, you don't need to worry about that. Come on, get your butt up and over here."

I got up from the sofa, and it seemed to take so much energy. I took my usual position, next to the piano.

"We're not doing anything until you stand up straight."

I stood up as straight as I could.

"I've changed my mind. The song can wait. Let's do a few exercises to loosen you up."

As I lay there on the floor with my palms on my belly, my head began to swirl with the rhythm of the ceiling fan. I couldn't picture the flame the way I usually can.

"Come on, Z, stop lifting your chest. Concentrate."

I started coughing and sat up. "Would you mind terribly if we rehearsed next week? My mind just isn't on this."

"You could've fooled me."

"I'm just feeling a little confused."

"Well, talk to me, Z. If you come in here tense, and your mind is somewhere else, we're not gonna get anywhere."

"I know."

"Do me and yourself a favor. Go home. Try to relax. I know it might sound corny, but remember how good you used to feel when you sang in church?"

I shook my head yes. And I did remember. I felt free. And couldn't wait for Sunday to get here. I felt replenished after singing a solo. I'd look out at the congregation—in tears, fanning themselves, and shaking their heads up and down. And Daddy and Marguerite, looking so proud. But in those days, singing didn't take any effort, and I did it because I wanted to, and I wasn't concerned about going into a studio to make a record.

"Then surrender," Reginald was saying, "and let God back in your heart, and you'll feel the power of every single word you sing."

I tried to manage a smile.

"If you need more than a week, take it. I don't want to see you in here again until your attitude is more positive, understood?"

"Yeah," I said, and got my coat.

I cried all the way to the subway. As the train rattled along, I took out my Walkman and pushed the On button. I had forgotten that last time I'd put in Joni Mitchell, and it was near the end of "Don't Interrupt the Sorrow." I listened.

This song was too much for me tonight, so I turned it off and listened to the rhythm of the shaking train until I came to my stop.

*   *   *

Everything was perfect. Franklin surprised me and cleaned the whole apartment. He even cleaned the oven and the refrigerator, washed windows, and mopped and waxed what he called "his" floors. He insisted on doing the laundry too, which I begged him not to do—because I've seen what happens to clothes that he washes. Fortunately, everything was still the same color when he dumped out the laundry on the bed. Nothing was folded, and everything was wrinkled, but I let him know how much I appreciated it. He's been trying so hard to be helpful, which is why I decided not to mention the school issue again until he did.

I spent the morning in my music room, trying to let God into my heart, but He must've been too busy or sensed I wasn't sincere. You can't fool God—that much I do know—and even He probably knew I sounded lousy. So I gave up.

I went to the grocery store instead. I started cooking as soon as I got back. I made two large pans of stuffed shells, a gorgeous salad, asparagus tips, garlic bread, and homemade cheesecake. I bought enough wine for twenty people instead of nine. Everybody was supposed to be here by six.

At five o'clock, the phone rang. Franklin was blasting Evelyn "Champagne" King's "Love Come Down," and I had to ask him to turn it down.

It was Claudette. "We're not gonna be able to make it, girl. Little George has had a temperature all day, and now it's up to 105. I'm taking him to emergency. I'm really sorry, Zora."

Next was Darlene. "I've got cramps so bad I can't even walk. Tell Franklin I'll try to get out to see you guys next week, okay? I'm sorry, Zora. I was looking forward to this too."

Portia. "Girl, I got a wisdom tooth pulled yesterday, and the whole right side of my face is swollen and hurts like hell. I can't go nowhere looking and feeling like this."

Marie. "I just got your message five minutes ago. I've been working in Florida for the past two weeks, and I'm wiped out. Let's get together soon, though, and tell that handsome man of yours I said hi."

Judy. "I've got a brand-new presentation to make on Monday morning, and one I'm finishing up now. I'm still proving myself, you know, and I can't afford to blow it. I'm so sorry, Zora, but do give Franklin my regards. Maybe one day I'll get to meet him. Let's try to get together for lunch or something real soon."

I hung up the phone, and by the time I told Franklin, the phone rang again. There was nobody left to cancel, so I couldn't imagine who this could be.

It was Marguerite.

"Your Daddy's in the hospital, chile. He told me not to call you, but he's crazy. It ain't too serious. But look like he got a peptic ulcer. He gon' be in there for a good week, until they finish running tests. Don't you worry none. I just thought you should know. How you doing? And how's Franklin?"

"Fine," was all I could muster up.

"Jake is in the driveway, blowing for me. We on our way up to see your Daddy now. We'll call you soon as he get home. And don't you worry, he's in good hands."

I hung up the phone and looked at all the food, then at Franklin.

"Who was that?" he asked.

"Marguerite."

"Something wrong?"

"My Daddy's in the hospital, but she said he'll be all right."

"What's wrong with him?"

"She said ulcers."

"Well, at least it ain't cancer, or a heart attack, or some shit like that. You okay?"

"Yeah, I'm okay."

"I know you disappointed, baby. You done cooked all this damn food, and ain't nobody but me here to eat it."

I looked down at all the games. Scrabble. Trivial Pursuit. Monopoly. A deck of cards.

"Well, I'm hungry as a motherfucker. You mind if I eat now, baby?"

"Help yourself," I said, and went to find my purse.

14

I found my GED, so I went back down to that school, talked to a counselor, and signed on the dotted line. Wasn't nothing to it. They told me I could go at night, so I can still work during the day. I'm gon' take three classes. Me. It even sounds funny, but what the hell. I gotta take some kinda English too, 'cause they gave me this test and it was obvious that I can't write for shit. When I told Zora, she said she would help me. I'm gon' give her the opportunity too. I can't start until this summer, but that's okay with me.

Why is it that the shit that can change your whole life is always somewhere in the damn future? 'Cause right now my so-called constitution still ain't got a single brick in it. And when you get right down to it, my shit is shaky as a motherfucker, 'cause I'm still in the same fuckin' position I was in when I met Zora. Which is why I'm trying to speed up this process. Hell, I been watching how she dedicate herself. Damn near every day, she close that door and practice. No ifs, ands, and buts about it. And what have I been doing with any consistency? Pissing, and begging the white man for a job. I can't keep doing construction, that much I do know. It don't take no brains to throw bricks and shit, and I got one I wanna use. Besides, this shit is starting to take its toll on me physically and mentally. But hell, for a man who's been trying to build a life without no foundation, I guess something to look forward to is better than nothing.

I was sitting by the window, going through one of my how-to books, to get some ideas and measurements about a coffee table I'm thinking about making. My black beans and rice was simmering, and for some reason I had put on one of Zora's lesson tapes and was listening to it. Reginald was talking about her stage presence, and how much fuller her voice would sound once it was recorded, dubbed, and mixed. I keep forgetting that this is what all this singing and shit is leading up to. A record. If my shit is still dragging by the time she make one, where is that gon' leave me? She gon' be traveling all around the damn world, staying in fancy hotels, meeting all kinds of people—men—with a pocketful of money, driving Mercedes Benzes, not trying to scrape up a grand to buy a used Chevy. People always change when they get successful, don't they? Some of 'em forget who stuck by 'em all through their little apprenticeship. You gon' be one of 'em, baby? You gon' be ashamed of me when you make it? Well, don't worry. By that time, ain't gon' be no dirt under my fingernails. That's a promise. You ain't the only one with a master plan, and from here on out, everything I do is gon' add another brick to my foundation. I took her tape out and put in The Whispers' "And the Beat Goes On." I blasted it.

Every few minutes I saw icicles falling from the roof. It's about damn time. I don't wanna make the table outta pine, but shit, I can't afford the wood I'd love to use. Cherry. Maybe I'll go ahead and spend a few dollars—get a nice piece of walnut or oak. Zora always accusing me of being a cheapskate.

I got up to stir my beans, when the phone rang. Don't nobody usually call here this time of day, and Zora won't be
home for a while, but I answered it anyway. It was Jimmy.

"What's up, dude?" I asked.

"I'm in a jam, Frankie."

"What kinda jam, man?"

"Jail, and you the only person I could think of with a phone
that might come to my rescue. Can I count on you, Frankie?"

"How much we talking about, Jimmy?"

"Two fifty."

"Damn. I ain't got that kinda cash, and Zora ain't here
right now."

"I'm all fucked up, man."

"Look, give me till the morning, and let me see what I can
come up with."

"Frankie, you a real friend, dude. This whole thang is a
case of mistaken identity. They done accused me of shooting
some Puerto Rican I don't even know. I'll tell you about it if
I see you tomorrow. I'm in Brooklyn, on Adams—your old
spot."

"Yeah, right. Check you later."

Before I got a chance to hang up and think about how I was
gon' ask Zora if I could borrow two hundred and fifty bucks,
there was a click in the phone. I didn't know if I should tell
her the truth or make up something. I pushed down on the
dial-tone button.

"Frankie?"

"Kendricks?"

"Yeah, man, it's me. I don't care where you working; have
your black ass down here tomorrow by seven sharp. We got
sixteen spots at that same site with the city. I didn't wanna call
you till it was definite."

"Man, for the last few months, all I been doing is shitwork, freezing my nuts off—but at least it's steady. Kendricks, don't have me giving this up for no bullshit."

"How much you making?"

"Eight fifty."

"Well, Frankie, there's been some changes going on down here. We done put so much pressure on these guys, man, that this time they came to us. I promised the contractor I'd bring him sixteen good workers, so all I can say is, if you snooze you lose."

"Is this union or what?"

"The contractor gave me his word that if my men came in at thirteen, didn't fuck up, and proved they could do the work, then you can get your book in less than a month. Will I see you in the morning, man?"

"Wait a minute. You ain't told me what's going up."

"You know the old Metro Theatre building?"

"Yeah."

"They through with the demolition and start pouring tomorrow for the Transit Authority's new offices."

"No shit?"

"No shit."

"I'll be there."

Before I got a chance to get excited, the fuckin' phone clicked again. What the hell is going on? I shoulda read my horoscope today, and maybe I'da been prepared for all this.

"Yeah," I said, in a tone that woulda made anybody wanna hang up.

"Franklin, it's me, Darlene."

"Well, this is a surprise, Sis. How the hell are you?"

"Not doing so well, I guess."

"Why? What's up?"

"I'm in the hospital."

"The what? Where? What's wrong? What happened? You okay?"

"Yeah, I'm okay. I've just got a concussion. I accidentally fell off a subway platform, can you believe it? Luckily, a train wasn't coming, but I blacked out. So I'm up here at Columbia Presbyterian for a few days."

"You fell off a subway platform?"

"My heel got stuck on something, and I still don't know what."

"You call Moms and Pops?"

"No, and don't you call 'em either. You're the only one I want to know where I am."

"So you're okay, then, right?"

"Sort of. They want me to take some tests."

"What for? All you got is a concussion. What kinda tests?" She didn't say nothing.

"Darlene?"

"Psychological."

"Psycho-who?"

"You heard me, Franklin. They just want to make sure I didn't jump."

"Jump? Is that what they think you was trying to do? Darlene, is that what you *was* trying to do?"

"I said it was an accident, didn't I? I didn't think you'd believe me. Anyway, I'm tired. I just wanted you to know where I was, and don't bother coming up here to see me. I'm gonna be fine."

She hung up before I could say anything else. I don't believe this shit. What kind of fool do she think I am? She did try it again. But why? Things couldn't be that bad, could they? All I wanna know is, what the fuck is going on that would make my sister jump off a damn subway platform?

*   *   *

Hospitals give me the creeps. I don't trust doctors and especially nurses. Your fuckin' life is in their hands. Everybody
know that a lot of 'em is racist—all you gotta do is read the
Post.

I found out what room Darlene was in and started following the arrows. Water was dripping on top of my work boots
from these flowers I bought her. I didn't know what I was gon'
say to her, really, but I just wanted her to know she didn't have
to deal with this shit by herself. That's probably what's underneath all this—the girl just lonely as hell. Life *can* be a bitch
when you ain't got nobody—but goddamn.

Darlene looked like shit when I opened the door. Her Afro
was matted to her head, and the whites of her eyes was brown.
She looked like somebody had blowed her up, the way her face
was all puffed out. She was watching *Family Feud* and wasn't
surprised when she saw me.

"Here," I said, handing her the flowers. Then I bent down
and kissed her on the cheek.

"Franklin, I told you, you didn't have to come."

"Well, at least pretend like you glad to see me, damn."

"I'm glad to see you," she said, trying her damnedest to
smile. "Thanks for the flowers."

I pulled up a chair and sat close to the bed. She crossed her
legs under the sheet, but they so long, her feet still touched
the foot of the bed. Maybe the fact that she almost six feet tall
intimidates motherfuckers, and they don't know how to move
in on her. Naw. It's that attitude of hers. It's negative. But I
didn't come all the way up here to size her up, then cut her
down. "So how you doing?" I asked.

"I'm okay, really."

"Darlene, I'm not somebody in the street. Tell me what the
real deal is, would you? Talk to me."

"I already told you, Franklin."

I pushed my chair closer. "Look, Darlene, if something is bothering you, you gon' have to tell somebody, or it's just gon' keep doubling up on you till you explode. It ain't worth it—take it from me."

She got tears in her eyes. At least that was a sign of life.

"Come on, talk to me."

"I'm trying."

I figured she'd be better off if I didn't push, so I lit a cigarette, even though I knew I wasn't supposed to be smoking in here. She dropped her hands in her lap and sat up straight, looked straight ahead and then at me.

"You always have been able to read me, Franklin." Then she let out a long sigh, like she'd been jogging or something. "I just don't know what I'm doing anymore. I'm confused about everything. I don't know what to say. Or even where to start."

"It's okay, Sis," I said.

She reached over and got a Kleenex and started wiping her eyes and blowing her nose, but I guess them tears was on cruise control.

"I'm tired, Franklin. Haven't you ever just felt tired?"

"Hell, yeah, but not so tired I wanna die. Life is a bitch—let's face it—but for every five fucked-up things that happen, there's one good thing to make up for it. If you was to take a little time and check it out, there's always another door around the corner that you can probably turn the handle and get through to the outside. You get my drift?"

"Franklin, that's so idealistic it's not even funny. Have you started meditating with Zora, or what?"

"Fuck you, Darlene." I exhaled and realized what I just said. "I didn't mean that."

"How old am I?"

"Thirty-one," I said.

"And what have I done with these thirty-one years?"

I didn't really know what to say or how she wanted me to answer.

"Nothing," she said, before I had a chance to think of a convincing lie.

"That's bullshit, and you know it."

"I can't finish anything I start. Can't keep a job. Don't have any friends to speak of. I haven't had a boyfriend in over two years. Haven't been kissed, touched, fucked—or even noticed—since I don't know when. I can't even remember what having a date feels like. When my phone rings, it's usually a wrong number. I can't have kids, so I can't even look forward to that. When I think about my future, you want to know what I see, Franklin?"

"What?"

"Pitch black."

"C'mon, Darlene."

"You don't know what all of this feels like, pressing down on you day in and day out."

"I think I can imagine."

"No, you can't."

"So 'cause you going through a lonely and miserable phase, you think that's a reason to say fuck it and just give up?"

"Who said I was giving up?"

"Nobody."

"I just said I was tired."

"How tired?"

"I don't know, Franklin, I really don't know."

"Look. I ain't no woman, and I'm used to picking up the phone instead of waiting for it to ring, but one thing I do know is that this kind of shit passes. Ain't you into women's lib?"

"What's that got to do with anything?"

"Shit, take some initiative. All these women out here going after what they want, they ain't sitting around waiting for too much of nothing. You oughta try that shit. How long you gotta stay in here?"

"Two more days."

"Tell you what. I'll be back here to pick you up. You coming home with me and Zora for a few days. We can hang out. Talk shit. Play some Scrabble. Do some boogying. You need to relax, stop thinking so hard about everything, and stop taking everything so damn serious. I think what you really need to do is have some fun."

"Fun?"

"Yeah." I smashed my cigarette out and kicked it under her bed, then stood up. "Look, I just don't want nothing fucked up to happen to you—you got that?"

She looked up at me and smiled. On that note, I split.

Wasn't no sense in lying. It always backfire anyway, so I figured I'd tell Zora the truth. Jimmy was in jail, and he's my buddy and needs my help. With the new job and shit, she'd know I was good for it. Only she wasn't home when I got there. I had rehearsed this whole thing too. Wasn't no voice class tonight, and I wondered where she was. Just as I was about to reach into the refrigerator, I saw her note on the counter: "Spending the night at Marie's. She's in trouble. See you tomorrow after school. Call me at 555-9866 if you need me. Love, Z."

If I need you? It never fuckin' fails. Whenever I *need* you, your girlfriends beat me to the punch. Maybe I ain't the only one you fuckin'. I took my beans and rice out the refrigerator and put 'em on the stove. Then I caught myself. Don't do this, Frankie. Don't even take the shit out this far.

Jimmy was counting on me. But I wasn't about to call Zora. Not now. What was the point? While I ate, I was trying to think of who I could call that could lend me some money—tonight. Damn sure couldn't call Darlene. Shit. And I gotta be down at A Dream in the morning by seven. I was finished eating by the time I thought of Lucky. I dialed information and got the number of the nursing home where he worked. He was there.

"Hey, dude, what's up?" he asked.

"I'm in a jam, Luck. The ole lady ain't here, and a friend of mine—You remember Jimmy?"

"Yeah, what about him?"

"He's in jail on a bum rap, man, and needs two fifty to get out. I promised him he could count on me. I start a new job tomorrow—serious money involved—and was gon' borrow it from my woman, only she's at one of her lonely-ass girl-friends' house. You good for it until next week?"

"I wish I could help you, brother, but I'm thinking about changing my name, 'cause I ain't had a drop of luck in weeks. My shit is raggedy, and the lady I been staying with is ready to throw my ass out on the street. I know you ain't gon' believe this, but I'm trying to clean up my act. I'm thinking about going to GA. I'm sorry, man."

"What the fuck is GA?"

"Gamblers Anonymous."

"I hear you, brother. But look, stop by sometime, with a brand-new deck, motherfucker, 'cause I miss kicking your ass."

"Go to hell, Frankie. Say, you still with that fine school-teacher?"

"Yeah."

"Is she still as good to you as she is for you?"

"I'm beginning to wonder about that myself, man. Check you later."

I hung up and sat there on the stool, staring over in the corner at my wood. I couldn't think of nobody else to call. I wasn't sleepy and didn't feel like watching no TV. I pulled the stool over to my worktable and picked up the mallet and a gouge. But it wasn't what I needed. I felt like carving. I picked up my drawknife and pulled it through the wood. When I looked out the window, it was snowing again. I lit a cigarette and took a few strong drags, then put it in the ashtray. The Whispers tape I'd had on finished, and it was too damn quiet in here, so I got up and put on a old Earth, Wind & Fire. The first song that came on was "That's the Way of the World." I walked back over and put my hand on a curve of the wood. It was rough. My tool roll was on the shelf underneath, so I picked it up and spread it out, but I was still looking at the wrong tools. It's too soon to be whittling or even thinking about carving.

I got up and poured myself a drink. I don't know what I'm gon' tell Jimmy. I swallowed the shit, and it burned going down. By the time this tape ended, I had smoked at least ten cigarettes and polished off the pint. It was quiet as hell again. I didn't feel like putting in another tape. I wish Zora was here. It don't feel this quiet when she's here. I leaned back against the refrigerator and kept watching the snow through the window. I wondered if there was really anything I could do to help my sister. Her spirit been broken. And I ain't had much experience repairing 'em. I swear, I wanted to call Zora and tell her that I needed her here with me more than her silly girlfriend. Hell, I'm her man. But that woulda been tacky as hell. And hearing her voice and not being able to look at her wasn't gon' do me no good. I wanted to talk to somebody about everything, but where would I start? It didn't make no difference noway, 'cause I couldn't think of nobody. I lit another cigarette, exhaled, and one thing was real clear to me. I really ain't got no friends.

15

Who was I to think I could save somebody else's life? Shit, my own energy level has dropped so much that with the exception of loving Franklin—and sometimes that alone uses up most of it—everything else I do feels mechanical. From teaching to eating. I'm surprised he hasn't noticed—or at least he hasn't said anything—about these ten pounds I've put on. I don't know, maybe I'm just scared. Scared that I'm not as good a singer as I thought I was. Scared that even if I do make the demo, it'll go unnoticed or I'll get some mediocre contract that won't make any kind of splash. That I won't have affected anybody. And whose fault would that be? I think my whole problem is that I'm too self-centered. If I could just stop thinking so much about Zora and stop doubting myself so much, maybe I'd not only have more energy but have a little more compassion.

I've been trying to prove this to Franklin—that I really do care what happens to him—but I guess it shouldn't start and stop with him. Besides, Marie is my friend. And she's in bad shape. Nothing helps you to stop focusing on yourself better than when someone you care about needs you. So when she called, I was grateful for the diversion. She was hysterical and—as usual—drunk. When she'd come home this evening, she said, there was a seventy-two-hour eviction notice stuck on her door. "I don't know what I'm gonna do, Z. I can't handle this shit anymore. I swear to God, I need a fucking break. A woman goes through all kinds of changes trying to get one foot in the fucking door—Tell me something, do you think I'm funny?"

"Of course you're funny, Marie."

"Yeah, but the men in this business sure know how to cockblock. Let's face it: I'm not Richard Pryor or Bill Cosby, am I?"

"No, but you've got your *own* style, which is much better than being a carbon copy."

"Speaking of styles—Shit! Hold on, I've gotta—"

When she didn't come back to the phone after two or three minutes, I decided to get over there to make sure she was all right. Tonight, though, I was not about to play her little game with her. Yeah, I'd listen to her sad story, but as soon as she finished, I was going to cut the bullshit—meaning I wasn't going to feel sorry for her like I've done before. I was going to tell her exactly what I've been thinking for the last couple of years. If I had to stay there all night to ram it into her head until she agreed to get help, then that's what I was going to do. I packed something to wear to work, and was writing a note so Franklin wouldn't be worried, when the phone rang. It was my Daddy, making kissing sounds in my ears. He was home, and feeling like his old self again.

I stood in front of Marie's building. Thank God her lights were on. It must've started snowing while I was on the train. Boy, was it pretty. I hope Franklin doesn't get mad about my not being home when he gets there. I rang her buzzer, and she buzzed me in. Maybe she was expecting somebody else. I took the elevator to the fifth floor, and when I got off, I could see that her door was cracked open. I walked in but didn't see her. How could Marie live in such a tiny place all these years? I'd go crazy living in one room, that much I do know. Newspapers were strewn all over the floor, along with the clothes she'd probably worn the past week. And the smell. A combination of Russian vodka—which was sitting on the cocktail table, open—and packs and packs of cigarette smoke. I tried to open a window, but it was stuck.

"*I'll be right out!*" she yelled from the bathroom.

I didn't know where to sit, so I cleared a space from one of her director's chairs. When I heard the bathroom door open, I looked at Marie but didn't know what to say. The girl was butt naked.

"I knew you were coming. I've got ESP, Z, did you know that?"

"Why don't you have any clothes on?"

"It's hot in here. Why? Does it bother you?" She sashayed over to the couch and poured herself another drink.

"No, it doesn't bother me, Marie. But you look a little ridiculous, and it was really stupid of you to buzz me in without asking who it was and leaving your door open like that in your condition. Have you forgotten that this is New York City, or what?"

She flopped down on the couch, right on top of those dirty clothes. I got up and went over to her closet. At least twenty pairs of shoes fell out when I opened it. God, what a mess! No wonder she drinks. "Marie, where's your bathrobe?"

"I don't need it, and I don't want it!"

"Fine," I said, after I found it and threw it in her lap. Then I sat back down. "Okay. So. How much do you need to stop the eviction?"

"Do we have to talk about that now? I was just starting to feel good. How about some music?"

"Look, you're the one who got yourself into this mess, and

I came over here to see what I could do to help you get out of it. Do you have any coffee?"

"Coffee? Who needs coffee when I've got vodka? How stupid, Z. Come on, have a drink with me."

I refused to answer her and got up and walked over to the corner that was supposed to be the kitchen. Dirty dishes were piled in the sink, and roaches were crawling everywhere. I felt my skin itching but tried not to think about it. I found the Joy and decided to clean up some while I made a pot of coffee. "How much?" I asked again.

"Shit, Z. About eight hundred smackeroos." She started laughing after she said it.

"I can lend it to you," I said before I even realized it. This was part of my studio money, which Franklin had no idea I'd saved. I never spent that five hundred dollars my Daddy gave me, but I wasn't about to use it for a stupid car. For some reason, after looking at Marie, knowing how hard she's been trying to get work, it felt like this was worth it. I couldn't let her get thrown out, I just couldn't.

"You don't have to do this, Z. I don't know when I'll be able to pay you back. And hey, I'll be okay, really."

I turned the fire up under the water and put extra coffee inside the filter, because I knew it would take something close to espresso to sober her up. The sink was full of bubbles, and I figured I'd let some of the food soften up and soak off for a few minutes. I went and got my checkbook out of my purse. I was writing a check, when I looked over at her. She was spread-eagled on the couch, the bathrobe was on the floor, and she was massaging her breasts like she was in here by herself. "May I ask what you're doing?"

"What does it look like?"

I ripped the check out of the book and threw it on the cocktail table. I heard the water boiling and got up. "You need help, Marie. Have you ever thought of getting some? I mean, joining AA or something—anything?"

"Yeah, I've thought about it."

"So why don't you go?"

"I just haven't had time."

I forgot. You can't talk to a drunk when they're drunk. Nothing sinks in or adds up. So I figured I'd keep my little speech to myself. "Do you have any rubber gloves?"

"Try under the sink."

I was afraid to open the doors, but I did it anyway, and to my surprise, the gloves were actually visible. I poured water over the coffee and looked inside the cabinet for a cup. I decided it would be best to rinse it off first, which I did, then filled it and took the coffee over to her. At least she wasn't rubbing anything now, but she looked like she was in a trance or something. She was gazing up at the ceiling. "Drink this," I said.

"I don't want any coffee. I thought you were making it for yourself."

"Look, Marie, I don't know who you're trying to kid, but you need to think about cleaning up your act before taking it back onstage. Staying drunk won't get you out of this, and it won't help you get another gig, but you know that."

"You didn't come up here to lecture me, did you?"

"No," I said, and walked back over to the sink. I put the gloves on and stuck my hands into the scalding water, but I didn't feel its intensity.

"How is Mr. Franklin doing these days?"

"Fine," I said.

"Is he fucking you good?"

"Why?" I asked, as I put a plate into the dish rack. But Marie didn't answer me. I cleaned and rinsed another plate, and was about to put it into the rack, when I felt her standing behind me—but I didn't move. The next thing I knew, her hands had slid underneath my armpits and moved to my breasts. She couldn't possibly be this damn drunk. I dropped the plate in the sink and spun around, but Marie didn't budge. My face was against her neck—since she's so tall—and I pushed her. "Are you losing your fucking mind, or what, Marie?"

She was grinning. "Don't act so surprised, Zora."

"Surprised? I've known you for almost two years, we're supposed to be friends, I come all the way up here to help your drunk ass out of a fix—and you put your hands on my breasts and don't think I should act surprised?"

"I've been wanting to touch 'em for a long time."

"Marie, stop it. Right now! Go sit your drunk ass down and think about what you're saying and what you've just done. Come on." I really didn't want to touch her, but I shoved her out of my path anyway.

"I know exactly what I'm doing and saying."

"You need help, I swear, you need some damn help."

"I need you to put your arms around me, that's what I really need," she said, and started coming toward me again. That's when I hauled off and slapped the shit out of her so hard she fell on the floor.

"You're past drunk if you thought I'd let you get away with some shit like this."

She struggled to get up but didn't have the energy. Then she started crying, but I didn't feel sorry for her in the least. I reached for my coat and purse and walked over to the door.

"Don't go, Zora, please. I'm sorry."

"Sorry? Do you pull this shit on all your girlfriends?"

"No. Just you."

"Oh, am I supposed to feel privileged, or what?"

"I said I'm sorry."

"Why didn't you tell me you were like this, huh?"

"Because you never asked."

"Right. Look, you've got a choice, Marie. Give that money to your landlord, or fuck it up. But if you're out on the streets in three days, don't call me, okay?"

"I'm sorry, Zora. Where's the coffee? I'll drink it." She tried to get up again, but without any success.

"Look, I'm still your friend, and I'm going to pretend like this little scene here never even happened. But try to pull a stunt like this again, and this friend is history—you got that?"

All she could do was nod. I left her there on the floor.

The apartment was dark, and I couldn't wait to slide under the covers and feel Franklin. I needed him to put his arms around me and hold me all night. I couldn't believe what Marie had tried. All the way home, I kept thinking about her and how pitiful she was. Why couldn't I have read the signs? I wasn't about to tell Franklin what had happened, because he wouldn't empathize at all, with me or Marie—I know him.

I peeked inside the bedroom, and sure enough, he was lying there asleep. I took my clothes off as fast as I could and stood next to the bed and looked down at him. God, was he handsome, even in his sleep. I watched him breathe and could smell his body heat from here. My crotch started throbbing, and I was excited at the mere thought of what I was going to do. But I felt dirty, so I turned and walked to the bathroom and quietly closed the door.

I took a one-minute shower and was back before I knew it. Now my breasts were throbbing. All I wanted to do was feel his heartbeat against mine, smell him, rub my ears against his muscles, touch his tongue, and feel him inside me. I didn't care what shape it was in. When I crawled into bed and put my hand around it, it felt strong and firm. I stroked it, then climbed over his thighs—which seemed warmer than usual—and eased down on him. Shit, Marie doesn't know what she's missing.

My hips began to move without any help from me, and that's when I felt Franklin's hands begin to slide up and down my back.

"You came home?"

"I came home," I said.

He leaned forward and kissed me. When I closed my eyes, I could still see him. The hair on his chest brushed my nipples, and he pressed me so close that our heartbeats caught up with each other. I felt soft and electric, weak and strong. Then those wonderful hands of his cupped my hips. I was floating on him now, and when he looked at me as if he was asking me a question, the answer came all at once.

"Mornin'," I said, trying to wipe the grin off my face.

"So what was you on last night?"

I started laughing. "You."

"You ain't woke me up like that in a long time. I love it when you want it. You act hungry, and you know how to give it up when you hungry."

"Well, I'm glad you were here to wake up."

"Sometimes I wish I was a woman, you know that? You make me jealous as hell when you come three and four times in a row and shit."

"If I didn't have the right man, it wouldn't be possible. What are you doing up so early?"

"Starting a new job today."

"Really," was all I could say.

"Yeah. You seen my gray thermal undershirt?"

"Look in the third drawer, under the red one. You have time for coffee?"

"Yeah, but make it quick."

"Make it quick, make it quick. . . ."

I got up, and instead of going directly to the kitchen, I walked over and plastered a sloppy kiss on his lips—bad breath and all. "Go brush," he said, and started laughing. "So what's the deal with Marie?"

"She'll be okay, I guess. She's an alcoholic, you know."

"I think you told me that. So what happened? I thought you was staying the night. Did you miss your Daddy that much?"

"Yeah, I missed you. But to be honest, her place was a mess, she was sloppy drunk, and all she needed was some money."

"You lent her some money?"

"Yeah, I had to, or she would've been out on the street in three days. She got one of those seventy-two-hour eviction notices."

"Just how much did you lend her?"

"Why?"

"I'm just curious."

"Eight hundred."

"Eight hundred fuckin' dollars!"

"You don't have to scream, Franklin."

"You mean to tell me you lent a drunk almost a grand?"

"So what? She's my friend, and she needed my help."

"Yeah, but you couldn't help me when I needed it for a car."

"Franklin, the girl was getting evicted. Haven't you ever been in this kind of position?"

"Yeah. As a matter of fact, I'm in this position right now. Jimmy's in jail and needs to borrow two fifty and I was gon' ask if I could borrow it from you—but I guess that's dead."

"What's he in jail for?"

"What difference do it make? Why didn't Marie pay her rent?"

"I can still lend it to you, Franklin."

"Where you getting all this money? This ain't your studio money, I hope."

"Sort of."

"Look, *I* can pay your money back, but what about Marie?"

"It's a chance I'm taking."

"Yeah, right. When Reginald is ready, and you ain't got the cash, what you gon' do then?"

"I'll have it, don't worry."

"I just wanna make sure you get this demo tape, baby. You been working on this thing for a long time, and I don't wanna see everything go down the drain over some bullshit."

"It won't, but sometimes things take longer than you think. You should know that better than anybody, Franklin. And besides, that's what's wrong with the world now. We need to exercise more faith in folks, you know?"

"Well, with this new job, together our shit could really kick off. I was thinking, we should try to get outta here by spring—get a bigger place, you know?"

"Why don't we wait and see how long this one lasts?"

"I hear where you coming from, baby. And you right. I ain't even gon' tell you none of the details. I'ma let the paycheck and my union book tell the whole story."

"Franklin, do me a favor. Understand that it's not you I don't have the faith in. It's them. I've seen you get your hopes up so many times, and then the big letdown."

"I hear you. Oh, by the way, speaking of letdowns, would you mind if my sister spent a few days with us? She's sorta been under the weather."

"No, I don't mind. What's wrong with her?"

"I don't know. She's just been real depressed and shit, and I figured we could cheer her up. Will you help me, baby?"

"I'll try."

"Thanks," he said, and reached out to hug me. "I'm so glad you came home last night, 'cause I was beginning to wonder who you cared about more—me or your girlfriends."

"Franklin?"

"Yeah?"

"I love you."

"Tell me again."

"I love you!"

"Tell me that you'll never leave me."

"I'll never leave you."

"Even if our shit looks like it's going down the drain?"

"Even if our shit looks like it's going down the drain."

He threw me on the bed and squeezed me. "I love you too," he whispered. "Yes, I do, I do, I do."

16

Kendricks wasn't bullshitting. I got put on as a concrete worker, which means I'ma spend all damn day building forms, then holding 'em in place, then stripping concrete when it's finished. But it's okay. Hell, I'ma be making $13.96 an hour, and I'll be eligible to join Local 168 after working seven days, if the Italians don't have no objections. My foreman's name is Bill. After he saw how good I was—at least how hard I worked—right before quitting, he pulled me aside, away from the other brothers, and said, "Look, Frankie. You mind if I call you Frankie?"

"Naw. Everybody calls me Frankie."

"Well, if what you showed me today is any indication of how good a worker you are, you can look forward to staying on."

"Meaning what?"

"Meaning we've got five or six more jobs lined up after this one here, and if you don't fuck up, have your ass in here on time, do what's expected of you, and don't slack off none, you can go places. Be part of the crew—understand what I'm saying?"

"Yeah, I understand."

"And this is between me and you, not the world—got that?"

"I got it."

All he meant was I was probably the only black he was even thinking about keeping. These motherfuckers really know how to put you on the spot. But fuck it. I wanna know what it feels like to bring home a paycheck for a few months without no breaks.

As I walked over to the shanty to get out of these dirty clothes, I started wondering if there was any other way to determine your worth as a man besides how much money you make.

One thing I love about Zora is that she keeps her word. The two fifty was laying on the counter, just like she said it would be. That meant she had to get her clothes on, run to the cash machine, then back home, and then back to the subway to get to work. To tell the truth, I don't know if I'd go through these kinds of changes for any of her friends.

I got the creeps again, being in that jailhouse. No shit. It brought back memories like a motherfucker. I paid Jimmy's bail and was sitting there waiting for him. Paperwork is a bitch, but it don't take 'em but a minute to lock your ass up.

I was reading my horoscope in the *Daily News*, when Jimmy thumped me on the head.

"Thanks, brother. I owe you."

"What you drinking? I wanna know the truth about what went down, man." I folded my newspaper under my arm, and we left. We stopped in the first bar we came to on Atlantic Avenue.

"Remember Sheila, man?" Jimmy asked.

"I heard you mention her, but I wouldn't recognize her if I saw her."

"Anyway, she's Puerto Rican. I shoulda never wasted my time and money being around her, I swear. Hindsight is a bitch, ain't it, man?"

"Get to the fuckin' point, Jimmy."

"Wait a minute. Why ain't you drinking?"

" 'Cause I just started a new job today, and I don't need my head to be all fucked up, that's why."

"Well, anyway, we got a little set going at Sheila's pad, and there's this loud-ass knock on the door, man. Everybody run and shit, start flushing shit down the toilet and what have you, but turns out it ain't the man, it's some dude Sheila owe all this money to, and as usual, she ain't got it. He told Sheila she was dead, and this other dude, Jesús, was sitting in the kitchen, another PR, and he was so fucked up, all he heard was the word 'kill,' and he came out through the kitchen like Clint Eastwood and shit and shot the motherfucker."

"So I don't get it. Where do you come in?"

"It was my gun, motherfucker."

"What was he doing with your gun?"

"What difference do it make? The bottom line is, the cops show up out of no-fuckin'-where man—I mean, the mother-fucker wasn't even cold yet—and Jesús split out the kitchen window and leaves the gun and naturally they trace the shit to me. And here I stand."

"When's your court date?"

"Sometime the end of next month. You know any good lawyers, man?"

"Me? Be serious. But Zora might. As a matter of fact, one of her girlfriends is a lawyer. I'll ask her tonight. You wouldn't lie to me, would you, motherfucker?"

"I swear, Frankie, I ain't shot no-goddamn-body. I swear. I may do some illegal shit, but I ain't one for killing mother-fuckers. I keep my piece to stop these son-of-a-bitches from misusing me, that's all. It's more like insurance."

"So where you going from here?"

"I don't know, man, I don't know."

"I suppose you broke?"

"Do a Chinese have slanted eyes?"

I took a twenty outta my pocket and gave it to him.

"Thanks, Frankie. I think you about the longest friend I ever had, and considering what I'm into and you all straight and shit, I don't get it, man."

"That's what's wrong with the world now, dude. We need to have more faith in people, 'specially our friends."

"Well, I appreciate it. And I ain't gon' disappoint you, man. I'ma pay you back."

"Look, you ain't gon' be in the streets and shit tonight, are you, man?"

"Naw, naw, naw. I got lots of places I can go. I just ain't thought about it yet."

"Well, you got my number, and call me in a few days, and I'll find out what Zora can tell me, okay?"

"Bet."

We both got up and shook hands. I went left. Jimmy went right—only he was still standing at the curb by the time I turned the corner.

"Room 304, please."

"I'm sorry, sir, there's no one in that room."

"Check your records. There should be a Darlene Swift in that room. She ain't supposed to be released until tomorrow."

"She was released this morning, sir. Is there something else I can do for you?"

"No," I said, and hung up. Now, why the fuck she tell me that lie? I picked up the phone and dialed her number but didn't get no answer. That's when I decided to call out to my Moms and Pops' house. If she wasn't out there, I didn't know what I was gon' do. The girl is a schizoid, I swear to God.

"Nnhello."

Just for the hell of it, I figured I'd be nice and see what happened. "How you doing, Moms?"

"Franklin?"

"You got another son I don't know about?" I pretended like I was laughing, but she didn't think it was funny. Once a bitch, always a bitch.

"No, one is quite enough. You wanna talk to your Daddy? He's right here, hold on."

"Hello, son. How've you been?"

"Fine, Pops. You seen Darlene?"

"Yes, she's right upstairs. She just got out of the hospital, did you know that?"

"Yeah, I knew it." She's such a fucking traitor, I swear to God. Didn't want me to call 'em, but yet and still she picks up the goddamn phone and not only calls but goes out there.

"She's not feeling like herself lately and needs to get some rest and relax."

"And you think she's gon' be able to do that out there?"

"Your mother's doing everything she can to make her comfortable."

"Yeah, I bet."

"You want to talk to her, I can call her to the phone."

"Naw, don't bother. Just tell her I'm glad she's okay, and if she needs something, she got my number."

"I'll do that son. So tell me—"

"Later, Pops."

All three of 'em deserve each other, that's about all I can say.

When Zora walked in the door, I swooped her up in the air.

"What's going on, Franklin?"

"I'm in like Flynn, that's what."

"I'm glad to hear it."

"I been thinking."

"Again?"

"Seriously, baby. Let's start looking for another place, something where we can both stretch out and do our thang."

"But you just started working today, Franklin. Don't you think you're jumping the gun a little?"

"Naw. I'ma be honest with you, baby. I ain't never felt like this was *our* place. Your name is the only one on the lease, and if you wanna know the truth, I feel like I'm living with you but it's still *your* pad."

"You've never said anything like this to me before. Why now?"

I put her down. "Things is changing. Hell, I'ma be going to school, you gon' be singing and shit. This place is nice, but it's too small. I feel too damn self-conscious whenever I wanna do some woodworking. I would like to have a room where I can leave the sawdust on the floor without worrying about how the pad looks. Can you understand that?"

"Yeah, I can understand that."

"So I'll call up Vinney and tell him we'll be moving by the end of the month."

"Franklin, when is Darlene coming over?"

"She ain't. She changed her mind."

"Is she okay, or what?"

"Yeah, she's okay. She's out to my Moms and Pops'."

"So where should we look?"

"Park Slope, Cobble Hill, Boerum Hill—anywhere but around here. I'm about fuckin' sick of these changing neighborhoods. I wanna live on a street where ain't no damn scaffolds, for a change."

"We're going to have to pay for that, you know."

"So what? There's a price to pay for everything."

*　　*　　*

On payday my check was $569.32. I couldn't believe that shit, for only a week's work. But then again, I been working over- time every single night, and gon' keep on working it too. I mailed Pam a hundred, paid Zora her two fifty back, and put a hundred in the bank. I kept the rest in my pocket.

For some reason, I couldn't bring myself to ask Zora about that lawyer friend of hers. As much as I hated to admit it, Jimmy was on his own. I bailed his ass out, and besides, I wanna get away from all this riffraff. Maybe thisa teach his ass a lesson. That it's time to get away from all them motherfuck- ers he hang out with and turn his back on dealing dope. Wishful fuckin' thinking, I know.

During the second week at work, I noticed something funny. Out of the sixteen brothers that got put on, I didn't see but about four of us on the site now. I wanted to know what the deal was, so I went over to this dude Juney and asked him.

"You talking to the wrong man, brother. All I know is, I'm here, and come Friday, I get paid."

When I got home from work, I decided to call Kendricks to find out for myself.

"They didn't work out," he said.

"What you mean, they didn't work out?"

"The foreman said they wasn't doing the work, so he let 'em go."

"And you believed that shit?"

"Look, Frankie, if the man said they wasn't doing the work, what am I supposed to do about it?"

"Nothin'," I said, and hung up.

On payday, Kendricks showed up.

"You trying to get 'em back on, man?" I asked.

"No. I just had some loose ends to tie up."

They couldn'ta been that loose, 'cause they was tight enough to fit in that brown envelope he left with.

17

My instincts are telling me that this is going to be a mistake.

Franklin just had to open his big mouth and tell Vinney we'd be out of here by April 1, and Vinney rented the place just like that. So who was the one who had to rush around looking at places because Franklin hasn't had time? Me. It's been three and a half weeks now, and not only did he join the union but he's gone overtime-crazy. I know I shouldn't complain, because I've never seen him so confident and full of energy. But on the other hand, I can't help but worry about what's going to happen if he gets laid off. All this time I was under the impression that once he joined the union, all our problems would be over, but I found out that that's not the case. All the union does is guarantee health benefits and a retirement fund. He can still get laid off.

At any rate, I found something nice in Boerum Hill. It was two floors of a brownstone with two bathrooms—thank God—and cost $750 a month. "We can handle that," was what Franklin said when I told him. He didn't even want to see it. "You got good taste, so I know it's probably more than decent."

Our new landlord—a fat, white-haired Jewish man—didn't

even bother to check our references. He was more impressed by the fact that I'd been to college, was a teacher, and was able to bring him back a certified check for fifteen hundred dollars the same day. Although Franklin proudly forked up over a thousand, it broke my heart to withdraw all but two hundred of my studio money. I'm beginning to wonder if maybe it's not the time for me to pursue my singing, because all kinds of roadblocks keep popping up to prevent it. We'll see.

"What kind of work does your husband do?" Sol asked, as I signed my half of the lease.

"He's not my husband, but he works construction," I said.

His bushy white eyebrows rose up, and I wanted to tell him that this was the eighties, so don't act so damn surprised.

The day before we were moving in, Sol finally met Franklin. "You look like a football player," he said.

"I ain't never played no football," Franklin said, while he signed.

"Basketball?"

"I watch it on TV."

"There won't be any loud parties, hey?" he asked.

"Why?" Franklin asked.

"Oh, I was just wondering. Nothing wrong with a party every now and then."

Franklin slammed the front door and left Sol sitting on the steps, chewing his cigar and tapping his cane on the sidewalk.

When we got upstairs, he said, "I can already tell that I don't like that motherfucker."

We bought every kind of cleaner and disinfectant you could think of. I told Franklin that I couldn't put our food and stuff into this refrigerator or these cabinets until I knew they were my kind of clean. Sol had said there weren't any roaches, but I knew that was bullshit. This was New York, and as soon as I opened the cabinets, I saw their eggs in the corners.

There are two things I hate doing: cleaning the oven and cleaning the refrigerator. Franklin said he'd do it. I swear, I love that man. My job was the cabinets and bathroom. Before I got started, I decided to go to the corner and get us both something to eat. I was starving. When I came back, Franklin had all the burners sitting on the windowsill and the shelves from the refrigerator in the sink, and he was singing "Billie Jean" along with Michael Jackson, blasting on his boom box.

I sprayed some stuff inside the medicine cabinet and on all the bathroom tiles, then I sat down and ate my sandwich. The combination of Comet, Fantastik, and ammonia started making me feel dizzy and light-headed, so I walked back into the living room. It wasn't any better out there. My roach spray and Franklin's Easy-Off fumes felt like they were caught in my throat, and all of a sudden I thought I was about to throw up.

"Franklin, I've got to get out of here for a few minutes. We've got too much stuff going in here, and it's making me sick."

"Go on, baby. This shit is starting to get to me too."

I heard him opening the windows, but I still had to leave. I went downstairs and sat on the front steps. My head was spinning. The cool spring air helped, and after ten or fifteen minutes I felt better, so I went back upstairs. Now he had the boom box blasting on WBLS, and he was singing "Baby, Come to Me," along with Patti Austin and James Ingram. After another ten or fifteen minutes, I started feeling nauseous all over again.

"Franklin, I can't take this."

He turned the volume down. "What'd you say?"

"I said, these fumes are really getting to me."

"This shit *is* strong, ain't it? Look, I can do the rest of this shit. As long as I got some music, I can clean all day. Why don't you go on back over to the other place and finish up the rest of the packing."

He only had to tell me once.

It took us about two weeks to get the place in any kind of order, but finally we had everything where we wanted it and some space to ourselves.

Franklin was watching *60 Minutes*, I was cooking dinner, feeling great, and singing "Sweet Dreams" by the Eurythmics, and I happened to look up at the Sierra Club wilderness calendar. A herd of elephants were coming toward me, and that's when it hit me. I hadn't gotten my period yet. "Shit," I said.

"What's wrong, baby?" Franklin yelled from the living room. He was working on measurements for the wall unit he was going to build us.

"Nothing," I said, and flipped back to March. Three baby lions were squirming and fighting for their mother's nipples. This was impossible, I thought. Like always, I circle the day I'm due, which was supposed to be the twenty-eighth. I turned the calendar back to April and stared at the eleventh, which was today. That's when I remembered the night I'd come from Marie's and was so hot and bothered that I never got around to putting my gook in. How stupid. How fucking stupid.

"What's going on in April that you gotta be staring at it?" Franklin asked, walking up behind me.

"Franklin, my period's two weeks late."

"So I guess that means we having a baby. Good thing we moved, 'cause at least we got someplace to put it."

"Are you crazy?"

"What makes you think I'm crazy?"

"I can't have a baby right now."

"Why not?"

"First of all, we're not married and you're not even divorced; and second of all, I'm just on the verge of going into the studio; and . . . what would we do with a baby?"

"Love it."

"Love it?"

"I'll have my divorce before it's born. I promise."

He must be losing his fucking mind. "Franklin, let's be realistic."

"I am being realistic, baby. I want you to have my baby."

"Simple as that, right? Look. You never know how long a job is going to last, and we just moved into this expensive apartment. Just when things are starting to look good, you want me to up and have a baby?"

"You done already got rid of one of my babies. And I ain't letting you kill this one. But I guess now ain't the time to bring that up, is it?"

"Go ahead, lay a guilt trip on me."

"I'll work two jobs, if that's what it'll take, baby."

He looked so sincere I actually believed him and felt like saying okay. I wished it was that simple. What would I tell my Daddy? And Portia and Claudette and Marie? And the school? "First let me get the test and make sure. It could be that I'm just stressed out from moving and everything."

"You pregnant, baby," he said.

"What makes you so sure?"

"Remember when we was doing the cleaning in here?"

"Yeah."

"I knew you was pregnant then, and that's why I made you get out the house. I've told you and told you, baby: I know when your period is due. Anyway, I want a daughter."

"Franklin, stop it! I'd be crazy to have a baby now, and you know it."

"Okay. It's your body. Do whatever you want with it. Be selfish. Don't think about me. I mean, all I did was stick my dick in you, right? I ain't gotta have the baby, right? So whatever you decide to do is okay with me. Really." He looked at me while I checked the rice. "Really," he repeated. "I'm going to the store. You want anything?"

"Nothing I can think of."

I didn't put enough water in the rice, burned the lamb chops, scorched the zucchini, and put too much salt on the salad. When Franklin came back, he had already opened his fifth of Jack Daniel's. He hasn't had a drink since he started working.

"Dinner's ready," I said anyway.

"I ain't hungry," he said, and picked up his boom box, walking toward the door with it and his bottle. "I'll be back."

"Where you going?" I asked.

"Nowhere," he said, and slammed the door.

I heard the music outside the front window and walked over and looked out. He was sitting on the stoop, smoking a cigarette and sipping from the bottle, which was inside a brown paper bag. I swear I wasn't trying to hurt him. But this was my life too. I sat down on the couch. My picture of "Running Men" was crooked, so I got up to straighten it. All of a sudden, I wished I had some grass to water, or a mother to call.

Was I being too cold and selfish about this? The truth of the matter was, I was just scared. Confused. I want to do the right thing, but this isn't how I dreamed it. I've always wanted things to be right whenever I did have a baby. To be married to the man I loved. To have made my mark in the music industry. To . . .

I put my hand over my belly, which felt thick. There was some kind of throbbing going on, and it felt like my period. But I'd been feeling like this for at least a week now. Okay,

Zora. Calm down. Be realistic. You're just trying to find a way to justify not going through with it. You're good at justifying things you can't deal with, aren't you, Zora? But just remember, this would make four. Shut up. You've gotten off too easy as it is. Would you just shut the fuck up! You're a selfish little bitch—go ahead, admit it!

"You coming to bed, baby?" Franklin asked.

I didn't hear him come in the door, and I jumped. Somehow I was sitting at the dining room table, even though I don't remember walking over here or sitting down. He set the half-empty bottle down in front of me. "In a few minutes," I said.

I turned out all the lights and then took a fifteen-minute shower. I was hoping he'd be asleep by the time I got out, but he wasn't. I got under the covers, and he put his arms around me. I collapsed inside his arms and buried my face in his chest.

"Please don't kill my baby, Zora."

"Franklin, don't start, please. You're drunk."

"What makes you think I'm drunk?"

"You've drunk a pint of bourbon, that's why."

"I still don't want you to kill my baby."

"I don't want to *kill* your baby."

"Then why you doing this to me? I love you and want you to be my wife, and I want you to have my baby."

"Franklin, didn't you say earlier that it was my body?"

"I was lying. I mean, shit. You taking this fuckin' intellectual approach about a emotional situation. At first I figured I'd go along with it. But fuck it. I had to get high to tell you what I really felt. What you talking is a bunch of crap. It ain't never gon' be no perfect time to have no baby. But I do know one thing. That's my baby you carrying inside you, and I don't want you to kill it. And you may think I'm drunk, and maybe I am, but I swear to God, I'll get my divorce, and I'll bust my nuts and work three jobs if I have to to take care of y'all. Look at me, Zora."

God, he was making this so hard. I broke away and looked up at him. I loved him. I wanted to have his baby. But why now, God? That's all I wanted to know.

"You won't regret it, baby. I swear you won't."

I didn't want to say anything I might regret later, so I eased away from him and put my head on my pillow. "Can we just sleep on this?" I asked.

"Why not?"

In the morning, I felt his lips brush across mine, but I pretended to be asleep until I heard the front door close. When I got up, I saw a note Franklin had left me on the kitchen table. "I want us to be a family."

I called in sick.

I took the subway to the Women's Center in Manhattan and cried all the way there. After the test, I sat in the waiting room with twenty or thirty other women. Some of the men paced. This was the very same place where I'd had my last abortion. No matter how many times I blinked, I kept seeing that table, those white gowns, that IV bottle, and the plastic needle in my arm. My mouth was beginning to taste like gas, and I heard somebody say, "Start counting backward from a hundred." "I can't," I said out loud, and a few people looked at me. I cannot climb up on one of those tables again. I had promised myself that that would be the last time. Besides, how many times can you do it without feeling guilty? Once. Twice. Three or four times? Isn't it about time, Zora, to grow up and take responsibility for your actions?

"Zora Banks," a voice called.

I jumped up. My heart was racing, and the next thing I knew, I was sitting in a little beige room. The young blond woman was all in white, and in her hands was a little white dial.

"Have a seat."

I sat down, I think. I looked around the room. There were pictures of little unborn babies at different stages, and a plastic sculpture of a fetus.

"How do you feel?" she asked me.

"Nervous."

"Well, I hope I've got good news for you," she said, turning the arrow on the little dial. "Your baby—if you choose to have it—will be born right around New Year's."

Be born. Be born. Your baby will be born. I couldn't say anything. I was trying hard not to cry, and she looked over at me real nice and put her hands on top of mine.

"You're not happy about this, honey?"

"Did you say *my* baby will be *born* around New Year's?"

"If everything is accurate, you're about six weeks pregnant, which gives you a delivery date of January first."

Delivery date. Deliver me. Six weeks. Pregnant. Me. So it was real. Me. Six weeks pregnant. And with Franklin's baby.

"Do you need some time to think about this?"

Something weird started happening. My heart was beginning to feel lighter and lighter. Instead of my feeling burdened by the whole notion of giving birth to a child by a man I loved, all of a sudden it made perfect sense. It was *time* for me to do this, and regardless of what the outcome, I was going to do it. I looked at the embryos on the wall and tried to imagine what mine looked like. I was going to have a baby. For the first time in a long, long time, it felt like I was actually going to finish something I had started and would be able to see tangible results.

"Ms. Banks, are you all right? Do you need some time to think about this?"

"No," I said, feeling a grin emerge on my face. I stood up and looked down at her.

"Well, you're smiling," she said.

"It looks like I'm going to be a mother," I said.

I walked forty blocks before I realized I'd walked at all. Just like that, I had made a decision to bring a life into the world. Me. A mother. My whole life was about to change, by one decision. I stopped at Forty-eighth and Madison and went into a Japanese restaurant. I ate twenty dollars' worth of sushi. There are plenty of women who sing and have children, I thought. Daddy'll be happy, once Franklin and I are married. Me married. By the time I paid the check, I felt as if someone had shot me up with laughing gas.

Once I got outside, it seemed like everything that was green was now a bright metallic green. I could actually smell the tiny trees, diamonds bounced up from the sidewalk, people smiled at me, and I just knew that everybody could tell I was going to be a mother. When I got home, I called my neurologist and told him I was pregnant and that I hadn't been on any medication in over four years. I didn't mention the few pills I'd taken a while back; I assumed they wouldn't make a difference, because the last time I went to take one, I noticed they had expired the year before. I told him I'd had only one seizure, after having drunk some alcohol, and he said that there was no way he could predict what was going to happen. Since my disorder wasn't inherited and because I wasn't on any medication, he thought it might be in my best interest to start taking it again. Fuck him, I thought. My chances of having a normal baby and even a normal pregnancy were a helluva lot higher without phenobarbital flowing through my bloodstream and into my baby. He suggested that throughout the pregnancy my doctor monitor my blood pressure. That I'd see to.

*   *   *

The rest of the day dragged on and on. Don't work any over-time today, Franklin, please. He walked in the door early—it was four o'clock.

"Hi," he said.

"Hi," I said back. Then I smiled at him.

He smiled and his dimples dug into his cheeks. Not saying a word, he walked over and put his hand on my belly and made circles. Then he put his arms around me and pulled me in. His warm lips pressed against my cheek, and then he pulled away and stroked my hair. His eyes were glassy, but he wasn't crying. He bent his head down and put his lips against my ear. "Thank you," he whispered. "Thank you."

18

Zora's getting fat and lazy. Sickening, really. Every time I look up, she pulling up her blouse, staring at her stomach in the mirror. She's taking this baby shit a little too far, if you ask me. Her titties is even juicier now, only she can't stand for me to touch 'em. I got to beg for the pussy too, 'cause if she ain't too tired to participate, she "just don't feel anything down there now." I swear to God, you'd think she was the first woman on earth to ever be pregnant. I'm just glad the whole thing don't take no longer than nine months; we got five more to go.

I already warned her: "If you turn into blubber after the kid is born, we gon' have problems." So far, all she been craving is fruit salad, but like they say, it ain't over till the fat lady sing. The thing I do like is how much she starting to look like a peach. What they say about pregnant women is true, I guess, 'cause Zora is definitely glowing.

She ain't said another word to me about the divorce except, "If we aren't married by the time the baby gets here, we're going to have even bigger problems. But I'm not going to mention it again." I took this as a threat. The real deal is, she just worried about what the fuck everybody gon' think. She must not realize that this is the eighties, and don't nobody really give a fuck. All the movie stars is having babies and they ain't got no husband, but she says, "I'm not a movie star." And all I said was, "Yes, you are, but don't worry about it, baby."

She done even put her singing on hold, 'cause she said she's too worn out after she get outta school to catch the train all the way to Manhattan. Hell, that was one night a week I could count on being by myself. And I miss it.

"Let's do something," she said. We was playing Scrabble, and she was kicking my ass for a change.

"Like what?" I asked.

"Like go to the jazz festival in Saratoga. Spend the weekend. We haven't done anything this whole summer, Franklin."

"When is it?"

"In two weeks."

"Get the tickets, then."

"Are you sure you'd like to go?"

"Yeah. Who's gon' be there?"

"Chaka Khan, Gladys, B. B. King, Ray Charles, Pat Metheny, and I forget who else, but it's a great lineup."

"How much will the whole thing cost?"

"I don't know, but what difference does it make?"

"I told you I'm looking for a car."

"Here we go again with this car business."

"Okay. So when your ass go in labor, you want me to call a cab, or we can catch the subway—is that how you wanna get to the hospital?"

"No."

"Okay, then. It's your turn, baby."

"We don't have to go, Franklin."

"I wanna go. And you right, we ain't done nothing exciting all summer, and we could stand to break this shit up."

"Are you bored?"

"Did I say I was bored?"

"No, but the tone of your voice is hinting at it."

"I could just use some pussy tonight, if you wanna know the truth."

"Okay."

"I don't wanna play no more. You won. Come on."

"Franklin!"

I was already getting up. Shit. "What?"

"Nothing," she said, and started putting away the letters.

I was on top of the covers, waiting for her to do her shit. I ain't never seen a woman got to go through so much preparation just to give her man some pussy. But I waited.

"Promise you won't pull too hard or bite my nipples."

"I promise."

"And you won't jab me."

One more word, and Tarzan was gon' deflate. "Get in the bed, Zora."

She got in and put her arms around me. I rolled over on top of her.

"Franklin, you're hurting my stomach. Move up some."

"I'm sorry, baby," I said, and put all my weight on my palms and pressed 'em against the sheet. I tried to put it in.

"Ouch, Franklin. "

"What's wrong?"

"I'm not even ready for this," she said.

"You ain't never ready. Just be quiet for a minute, would you?"

I licked my fingers and then rubbed them against her. She was still dry as hell when I tried it again, so I got up and went to get the Vaseline and smeared that all over it and Tarzan. This time, it slid right in. She was hugging Tarzan tight, but she wasn't helping none. So I just took off.

Ten minutes later, I rolled off of her.

"Did you feel anything this time?" I asked.

"You don't wanna know," she said.

She turned her back to me, and that's when I realized she had been crying, 'cause my neck was wet and I wasn't doing no sweating.

"What's wrong, baby?"

"What makes you think something is wrong?" She still wouldn't turn toward me.

"You crying?"

"No, I'm not crying. Don't be ridiculous."

"Yes, you are. Turn around here." I reached to turn her toward me, and any fool could see them big crocodiles, even in the dark.

"Talk to me, Zora. What's wrong?"

"I feel like a piece of meat."

"Why?"

"Because for the past month all you've been doing is asking me to fuck you, and then when I do you just hop on top of me and bang me for a few minutes and then roll off, just like you did tonight."

"But you said you wasn't getting nothin' out of it, so I was trying to spare you."

"Franklin, you don't kiss me or touch me like you used to do. Did it ever occur to you that that might help?"

"Shit, every time I put my hands somewhere, you say it hurts. What the fuck am I supposed to do?"

"Hold me sometimes."

I reached over and put my arms around her. She was asleep before I knew it. I sat up and lit a cigarette and looked down at her. Is this what I gotta look forward to for the next five months?

19

"**Y**ou're what?"

"You heard me—pregnant."

"Damn," Portia said. "And you gon' have it and shit?"

"I'm four and a half months—I guess so."

"So when you and Franklin getting married?"

"Before it gets here."

"Well, girlfriend, I think we're on the same wavelength."

"What do you mean by that?"

"When's your due date?" she asked.

"January first—can you believe it?"

"Mine is December eighth."

"What did you just say?"

"I said, 'Mine is December eighth.' "

"Wait a minute. Portia?"

"I'm here." She was laughing.

"I know damn well you're not telling me you're pregnant too."

"Yes, I am."

"I can't believe this shit. You, Portia? Miss Never-settle-down herself?"

"Who said I was settling down?"

"Whose is it?"

"Arthur's."

"But he's married."

"So what? So is Franklin." I know she didn't mean to, but it felt like she just slapped me in the face.

"Don't misunderstand me, Portia. But I mean, tell me the particulars, girl. Franklin's in the process of getting his divorce. What're you and Arthur gonna do?"

"I don't want him to get a divorce."

"Are you crazy?"

"No. I don't love him. When I missed my period, I just said fuck it. This time out, I'm going through with it."

"Does he know?"

"Hell, yeah, and he's excited as hell. His wife knows too. Simple bitch. He wants to get a divorce and shit, but I told him to keep his little ass right where he is."

"But what and how . . ."

"Look, girlfriend. I ain't gon' be the first woman out here by myself with a child. Arthur's loaded. He's already giving me money. I could quit my job right now if I wanted to. This baby is already paid for; and he's starting to get on my nerves. I told you he was a fool, didn't I?"

"So why do you want to have his baby?"

"Because I'm tired, girlfriend."

"Tired of what?"

"Of running the streets, of getting high, or not doing anything constructive with my life. This is important."

"I don't believe this shit."

"Believe it, girlfriend. And believe that I'm getting the fuck outta New York too."

"And going where?"

"Back to Nashville."

"Get the hell outta here, Portia. Why? And when?"

"Because I wouldn't raise a dog here, that's why. I'm leaving before Labor Day, that much I do know."

"Did you tell your parents already?"

"Yeah."

"And?"

"They're happy for me. Big Daddy was ready to take the train up here and kill, until I set him straight. I told him this was my decision, that I wasn't no damn baby, I was just having one. Simple as that. My Mama been *here* herself, so she just told me to come on home, where I'd be safe."

"I can't believe this. Portia McDonald pregnant?"

"Shit, look at you."

"I haven't told anyone except the school. As a matter of fact, I lied, Portia."

"To who about what?"

"The school. I told them I got married over the Fourth of July."

"Why? You ain't gotta lie about no shit like that. Girl, this is the twentieth century. If you wanna have a baby with no husband, that's your fuckin' business. They can't fire you."

"I know that. It's just kind of embarrassing. I never planned on having a baby without being married, you know."

"Shit, I never planned on having a baby, period," she said.

"Why didn't you tell me sooner? That's what I wanna know."

" 'Cause I wanted to make sure it was too late to change my mind. Friends have a way of influencing you, and I didn't wanna be influenced. I wanted to make a decision like this all by myself for a change."

I swear, this did not sound like the Portia I knew. But when she said, "Look, girlfriend, let's get together and compare guts," I knew it was her.

* * *

There are some things in life you dread having to do. Facing opposition is one. Or your Daddy. I couldn't figure out how to tell him over the phone, and I decided to just wait. I couldn't lie to him about being married. That would be like asking God for something I didn't deserve or need, so I decided to wait.

Franklin was working overtime, as usual, and for some reason I found myself sitting in my music room in front of the piano. I've missed my voice classes, even though I've pretended I haven't. What's funny is that since I've been pregnant, it seems like I feel everything two or three times as much. I've written at least five good songs in my first trimester alone, and I can't lie: Writing 'em felt almost as good as singing 'em.

I pushed Play on the tape.

> I've been out on this cliff before
> with men who swore they could
> teach me how to fly
> so I jumped off
> while they peeked over
> and watched me hit
> the bottom from way up high.

Was that really me, sounding like Odetta? I could feel the tears welling up in my eyes. "Don't," I said aloud, but my heart just refused to cooperate. To tell the truth, I didn't know why I was crying. I turned off the tape and sat there on the bench. Then the weirdest thing happened. I felt something flutter in my stomach. I was trying to figure out what I'd eaten that might've caused this, but before I could think about it, it happened again. I put my hand over my stomach and waited. I felt it move again. At that moment, two things occurred at once. Number one was that there was something coming to life inside me. And number two, I was scared as hell.

20

I took the day off, went out, and bought myself a pair of black linen pants and a good white shirt to wear to the concert. I trimmed my mustache and shaved extra close and wore Zora's favorite cologne. Even with her little round belly, she still looks pretty. Since I can finally see the evidence of my work, it's beginning to sink in that I'm gon' be a daddy again. Ain't no sense in me lying—I didn't really plan on having no more kids, but I love Zora and I wanna keep her. I guess this was one way of guaranteeing it.

I had to help her up the bus steps. She wobbled down the aisle and took a seat by the window, then I sat down. As usual, my legs wouldn't fit, so I stuck my knees out in the aisle. They don't make seats on buses and shit for tall people. All the motherfuckers that designed public transportation musta been under six feet.

But we was on our way.

For the first time since we been together, I was paying for *everything*—the concert, the hotel, food, even this bus ride—and it felt good. Zora fell asleep on my shoulder, and for two of the four hours' worth of the ride, she squeezed my hand in her hand. Even though she ain't giving up the pussy like she used to, I still ain't never been with a woman as sensuous as her. I squeezed her hand back and stroked her hair until the bus pulled into this rinky-dink station. "We here, baby," I said. And she sprung up.

"Doesn't look like it," she said, and rubbed her eyes.

The first thing we did was get a newspaper to find a place to stay. Everywhere Zora had called before we got up here was booked. The best places was in town. But we took our chances. To make a long story short, we ended up in this dumpy place that looked like the Bates Motel. We took a cab, and on the way out there, Zora was reminiscing out loud and shit, 'cause she been up here before, with some dude named Dillon, which I damn sure didn't wanna hear about. She kept pointing to restaurants she had ate at, stores she had spent boo-koo cash in, and showed me this dark-ass road that led to some famous artist colony. She told me about the natural hot springs, which she couldn't even think about getting in in her condition, but I told her I was gon' check it out.

Every motel we passed had the No Vacancy lights on. Half of New York City was up here. But when we finally saw a vacancy sign, the cab pulled in. The man behind the desk even looked weird, and I almost called him Norman. Zora thumped me on my back when I started laughing, and the old man starting laughing too. He showed us the pool first, then opened our door. I could smell mildew, but I didn't say nothing. But for forty-seven dollars a night? There was two lumpy double beds in the room. The mirror was so old it was foggy, and I was surprised to see the TV was color. And I ain't never seen a bathtub as small as this one. It was only half a one, but deep enough to soak—if you was short. Zora turned on the air conditioner, and it sounded like a truck was going through the damn room. And since we was off the side of some dark-ass road, about four miles from town and civilization, once we got settled, it wasn't like we could walk down Atlantic Avenue and shit. We was in for the night. It's a good thing I brought my own bottle.

I ain't heard birds tweeting and crickets chirping since I was down South. One thing I do know—ain't no way in hell you could pay me to live where there ain't no streetlights or people hanging out on a corner. What you supposed to do if you run outta cigarettes? The only thing we would probably find out in this motherfucker would be snakes and horses. But I ain't complaining, 'cause this is really the first vacation I ever took in my life. The best part about it is I'm with the woman I love—even though she ain't fuckin'.

Zora beat me up. I watched her putting on her makeup in the bathroom. When she backed up some, I saw that her ass was almost as wide as the whole door. Her titties looked like two oversized coconuts and those little bird legs didn't look like they could stand all hundred and sixty-five pounds. "Come here, baby," I said. She jumped, 'cause she thought I was asleep.

"Franklin, don't do that, please. You scared the shit out of me."

"Why you up so early?"

"I'm hungry."

"So what else is new?"

"Do you realize it's almost ten o'clock?"

"Get the fuck outta here. We slept that long?"

"I guess we needed it."

I got up out the bed. I was gon' try to hug her, but that belly of hers stopped me from getting as close as I wanted to, so I just patted it. "How's my daughter doing?"

"You don't know it's a girl, and what if it's a boy?"

"I want a daughter."

"Anyway, it's moving for real now, Franklin. This morning, unless I'm crazy, I saw a lump rise in my stomach."

"Why didn't you let me see it?"

"Because I didn't want to wake you up."

"Well, next time wake me up. You think you gon' be able to do all this walking we in for today?"

"I'm just pregnant, Franklin, not handicapped."

Coulda had me fooled. But I wasn't about to say no shit like that. She'd be in tears. I jumped in the shower and started thinking about the lineup tonight. Ray Charles and B.B. King. Shit. And Gladys and Steely Dan—which is who Zora loves. She got at least twenty albums by white people, more than any black person I know—and two by Joni Mitchell, who looks like a transvestite if you ask me, and Fleetwood Mac, which she plays to death. I can't say I hate white-boy music, but I swear to God, what makes me sick to my stomach—no, mad as hell—is the fact that most of 'em imitate black singers and musicians, but the white boys make all the fuckin' money. And some of 'em don't even sound that damn good. Steely Dan and Pat Metheny—I'll give credit where credit is due.

"I *would* like to get some sun today," I heard her say. Figures. She worse than white girls when it comes to laying out in that hot-ass sun, watching herself turn colors. But I didn't say nothin'. I got out, dried off, and put on a pair of slacks and a shirt.

"I wish you would wear shorts once in a while, Franklin. As hot as it is outside, and you're wearing long pants."

"I told you faggots wear shorts. I don't own a pair and don't intend to."

"Some notions you just take too far, I swear. But if you want to burn up, fine with me. And you've got such pretty legs."

"I wish I could give you a few inches." I started laughing,

but she didn't. "I didn't mean that, baby. Your legs is fine just the way they are."

Since there wasn't no phone in the room, I went to call a cab. He said he'd be here in six minutes. So we sat outside on the lounge chairs by the pool and waited. Norman waved to us. Me and Zora both started laughing and waved back.

"Thank you for bringing me up here for the weekend, Franklin," she said, outta nowhere. It was nice to hear, and nice to know she appreciated it.

"You're welcome, baby. We gon' do more of this kinda stuff too. I promise."

Then we just sat there like dummies, looking around at all the greenery. Trees was everywhere. And flowers too. It was pretty, and we could see the mountains and shit. I know one thing—it smelled a helluva lot fresher out here than it did in that fifty-dollar room.

We ate breakfast at this pretty restaurant that Zora picked out. The food was overpriced, but it was good. It was hot as hell up here, and the white people looked miserable. We passed this miniature-golf place, and I wanted to check it out, but Zora said she didn't want to. It was too hot to be doing that kind of stuff, so we took a cab straight back to the Bates. Zora got in a big bathing suit, which was kinda ridiculous, and dived in the water like a damn fool. I got a Heineken out the cooler I'd bought in town and came out and joined her. She was moving through the water like a baby whale, and I just watched. I ain't that good a swimmer and didn't feel like embarrassing myself, so I sat under one of them umbrellas and drank beer.

Then here come this white dude. He sat right down beside me. He musta been in his early thirties, looked like Robin Williams, and was either a alcoholic or sunburned.

"Hi," he said.

"How you doing," I said.

"What does this place remind you of?" he asked.

"The Bates Motel."

He started laughing. "That's exactly what I told my wife. You guys here for the concert?"

"Yeah."

"We are too. From Long Island. We just had our second kid three months ago, and I swear to God, if we spent one more weekend behind closed doors, I was gonna freak out."

"I know what you mean. Sometimes you just gotta get out the city to regroup, do it to the ole lady in a different bed."

He started laughing. I couldn't believe I was talking to this white dude all friendly and shit. The bottom line was, when you got right down to it, we was both men.

"Did you guys drive up here?"

"No," I said.

"Well, look. We're going to the same place; doesn't make any sense to take a cab. We're in room sixteen. We wanna get there around seven, so give a knock if you want a lift."

"I'll do that. First I gotta see what the ole lady wants to do for dinner."

He threw his hands up in the air and then dived in the water. Zora was drying off and rubbing suntan lotion on her legs. I musta drank four beers, and the heat was getting to me, so I went to lay down for what I thought was a hot minute. When I felt Zora ease next to me and put her arms around me, my first thought was, maybe she felt like it. So I kissed her a few times and then I tried, but some of the weirdest shit happened. Not only did she not resist, but Tarzan wouldn't cooperate.

"What's wrong?" she asked.

"I don't know. Maybe I just had too many beers." I waited ten minutes and tried it again. Dead. I think I know what the problem is. It's that big belly. It's working against me. But I didn't say nothing to that effect, 'cause that would just hurt her feelings. "You hungry?"

"A little. I ate one of the mangoes from the cooler."

"What time is it?"

"Quarter to four. Let's shower and go into town and walk around, eat, then walk to the concert."

"Okay, but that white guy asked if we wanted a ride."

"Well?"

"I don't feel like getting all friendly. I came up here so me and you could be by ourself. Besides, we'll never be able to get rid of him."

"If he was black you wouldn't be saying this, would you?"

"I don't know." I jumped up and took my shower and got dressed. Then I went and knocked on his door and told him thanks but no thanks. Told him Zora was starving right now, and he understood. Told him we might check him out tomorrow.

Zora wore this white dress and looked like a black angel. Big belly and all. The cab was there in no time. When we cruised into town, the streets was packed. We got out in front of this knickknack store, and for the next hour and a half, I was bored to death. Zora had to walk into every single store we passed. Finally, I said, "Look, we ain't gotta see everything that's for sale, do we?"

"Franklin, don't be such a drag. How often do we get to see this kind of stuff? Relax."

She just had to whip out one of her credit cards. To make me look like I couldn't afford to buy what she wanted. She already starting to call all the shots, and it ain't like I don't want her to have fun, but damn, I feel like her help, 'cause all I'm doing is carrying her bags. This weekend ain't starting out on a good note, I can see that already. She just bought some

kinda picture for ninety fuckin' dollars. I guess it was pretty—
most of the shit she usually buys is—but I didn't even wanna
look at it. Since we wasn't going straight back, the lady said
she'd hold it there until tomorrow.

"I want to get some T-shirts," she said, when we walked in
front of a T-shirt store. At least it was something I use.

I followed her in, just like a damn kid, and when she spotted this yellow one with a red and orange horse on the front
that said "Saratoga Springs" on top, she turned to me.

"What do you think?"

"What difference do it make?"

"Franklin?" she said, putting her hands on her hips.

"Get it."

When I heard her ask for a extra-large for me and a
medium, I cleared my throat. "When you think you gon' fit
into that?"

"After the baby, when do you think?"

"Yeah, right." I wanted to say, Keep dreaming, but I
didn't.

"I'm about starving now, are you?" she asked, after we got
outside.

"There's a store we passed that had some wood sculpture in
the window, and I wanna go back and check it out."

"Right now?"

"Why not now?" I asked.

"Franklin, I'm hungry. Why didn't you say something when
you first saw it?"

"Forget it," I said.

"No. Come on."

"I said forget it. What you got a taste for?"

"Seafood," she said.

We walked down a few doors and saw this place called Vi-
vian's, and they had a special on prime rib. I always wanted to

try that, so I said, "Let's go in here." To my surprise, she didn't object. There was stained glass everywhere, and plants hanging from the ceiling, and everything was made outta wood. Once we was seated, the waitress asked if we wanted anything from the bar. Zora said no. I asked for a double Jack. She just gave me this look.

"Why you looking at me like that?"

"I was just thinking that if it's a boy and he looks like you, how handsome he'll be."

"And if she's a girl and looks like me, then what?" My tone was nasty, even though I was trying hard not to sound like it.

"Franklin, why are you getting so cynical all of a sudden?"

"Am I? I didn't mean to sound cynical, baby. You right, I'm just a little hyped up, I guess."

"Don't you think we should start thinking about names?"

The waitress came back with my drink and took our order. I got the prime rib and Zora ordered lobster. Just 'cause I told her she could eat anything she wanted to this weekend, she had to get the most expensive thing on the damn menu. "Yeah, but not today."

"Franklin, are you getting a bug up your ass about something?"

I threw my hands up in the air. "Diana if it's a girl, and you name it if it's a boy."

"Diana? Are you serious? Why not Pollyanna?"

"Look. You asked, so I told you. I like that name and always have."

"Well, I don't like it. I couldn't even imagine looking at a baby of mine and saying, 'Hi, Diana.' "

"Fuck it, then, Zora. If you can think of one better, lay it on me and I'll tell you what I think. I'm sure you'll have it all figured out."

"What's that supposed to mean?"

"Nothing," I said. "Nothing."

By the time the food got there, I had had two more drinks. We ate with hardly no conversation between bites. The prime rib was dynamite, and even though I can put it away, I couldn't finish all this meat. I knew Zora was gon' eat every drop of hers, which she did, and didn't even offer me none. I got a doggie bag and paid the check, which came close to sixty fucking dollars. I couldn't help but thinking how much that would buy at the grocery store. Damn. This weekend look like it's gon' cost me close to three hundred bucks. I see why people don't take vacations. All I'm gon' have to show for it is a damn T-shirt when it coulda been my down payment on a ride.

When we got outside, Zora looked at me. "You look awful handsome tonight, Franklin."

"Thank you, baby," I said, trying to lighten things up. "You got the tickets?"

"I thought you had 'em."

"They was on the dresser, and I thought you put 'em in your purse. Goddamn."

"Franklin, it's not that big of a deal. We'll just take a taxi back and pick 'em up. Simple as that."

"That's six dollars one way. Never mind. You got a dime on you?"

She gave me a dime, and I called the taxi. It was there in less than a minute. We rode out toward the Bates, and Zora just looked out the window. "These mountains are beautiful, aren't they, Franklin?"

"What mountains?"

When we got to the Bates, I ran in for the tickets and decided to bring my fifth with me. I was gon' need something, and I swear to God, I didn't know why I was jumping on Zora's case. I need some pussy, that's probably what the real

deal is. I'ma get me some tonight too. I don't care how tired
she is. The only reason Tarzan probably wouldn't stand up
earlier is 'cause she was the one who initiated it. Not that I
don't like her to be the aggressor, but she always likes to do it
in the daytime. My jones comes down at night.

We could hear music before we even got there. Hundreds
of people was walking with blankets and coolers. I was feeling
pretty mellow and ready to party now. We started walking up a
hill, and Zora was losing her breath. Finally, something she
couldn't do.

"Franklin, I need to stop for a minute. And I think my feet
are swelling too," she said.

"Aw, come on. We almost there."

I watched her struggle.

At least it wouldn't be dark until about nine, and since
most of the people was sitting on the grass behind the arena,
which was outside, with just a covering on it—that's where our
seats was—we decided to sit out there with the rest of the white
folks for a while. We didn't bring no blanket, but Zora wasn't
thinking about that white dress and flopped her fat ass on
down. I whipped out my bottle.

"Franklin, do you have to?"

"Look, would you get off my case."

She turned away from me, like she was trying to act like we
wasn't together. Fuck her. I was glad it was summertime,
'cause you get to see all the ass you want to. I looked around
at Zora and that belly. All of a sudden, I wished she wasn't
pregnant. All of a sudden, I realized that I wasn't married to
this woman, that here she was carrying my baby, another
woman controlling my destiny—again—and I was trying to figure out how I talked her into doing this shit in the first place.
I didn't want no more kids. She tricked me into this shit. She
knew I wasn't gon' tell her to get rid of it. Here I'm thinking

I can keep her, and I betcha she had this shit all planned. "I know one thing," I said. "These young girls is getting finer by the year." I didn't mean to say it out loud.

."Then why don't you go get yourself one?" she said.

I got up, threw her her ticket, and started cruising.

Not really. What I did was I walked around and polished off the most of my bottle. I don't even know why I said that shit. I got away from the crowd and ended up where the mineral baths was. They had these antique benches lined up, and I sat down on one. I lit a cigarette and looked out toward the mountains. Everything was happening too fast. Me and Zora. This baby.

After a while, I figured maybe she might think something weird happened to me. I fumbled in my pants pocket for my ticket and walked back. I went to the aisle where the usher was, so he could show me where our seats was. I could barely see Gladys Knight, but I heard her singing "Save the Overtime for Me." The man walked me to the right row. "Are you all right, sir?" he asked. I guess it was obvious that I was fucked up, but I said, "Don't I look all right?" and he didn't say nothin' except "Yes, sir."

Something wasn't right. As I got closer to our seats, I didn't see her. 'Cause she wasn't there. Everybody in the row had to stand up so I could get past 'em, and now they had to stand back up, 'cause I wanted to know where the fuck she was, find out what kind of game she was playing. I got back outside and looked on the grass, which now I couldn't hardly see shit, 'cause it was dark. Where the fuck was she? She probably wanted to make me look like a chump all along. Probably had this shit planned too. Couldn't stop by the store I wanted to go in. Didn't ask if it was something special I wanted to do. And the one thing I suggested, golf, she said it was too hot, yet she could lay out in the hot-ass sun and try to get black for two damn hours.

I musta stood around for at least a half hour, thinking maybe she went to the bathroom or something and would be right back. But she didn't come back. So finally I walked back out to the entrance, where you could get a cab, and there she was, sitting on a bench. I walked over to her. "What's wrong with you? Why ain't you inside, listening to the music?"

"Could you please not raise your voice?"

"Oh, so now you *telling* me what to do?"

"Franklin, you're drunk. When we sat down in the restaurant, I knew this was coming, but I didn't think you'd embarrass me like this."

"Oh, so you embarrassed, is that it? Well, whip-the-fuck-ee."

She got up off the bench when she saw a cab pull up, and I grabbed her by the arm.

"Where you think you going?"

"Back to the motel. You're making me sick. And what I want to know is, where's that piece of fine young ass you so desperately thought you could get? There's still time, so go get it, and please let go of my arm."

"You ain't going nowhere. I paid all this goddamn money for these tickets, and we came up here to have a good time and listen to some music. You the one who fucked it up. Whatever Zora wants to do, we do it. Even that baby was your big fuckin' idea. Well, I'll tell you what. I'm tired of you telling me what to do." I pushed her in the cab and slammed the door. "Don't be there when I get back. No, I'll tell you what—don't look for me tonight, 'cause I'm gon' get me some unpregnant snapping pussy, some good pussy, from somebody who wants to give it up at night!"

The cab pulled off, and that's the last thing I remember.

21

I hate his fucking guts.

Couldn't just go away for the weekend and have a good time, like normal people. No. He had to show his black ass. He was deliberately trying to start a fight with me. But why? That's what I don't understand. I didn't do anything out of the ordinary. Did I? Franklin's got problems and doesn't even know it. He's so used to being broke and miserable he doesn't know how to relax and enjoy himself. And even though I never wanted to believe this, I think he's an alcoholic. He can't just have a few drinks; he's not satisfied until he's drunk. Since I've been pregnant, he hasn't once said I was beautiful. So now the baby was all my idea, huh? Is this what happens when a man gets scared? He's got to turn things around to put the blame on you? He never finds the good in anything. And one thing has become crystal clear to me now. He's more like his mother than he realizes.

I wasn't about to be at the motel when and if he came back ranting and raving like a lunatic. I cried all the way in the cab, and the baby was moving, and I swear to God, I wished I could've reached down and yanked it out of my stomach and thrown it out the window. What have I gotten myself into? Here I am five months pregnant by a man I love but am not married to, and have no idea when and if it'll ever happen, or now if I even want to marry this asshole. He begs me not to get rid of it, then turns around and accuses me of tricking him. All I wanted to do was sing. Fall in love, and sing.

I paid the driver and could barely get the key in the door because I was shaking so bad. I was scared of my own man. He had grabbed my arm like I was some stranger. I threw all my clothes and toiletries into my suitcase and slammed it shut, then I counted to see how many dimes I had and went back outside to use the telephone. I kept looking up at the road to make sure when I saw a cab it wasn't turning in here. I was prepared to run. My heart kept beating so fast, I thought I was going to have a heart attack right then and there. I bet that'd make him feel bad—coming back here and finding me and his unborn baby on the cold cement. I bet that'd sober him up. I was being too dramatic about this. Stop it, Zora. Get ahold of yourself. I took a deep breath and told my heart to slow down, relax. When it felt like it was trying to cooperate, I called to see what time the next bus was leaving. But there weren't any more buses going to Manhattan tonight. Trains. No more of those tonight either. Then I started looking for vacancies at other hotels and motels, but everywhere I called was still booked. Shit.

I took another deep breath and convinced myself that he wasn't coming back. Simple as that. I walked back into the motel room and locked the door. Then I sat down on the bed. This was all wrong. All of it. I'm supposed to be married. I'm supposed to be in the studio, or coming out of the studio, with my demo. I'm supposed to be waiting to hear from some producer, telling me I've got style and a strong voice and they want to record me. How did I get to this place? When did all this happen? I was out of tears now, so I turned on the TV and was half-ass watching it. Every time I saw a headlight through the curtains, I panicked. I decided not to put on my gown, just in case. And sure enough, I heard a key turn in the door and jumped from one bed to the other.

"Don't jump, baby. Ain't nobody gon' do nothing to you."

"How did you get here, Franklin? I didn't hear a cab."

"I walked."

"All the way from town in the dark?"

"I needed to walk."

"Why are you acting like this? This is our first time doing anything fun, and you fucked it up."

"No, you fucked it up, baby."

"What did I do?"

"It's what you haven't done. Look, I wanna say I'm sorry, but I ain't, at least not yet. Just let me have some pussy, sleep this shit off, and I'll see how I feel in the morning."

"Are you crazy?"

"Naw, and I wish you would stop asking me that shit."

"What do you think I am, some kind of fucking machine or something? We go to a concert, sit on the grass, and the next thing I know, you're checking out all the young girls and telling me how fine they are. And since you couldn't find any, you come back here and expect me to fuck you?"

"I didn't look for none."

"Tell me this: What would you have done if I'd have said some shit like that to you about all the fine men around?"

"They wouldn't be looking at you, 'cause you fat and pregnant."

"Well, fuck you too."

"What did you say?"

"You heard me."

The next thing I knew, he hauled off and slapped me so hard my head hit the headboard on the bed. I don't know what I saw, but something silver was swirling around in front of my eyes, and I felt the right side of my face stinging. Before I realized it, I jumped up and threw the lamp at him, but he dodged it.

"You motherfucker!"

He started coming toward me, but then he stopped dead in his tracks. I pushed myself back against the headboard, with the clock radio in my hands, ready to throw it.

"Put the radio down, baby. This is crazy. I'm wrong. I ain't had no business putting my hands on you. I'm sorry. I swear to God, I'm sorry."

"Don't come near me, Franklin, or I'll bash your fucking head in." The baby started moving, and I had to change positions. How was I going to get out of here? This had to be a nightmare, because Franklin had just hit me. And I'd just thrown a lamp at him. This is what I've heard about all my life. Men and women fighting. I've always wondered how people that love each other find it in their hearts to deliberately hurt each other. Now I know. No, I don't, because I don't understand this. I was crying again and needed to blow my nose, but I wasn't about to put the radio down. Franklin sat at the foot of the bed and put his head in his hands. It sounded like he was crying, but I wasn't impressed. I saw a Phil Donahue show about this once, and most of the women said after they hit you, they'll do anything to get you to forgive 'em. Crying was on the top of the list.

Then someone knocked on the door. "Is everything all right in there?"

"No!" I yelled.

"Yeah, we just knocked over a few things," Franklin said. "I'm not gon' touch you," he said. "I swear to God."

"Would you just leave?"

"I ain't got nowhere to go," he said.

"That's not my problem. You're the one who said you

didn't want to come back, so would you leave, please. I don't care where you go."

To my surprise, he got up and walked out the door. Then, like a damn fool, I didn't want him to leave, but I couldn't bring myself to go after him. That's another thing the women on the show said always happened. All I knew was that I was confused. I got up and peeked out the curtains and saw him go sit by the swimming pool.

I couldn't believe it. Franklin started taking his clothes off and stripped down to his briefs. Then he eased into the pool and was standing in almost six feet of water, which was just over his shoulders. He stood there for a few minutes, dunked his head under a few times, then started doing a dead man's float. Once he reached the other end of the pool, his arms reached up and pulled, and he was moving through the water like a torpedo. He could swim! But why'd he tell me he couldn't? He did at least ten or twelve lengths, then got out and put his shirt over his shoulders and sat down on a lounge chair.

I stood there and watched him reach into his shirt pocket and get a cigarette. He used one to light another one and must've done this at least six or seven times. I knew he had to be freezing, so finally I opened the door. "Franklin," I said, "come on back in before you catch pneumonia."

He got up slowly, and when he entered the door, I handed him a towel.

"I'm sorry, baby. I swear to God I am."

"Look, Franklin. I don't understand what's going on, and right now I'm so tired I don't know if I want to use the energy to find out. But promise me something."

"What's that?"

"That you'll cut down all this drinking."

"Looks like I'ma have to, if it's fuckin' with me like this."

"And this I'm not asking. If you ever so much as raise your hand to me again, if I don't kill you first, your ass is going to jail. I mean that from the bottom of my heart."

"I swear, baby, I ain't never hit you before when I was mad, have I?"

"No."

"Let me see your face over here in the light." I walked over, and he held my face gently in his big hands. "Damn, I'm sorry." I turned to look in the mirror, and the whole side of my face was red. He put his arms around me and held me for the longest.

"Do you think it's possible we can enjoy what's left of the weekend?" I asked.

"I'm gon' give it my best shot," he said.

In the morning, Franklin was up at six, waking me.

"Come on. Let's go look at the horses and have breakfast at the track. I read about this boat ride up in Lake George. We can do that and be back in time for the concert. I called another hotel, not motel, in town that'll have a vacancy later, so we can stay there tonight. I wanna make this up to you, baby."

"How much is it?"

"Let me worry about that."

"But what about this room? We've already paid for it."

"So what? It's only money."

I looked at him hard. The baby started kicking. My heart was giving in, and my shoulders began to fall. "Just give me a few minutes to shower, and I'll be ready."

Franklin kept his word. The whole day felt like a dream, and as we sat on the deck of the *Ticonderoga*, I kept looking over at him to make sure he was the same person who had hit me last night. He wasn't. He was the same tall black handsome man I had fallen in love with. We sat out there in silence, watching fifteen miles of waves and trees. When small boats passed us, the people in them waved, and we waved back.

Franklin didn't so much as drink a beer.

We sat in our reserved seats at the concert that night. The baby danced, and Franklin held my hand. When Chaka Khan finally slowed down and sang "Stop on By," my head was on Franklin's shoulder. We walked back to the hotel, which was beautiful, and I saw that it cost him ninety dollars for the night, but I didn't say a word about it. I even felt like making love, but Franklin told me to just go to sleep and rest. By the time we were on the bus home the next day, the entire weekend felt like it didn't really happen. Nothing fit together, except Franklin's head on my shoulder and his hands on my thumping belly.

22

The foreman called me into the shanty.

I was glad, 'cause it's cold as a motherfucker out here now, even though it's only the end of October. Shit, feel like it's getting ready to snow. All I'm hoping is that he gon' tell me, when we start the next job in a few weeks, that it's gon' be inside.

"Frankie, would you like some coffee?"

"Yeah," I said. The tone of his voice was off, and something told me in a split second that it wasn't gon' be no next job. I been through this routine enough to know.

"Naw, I changed my mind. I don't want no coffee."

"Well, you know I don't make the decisions around here . . ."

"Mel, get to the point, would you? Am I going to the next site or not?"

"Afraid not, Frankie."

"What happened? Too many blacks on the job?"

"Nothing like that. The contractor's cutting back. He's got too many men on the next crew."

"Yeah, right. So when do we, or should I say I, end here?"

"Two weeks."

"And the fact that I've been busting my nuts, working overtime damn near every other night, ain't missed a day, ain't been late, and knowing I coulda probably had your job, ain't got nothin' to do with this, do it?"

"Frankie, you're one of our best workers, but this isn't my decision."

I got up and went back outside. I put my work gloves back on and found my lunchbox.

"Where you going, Frankie?" I heard him yelling.

"Home. And fuck you too."

I went down to my union hall and told 'em what happened. They told me I hadn't been fired or laid off, that what I had just done was quit. "What else you got?" I asked.

"Nothin' right now. Stay in touch."

The union hall is just as racist as the rest of 'em. They all work together, really, and I don't even know why I bothered going down there in the first place. But it don't matter, 'cause I need a break anyway.

So I went home.

It was cold as a motherfucker in here too, but since this is New York, the landlord controls the heat. I was ready to fuck with somebody, so why not Sol? I went downstairs and knocked on his door.

"Come on in," he said.

When I walked in, I swear to God, the smell was enough to knock you down. Between them nasty-ass cigars he smoke, all this old shit he calls antiques, three handicapped cats, and two mutts he calls dogs—and he probably ain't bathed since I don't know when—I just said, "Naw, I'll stand right here." I was in the doorway, with the door still open. "How about some heat?"

"What, you think it's cold? This is gorgeous weather. It's fall, Franklin."

"Look, Sol, as much rent as we paying you, it's cold as hell up there, and I'm asking you to turn up the heat. It's forty-something degrees outside. Fuck fall."

"Take it easy, Franklin."

"You gon' turn on the heat?"

"There's a way to ask people to do things," he said, and reached for his cane.

I turned to go back upstairs and saw one of them damn cats. This one had white pus and shit all around its eyes and only three legs. I wanted to kick it, but I stepped over it.

When I got upstairs I poured some water in the Mr. Coffee, but before it started brewing, I knew coffee wasn't what I needed, so I turned it off. I got the bottle of Jack Daniel's from the cabinet and poured a tall one. I guess I'ma just have to go down to the union hall every single day till they put me on somewhere. And I'll go down to the organizations too. What the fuck. This is the wrong time to be getting axed. I got a baby coming in less than two months. I got Christmas and two kids who gon' expect me to be Santa Claus. I got a divorce I gotta pay for. And I gotta tell Zora this shit.

I felt somebody shaking me.

"What, what, what?" I asked. Shit, I didn't know where I was, until I looked up.

"Franklin, what's wrong? What are you doing home so early?" I wanted to answer and sit up at the same time, but a jackhammer was beating away in my head, and I couldn't do or say nothing. The inside of my mouth felt like it was full of cotton.

"Franklin?"

She had backed away now and walked clear to the other side of the living room. Good. Now I don't have to look at her. Her belly came to a big point, and that was Zora, all right, with my baby inside her. "I'm sick."

"You're drunk," she said.

"That too."

"What's the reason this time?"

"I got laid off."

"But the union can help you, right?"

"I been down to the union."

"And?"

"Ain't nothin' happening."

"I thought that was *one* of the reasons for joining."

"I ain't never said getting in the union guaranteed me no job."

"I know that, but you said it'd be easier."

"All I said was it guaranteed they gotta pay you union wages, and you get benefits."

"But don't they look out for you?"

"Yeah, if you ain't black."

"Don't start that again, Franklin. You use that as an excuse for everything."

"Don't tell me what I do. I ain't in the mood for it right now. What's for dinner?"

"You've already had yours, I see."

She held up the empty bottle. I know damn well I didn't drink all that. But I guess I did. "Look, I'm feeling like shit, baby. I just lost my job, and I ain't had nothin' to eat all day. Could you just cook me something until I get my head together, and then I can think straight."

She didn't say nothin', but went upstairs to the bedroom, came down in my Saratoga T-shirt, and walked over and opened the refrigerator. She took out a plastic container of liver and threw it down on top of the cutting board. Then she snatched a box of rice from the cabinet, filled a pot with some water, and this went on till everything was finished.

I managed to sit up. "Thank you, baby," I said, and walked over to give her a little kiss on the cheek, but she turned away.

"It's ready," she said, and sat down on the couch and turned on the TV.

So she's pissed. So I'm disappointed. So everything is everything.

I had just cleaned my plate, when the phone rang. I waited for her to answer it, but she didn't. It rung about six times, when, finally, I said, "Ain't you gon' answer it? You know it's for you."

"You live here too. You answer it."

So I picked it up. "Yeah," I said. It was that faggot she used to hang out with, Eli. The one she had me thinking was her man when I first met her.

"It's your old boyfriend," I said. Her eyes lit up, and she took the phone from me. I went to the upstairs bathroom and ran a hot tub of water. What I needed to do was sweat. By the time I got out, it was damn near nine o'clock, and I still felt like shit, and I looked around downstairs and didn't see her. She was probably in the bed, so I went back upstairs—one step at a time, which was a sign that I was still fucked up. The liver and rice helped, but can't nothin' get alcohol out your system but time.

Sure enough, she was under the covers.

"What'd the faggot have to say? He need some pussy?"

"Spare me, would you, Franklin?"

"What did he want?"

"Why?"

"He ain't been calling you. Why now?"

"Reginald's sick."

"So what?"

"You can really be callous, you know that?"

"So what's wrong with him? He got that faggot disease that's out now, AIDS?"

"No, he does not. He's got something called shingles."

"What the fuck is that? A new faggot disease that just came out?"

"It's some kind of nervous disorder where your whole body gets covered with bumps. *Anybody* can get it."

"So what's the big deal?"

"The big deal is it can take up to three months for him to recover, and Eli wanted me to know in case I was ready to start my sessions back before he was okay again."

"How'd he get the shit in the first place?"

"I just said it has something to do with nerves. It's related to herpes."

"Figures. Them faggots fuck anything that'll bend over. God is punishing all of 'em. A dick was meant to be stuck in some pussy, not another man's ass."

"Franklin, you're the one who's being punished, for having such a fucked-up attitude. The only person you feel sorry for is Franklin, isn't it?"

"Oh, so now you gon' turn the shit around and put it on me, huh?"

She lifted the covers and threw 'em back, then started to get up.

"Where you going?"

"To sleep downstairs on the couch. I can't stand this."

"I don't want you to sleep on the couch. I need you here with me."

"You need, you need. That's all you think about is what Franklin needs. Well, masturbate."

"I'm tired of masturbating. It's a shame when a man got a woman and gotta stroke his own dick just to get off. But I didn't say nothin' about fuckin', did I? All I said was I need you."

"That usually means fucking."

"If you sleep on the couch, I'm coming down there too."

"Franklin, could you give me a break for once?"

"I'm hurting, baby, can't you see that?"

"What I see is that you've been drinking all day and you're laid off again and starting to feel sorry for yourself, and I can't stand it. Not tonight."

"Then take your fat ass on downstairs. Go. Now! Get the fuck outta here. I don't need you anyway."

She walked on out, and I heard her grab some blankets from the linen closet. I wanted to push her down the stairs, but instead I laid on the bed and turned on the TV. I picked up Tarzan, but he probably died sometime this afternoon. I couldn't think hard enough to make him hard, so I fell asleep.

Static woke me up.

It was daylight. My head felt better but not good. I got up and went downstairs. I didn't smell no coffee, nothing. The couch was empty, and wasn't no blankets on it. Zora was already gone. I looked at the clock, and it was after nine. Damn. I took a quick shower and left for the union hall.

I got a different story: Don't call us, we'll call you.

So I went down to A Dream, but it was closed. Closed? What the fuck is going on? I knew I was fucking up a whole day, but damn, something was up, and I wanted to find out. I went back down to the site and found Mel.

"What d'ya want, Frankie?" he asked.

"Look, I know I was rude and shit, but I wanna know what happened. What's the real lowdown on why I ain't going to the next job?"

"Like I told you. There's been a lot of shit going down, and it involves jail."

"Jail?"

"Indictments."

"The organization got anything to do with this?"

"Don't you read the paper, Frankie?"

"Yeah, but not in the last few days. Tell me what the fuck is going on."

"Turns out the feds have found out that quite a few of your so-called affirmative action organizations been taking payoffs to keep your kind off the sites."

"Get the fuck outta here, man. Kendricks?"

"Why don't you ask him?"

"I been down there, but it's closed."

"Then that should tell you something. Look, I got work to do. You get on anyplace?"

"No. Not yet."

"It's gonna be hard, I'm telling you that right now."

"So you hiring?"

"No, but what I do have is a hundred bucks."

"For what?"

"So you can stay home."

"Where is it?"

He reached in his pocket and handed me a hundred-dollar bill. I just looked at him, then at the money, turned, and walked away.

23

I'm going crazy.

Here it is the middle of November, and Franklin's still not working. I'm trying to be patient, and understanding, and all that, but it's getting too hard. All I do is go to school, come home, cook, watch *Wheel of Fortune,* and then play Scrabble with Franklin to make the night go by. I take a shower and stare at myself in the mirror for a good ten minutes and get into bed and pray he doesn't want to do it. He's down to once a week now, and he's still got that ten-minute problem. I'm sure it's me that's causing it, but I'm sorry. I'm pregnant, and there's nothing I can do about it now.

And sure, I'm up to 180 pounds, but I'm not the only one in this house who's put on weight. Since Franklin's been off work, I guess he spends a good part of his day eating, because he's put on a good twenty pounds himself. He can't even wear his blue jeans anymore; all he wears is sweats. But I don't say anything about his weight either. Just last night, I was rubbing my stomach and hips with Nivea—like I've been doing every night since I first found out I was pregnant—and he walked into the bedroom butt naked. He looked at me.

"Why you put that stuff on every night?"

"To keep my skin lubricated."

"You think that's supposed to stop you from getting stretch marks?"

"It might help."

"Every woman I ever knew that had a baby's got stretch marks, so don't get your hopes up. You gon' have to lose about fifty of them pounds to start with."

"What about you? How do you plan on losing yours?"

"This is just from being at home. As soon as I start working out again, I can knock this right off."

"I might join a gym myself," I said.

"Just don't join the one I belonged to."

"And why not?"

" 'Cause all the dudes'll know you my woman. If you lose the weight, then they gon' try to hit on you, and if you don't, I don't want them to know you my woman."

"You really know how to make me feel good, you know that? Do you get a kick out of hurting me, is that it?"

"I'm not trying to hurt you. I'm just telling you how I feel, that's all."

And what did I do after that? Went back into the bathroom, pulled up my nightgown, and looked at my breasts and stomach very, very hard. I didn't see any stretch marks. I'll show that bastard. If he thinks I'm going to stay fat after this baby, he's got another thing coming.

I finally wrote Daddy a letter and told him everything in such a way that he apparently understood, because he called and told me not to worry about anything. He was actually excited about having a grandchild. He also told me that Franklin had told him his whole situation, and when the time was right, Franklin was going to do the right thing. "Just give him some time, and let me know if you need anything—anything at all," he said. Marguerite sang a different tune altogether, but I wasn't interested in that melody.

Something's going to have to break, and soon, because I can't go on like this much longer. I've spent a fortune putting the baby's things in layaway, because I'm almost up to my limit on my Visa, and besides, some kind of way Franklin's got to help. I've still got a few dollars of my studio money left, but I'm keeping it for that purpose and that purpose only.

I can't give up everything.

And I need to get out of this house. I haven't seen Marie or Claudette in ages. Portia's gone already, and I miss her loud mouth more than she'll probably ever know. Every day when I get home, he's always here. Once, I'd like to just come home and he'd be gone. Out. Anywhere. But I'm Franklin's sole source of entertainment. I fill up his social calendar, and what's so sad is that somehow he's become the same thing for me. This is not healthy—at least it doesn't feel healthy. We're supposed to be happy. Looking at baby furniture together. We're supposed to be married. But at this point I'm not mentioning it, because I'm not so sure anymore if I want to be his wife. I'm just keeping my mouth shut until the baby gets here and see what he does.

Today when I came home, he was upstairs in the bedroom, laughing out loud. As usual, he was watching *Love Connection*. The house was a mess. The same dishes from last night were still in the sink. His towel was in the middle of the bathroom floor, and a plate where he must've eaten was sitting in the middle of the living room floor. So were the crumbs. Ashtrays were overflowing, plants were drooping; he must've been doing his woodworking, because he'd tracked sawdust all through the house.

I went upstairs, and he was spread-eagled across the bed, with his legs, dirty sneakers, crossed and pillows propped up behind his head. He was eating Doritos and had a sheet of sandpaper and a piece of wood in his hands. On top of my two-hundred-dollar comforter. But I didn't say anything.

"Hi, baby," he said. "This show is a gas. Some of the things these people do on a date'll crack you up. Come here, sit down. How was your day?"

Just like that. Like he didn't have a care in the damn world.

"Fine," I said.

"What's for dinner, baby?" he asked, lighting a cigarette. "I'm starving."

I hadn't even hung up my coat yet. "Your guess is as good as mine. I don't feel like cooking tonight. Just what've you been doing all day, Franklin?" I asked, looking around. The bedroom was a mess too. His socks and underwear were all over the floor, and cigarette ashes were at the foot of the bed. I saw his empty glass but didn't say anything.

"Why?"

"I just wanted to know if you looked for work today."

"It's too cold."

"Yesterday it was too cold."

"And it's too cold today. Probably be too cold tomorrow too."

"What about the rent?"

"What about it?"

"You think I can pay seven hundred and fifty dollars by myself?"

"You're superwoman. You'll think of something."

"Franklin, what's happening to you?"

"Nothing. What makes you think something is happening to me?"

"For the past three and a half weeks, I've been trying to be patient. Ever since you got laid off you've spent exactly three days looking for work. This isn't right."

"I'm just taking a little vacation. I'm tired."

"Tired?"

"Yeah, tired."

"What about me?"

"What about you?"

"I'm having a baby, in case you haven't noticed."

"Ain't nobody noticed more than me."

"Aren't you the least bit concerned about it? And what about the bills and the rent? Don't you care?"

"Yeah, I care, but it just ain't nothing I can do about it right now."

"If you would get up off your black ass and try, you might."

"Don't swear at me, Zora."

"Look, Franklin, I'm getting scared. This is all wrong. Everything is all messed up."

"Don't worry. I told you, I'm taking a little vacation, but it'll be over by Friday. I'll go out and get a fuckin' job, and we'll be back where we started."

"Which is where?"

"You tell me."

With that I just turned and walked away. I went downstairs and picked up the telephone. I didn't even know who I was calling. Claudette answered. But before I had a chance to say hello, Franklin pressed down on the receiver.

"You ain't gotta call none of your girlfriends and blab all our business."

"I wasn't about to blab all of our business, and so what if I was?"

"Why don't you talk to me?"

"About what?"

"Anything."

"Franklin, this is getting a little ridiculous. I can't talk to you. You get on the defensive about everything."

"You know, you women are all alike. When I was little, my Moms used to pull this same shit on me."

"And just what shit is that?" I didn't feel like hearing another story about his mother, but if we were going to have it out, I wanted to get it over with.

"She never wanted to hear my side of anything. I was always wrong."

"You're saying I'm like your mother?"

"Did I say that?"

"You're implying it. Well, let me tell you something, Franklin. I'm about sick of you blaming everything that happens to you on your mother, and I'm sick of being compared to her every time I do or say something you don't like."

"She fucked me up."

"I'm ready to agree with that."

He went to the cabinet and got a bottle out, but I didn't dare say anything. I watched him pour. Then I watched him take a long swallow.

"My Moms stripped me of my manhood before I was a man."

"No one can strip you of anything unless you let them."

"Do you know what it's like not to feel loved by your own mother?"

"Mine died when I was three."

"But your Daddy loved you."

"And still does."

"Well, growing up in a house with all girls, and one who was the favorite and got anything she wanted, and I got treated like shit, ain't helped me one bit."

"You can't sit here and expect me to believe that your mother *never* showed you any love."

"Why would I lie? What I'm saying is that if she did, she had a fucked-up way of showing it. Do you know how bad that can make you feel inside, knowing that your own mother don't give a shit about what happens to you, huh?"

He took another long swallow. I didn't feel like answering. I wanted to tell him to just grow up. But I didn't.

"And my Pops. He's pitiful. Sometimes I'd like to kill both of 'em. He's a faggot. Just let her run all over him, let her run everything. Didn't have no balls. And that's why I made up my mind a long time ago that I wasn't never gon' let no woman run me. Never."

"So what has this got to do with anything?"

"Baby, I got a lotta things going on inside me that you don't understand, and it don't seem like you trying."

"Like what, Franklin? Like what?"

"Like not being able to find a job. I been out there at least ten different times. I just got tired of telling you that nothin' was happening. And yeah, I could get some shitwork, making five dollars a hour, but I'm tired of that. Tired. Can't you understand that?"

"Yeah, but we've got a baby coming—can't you understand *that*?"

"All I'm saying is bear with me. If you love me, then prove it."

"What do you think I've been doing for almost two years?"

"You've done a pretty good job of it—till now."

"What's that supposed to mean, Franklin?"

"You and your little singing career. Don't get me wrong, baby. You can sing, and I wanna see you make it. But you put everything before me."

"What are you talking about now?"

The glass was empty.

"You done got carried away with these extracurricular activities at school. Everything is the kids this and the kids that.

You used to wanna fuck me anytime I wanted it. You used to talk to me. You used to wanna play Scrabble with me all the time. We used to have fun. You used to not mind cooking for me. Now I gotta beg for everything. Just a little attention, that's all I want. To know that I matter."

He sounded so pitiful I wanted to throw up. The only reason I'd been staying after school was because I didn't want to come home. Every time I turned the key in the door I automatically got depressed. But now I was thinking, *had* I stopped doing all those things? *Was* I making him feel like he was just another piece of furniture? I hadn't meant to. Really I hadn't.

"Franklin, you do matter. But I don't know how much I have to do to prove to you that I love you. You're making it awful hard. How do you think I feel? Here I am eight months pregnant, living with a man who's not only unemployed but who's not even my husband. When we started out, you had dreams. I had dreams. You had me believing you would go back to school, get your divorce, and start your own business. And look at you."

"You don't have to tell me to look at myself. What you think I do in here all day?"

"Well, the rent's due in two weeks, and if I pay it, then that means the phone'll probably get turned off or the lights, or I'll get behind in my credit card payments."

"That's all you can think about is the fucking bills? What about me? You ain't heard a word I said."

"What about you! Is that all you think about, Franklin? Look, let's just stop this conversation, because it's going nowhere."

"Yeah, 'cause I ain't in the mood for no arguing. What about dinner?"

This motherfucker must be deaf.

24

I got a rinky-dink job that lasted a week. I only took it to shut Zora up. She was really getting on my nerves, and I figured I better do something to break up the fuckin' monotony. I didn't know what I was doing, really. All I knew was that I was tired of repeating myself and getting no-goddamn-where. After a while, a man gets worn out, beaten down, and you ain't got nothing left. No drive, no will, no fuckin' energy. My dick don't even get hard unless I talk to it. I ain't saying it's all over, and I ain't saying I'm giving up. All I'm saying is that right now I'm tired as hell. And too many things is coming at me at once. This baby. Zora. Work. My kids. I ain't got but ten bucks in the bank. What happened to all the fuckin' money I made this year? Rent. School clothes. Union dues. Groceries. Rent. Sneakers. Light bill. Groceries. Rent. Derek's dirt bike. His Prince concert. His First Edition concert. Groceries. And rent. And I'm still on foot. It seem like the more that's expected of me, the less I'm able to do. I can't take feeling like this either. I swear to God, I can't.

I'm trying not to drink, but that's hard as hell to do too. My woman ain't satisfying me. I ain't satisfying myself. I'm pissed off at myself, to tell the truth. Here I am almost thirty-four years old, and what I got to show for it? A $750-a-month duplex that ain't mine. And some wood and old tools. That's it, when you look at it straight. Somewhere in my head is my Moms' voice, saying, "I told you you wasn't gon' never amount to nothin'." And this just makes me grit my teeth. I'ma prove her wrong, if it's the last thing in life I do.

I know I been a lazy motherfucker. And Zora's right. She don't need to be coming home from work to a nasty house. So I decided to surprise her. Clean up the place. Maybe if I put a little more energy into this thing, change my attitude, shit might pick up. We gon' see.

I tore the place apart. Refrigerator, oven, all of it. Picked up all the plants off the floor and set 'em on the tables, and sprayed the bathroom walls with Soft Scrub. I poured Comet in the tub and sinks, and put in a Maze tape. Them motherfuckers can sing they asses off. "Joy and Pain" was blasting, and even though it was snowing, I had the windows open. It's hard to clean and party to this kinda music without a shot, so I poured myself a little one. Shit, I was sweating, and I musta played Maze at least three times before I changed it and put on Stephanie Mills. Now, that's my girl. I ain't never heard nobody so little hit so many big notes. Zora can learn something from this girl. And I seen her live once. Talk about energy. She runs back and forth across the stage like lightning, and seem like her little feet don't even touch the damn floor. And them little hips can rock it, I swear to God.

By the time *Love Connection* was almost on, I was finished with everything except waxing the floors, and since I wanted everything to be nice when Zora got home, I said fuck *Love Connection* today.

She had went out and bought all this baby stuff. Spent a goddamn fortune. She didn't seem to be too worried about the rent, when it came to that baby. I think she's going a little overboard, really. You should see the kid's room. You'd swear we was rich and white. I didn't bother cleaning in there—'cause needless to say, it wasn't dirty.

I figured I'd watch *The People's Court* while I changed the sheets. Then I would cook, so it would be warm by the time she got home. Judge Wapner don't give a motherfucker a break, I swear. It was real stupid today. Some people was arguing over a damn dog. I turned it off and got myself another little drink. Shit, I forgot. Tonight was her Lamaze class. She don't talk to me about it, 'cause when she first asked me if I'd go with her and I got so drunk that all I did was stand outside and look up at the window 'cause I was too depressed to participate, she cussed me out, and now her white girlfriend, Judy, is gon' be her coach.

I wasn't even high yet, so Zora wasn't gon' be able to say nothing to me about being drunk when she got home. I decided, since I had at least a good two hours to kill, to go into my woodworking room. Now, this was a mess, and I wasn't about to clean this shit up. Not today. As a matter of fact, the worse it looks, the better I like it. Make me feel like I'm accomplishing something, although I ain't finished nothing in here in I don't know when. That's what I need to do. Concentrate more on my wood. We could use a real bookcase, not bookshelves, to put all these damn books. Most of 'em was still in boxes. And that bed we been sleeping in ain't never been big enough. Maybe I'll make a new frame king size. But that takes money too. Shit.

I was moving some of the big pieces of pine over in a corner, when the phone rang. I hope it ain't none of Zora's sorry little girlfriends. I don't feel like talking to none of 'em. It was my Pops. I shoulda known it was gon' be bad news. Darlene done had a nervous breakdown and was in Bellevue. He ain't even been up to see her 'cause he working on the basement 'cause my Aunt Delilah is coming up from South Carolina. Big fuckin' deal, I thought, but I didn't feel like saying it. I told him I was about to be a daddy in a few weeks and he couldn't understand why I hadn't told him before now. I wanted him to think about why. I told him Merry Christmas and hung up.

It was too late to think about getting on a train going up to Bellevue tonight, but I called. Darlene didn't have no phone in her room, and when I asked how she was doing, the nurse just said she wasn't able to give that information out over the phone. When I asked what time was visiting hours, they said she didn't want any visitors. "But I'm her brother," I said.

"She's given explicit instructions not to allow any visitors whatsoever. I'm sorry, sir."

"Well, when is she getting out?"

"You'll have to talk to her doctor about that."

"And what's his name?"

"Hold a minute while I get her chart."

I poured myself a drink while I waited. No visitors. Darlene is taking this shit too far. When the nurse came back, she gave me a number for Dr. Pavlovich.

"Thank you," I said, and hung up.

Well, tomorrow I'ma call him to see if he'll tell me what the real deal is. That's my sister up there falling apart. I know my shit is raggedy, but I'll be damned if I'd let anybody or anything wear me out like that. I guess the word for her is "vulnerable." She's too goddamn vulnerable.

I was kinda fucked up by the time *Wheel of Fortune* came on, and believe me, I was trying not to get like this. Sometimes there's just too much empty space that's anxious for something—anything—and the only way I know how to numb it is with a few drinks. I know I got a problem, but I ain't no alcoholic. These is just rough times.

*   *   *

"Franklin! You cleaned the house?"

"Dinner is ready for you too, baby."

She looked so surprised and so damn happy, I couldn't help but thinking that maybe I shoulda been doing this all along. Maybe it woulda eased some of this friction. Our shit has got so thick you could cut it with a knife. It sure felt good seeing a smile on her face.

She walked over and put that big belly against me and wrapped her arms around me and kissed me on the cheek. That was all I needed. "Thank you," she said. "Thank you so much."

"The rice stuck a little bit, and maybe the chicken still got some blood in it. Matter of fact, I know it do, but it was brown, so I took it out. If you don't eat it, it won't hurt my feelings."

"We can put it in the oven for twenty minutes, and it'll cook on the inside. Don't worry about it."

"So how was your day, baby?"

"Good. A lot of the teachers threw me a surprise baby shower, and, Franklin, you won't believe all the stuff they got for the baby. A bassinet, one of those little seats, a changing table—you know how much those things cost?"

I shook my head no.

"Me either, but they're expensive. And I got so many sleepers and undershirts and five boxes of newborn Pampers. Will you go out there with me one day next week and help me bring it home?"

"Yeah. That was nice of 'em to do that."

"Sure was. So how was your day? I see you were real busy. This was thoughtful of you, really, and I appreciate it."

"No problem. I just been down, baby. So down I can't even explain it to you. I know I been fuckin' up, and I know I ain't

been the easiest person to live with, but shit is about to
change. I'ma do something, but don't ask me what right now,
'cause I still ain't figured it all out yet. One thing I do know
is that I'ma have to figure a way to get outta construction. The
money is good, but you only as good as the day you working.
And with the baby and everything, I need something I can
count on. Bear with me, would you, baby?"

"I'm trying, Franklin. That's what I've been doing, is trying."

"Sit down. Relax."

I told Zora that my Pops had called, and what he said. Zora
was surprised, but not shocked. We was about to sit down and
eat when she told me that she was going out to Claudette's on
Sunday and it was for women only. Didn't hurt my feelings
none 'cause a game was coming on. I told her to have a good
time.

The next morning, Zora went to the Laundromat and I called this
doctor. They musta had me on hold for damn near ten minutes,
but I wasn't hanging up till I found out what the deal was.

"Yeah, Dr. . . ." I looked at the little piece of paper to get
his name straight, but he beat me to it.

"Pavlovich."

"Yeah, right. I'm Darlene Swift's brother and I was told by
the nurse at the hospital that she's under your care, and I just
wanna know what's wrong with my sister and if she's gon' be
all right."

"Well, there's only so much I can tell you."

"I'm listening."

"She's suffered from what I like to call an emotional im-
balance, which caused her to experience a temporary breakdown."

"So she had a nervous breakdown is what you're saying,
right?"

"Well, it's a little more complicated than that. Your sister has a very low self-image. From what I gather, she's been depressed for a very long time. I'm going to try to get her to talk to me, to see if we can get her back on her feet."

"You a psychiatrist?"

"Yes, I am."

"Well, when she gon' be able to come home?"

"Sometime soon, but I've advised her that she shouldn't be alone for a while. I spoke with your father just this morning, and he's agreed to let her stay at home until she's more confident and strong enough to handle everyday affairs on her own."

"Is she suicidal?"

"I can't answer that question."

"You gon' dope her up?"

"She'll be given antidepressants, if that's what you mean."

"One last question, Doctor. Is she gon' be all right? I mean, she ain't crazy, is she?"

"No, she's not crazy. If she's amenable to treatment—being open about her difficulties—and if she's willing to confront what may be bothering her, that'll be a beginning."

"Thanks. Thanks a lot."

I went straight to the dictionary and looked up "amenable." All I can say is if she ain't, she better be.

25

When I walked into Claudette's house, the first thing I saw was crepe paper everywhere. Then a group of women—half of whom I didn't even know—popped through another doorway and yelled "Surprise!"

"Claudette," I said, when I spotted her, "you didn't have to do this, and you know it."

"It took me long enough to get your behind out here. We've had this planned since October, girl."

She introduced me to nine or ten of her girlfriends, and they knew all about me. The dining room table was stacked with gifts, and a stroller sat right next to it. I really couldn't believe this. And Claudette's house was gorgeous. It'd been so long since I'd been out here.

"Zora?" This voice came from behind me. It couldn't be who I thought it was.

"Marie?" I said, turning. This kind of affair wasn't her style at all, but it was Marie, all right. And she looked good.

"How goes it, Miss Z?"

"Fine. But what about you? You're the one who's looking like a million dollars."

"Well, girl, so much has happened since the last time I saw you. I'm gonna be in a movie! For real. And I'm not drinking, either. Don't look at me like that—it's the truth. It's been sixty-two days, I swear to God. Anyway, I haven't felt this good in years. And to make a long story short, I've got gigs coming out of my ass. My material has gotten so much better—I can't believe it. And I've been meeting some dynamite people, one in particular I'd like you to meet. As a matter of fact, she's here with me. Her husband is a big record producer, girl, and I told her about you and I told her you wrote music, and her husband would like to hear your demo. I'm not bullshitting. That's the least I can do, considering."

"Are you putting me on, Marie?"

"He's produced all kinds of people. I'll tell you all the details later. But let me just ask you this: Does Columbia Records ring a bell?"

"Get out of here."

"I brought something for the baby, but this is yours." She reached in her purse and handed me an envelope. "All eight hundred. Thanks, Zora."

"Are you serious, Marie? Are you sure you can afford to do this now?"

"I'm telling you, Z, things have been happening. Nobody is more surprised at this shit than me."

It couldn't have come at a better time.

"Come here, girl," Claudette said, pulling me by the arm. "Let's get a look at this belly. Somebody get the camera. Lord only knows when I'll ever see this girl in this condition again."

"First, I need to go to the bathroom."

"Ladies, how many of you remember those days?"

At least ten of them yelled out, "I do!"

"When you come back," Claudette said, "I've got a surprise for you, so hurry up."

When I came back out, everybody was sitting in the living

room like they were waiting for something. "What's going on?" I asked, and sat down too.

"Nothing, bitch!"

Portia! She walked into the room holding this little bundle in her arms, and I couldn't believe this shit. "Portia? Is that really you?"

"No, it's your fuckin' imagination." Then she started laughing. It was easy to see that she wasn't a size seven anymore, but the girl still looked good.

"What are you doing here? When did you get back from Nashville? What did you have? When did you have it? Why didn't you call me? Let me see!"

She opened the blanket and the eyes of a cute little brown baby in pink were squeezed tight. She looked so new.

"She came early. Her name's Sierra. Six pounds six ounces, and I didn't stay in Nashville 'cause I'm getting married."

"Wait a minute," I said. "Let me sit down."

"You're already sitting down."

"You're getting what?" I said.

"Married. To Arthur."

"But I thought . . . never mind. Congratulations! Does this make you happy?"

"Very. I was bullshitting, girl. I love the motherfucker, but I was just scared, and since he was, you know . . . But hey, he was at the hospital and everything, he was right there, and I ain't used to nobody being there for me, and by the time she got here, his papers was final."

"Get out of here!"

"I'm serious, girl. I'm serious. He's a good man, and I just didn't wanna admit that I was all strung out and shit over no you-know-what. You get my drift?"

"Of course I do."

"So how's Franklin?"

"So-so."

"He treating you right?"

"As well as he can."

"What about *his* papers?"

"He hasn't gotten 'em yet, and I'm not pressing him. So much has happened that I'll have to tell you about it another time. Not now. I can't believe you're here, Portia, and I'm so glad you're back. I swear I am."

Then she bent down and whispered in my ear. "What about the seizures?"

"I've been monitored like you wouldn't believe. And so far, everything's gone smoothly. I'm not even worried about it."

"All right, everybody. There's plenty of food in the kitchen, some games we're supposed to play, and then we want Zora to put on this stupid hat and open the baby's presents," Claudette yelled.

After the games, boy, did we eat and eat and eat. I should really speak for myself. I held Sierra and didn't want to put her down. Marie introduced me to JayJay, the woman whose husband was the producer. She seemed pretty down-to-earth. Lived in Teaneck, New Jersey, and invited me over after the baby was born to meet her husband.

When it came time to open the gifts, I was past elation. This was just too much. I sat in a chair they had put in the middle of the room, and everybody watched. I couldn't believe all the money these women had spent on my baby. I wouldn't have to buy another thing, not another thing.

"I don't know how I'm going to get all this stuff home," I said.

"Girl, when we do things around here, we do them right. Go look out the window," Claudette said.

I walked over and pulled the curtain to the side and saw a

big black limousine parked out front. "Are you guys nuts? What do you think I am, a movie star or something?"

Portia walked over and put her hands on my shoulder. "Get used to it, girlfriend."

Portia and I agreed to talk tomorrow. She said that Arthur had told her she didn't have to do any more court reporting, and when the baby was four months old she was going back to school. She didn't know what classes yet, but she was going. Marie and I agreed to stay in touch, and she would let me know when she'd be back from California.

On the way home, I couldn't believe how soft the leather seats were and how dark the windows were. I leaned back into the cushions and felt important. I just wished it could last.

The following week, Franklin and I were back to where we were three weeks ago. The house was a mess, and I'd been letting it stay like that just to be ornery. But Christmas was only four days away, and I was finally getting the spirit, so I decided to go ahead and give the place a good once-over, since my days waiting for the baby to get here were numbered. Franklin even agreed to help. And since he didn't have any money, I went out and bought his kids some Christmas presents. He's been back in the dumps, but I've been too preoccupied with myself to worry about him.

We had torn the place apart—disinfected everything, cleaned the woodwork, moved furniture, you name it—and finally, Franklin said, "Look, baby, why don't we take a Scrabble break?"

"But where can we sit?" I asked.

"I'll move some of this shit off the couch. When we finish, I'll put all the plants and stuff back and finish the floors. How's that?"

"Fine."

"Set 'em up," he said.

He got the egg timer out, and I was disappointed when I saw my letters. All I had were three *i*'s, two *o*'s, a *u*, and a damn *p*.

Franklin was grinning. He gives it away every time when he's got good letters. And as usual, he was shifting them back and forth, back and forth, until it got on my nerves. "Would you make your word today, please?"

"Gimme a minute, baby. I don't wanna break your heart when you see this."

After fifteen minutes of this, he was winning, of course. I was just about to make a word that would get me a triple word score, when all of a sudden it felt like I was going to the bathroom on myself, so I jumped up. "I've got to pee," I said. "I'll be right back. And don't cheat."

I sat down on the toilet and left the door open so I could watch him, because I've busted him before. Then this gush of water started coming out of me, and I knew this wasn't pee. And it just kept coming! "Franklin! Franklin!"

"I'm right here. What's wrong?"

"My water. My water. My water broke!" I was scared to death and couldn't move. Was this it? Was this really it? I started crying and still couldn't move. Franklin got up and stood in the doorway.

"I wish you could see the look on your face, like you just seen a damn ghost." He started laughing.

"This isn't funny, Franklin. Is it coming now? I don't feel any contractions. What are we supposed to do? And look at the damn house. Why'd I have to pick today to tear it apart? Franklin, I'm scared." I couldn't remember a thing I'd been told in my Lamaze class, not a thing.

He just kept laughing. "Take it easy, baby, take it easy. What I wouldn't pay to have a picture of you right now."

"Franklin, this isn't practice. This is real. I'm about to have a damn baby. I don't believe this shit. I really don't believe it."

"First of all, is the water still coming out?"

I hadn't noticed one way or the other. Then I realized it had stopped.

"Then get up slowly," he said. I couldn't believe how calm he was, but of course he's been through this before. "I'll call the doctor and tell him what's going on."

I heard him dial the number. I damn sure didn't want the baby to be born in the toilet, so I stood slowly and pulled my panties up, then my blue jeans. I didn't pull the top part over my belly, just in case the baby needed some breathing room. Baby? Up to now, it really felt like I was going to be pregnant forever and the baby was just a nice thought. But it's on its way now.

"Baby, do you feel any contractions yet?" he asked.

"No. You think it's dead?"

"She don't feel nothing yet," I heard him say. "Yeah, it's been moving. For the past hour that's all we been doing is watching it. Okay, I'll watch her. It's seven o'clock now. Twelve hours. Got it."

"Franklin, what did he say?"

"Take it easy, baby. First of all, you need to lay down over here on the couch, and I gotta get my watch and write down every time you feel a contraction. Don't you feel nothing yet?"

"Sort of like a flutter, but it doesn't hurt. It's supposed to hurt."

"Well, look. Lay down. It was your turn, wasn't it?"

"Franklin? Are you nuts? You mean to tell me you still want to play Scrabble, and I'm getting ready to have a baby? And look at this damn place."

"You ain't having it right now, and the doctor told me to

keep you occupied and we *can't* fuck, so will you make your word?" He was actually laughing!

"Oh-oh. Franklin, now I do feel something."

"What does it feel like?" He looked at the clock, got one of the Scrabble pads, and wrote down the time.

"Sort of like cramps, but it still doesn't really hurt."

"Well, the doctor told me if you ain't having 'em within ten minutes apart in five hours for me to call him back. He said you supposed to have this baby within twelve hours after the water break, or the baby might get infected."

"Twelve hours? What time is it now?"

"Ten after seven. Look, I can see we ain't gon' finish this game in peace. Why don't you go upstairs and lay down?"

"Am I supposed to walk up stairs?"

"What harm can it do?"

I got off the couch and walked up the stairs like I was handi-capped. I was surprised I made it in one piece. I lay down on the bed and looked at the clock, and that's when I felt something again. This one hurt a little bit, but not all that bad. Franklin turned on the TV. He had his little piece of paper with him and he lay down beside me. "How you feeling now, baby?"

"Tired," I said, and I did.

"Then try to get some sleep. We may have our work cut out for us yet, so get it while you can."

I closed my eyes and didn't think I'd really fall asleep, but the next thing I knew, something pulled in my stomach, and it woke me up. I grabbed Franklin's hand. "Franklin, it's hurting now."

He got out his pen and wrote. The clock said ten-twenty. Where'd the time go? "I think we should call the doctor, Franklin."

"It's only been three hours, baby. Not yet. You just lay back down and try to take it easy."

So I did, but this was getting serious. Every time I closed my eyes, one would wake me up, and I would grab Franklin's pants leg, his arm, something, and dig my fingers into him.

"Damn, these suckers is coming now, ain't they, baby?" he said, with his little fucking pen in his hand. His legs were crossed, and he had the nerve to get up and change channels.

I couldn't have answered him if I had wanted to; I was too busy gritting my teeth. Then I dozed off, and was awakened again. Finally, I snatched his little pad out of his hands and tried to count how many I'd had so far, and that's when another one hit me. I started crying. Franklin kept writing, and I kept crying. They were still only ten minutes apart, but by one o'clock, he called the doctor and told him. "When they're five minutes? Okay, we'll be there."

"What did he say—can I come now?"

"Nope. If they're not five minutes apart by five this morning, I'm supposed to take you then."

"I can't take this shit that long."

"That's what the doctor said, Zora."

I lay back down, and pretty soon this was unbearable. I mean really. It seemed like someone was shooting me with darts. I knew one thing already—I wouldn't go through this shit again if you paid me a million dollars.

"Come on, baby, let's go," Franklin said.

"What? What time is it?"

"Quarter to five."

"It couldn't be." But it was, and Franklin's little list was two whole pages. His eyes were beet red; he probably hadn't been to sleep at all. I felt sorry for him. Then I sat up, although I didn't think I could. "How are we getting there?"

"I've got a cab waiting downstairs."

"What about my little bag? And I need to take a shower, Franklin. I know I must smell. And my hair!"

"The bag is right by the door. And if you want me to tell the cabdriver to wait till you take your shower and do your hair, fine."

"Fuck you, Franklin! Did you call Judy?"

"I'll call her when we get there. Come on, Zora."

I had to walk slowly down the steps because these suckers were coming at me from every direction now. God, how do women do this three and four and ten times is what I want to know. I could hardly sit on the seat in the cab because it hurt. And why don't they get these damn potholes fixed? I held Franklin's hand so tight that it was wet.

"It's okay, baby," he said when he saw me banging my head against the glass. "You're just having a baby, not dying."

"Shut up, Franklin! Have you ever had a baby?"

"Yeah, twice."

By the time we got inside and they examined me, I was only four centimeters. The baby wouldn't be here for a while, the doctor said. "But it hurts," I said. "We know," was all the nurse said. "We know. Try walking around a bit. Where's your husband?"

"He's calling my coach."

"Well, ask him if he'll get you some ginger ale. That might help."

Ginger ale? This bitch must be on drugs. Franklin appeared and told me Judy was on her way. He went to get my soda, and when he came back, I could smell the alcohol on his breath. I swear, I wished I could've drunk some too. Anything to stop this pain. I drank the soda, threw it right up, and the nurse told Franklin to keep walking me. So he did. Back and forth, up and down that damn hallway I don't know how many times. Every few minutes I had to lean against the wall to hold myself up. Nothing should have to hurt this much, nothing.

Judy showed up about six-thirty. "How's it going, Zora?"

I just looked at her and wanted to slap her.

"Come on, it's my turn to walk you. You remember what we learned in class?"

"Fuck you and fuck that class," I said.

"Zora, it's that bad, huh?"

"No, I feel great."

"They told me this might happen too, so I'm not gonna take it personally."

After what felt like hours, I said, "What time is it?"

"Ten o'clock," Franklin said.

I was lying down on a couch now, and the pain felt like it was shooting everywhere inside me, no matter which way I turned. Finally, the nurse came out and got me, measured me, and said, "Is everyone coming?"

Franklin and Judy got up. They wheeled me into this white room and put me on another bed. Then the nurse got out this IV thing, and I asked what that was for. "We're going to have to induce your labor. You're still only six centimeters. This'll cause your cervix to open a little faster, but it may hurt a bit more."

It couldn't possibly hurt any more than this. But I didn't care at this point; I just wanted this shit to be over. She wasn't lying: This pain was worse than worse. Franklin and Judy sat at the foot of the bed, watching how big my contractions were when they appeared on a screen that I couldn't see. It was like a damn game to them. And every now and then Franklin would whip out his bottle and take a nip.

"This is all your goddamn fault!" I yelled.

He started laughing, and that's when Judy got up and came over to the bed to help me breathe right again. I swear I was trying to cooperate. The next thing I knew, I had a bowel movement right there in the bed. The nurse came in and said it was all right, that this was good. Give me a break, I thought.

Right after she changed the sheets, it happened again. And then I felt like I had to go just one last time. I pleaded with her to let me go into the bathroom while she changed these sheets, and that's when the doctor came in and started putting my legs up and everything, and I said, "Please can't I just go to the bathroom, just once more. Just once more."

"You sure can, and you can go right here. Just slide down a little bit more."

"I don't want to do it right here," I said. I was already kind of embarrassed but in too much agony to really give a damn. Okay, I thought, fuck it. If they want to see it, they can see it. It felt like this was the biggest bowel movement I ever had to make in my life. If I could just push down one good time, then I'd be ready to have this baby.

"We're ready," the doctor said. So I pushed. And boy oh boy, did it feel good. That's when I felt something plop out of me, and the doctor said, "It's coming. Keep pushing."

"What's coming?" I asked.

"The baby's head's in my hands. Just keep pushing, and we'll be finished in a minute."

"You've gotta be kidding," I said. Franklin was standing up, looking down. "Come on, baby, I see it! I see it!"

I couldn't believe this shit. It didn't even hurt now, but I pushed with all my might, and that's when everybody started screaming. All I knew was that I felt a great sense of physical relief.

"Congratulations, it's a boy!"

"What?"

Then the doctor held up this little pale wailing thing, and sure enough, it was a baby. I started crying. Was that all there was to it? I looked at what he had in his hand, and if Franklin had got out of my way, maybe I could've seen him whole. Then he ran over to me and kissed me on the lips.

"Thank you baby, thank you baby, thank you baby. We got us a baby boy!"

"Is he okay?" I asked.

"He looks fine," the nurse said.

By now the doctor was doing some other stuff down there, and the nurse had taken the baby over to this little scale to weigh and measure him and clean him up. And that's when I felt something else fall out of me. Even though I knew I was tired as hell, I felt as high as a kite. Like I was floating. I kissed Franklin back and looked at him. "But it's a boy," I said.

"I know, and I'm happy."

Judy walked over and kissed me and squeezed my hand. "You were great, Zora. You were just great. Congratulations!"

I lay there and kept staring over at the little pale body until the nurse wrapped him up in a blanket and put this little ski cap thing on his head and brought him over to me. "Do you know how to hold him?"

"I think I can manage," I said. I was grinning so hard, my heart felt like it was expanding. When she finally handed him to me, I sat up and cradled him in my arms and looked down at his wrinkled face. "Hello, Jeremiah," I said. "Welcome to the world."

26

While Zora was in the hospital, I got the house back in order. I bought her some flowers too, 'cause she deserved 'em. I don't know how women can go through all that pain and come out in one piece. Shit, Zora didn't mention nothing about no pain once she picked up Jeremiah. She said, to be honest, that whole part was vague, and she couldn't remember the pain, really. Shit. I was there.

I know one thing—he sure is pale. As black as I am, and as brown as Zora is, I can't understand why that boy ain't darker. If I didn't know better, I'd have my doubts. But I know better.

Of course she's breast-feeding. She said she had to, 'cause it's better for the baby. It'll stop him from getting sick as he gets older. My Moms didn't breast-feed me. I know that for a fact, and I can count on one hand the colds I've had in my whole life.

They'll be home on Tuesday, which gives me two days to come up with something. This morning I went down to the union hall and told 'em if they didn't get me a job within twenty-four hours, I was gon' turn all them motherfuckers in for collusion. I ain't stupid. And check this out: As I'm walking out the place, the guy says to me, "Hold on a minute. You don't get jobs by threatening people, son."

"I ain't threatening. It's just some things I know that you didn't know I knew, and some people too."

He shuffled some papers and then said, "Hold on. Maybe I got something here, good for about three months. Interested?"

"Depends."

"On what?"

"On where."

"Downtown Brooklyn."

"Starting when?"

"Today, if you get on over there."

"Consider me there," I said.

Three months was better than nothing, and I wasn't surprised when it was the same site I had worked at before. Mel was surprised as hell to see me, and both of us pretended like I never left. I couldn't wait to get to the hospital to tell Zora. This would make her day.

I was doing drywalls, thank God, which meant I was inside. I could do this shit with my eyes closed.

Zora was feeding Jeremiah when I got there.

"Hi," I said. She looked so pretty, and I'd even go so far as to say younger. She was glowing, maybe 'cause she was happy.

"Hi," she said back, grinning.

"How you and my man doing?"

"Oh, just fine. He's a greedy little varmint, I can say that much. Every two hours, here he goes. He's sleeping in here with me, did I tell you?"

"Where else is he supposed to sleep?"

"In the nursery, but I wanted him here. Might as well get used to it."

"How come he's so pale?"

"I don't know. Look at him. He's not all that pale."

I looked at him, and sure enough the boy was at least two shades darker than he was yesterday. How do that shit work? I wondered. Now we getting somewhere. "I was beginning to have my doubts, baby. He still got about five more shades to go before I believe he's mine." I started laughing. "Just kidding."

"You want to hold him?"

"Not really. He's too little. What if I hurt him or something?"

"Franklin, you won't hurt him. Here."

She handed him to me, and he didn't weigh nothing. It had been a long time since I held a baby, especially one that was mine. I looked down at him. This was my son, all right. "Look at that nose. That's my nose, ain't it?"

"If God is on his side, it won't be."

"Go to hell, Zora."

We both started laughing.

"Guess what?"

"You cleaned the house."

"Better than that. Yeah, I cleaned the house, but I got a job."

"Doing construction or something different?"

Now I felt kinda disappointed, 'cause I forgot I had told her I was gon' look for something outside of construction, but fuck it. I needed a job now, and I got one. Don't nothing pay like construction, that's for damn sure. "Sheetrock, and union scale, and it'll be good through the end of March. By then, I'ma thinka something with some permanence to it. I got another mouth to feed now, if you get my drift."

"I get your drift. How do you feel about this?"

"So-so. It's a job. It's work. It's a paycheck."

"Well, I'm glad to hear it, Franklin. I won't go back to work until the first of April, and you know we're going to have to find a baby-sitter."

"Don't remind me."

"Have you heard any more about your sister?"

"Just that she's out to my folks' house. I ain't called out there yet. I don't feel like it. I will, in due time."

"Franklin, thank you for giving me a beautiful baby."

"You're welcome," he said and handed Jeremiah back to me. Then he stood up. "Now hurry up and get your ass home, 'cause if I remember correctly, it was your turn, and I still got the letters on the table."

"You can't be serious."

"I am. Look, I just came to see the little munchkin and make sure you was still glad to be a mama and everything. I gotta be at work at seven, and I gotta wash my work clothes. I miss you, Zora. It's too quiet around there when you gone."

"I miss you too, Franklin. But when we both get home, you'll probably be eating those words."

She had that shit right. That bassinet didn't stay in Jeremiah's room more than two hours. Zora couldn't stand not seeing him. "What if he suffocates, and I'm not there?" Shit, it's a whole lotta babies sleep in their own room and don't die, but I didn't say nothing. So in he came, right next to our bed. Every time he cried, she jumped. Which was about every two hours. And every time I rolled over, her titty was out and stuck in his mouth.

The phone jumped off the hook. People I ain't never heard of was calling. And one by one, every last one of her girl-friends showed up. It was like they was rotating. Every time I'd come home from work, seem like a different one, or the same one that was here just the week before was back. It got to the point where I was sick of seeing all of 'em. Couldn't walk around in your own house butt naked after you took a shower. I wanted to take Jeremiah upstairs with me, but shit, couldn't do that either, 'cause all they came for was to drool over him and ask Zora questions.

Seem like a package came once a week too. From people from her church in Ohio that she couldn't even hardly remember. And her stepmother, Marguerite, she was pitiful. For the first month she sent boxes full of all kinda shit. I know I shouldn't be complaining, but I can't lie: I wasn't the star in this house no more. All the lights was shining on Jeremiah.

One thing I can say—and I don't know how this shit works, but right after Zora came home from the hospital, she had already dropped almost twenty pounds, and Jeremiah didn't weigh but seven pounds nine ounces. And over the next month and a half, she had dropped almost fifteen more. She said breast feeding helped. And the other thing was that that Nivea shit musta worked, 'cause she didn't have no more stretch marks than she had before she got pregnant. At least not on her stomach. I ain't never seen no shit like this, never.

By March, Jeremiah was a pretty brown. A little darker than Zora but not as dark as me. That was good enough for me. And he looked old enough to vote. Like a little man. I'm grateful that he wasn't no screamer either. As a matter of fact, he sleeps all night now, but Zora said she ain't putting his bassinet in his room until she's sure he's safe. Which is when? But I ain't saying nothing.

When the boy wakes up, he don't cry. Sometimes I walk over there and he's kicking his little legs up, and he's grinning and shit. The boy's well hung, which means he takes after his Daddy. This morning, I saw the bassinet kinda rocking back and forth, and Zora was out like a light, so I got up and picked him up and put him on my lap. I checked his Pamper, and as usual, he was wet. I ain't never changed no baby before, but I figured it would be stupid to wake her up to do some shit like this. I got it off of him, but he wouldn't stay still long enough for me to maneuver the damn thing to get it on him, so I just looked at him. "How about some fresh air on that little dick?" The boy just drooled, so I sat up against the wall and held him up on my lap. Check this out. The little chump kept trying to stand. No shit. He couldn't even hardly hold his damn head up, and he was grunting and shit, trying to stand. Squeezed my hands hard too. What a grip this kid's got. This kid gon' be in the Olympics, I'll put money on it.

I spoke too soon. 'Cause the next thing I knew, he stopped moving and looked dead at me. I thought he was getting ready to smile—something I been waiting on—but that ain't what he had in mind. I started smiling at him, talking baby talk and shit, and the next thing I knew, his little dick perked up and he was pissing in my lap. "Zora! Get this boy," I yelled. "You little chump," I said, laughing. And then he started his little jumping routine again.

"What's going on?" she asked, rolling over.

"Here, take this little pissy thing."

"Where's his Pamper?"

"I couldn't get it on. Here."

I handed my son to her and went to clean myself up. When I came back, he was up under her, just sucking away. I can't lie: I wished it was me.

When I got home from work today, wasn't nobody here but Zora and Jeremiah.

"Franklin, you've got to see this. Watch."

"Wait a minute. I ain't even in the door yet."

"You've got to see it now, because he might not do it again."

I stood there and waited. She did some cooing and shit, but I didn't notice nothing out of the ordinary.

"Did you see that?"

"See what?"

"Him smiling."

"Yeah," I said, lying. "That's nice. What's for dinner?"

"Spaghetti and meatballs."

"Again?"

"I was tired, and besides, I made enough for two days."

"You been home all day; you coulda cooked."

"You don't know what I do around here all day. Taking care of a baby isn't the same as just being home all day. Guess what?"

"Surprise me."

"Daddy wants me and Jeremiah to come to Ohio for a week, and he's already paid for the ticket. We're leaving day after tomorrow."

"You didn't ask me if you could go."

"What do you mean, 'ask you'? Since when did I have to get your permission to go somewhere?"

"What am I supposed to do while y'all gone for a whole week?"

"Franklin, please. You knew I was going home before I went back to work, so don't act so surprised."

"Have a good time, then. I gotta take a shower. Wait a minute. Let me ask you something. You gon' give me some pussy before you go, I hope."

"I'll put it on my calendar, Franklin. Okay?"

"When you gon' start giving that boy a bottle?"

"Why?"

" 'Cause every time I look around, you feeding him. How much he weigh now?"

"Ten pounds thirteen ounces. To tell you the truth, I bought him some formula today. I'm too tired all the time, so I'm going to supplement him with two bottles a day until I wean him."

"Good."

I went upstairs and got the water as hot as I could stand it. A whole damn week. What am I supposed to do without her?

When we got in the bed, I asked if we could put Jeremiah in his room, just for a little while. She hesitated but gave in. I swear, you almost don't know how to act when you ain't fucked your woman in damn near three months. I didn't know if Tarzan could still hang, but he surprised me. Then Zora fucked it up.

"Franklin, I can't breathe. You're putting all your weight on me. Could you just lift up some?"

"What you trying to say, baby?"

"I'm just asking you to lift up some. You've gained a few pounds yourself, you know, and I can't breathe."

Then Jeremiah started crying, and she just looked at me, like "I gotta go." When I rolled over, so did my dick.

Zora seemed too happy to be leaving. And she looked awful damn good too. Too good, if you ask me. I don't think she need to lose no more weight. She look fine just the way she is. But of course she thinks she's on a roll, and had the nerve to tell me that when she get back, she joining a health club, a new one that ain't far from the house. I wanna know where she got the money, but I ain't got the nerve to ask her. Since it is a new club and everything, they got this discount membership. I even checked it out, and I wouldn't mind joining it, but since I told her I didn't want her to join my club, I can't turn around and join hers, or can I? Maybe she got something up her sleeve. Maybe she saw something in that club she like besides Nautilus equipment and the damn sauna. Naw, don't start, Franklin. Don't start it, man.

For the whole week, she didn't even call. I wondered what she was doing, since she obviously had a built-in baby-sitter. Didn't she miss me? Hell, no; she got Jeremiah. All she do is live for that baby. I was tempted to go out and get me some pussy, just for spite, but by the time I got home from work, I was too beat to think about going to the bar. So what I did for seven days was ate tuna fish out the can, polished off the rest of that spaghetti, which tasted better than I remembered, and snacked on sardines and crackers and boiled rice. I went through two fifths of Jack Daniel's, and when I took a shower last night, I was embarrassed. My ass was bigger than Zora's. I got on the scale. Goddamn. When did I gain twenty-six fuckin' pounds? Shit. No wonder Zora didn't want my ass on top of her, but all I been wearing is work clothes and sweats; I didn't realize I had got this damn big. All this damn alcohol, and doing Sheetrock ain't getting it. And my fuckin' waistline is disappearing too. No wonder the women ain't staring me down these days. I used to damn near stop traffic, get double takes and shit. But them days ain't over. I'll be damned if I'll turn into flab when my woman's done had a baby and is starting to shine all over again. No way.

The day before they was coming home, she called.

"I miss you, baby," I said.

"I miss you too, Franklin. Has anyone called me?"

"Like who?"

"Like a woman named JayJay?"

"Naw. Who's that?"

"I'll tell you when I get home. Love you, and see you to-morrow."

I made sure the pad was spotless, so she wouldn't have nothing to complain about. I couldn't concentrate on my work for thinking about her. And right after lunch, I made a big mistake. Somebody was passing a bottle, and I started sipping. Then I took a break and went across the street and bought my own. By two o'clock, I was damn near seeing double. And when a slab of Sheetrock slipped out my hands and I fell back and it landed on my goddamn knee, it was all over. I couldn't walk.

I don't remember who took me to the emergency room, and I don't remember how I got home. All I know is that when I woke up, I was in my own bed, had a cast on my leg, and Zora was standing over me.

"Franklin! What happened to you?" she asked. She laid Jeremiah down. For me. She put him down for me.

"I got hurt on the job, baby, and I missed you. I missed you so bad," I said.

She walked around to my side of the bed and put her arms around me. Then she kissed me everywhere she could on my face. "Are you really okay, Franklin, for real?"

"I don't know, baby, I don't know."

"Can I get you anything? Does it hurt anywhere? Are you in pain?"

"Just right there," I said, pointing. "It hurts there."

"Would you like a pillow under it?"

"Yeah," I said. "A pillow would be fine."

"Are you hungry? Did they give you something for the pain?"

"Yeah, I took it already. But come here. Lay down here next to me and keep me warm."

She put Jeremiah in his bassinet and came over and laid

down next to me. She put her arms around me again, and I put my head between her breasts. I exhaled and dug my head in deeper.

"You been gone too long," I said.

"Well, I'm back," she said. "I'm back."

27

A baby can change your whole life.
Next to Franklin and my Daddy, I don't think I've ever loved any one person this much.

And I don't know where I've gotten all this energy. It's as if I'm on cruise control. While Franklin's at work, I put Jeremiah in his stroller, bundle him up real good in his snowsuit Portia bought him, and we take long walks. I want to say to everyone I pass, "Isn't he beautiful?" But I don't. The only thing that brings me down is this neighborhood. There's trash on the street, on the sidewalk, and I have to roll over it. I am certain of one thing: I'm not raising Jeremiah in New York. That much I do know. This is no place to grow up, I don't care what Franklin says. A child should be able to go out in the backyard and play, or the front yard, for that matter. No one in Brooklyn has a front yard. I've already made a vow to him: By the time he's three years old, we're out of here. With or without his Daddy. Record contract or no record contract. Don't ask me where I'd like to go. I haven't taken this dream that far yet.

And am I dropping pounds by the day? Yes, yes, yes. I never did tell Franklin that Marie paid me back my eight hundred dollars; something told me to keep my mouth shut about it. So I took $163 of it and joined this new health club right around the corner. Once I start work, on the way home this'll be my first stop. I have no intention of staying fat. None whatsoever.

Today, though, I had to interview a baby-sitter. I'd already waited to the last minute. This morning, Jeremiah and I had walked over to the city's day-care center, but they didn't have any openings for his age group. A nice black woman, who ran the program, was very helpful. "When you got to go back to work, baby?" she asked me.

"In two weeks," I said.

"Lord, don't you hate the thought?"

But before I could answer, she just kept on talking. She had to be around forty, but well preserved, and as petite as she could be, with the exception of that behind of hers. Her name was Betty.

"You know what? My cousin Mary baby-sits, and she's good with chil'ren. Got five daughters, honey." She looked down at my application. "And she live right around the corner from you. She live the same as what I do. In the Gowanus projects. You want her number?"

She wrote it down on a piece of paper, and as soon as I got home, I phoned. Mary sounded very nice and said she could come right over to meet us. She was there in less than twenty minutes. She was quite attractive, taller than I was, about five foot nine, and a little heavyset; she had long, crinkly hair. The first thing she did was pick up Jeremiah and smile at him. He smiled back at her. "What a handsome little guy. How old you say he is?"

"Three and a half months."

"My goodness. He's a little bruiser, ain't he? Is he on formula?"

"Yes."

"Baby food?"

"Cereal and fruit."

"That's good." She sat down on the couch and looked around. "You sure got a nice place here."

"Thank you." Jeremiah was jumping on her lap, and she was holding him right. I felt good about her. Very good. "So do you charge very much?"

"Whatever you can afford is fine. I just had a little boy what leave me after four years. Broke my heart, and all my girls is in school, and I could use some company. Whatever you wanna pay me is fine."

I couldn't believe this. Betty had told me fifty dollars a week would be plenty. When I offered it to Mary, she said that was just fine.

"Would you like to see my apartment first?" she asked.

As neat and clean as she was dressed, I assumed her house was the same way. Her fingernails were clean, and I didn't want to insult her just because she lived in the projects, so I said, "Maybe we'll stop by in a day or so to meet the rest of the family," which is what we did. And I was right. Her husband was just as friendly; they'd been married for twenty-one years, and all their daughters—who almost fought over which of them was going to hold and play with Jeremiah—were just as good-natured as their parents.

Franklin was hopping around the house in his cast when we got back. He'd been getting around pretty good, and had left before we had this morning to check on getting his workman's compensation. He was going to have to wear this cast for six weeks.

"I found a wonderful baby-sitter," I said.

"That's good. How much?"

"Fifty a week."

"Damn. That's two hundred a month, ain't it?"

"She's cheap, Franklin. Most day cares cost more than that."

Then he turned to Jeremiah. "Come here, you little crumb-snatcher."

Nothing made me happier than to see him playing with his son.

My first morning going back to work was weird. I was up at the crack of dawn, getting all Jeremiah's stuff packed in the diaper bag. I must've packed at least fifteen Pampers, six bottles of formula, baby wipes, rattles, two bottles of juice, three or four changes of clothes in case he spit up too badly—too much of everything. I was out the door by seven, and the poor thing was still asleep when I put on his snowsuit. Then I wrapped I don't know how many blankets around him. You could hardly see him as I pushed him in the stroller.

"My goodness, Zora, where is the baby?" Mary asked, then started laughing.

"Do I have too much on him, you think?"

"Chile, babies don't get no colder than we do. Don't worry about it, though. I can see you new at this."

"You're right. But, Mary, would you promise me one thing?"

"What's that?"

"That you take him for a little walk every day, or at least get some fresh air?"

"Chile, whenever the weather is good, we sit out on the bench all day. I can't stand being all cooped up here myself. Now you go on and have a good day."

By the time I got on the subway, I had this overwhelming feeling of emptiness and guilt, like I'd just abandoned my baby. I'd only known him less than four months, and I had already handed him over to somebody else. I looked around the train at all the other women and wondered how many of them had left their babies like I'd just done. How many of them had felt like this? Was I just being silly? And I wondered even more, as I looked at them reading their romance novels or *New York Times*, whether they were going to work because they wanted to or because they had to. I started crying and couldn't stop. I wished there was a way I could've stayed home with him for his first year—just to get to know him, watch him take his first step. I just prayed that I wouldn't miss out on that.

School was the same. Everyone was glad to see me.

"Miss Banks, we heard you had a baby boy. Is he as good-looking as you are?" someone said. I couldn't catch the voice, but I thought it might have been Luke, who the kids swore had a crush on me.

"Can he sing as good as you?" Maria asked.

I just laughed.

"What's it like being married?" Corinthia asked, leaning forward on her elbows.

I wanted to say, "I wish I knew," but instead I said, "It's great. Just great."

The day was uneventful. I wanted to call Mary on my lunch hour to ask if everything was going well, but I didn't want to get fanatic about this. After my last class, I had so much paperwork to attend to I couldn't get away until almost four-thirty. Normally, I'd be out of here by three forty-five. I couldn't wait to get to Mary's, and when I did, Jeremiah was sitting on one of her daughters' lap. She was ten.

"Hi, Miss Zora."

"Hi."

"Everything went just fine, Zora," Mary said. "He's such a good baby. The only time he cry is when he wet or hungry, huh?"

"I think so."

I started packing him up, and then Mary said, "Why don't you leave them bottles in the 'frigerator. You got enough to last a couple days, don't you thank?" She started laughing. "Y'all new mothers kill me. And you know what: If you wanna bring a box of Pampers and just leave 'em here, and a few clothes, it'll save you from lugging all that stuff in the morning."

I told her that was a very good idea, and it's what I did from then on.

Franklin hadn't heard a word about his workman's compensation, but he was getting around real well. And he had gained a few more pounds doing nothing but lying around the house all day. So this is what I asked him: "Would you mind picking Jeremiah up in the afternoons, since I take him over to the baby-sitter's? That's fair, don't you think?"

"Yeah; and no, I don't mind."

"Have you been doing any woodworking during the day?"

"I ain't got no wood and ain't got no money to buy none. I wanted to make us a dynamite wall unit to put all the books in, and a new bed frame—one that I can fit in—but it cost money."

"How much?"

"Well, I wanna put Formica on it. You know I don't make no bullshit, baby. I'm talking about real pieces of furniture—works of art. Something you'll be proud of. A couple of hundred; but a hundred would get me started."

I went in my purse and got it, since I had just got paid. And I don't know where my mind was, because the rent was almost due, and since he didn't have an income, I was going to have to pay all of it. Again. I was just getting sick of coming home seeing him planted in front of the TV.

"Thank you, baby. This is gon' be beautiful, I swear it is."

*   *   *

When I walked in from work the next day, Franklin was hard at work. "Where's Jeremiah?" I asked.

"Aw, shit, I knew it was something else I was supposed to do, baby. I'll go get him right now."

He forgot?

"Never mind," I said. "Never mind."

"I'll get him tomorrow. I promise. I was just so into this I got lost, baby. I gotta change my measurements again. I'm sorry."

The next day he didn't forget, but Jeremiah had pooped and Franklin acted like he didn't know how to change him and had left him on the bed, lying in it. I didn't say anything.

I had to go to the Laundromat, so I packed up the grocery cart and put Jeremiah on top in his baby seat. Franklin carried it downstairs for me. I washed five loads of clothes, and came home and cooked dinner.

By June, this routine was getting to be a little too much. When I asked Franklin why he couldn't watch Jeremiah or take him to the baby-sitter and pick him up, since he was home all day, he said, "I could get a phone call at any time of day about work, and what am I supposed to say—'I can't come 'cause I'm baby-sitting'?"

I never had time to go to the health club, and when I did, I was too damn tired. I'd been looking forward to having the summer off, but when I found out that Franklin wasn't getting any workman's compensation, because it turned out he'd been drinking on the job and it was all his fault—he had neglected to tell me that part—I had no choice but to sign up to teach summer school. We needed the money. Though his cast was now off, he was so into the bookcase—which was turning out to be even prettier than I expected—he asked if I could just bear with him a few more weeks, until he finished the bed.

Like a fool, I said yes.

A few more weeks lasted until September. And that's when I realized something. He didn't want to go back to work. Which I sort of understood. And granted, he was making himself useful around the house, but damn. This just felt so lopsided. I still loved the man, no doubt about that, but we were standing too still. I wanted him to do something. I wanted to be proud of him again. I wanted him to give me more reasons to look forward to spending the rest of my life with him. When we first met, Franklin excited me, kept me worked up. I never knew what to expect from him, and now I do. I guess the thing that hurts the most is knowing he has all this talent but isn't doing anything with it, except building furniture for us.

I mean, I've been hanging in there with him. I know I've gotten on his nerves, but he's gotten on mine too. I've often wondered, if I'd been off work the way he has, would he be as understanding. All I did know right now was that I'd been paying rent—everything, really—since March, and I couldn't stand it anymore. "Franklin, we need to talk," I said to him one Saturday morning after I'd asked him to watch Jeremiah while I went to the Laundromat, and he said he couldn't. "Why?" I'd asked. " 'Cause I'm gon' be using the power saw and drill, and I can't hear him when he cry and I don't want all this sawdust flying in his face. Take him with you. . . . Talk about what?"

"Everything."

"Not another one of these deep conversations. I know it's about my working, ain't it? But before you get all into it, let me tell you something. My knee still ain't right. It ain't no way I can go out there slinging bricks and shit, or it could go back out on me. Is that what you want to happen?"

"No, but you can do a lot of other things—"

He cut me off.

"Like what?"

"I don't know, but, Franklin, I can't keep this pace up. I'm paying for everything around here, and this month's rent is already late. After I pay the baby-sitter and rent and food and give you fifty dollars for wood and spending money, you know how much I have left out of my paycheck each month?"

"Naw. How much?"

"Sixty-eight dollars. This isn't right, Franklin, and you know it."

"Look, I'm almost finished with this bed, and that's when I'ma start looking. If you can't wait a few more weeks, I don't know what to tell you."

"You said the same thing in June."

"I'm saying it now too."

Something has happened to him, and I don't know what it is. All I know is this: If he doesn't have a job by Thanksgiving, he's getting out of here. I only gave birth to one baby; I'm not taking care of two.

I was starting to feel depressed all the time and didn't know what to do about it. If it weren't for Jeremiah, I don't know how I'd get from one day to the next. He's got six teeth now, and last night he took his first step—at nine months old! Franklin didn't seem all that impressed. I put him in the bath-tub—Franklin has never given him a bath—and sang to him while I bathed him. He likes it when I sing to him, and even sounds like he's singing too. After I picked him up and put his sleepers on, I gave him a bottle, and he was out like a light.

Franklin, as usual, had drunk his normal half pint—he'd cut down, he said—and had passed out on the bed with his clothes on. He was really starting to nauseate me.

But even though I was dead tired, I sprang up from the couch and walked to my music room. It seemed like a foreign place. I sat down at the piano and looked at it. The next thing

I knew, my fingers were pressing the keys, and a melody sur-
faced. And it kept coming and coming and coming. I couldn't
believe it. The magic was still there. I hadn't lost it at all. I
cried hard and looked out the window and up toward the sky.
"Thank you," I said, and I know He heard me. When I slid
away from the piano and stood up, I felt different. Unlike
anything I've ever felt in my life. As if something heavy had
been taken out of me and something light put in its place. I
opened the lid of the piano seat. It was full of music I'd written over I don't know how many years. And that's when something that I'd never even considered before, hit me. Not only
can you sing, Zora, but you can *write*. Do you have to stand
on a stage to sing? Do you have to make records in order to
affect people? I started pulling my bottom lip inside my
mouth with my teeth. God, hadn't I dreamed of what it would
feel like standing in front of those people with a microphone
in my hand? I sifted through the papers. These songs were
good, but I knew that when some of the melodies went
through my head, it wasn't always *my* voice I heard singing the
lyrics. Writing these songs was cleansing in and of itself. I always felt different when I finished. As if I'd been through
something, gotten over something, had a breakthrough of
some kind. Could I settle for this? Without even thinking, I
put the papers on the piano seat and walked down to Jeremiah's room. I just looked at him. What if I did get a record
contract and made it big? That would mean I'd be on the
road and away from home a lot. Wouldn't it? Jeremiah shifted
in his crib. I'm away from you enough as it is. "Too much," I
said aloud, and walked out of his room.

28

Since Zora thinks she's superwoman, I decided I was gon' let her be just that. She the one who think she got something to prove. All she do is throw shit in my face—how much she can do. Yeah, she's a good mother. She pays all the bills. She teaches. And now she's writing songs and shit again. I'ma get a job, but when I feel like it. She pressuring me all the time, and it seem like the more she get on my case, the less I feel like doing.

One thing I can say, though, is that I'm getting a whole lotta satisfaction working with this wood. It's the only thing I've made lately—besides Jeremiah—that I'm proud of. Zora don't seem to be that impressed by it. I do everything I can to get her to show me that she proud. When she come home, I got seven-foot boards laying right in the middle of the floor. And what do she say? "Franklin, do you have to do that here? Jeremiah can hurt himself."

All she think about is Jeremiah. He just done took over. It seem like he's her man, 'cause he get all the attention around here. I'm the stepchild. What she don't realize is how this shit makes me feel. And I'm tired of doing shit to get her attention, really tired. And even if I got a job right now, it wouldn't make no difference. Besides, I've had it with construction, really fuckin' had it. What she don't realize is how it feels to work and work and work at something and when you don't get no-goddamn-where you just lose all desire to do it again. That's exactly where I am, but it's kinda hard to get your woman to understand that you feel lost. Like I don't know what move to make next, and that's why I just concentrate on my wood. It's something I know I'm good at. It's something I can see the end results. I can look at it and say, "I made that." But Zora don't understand. All she think about is the bills. How lopsided this shit is right now, have been. But if she really loves me, she's just gon' have to stick by me while I get through this. Until I can think of something else to do.

Right now I can't think of nothing.

29

"Who you calling now?" he asked me.
"Why?" I asked.

"Whenever you come home these days, all you do is cook and then get on the phone. What about me?"

"What do you mean, what about you?"

"You could pay me a little attention sometimes."

"Like I don't?"

"Naw, you don't."

"Franklin, please."

"Franklin, please, my ass. It's that kid you love, not me. Now put the phone down."

"I've got to make a phone call."

"I said put the phone down and talk to me."

He snatched it from my hand, then yanked it completely out of the wall. "Now who you gon' call? Look at me, Zora!"

He was scaring me. Jeremiah was in his playpen, and in an instant my mind raced back to last summer up in Saratoga. But he wouldn't. He promised. "Franklin, take it easy, would you."

"Oh, so now you gon' tell me how to act, is that it?"

"What's bugging you all of a sudden?"

"Everything. You. This fuckin' kid. Me. Everything."

"Have you been drinking?"

"That's all you think about, ain't it, is how much I been drinking. Yeah, I been drinking." He opened the cabinet and pulled out a fifth of Jack Daniel's. It was almost full. Then he twisted off the top and took a long swallow. "You want some? That's probably what you need to loosen your stiff ass up. Here, take some."

He started coming toward me.

"Franklin, please. Stop it." I turned my head away, and he grabbed my face and looked me dead in the eye.

"Fuck it," he said, and threw the bottle against the wall. Liquor and glass splattered everywhere. "Just fuck it! Fuck you. Fuck this kid. Fuck everything!"

"Franklin, come here."

"Just leave me alone, would you? Make your goddamn telephone call. I'm outta here."

I just stood there for a minute and heard the door slam. What the hell was wrong with him now?

"Dada," Jeremiah was saying. I walked around the corner and saw him sitting in the middle of his playpen. "Dada," he said again, and I just started crying and touched his tiny hand. "Dada's gone," I said. "And good riddance."

I took Jeremiah upstairs so I could use the bedroom phone. I had written Reginald a note a while back and told him why I wasn't coming back for lessons, and he had left a message on my machine telling me that he was sorry, wishing me the best of luck, and saying that if I needed any connections or advice, to let him know. I just wanted to know how he was feeling these days. But he wasn't home. Judging by his voice on his machine, he was okay.

I was in bed when Franklin came in. I hadn't been able to fall asleep because I kept wondering if he was coming back or not.

Part of me wished he would just go away. Jeremiah and I would get along fine without him. He wasn't serving any purpose anymore. He seemed useless and hopeless and was draining me dry. Sometimes I'd walk through the house and think of when we first met, how beautiful it was. When I'd hear a certain record, I'd remember how much we used to laugh. But all that's changed. We haven't gotten anywhere together. He hasn't kept his promises. He's not doing anything with his life, at least anything I can see that would help me believe that one day we could actually be a happy family. And I'm tired. Tired of this boring-ass lifestyle. We never go anywhere. We never have any money to do anything except eat and go to work. This wasn't part of my dream, and I'm not settling for this bullshit. Jeremiah and I deserve better.

Franklin stumbled into the bedroom.

"Wake up," he said. "I know you ain't asleep."

"How did you know I wasn't asleep? It's after eleven o'-clock, Franklin. You know what time I go to bed."

"Yeah, you a deadbeat, all right. I need some pussy, baby."

"Franklin, please."

"Please, my ass. I want some pussy, and you gon' give me some tonight whether you want to or not."

"Oh, so you're going to rape me, is that it?"

"I guess so."

And he was telling the truth. He quietly walked over to the bed, pulled up my nightgown, and told me not to move. And I didn't. I couldn't believe this. This couldn't be the man I had fallen in love with. This couldn't be Franklin Swift doing this to me. But it was. He managed to get his clothes off, and to my surprise he was erect, which meant he'd had this whole thing planned. I wasn't about to try to fight him, because there was no telling what he might do. So I gave in.

He put all 238 pounds of his body weight on me, and even

though I could hardly move, I didn't say a word. I just lay there, numb as a rag doll.

He jabbed it in me as deep as he could.

"Franklin, take it easy. That hurts."

"I want it to hurt," he said. "Now move, goddammit."

So I moved.

In less than five minutes he was through.

"That's all I wanted," he said, and pushed me to my side of the bed.

I got up to go clean myself. "Get back here," he said.

"I'm just going to wash this stuff off."

"I want you to sleep in it, so you'll know you slept with a real man all night. Now lay down."

I got back in bed, and that's when I heard Jeremiah crying. I didn't know what to do, I was so scared.

"That's the baby, Franklin," I said.

"So?"

"So I can't just let him cry."

"So go get him. Ain't nobody stopping you. But do me a favor. Don't bring the little bastard in here. I don't feel like hearing it."

I walked into Jeremiah's room and picked him up. He was the only thing that felt real to me.

We slept on the couch.

In the morning, Franklin woke me up.

"I wanna talk to you," he said.

"Good, because you owe me an apology, Franklin."

"I don't owe you nothing."

I just looked at him. I swear, I wanted to spit in his face.

"I been thinking. Since you been doing everything around here anyway and shit, and since I don't feel needed or necessary, and since you probably had it planned on being a single mother all along, I'ma give you the opportunity to do just that."

"Just what are you saying?"

"I'm saying I want out. I need a break from you. From this kid. From everything. My head is all fucked up. I don't know what I'm doing, and I need to be by myself for a while."

"Oh, so you're leaving us?"

"Call it what you wanna call it. But by Thanksgiving, I'll be gone."

"That's fine with me."

"I figured you'd say that," he said, and was out the front door.

I lay there for a few minutes and didn't feel anything. Did he say he was leaving us? Jeremiah was still asleep, and just the thought of starting the day caused me to lose every drop of energy I thought I had. I wasn't going anywhere today. Leaving us? Then I suddenly felt this incredible feeling of relief. Leaving? Good. Go, I thought. We can make it a helluva lot easier without you. Go. Go. Go. I picked up my slipper and threw it at the door. "Go!"

Though I didn't go to work, I took Jeremiah over to Mary's house anyway. I needed to be by myself. To think. I didn't feel as drained as I had earlier, and something told me to pick up the phone and call that woman I'd met at my baby shower whose husband was a record producer. Before I knew it, I had dialed her number. Her husband answered the phone. I hadn't planned on talking to him, hadn't rehearsed my speech and had no idea what to even say to him, so I just told him what I'd been doing and where I'd been trained and all that, in one breath.

To my surprise, he knew Reginald, who had trained some of the people he'd produced. "Look," he said, "I'm always looking for new material. Do you have a tape you can send me?"

"I sure do."

"You've got it all copyrighted?"

"Yes, I do. Reginald made sure I did that. And look, I appreciate this, really, and don't feel obligated to get right back to me, because I understand how busy you are. Really I do. And if you don't like my music, my feelings won't be hurt." Then I realized I was lying. "Yes, they will."

He started laughing and told me he'd get back to me as soon as he came home from a road tour, which wouldn't be until the first of the year.

I didn't have anything but time.

30

I didn't have nowhere to go.

I was really calling her bluff, trying to see if she wanted me to go. Or better than that, I wanted to beat her to the punch. I knew my days was numbered and that she probably been plotting how she was gon' get me outta here. But my name was on this lease, just like hers was, so the only way I was gon' leave was by making the decision myself.

It ain't that I don't love Zora no more. It ain't that at all. I just done disappeared. I don't know who the fuck I am no more. And that pisses me off. I'm taking it out on her, I can see that. I'm jealous of my own son, and that shit ain't right, and I know it, but I don't know what to do with all this rage. All this anger I done accumulated. I gotta find the right outlet for it, though; that much I do know. And in order to do it, I gotta get away from her and Jeremiah. I gotta start all over. From scratch. The same way I was trying to do it when I first met her. When I think about it, I did the shit all wrong. If I remember correctly, it was my foundation I was working on, my constitution. Shit. But what did I do? Fell in love when I didn't have nothing to offer no woman of her caliber. And I knew that shit from jump street. She been to college. She already had accomplished something with her life, and she was still trying to do more. That was one of the things I liked about her. But now the shit is backfiring, pissing me off, and I know why. 'Cause I still ain't no-goddamn-where.

And Zora didn't even try to understand why I didn't wanna pick Jeremiah up from the baby-sitter. She didn't have no fuckin' idea how embarrassing that shit woulda been for me. So I used waiting for a phone call and my woodworking as a excuse—but that wasn't it. I couldn't stand the thought that all the people in that house knew I wasn't working, knew it was Zora paying her, and I didn't want to be looked at and see the question in their eyes, like, "What do you do all day?"

What I do all day is drink and stare at the walls and listen to music. Which is what I was doing today when the doorbell rang. It was the mailman. He had a package for Zora that wouldn't fit in the box. I brought all the mail upstairs and looked at that big brown envelope. It didn't have no return address on it, and I wanted to know what it was, so I opened it. I couldn't believe it. A fuckin' calendar of black men in bathing suits and shit. Why the fuck couldn't she wait till I was gone to bring some shit like this in here? I threw it on the kitchen table and sat back down on the floor and turned the music up. The longer I sat there, the madder I got. She ain't gotta throw the shit in my face, not like this. Here I been waiting for her to put her arms around me at night and tell me she don't want me to go, tell me she still loves me, still believes in me, but the deal is, she wants my ass outta here. I shoulda guessed. 'Cause ever since I told her I was leaving, she been strutting through this house happy as a little fuckin' lark. I been sleeping on the couch, 'cause I don't even want the pussy no more.

Ronald Reagan's wrinkled red face was on the TV, but I had the sound off 'cause I was mad that Jesse didn't win. I voted for the brother. The ashtray was overflowing when

Zora walked in with Jeremiah, and I was blasting the Temptations' new side, "Treat Her Like a Lady." I knew she was gon' wanna confront me, 'cause Thanksgiving was only four days away.

Jeremiah's cheeks was red. I looked over at the window, and it was snowing and dark. She looked worn out, but that's what she get, trying to be superwoman.

"Could you turn that down a little bit?" she asked me.

I didn't feel like it, but I did anyway.

She started taking off Jeremiah's snowsuit. She put him on the floor and he staggered over to me. I put him on my lap.

"Franklin, do you know what day it is?"

"Yeah, I know what day it is. Why?"

"You said you'd be gone by Thanksgiving, and you haven't started packing or anything."

"You got somebody else moving in here on Thanksgiving?"

"Be serious."

"So don't rush me."

"You're the one who said when you'd be leaving, and I've got arrangements I have to make."

"Like getting one of them motherfuckers on that calendar to come over and oil that dry-ass pussy?"

"What calendar?"

"That one right there, and if you don't want me to break your fuckin' neck, you better get it outta here. You got some nerve, you know that. I ain't left yet, and you already bringing this kinda shit in the house."

"Who told you to open my mail?"

"I did."

"Who was it that brought you *Players* magazine's calendar of naked women and hung it up in your workroom for you?"

"That ain't the point. All I'm saying is you got five minutes to get it outta here, or you gon' be sorry."

She jumped up and put it some-damn-where, and came and took Jeremiah from me.

"I need some more time," I said.

"For what?"

"To leave. I ain't got my plans worked out, and when I do, that's when I leave."

"Which is when?"

"I don't know yet."

"Franklin, I can't do this this way. It's not fair."

"Life ain't fair. But I'ma tell you something. You gon' be walking on eggshells around here until I do leave, 'cause with this stunt you just pulled today, I swear, I'd love to kick your ass one good time before I leave."

"Are you threatening me?"

"What it sound like to you?"

She went in the kitchen and started cooking. The phone rang, and she answered it. I freshened my drink. She kept on talking and talking and talking, just like I wasn't there. I think I'm beginning to realize how you love somebody and hate 'em at the same time. The fuckin' line is so thin. I heard her laughing and shit, while she fed Jeremiah. Finally, she hung up the phone and took him to the bathroom to give him his bath. She stepped over my feet and shit, like I was a piece of furniture.

Right now, I swear to God, I could kill her.

31

When I got Jeremiah's bottle out of the kitchen, I also got a butcher knife and slid it under my armpit. I did not say good night to Franklin. I walked back upstairs and tried to stop my knees from shaking. I didn't know what he was thinking or what he might do to me. Jeremiah was already asleep when I went into his room, so I brought the bottle back into my room. Then I thought about it. If Jeremiah was in here with me, Franklin might be less likely to do anything to hurt me, so I put the knife under my pillow, brought Jeremiah back in here, and laid him down next to me. And then I waited.

Franklin was playing all these old love songs—songs we used to make love to: Teena Marie's "Portuguese Love" three times in a row; The Whispers; Al Jarreau, Stevie Wonder, and Jeffrey Osborne. I kept my eyes open for hours, just listening and remembering. I could not believe that we had arrived here. The man downstairs was not the same man I fell in love with. He was Jeremiah's father, but not his Daddy. When did all this happen? And where was I?

I heard the record scratch. He was changing them, and probably so drunk he didn't even know he scratched it. Now it was Tina Turner he'd put on—"What's Love Got to Do with It?"

I lay there and cried, because I knew what it had to do with it. Everything. He must've played that record at least ten times in a row, and on full blast. I wanted to ask him to turn it down, but I wasn't crazy.

Then the music stopped.

And that's when my heart started pounding, because I knew he was probably on his way up here. I put my head under the pillow, my hand on the knife, and just lay there and waited for the door to open. But the next thing I knew, I felt a tiny hand wandering over my back, the weight of Jeremiah's twenty-one-pound body following, and when I opened my eyes, daylight streamed through the window.

"Good morning, pookah-pookah," I said, and he grinned, looking just like his Daddy. I got up and took him downstairs, afraid of what I might find. Maybe he had decided to go ahead and leave. But before I reached the bottom step, I saw him on the floor, sprawled out like a big black whale on an island of album covers. The living room smelled like an old bar, and the bourbon bottle was empty. He coughed about ten times but didn't wake up.

I tiptoed around him and got Jeremiah ready for the baby-sitter. Instead of packing enough things for the day, I packed enough for several. I took him to Mary's and told her the truth about what was happening between me and Franklin.

"Jeremiah's fine here. You go ahead and do what you gotta do, and don't worry about this baby."

I went to a restaurant and phoned the school and told them I was sick. Then I called Portia and told her everything and asked if I could stay with her a day or two, until I could figure out what to do next. She told me to come on over.

Her new place was beautiful. Her rent was paid and she was happy. I envied her. "Where's the baby?" I asked.

"With Arthur's Mama. Girl, they love her to death, and come get her so I can have a few hours to myself."

"That's good."

"So did this motherfucker hit you?"

"No, but he told me he wanted to."

"So put him out, since he don't wanna leave."

"How?"

"Get a fucking restraining order. The police'll make him leave."

"But his name is on the lease."

"That don't mean shit. He ain't paid no rent in centuries, and not only that but he's threatened you, and you're scared. That's all they need to know."

"How long does the process take?"

"Hell, hours of waiting, but are you scared to go back home?"

"Yeah."

"Then stand in line. He ain't the only motherfucker that's fucked up, you know. You want some coffee?"

"No. I should go now and get it over with."

"Damn, you gotta go all the way back to Brooklyn, you know. You know where the Family Court is?"

"Yeah."

"Right in there."

After Portia left for school, I didn't have the energy to go anywhere, so instead I watched soap operas all day—something I've never done. By the time Portia got home, President Reagan was holding a press conference on every network. Shit. I didn't even vote. Arthur cooked dinner, and I tried to eat, but couldn't. I finally just fell asleep on the couch.

In the morning, I took the subway to Brooklyn, and the ride felt like it lasted a week. By the time I got to court, it was five after nine. There were only two or three people in front of me. What was I going to say? It turned out that I told the truth. And it worked. They gave me the form and said that I had to get it served on him. But how was I going to do that?

I sat in the waiting room for at least another half hour, just thinking. This was stupid, I thought. Stupid, stupid, stupid. I walked over to the phone booth and dialed. Franklin answered the phone.

"Where you been?" he asked.

"It doesn't matter," I said.

"What you trying to prove, Zora?"

"Franklin, you've scared me so bad that I can't stay in the same house with you another day."

"Didn't nobody tell you to bring no fuckin' calendar of naked men in here, did they?"

"I want you to leave today."

"Oh, so you *telling* me to leave, is that it?"

"Yes."

He started laughing.

"I didn't think we'd get to this point, Franklin, really I didn't. I have loved you from the beginning, and you know it. I've tried to be understanding, tried to be supportive, but it doesn't seem to have done any good. You've gotten hostile and angry and lazy, and I can't take it."

"Spare me the sentimental bullshit, would you. I told you, I'll leave when I'm good and ready."

"I've got a restraining order."

"You got a what?"

"I'm at the courthouse now, and it's in my hand. If you're not out of there by tomorrow, the police'll come and make you leave."

"You mean to tell me that you went to the *white* man to get me outta here? The fuckin' *white* man? You bitches is all alike, I swear to God. You know what? I'm taking half of everything I paid for in here, and you wanna know something else? Fuck you and the *white* man."

He hung up.

I took the train back to Portia's, even though I was only ten minutes from Mary's house and I wanted to see my baby. But I couldn't chance it. Then I wondered if Franklin would go over there, so when I got to Portia's, I called. Mary said she hadn't heard anything from him, and if he came over she would just not let him in and would tell him that Jeremiah wasn't there. I thanked her and felt relieved, in a way.

Portia was at school all morning, so I sat around looking out the twenty-four-story window at the cars that looked like matchboxes, the people that looked like ants, and the smoke-stacks in Brooklyn. I called the phone company and told them I wanted the number changed to an unlisted one. How soon could they do it? Tomorrow, they said. Tomorrow. What now? I wanted to call my Daddy, but I couldn't. He would be too worried.

When Portia came in, she had Sierra with her, and that's when it hit me that I hadn't seen my son in more than twenty-four hours now.

"What happened?" she asked.

"I did it, and I called him and he was pissed off, of course, and said he was taking half of everything, even though he said he wasn't leaving until he got ready."

"Fuck him. You wanna go home?"

"Not right now. I'm still scared."

"All we gotta do is get the police to go with us. We'll do it tomorrow. I don't have no classes, and Ma Dear'll pick up Sierra at eight and we can go out there together. Okay?"

"Okay," I said.

The policeman went in first. I was still terrified that he'd be in there, with a gun, aimed at me. But he wasn't there. The policeman turned toward me and Portia.

"The place is a wreck, ma'am. He must've gone a little crazy."

I wanted to see for myself what he meant, and when I stepped inside, I felt a cold breeze hit me in the face. All the windows were wide open, and the first thing I saw was sawdust all over the floor. The seven-foot bookcase Franklin had built was chopped up into tiny pieces and piled in the middle of the floor. I walked upstairs to the bedroom, and he'd done the same thing to the bed. Even the mattress had been shredded.

"That sick bastard!" Portia said, as she walked through the place with the policeman.

"Well, he's definitely not here," he said. "Are you going to be okay?"

"Yes," I said.

"Just make sure you carry that restraining order on you at all times. And I'd get these locks changed if I were you."

I just nodded, and he left. I looked around the remainder of the place, and then ran to my music room and opened the door. It was still intact, thank God. I guess he hadn't gone completely nuts. But he'd taken all the books off the shelves and strewn them on the floor. I went to the kitchen, and he'd unscrewed a plastic rack he'd put up and left half of it hanging from the wall.

"This motherfucker was a sicko, Zora. Be glad he's gone."

I went into the bathroom. The shower curtain was hanging off the pole, and half of the plastic cylinder that we had bought for a dollar to cover the ugly and fading gray pole was missing. That motherfucker.

"We better get started cleaning this shit up," Portia said.

"I can't right now. I swear to God, I can't."

"Well, I ain't leaving here till you get these locks changed, girl."

While Portia looked through the yellow pages and found a

locksmith, I noticed that some of the albums on the floor had been cracked in two. He had disconnected the stereo and cut the cord on the television. I guess this was all my fault. I had turned against him, just like everybody else.

Portia started cleaning the place up, so I began to do the same. By the time the locksmith showed up and changed the lock—which cost me close to a hundred dollars—I was exhausted.

"I think I should spend the night," Portia said.

"No, you don't have to," I said. "He's already gotten his rocks off. He won't be back. Franklin does not like jail."

"You sure?"

"I'm sure. The locks are changed, and there's no way he can get in here."

"What about Jeremiah?"

"I don't want him in here tonight. Not until everything is back to normal."

"Normal?"

"You know what I mean. I'll stay here tonight, and when I wake up, if nothing's happened, then I'll go get him."

"You sure? I think I'll feel better if I just stayed. Arthur won't mind. And I don't want nothing to happen to you, girl-friend. This motherfucker is crazy."

She called Arthur, and I flopped down on the couch. Why did you have to do this to us, Franklin?

I was glad Portia stayed. That was the only reason I was finally able to fall asleep.

"You call the police if he shows up, you got that?" she said in the morning.

"I will," I said, and meant it.

After she left, I went to pick up my son. I can't lie: I was scared as hell, because I kept thinking Franklin might be hid-ing between buildings, just waiting for me. I looked over my shoulder until I got to Mary's house. He hadn't showed up there. Jeremiah was happy to see me, which helped. I picked him up and hugged him and rubbed my cheeks against his.

"If you need to leave him over here again anytime, you just let me know," Mary said. "This don't make no kinda sense. You'd think he would at least think about his baby."

I couldn't say anything to that.

Living alone—without him—took some getting used to. The first few weeks were the worst. Every time I walked into the apartment, I kept hoping he'd be there, just like he'd always been, watching *Love Connection*. I looked for stray socks on the floor, but there weren't any. No sawdust was tracked through the house, no coffee stains were on the counter; there were no towels on the bathroom floor, no overflowing ashtrays. I didn't have anything to complain about now.

Some nights, after I put Jeremiah to bed, I'd take a hot bath and wait for Franklin to walk in to wash my back or stick his hands in the suds and rub between my legs. My breasts would throb and harden at the thought of his tongue licking them, but I'd look down and see my own hands. I'd glance up at the mirror, hoping I could watch him shave, just one more time. I'd dry off and sit on the couch and look around the room, which felt much bigger since he'd been gone. Too big. I wanted to tell him to take his dirty boots off while he lay on the couch, but he wasn't there. I wanted to run my hands through the hair on his chest, but he wasn't there. I wanted to rub my cheeks against his cheekbones, but he wasn't there. I no longer had a man to cook for; I cooked for a family of three anyway. In the mornings, I still brewed a large pot of coffee and had to stop myself from yelling to him that it was ready. I no longer had anyone to play *Wheel of Fortune* with, so I stopped watching it. I started to throw the Scrabble game

in the trash one day, but something told me not to. I truly
hated living without him. And even though Jeremiah helped
me get through many a day, it still felt like someone had a
shovel and was digging in the middle of my heart.

It was usually dark by the time I picked up Jeremiah at
Mary's. And for the longest time, I felt like someone in the
Mafia who had a contract out on her. I was forever looking
over my shoulder. I had nightmares that Franklin hated me so
much he crawled through the fire escape window and was
standing over me in the middle of the night. I'd wake up
sweating and walk into Jeremiah's room to take him back to
bed with me. I was always cold and needed something warm to
touch me. Sometimes I would lay Jeremiah on top of me, just
so I could feel his heartbeat. When I'd try to go back to sleep,
the hissing of the radiator would mesmerize my ears, and I'd
listen to it for hours. I often thought I heard a key turning in
the lock, but I knew it was my imagination.

Right before Christmas, I was downtown, doing some shopping, and I saw a tall, handsome man coming toward me. It
could've been Franklin. I was about to cross the street and run,
but something told me not to. I was going to have to face him
sooner or later, and at least we were in public, so I stood there,
grasping the stroller handle tight and letting the cold wind whip
me in the face. My heart was thumping hard, but by the time he
was close enough to identify, I realized it wasn't Franklin at all.

I felt disappointed.

Christmas was bad.

I was a month late with the rent, but said fuck it. I bought
a five-foot tree, and even though it had been raining outside
for two days, I was determined to have a nice holiday without
him. I had dragged the tree up two flights by myself and spent
half the night decorating it with blue and gold bulbs and a

hundred tiny blinking lights. Jeremiah pulled at the tinsel and was hypnotized by the lights. I bought him seven toys, some corduroy coveralls, his first pair of blue jeans, shirts, pajamas, and some red slippers that zipped.

On Christmas Day, as I watched Jeremiah tear up and try to eat the wrapping paper and cardboard boxes, ignoring the toys, I kept waiting for the buzzer to buzz. But it didn't.

On New Year's Eve, I baby-sat for Portia and Arthur.

I put Sierra and Jeremiah in the big four-poster in the master bedroom and pulled the white comforter up over them. Walking into the living room, I sat at the window. It was so quiet in here it was scary. So I turned the radio on to WBLS, and Angela Bofill was singing "I Try." The words worked their way through me, and I started singing right along with her:

> I try to do
> The best I can for you
> But it seems it's not enough
>
> And you know I care
> Even when you're not there
> But it's not what you want
>
> You close your door
> When I wanna give you more
> And I feel so out of place
>
> And you know it's true
> Don't you think I'm good enough for you
>
> Can't you see
> That you're hurting me
> And I want this pain to stop . . .

I reached over and turned the radio off, then walked back to the window and opened it almost all the way. There was a wet cold outside, and the air felt good. I sat at the window for almost an hour, listening to the cars speeding in the distance on the expressway, watching the tiny people hurrying to get wherever they were going before midnight. The sky was navy blue, and snow started falling in miniature dots.

I got up and put on my pajamas and poured myself a glass of ginger ale. Then I looked at the clock. It was five minutes to twelve. I walked back into the bedroom and turned on the TV. Outside, I could hear firecrackers. They were already starting the countdown in Times Square. Four minutes till the New Year. A new year.

This hurts.

I watched the snow again and clinked my ice cubes.

Three minutes to go.

Together forever, but here I am again, all by myself.

Hundreds of firecrackers were going off now, and they sounded like they were all coming from inside this building.

Two minutes to go.

I straightened the comforter under Jeremiah's chin.

One minute.

I heard screaming and yelling coming from the television, and then I saw the big red ball drop.

I turned toward my baby and saw two tiny black eyes staring up at me. I lifted him out of bed and squeezed him against my chest. I whispered, "Happy New Year, Jeremiah." He closed his eyes again so I laid him back down, though I didn't want to let go of him. I needed to hold something. I needed someone to hold me. Sierra didn't budge.

I tried to fall asleep, to undream everything that's happened, but it was no use. I raked my fingers through my hair, thinking I could scratch away this pain, but I couldn't. That's when I noticed the moon through the clouds. I couldn't take my eyes off it. I looked at it so hard that it seemed to split wide open. It let light in, and that's when I collapsed and said out loud, "Fuck this shit."

I swear, I saw every single one of their faces. Not just Franklin's, but Dillon's and Percy's and Champagne's and David's—all of 'em. All the men that I'd let consume the past ten years of my life. How many times have I let myself deflate and crumble inside their hearts, dived into their dreams and made them my own? How many times have I disappeared into the seams of their worlds and ended up mourning, just like I'm doing now? Just how much are you supposed to give? When do you know it's time to stop? And what am I going to do with this ton of love in my heart? Is there a man out there somewhere who will welcome the weight? Who will savor it and love me right, for once? And what about the passion that's freezing in my bones right now? What am I supposed to do with it? Wait until someone else comes along and thaws me out? How many more broken promises will I have to endure? Is there a man out there who can keep a goddamn promise?

Franklin.

Didn't I make you float? Didn't I give you spring in winter? Didn't I show you rainbows and everything else that moved inside me? I gave birth to your child because I loved you. I stuck by you when you were broke, because I loved you. I stuck by you for *everything,* because *I loved you.* So tell me, goddammit, wasn't that enough?

32

I fucked up royally this time. Of all the sneaky-ass ways to make her point. Calling the white man on me. Zora knew that would do it—set me off. She always knew how I felt about 'em. And after I hung up the phone, the whole room just caved in on top of me. Yeah, I had threatened her, but I didn't mean that shit. Couldn't she see that I was just in pain? Naw, 'cause she didn't look. And yeah, I had told her I was leaving, but all I wanted her to do was ask me to stay. But she didn't. She was tired of my shit, and I was tired of hers.

I sat there in that empty-ass apartment, looking at all the stuff I made, and just like somebody had wound me up, I left. I stopped at the liquor store and bought a fifth of Jack Daniel's and drank it while I walked all the way to Just One Look. Why she have to do this to me? All she think about is herself and that kid. Is this what you do to somebody you supposed to love? I thought this shit was about thick and thin, hanging in there, getting through the rough parts, but I guess I was wrong. When I got there, I sat down on the barstool and waited. Sooner or later he'd be coming in here, I just knew it. When I felt somebody thump me on my head, I knew it was Jimmy.

"Who beat you up?" Terri asked.

"Everybody, and I hope not you too."

"I'm here to save you," she said, and bent down to kiss me on my cheek. This time I couldn't afford to resist. I was so fucked up that I pushed her face around and kissed her right there in the bar.

She stepped back. "Frankie? What's happened to *you*? You woke up from the dead, or what?"

"I'm in a jam, Theresa."

"And?"

"I need someplace to stay for a few weeks."

"And you asking me?"

"I know I was in a shitty mood the last time I saw you, but things have changed."

"Look, Franklin, let's not kid ourselves. You look like that woman just broke your damn heart, and ain't no sense in you trying to pretend like you want me. If you need a place to stay, you've got a place to stay, all right?"

I looked at her. I ain't never gave her enough credit.

"Thanks, Theresa. I appreciate this."

"So when you wanna come over? Now?"

"Naw, not now. I got something I gotta do first. What time you leave for work?"

"I'm on vacation for three days."

"Then look for me sometime between tonight and tomorrow."

"You black motherfucker!"

Now, *that* was Jimmy.

I turned to look at him and couldn't believe my damn eyes. Jimmy musta lost thirty, forty pounds.

"Hey, Jimmy. How you been, man?"

Theresa tapped me on the shoulder and said she'd see me later.

"You blind or something? Good, man. Damn good. What about you?" he asked.

"I need something," I said to him.

"Get the fuck outta here, Frankie. Like what?"

"Anything and everything. The works."

"You must be losing your mind, man. What's going on?"

"Nothing, man. You got anything or not?"

"It's that woman, ain't it?"

"Maybe, maybe not. The world don't stop because of no fuckin' woman."

"She broke your fuckin' heart, is that it? What'd you do to her, Frankie? Huh?"

"Nothing. Not a goddamn thing. I'm outta there."

"Well, what happened? Talk to me, Frankie. Goddamn."

"She called the white man on me, man. Can you believe that shit?"

"So what did you do to her?"

"I didn't bring home the bacon."

"So why not? You was working, wasn't you?"

"Not in the past few months."

"Why not?"

" 'Cause I got hurt on the job, and then I didn't feel like it."

"So you got what the fuck you deserved, motherfucker."

"Go ahead, rub salt into a open wound. What you got?"

"Frankie, it ain't no need in you totally fuckin' up, man, come on. Dope ain't even your thang. Why let some woman lead you in the wrong direction, man?"

"I just need something to get me through tonight, that's all."

Jimmy looked at me and sighed. "All right, I'ma let you have this shit, but don't come back, man. 'Cause if you do, the answer gon' be no. I know I still owe you some money, but this ain't how I planned on paying you back. And you don't wanna get back into this shit, Frankie. Look at me."

"Yeah, well, thirty more pounds, and that's when you should quit."

"I'll be right back."

He was gone a few minutes, and when he came back, he handed me a little brown lunch bag. I asked him what ever happened about the court thing, and he just said they threw it outta court for lack of evidence. That was good enough for me. I split.

Some things you never forget. Like how easy it is to tie yourself up and where to hit it. The cocaine went straight to my brain and exploded. Blood dripped on the bathroom floor, but I didn't give a fuck. The only thing on my mind was getting my shit together so I could get outta here. But first I wanted to make sure Zora was gon' know I was gone. I ran upstairs and got my power saw and came back down. I started throwing books off the shelf and was pissed when wasn't no more left to throw. This bookcase was a work of fuckin' art, and she didn't even appreciate it. I ran back upstairs and got my ax and started chopping. I heard the wood crack, and I had to move out of the way when the damn thing almost fell over.

After that I just went crazy. I'd go to the bathroom and cook up some more and do it. I was breaking up things so fast I couldn't even slow down long enough to realize what was mine and what wasn't. By the time I finished, it was so much sawdust in here that I couldn't breathe, so I opened all the damn windows. My heart felt like it was gon' pop outta my goddamn chest, and it wouldn't slow down. What the fuck was I doing? And what did I just do? I had to get outta here, go somewhere, but I didn't know where.

I slammed the door and ran downstairs, since walking was outta the question. I was all the way in Queens when I saw the fuckin' sun come up. My mouth felt like chalk was in it, but at least my fuckin' heart had slowed down. I finally came to a park and sat down on a bench. But I couldn't sit up, so I laid down.

When I woke up, I didn't know where I was. All I did know was that I didn't have no address or no woman no more.

It didn't take me but a couple minutes to grab my shit and get it outta there. I couldn't believe the mess I made, but fuck it. I had a cab wait for me while I made three trips. I almost couldn't close the cab door on the last one.

Terri was thoughtful. She tried her best to do everything she could to make me comfortable.

"You don't have to feel obligated to sleep with me unless you just want to," she said, handing me some blankets.

I really didn't wanna sleep with her, but I needed somebody close to me, even if all I could do was pretend it was Zora. "Would you mind if I slept with you tonight?" I asked.

Her face lit up, and she grabbed back the blankets.

In the morning, I made myself a vow. If I was gon' clean up my act and get my shit together, I was gon' have to make some changes. Number one, I was gon' have to cut out all this fuckin' drinking. Number two, I was going back to school. And number three, even though I missed Zora and my son already, I wasn't gon' show my face over there until I felt strong enough to look her in the eye and tell her that I was sorry.

It took three months.

33

When I heard the buzzer, I almost dropped Jeremiah on the floor. The only person that pressed on it like that was Franklin. I ran toward the door. Then I made myself slow down. I was nervous. Didn't know what to expect. I clutched Jeremiah, and from the top of the stairwell, I saw Franklin's broad shoulders spread across the glass in the door. When I got to the bottom step, I looked at him.

"Ain't you gon' open the door?" he called through the door.

"Are you going to kill me?"

"Yeah, I got a gun full of bullets I been saving just for you. Come on, Zora, I just wanna see my son."

I opened the door slowly and then backed away. My heart was beating like 100 mph. Jeremiah was drooling on my sweatshirt.

"He's getting big, huh?" he said.

I nodded and turned toward the stairs, still clinging to Jeremiah and afraid that Franklin just might have a gun, if he hated me as much as I thought he did. I reluctantly went up the stairs first. A man wouldn't shoot a woman in the back.

The first thing he did once we got inside was look around.

I guess he wanted to see what I'd managed to salvage, and I was glad I had replaced lots of things. The place looked even better than when he lived here. I put Jeremiah down on the floor. Franklin had on a leather jacket, which I had never seen before, and he didn't take it off or that Sherlock Holmes hat he was wearing. He looked like he was back down to his old size, and for some reason he looked much taller than I remembered. Jeremiah walked over and pulled his pants leg. He looked like a toy standing next to Franklin. Franklin smiled at him and picked him up. I found myself smiling too. This is his Daddy, I kept thinking to myself. His Daddy. He kissed Jeremiah on the lips and held him away and looked at him. "How you doing, my son, my son?"

This broke my heart.

"He's got so big. Look at the feet on this kid," he said. Jeremiah was touching Franklin's face, and Franklin rubbed noses with him. Jeremiah giggled, and then Franklin started looking at me. He put Jeremiah down.

"Thanks," he said. "That's all I wanted, to see my son."

Before I knew what to say, like, "Please don't leave yet," he already had his hand on the doorknob. The next thing I knew, he was out the door. I ran to the top of the stairs and yelled down, "Anytime you want to see him, you can, Franklin. He'll always be your son."

I didn't hear him answer, so I went back inside the apartment and flopped down on the couch. Jeremiah was climbing on a chair, trying to get something. I could hardly see through the tears in my eyes—he was a little blue blur. I wiped my eyes clear of all tears, but others replaced them.

I still didn't know where he lived or how I could get in touch with him if I wanted to. And like everything else I'd done, with the exception of giving birth, I wished I could rewind this movie and take it from the top.

*   *   *

Jeremiah was running through the house when the doorbell rang again, not fifteen minutes after Franklin had left. My heart jumped. I wanted to tell Jeremiah that that was probably his Daddy, coming back. After seeing us, he realized he missed us and still loved us and had had enough time to think and get his head back together.

I raced downstairs as fast as I could. I was going to run into his arms and squeeze him and tell him how much I still loved him and how much I've missed him and God, was I glad he's back. But it wasn't Franklin. It was someone else, just as big. His chest took up the whole window, and I couldn't see his face. Until he bent down. It was Franklin's father.

I opened the door, wondering why he was here.

"Hello, Zora. I'm so sorry to bother you like this, honey, but can I come in?"

"Sure, come on up."

"Would you look at my grandson? Come here, fella."

He reached and took Jeremiah out of my arms, and I started upstairs, trying to figure out what he was doing here. I knew something had happened.

"Can I get you something?"

"No, baby. Where's Franklin?"

"Franklin doesn't live here anymore, Mr. Swift."

"You two just had a child. When did all this happen?"

"Right after Thanksgiving."

"Where's he living?"

"I don't know."

"Well, doesn't he stay in touch?"

"As a matter of fact, you just missed him by a few minutes. It was the first time he's been back. But he didn't tell me where he's living. I think he'll come back soon."

"Well, what in the world happened, baby?"

"It's a long story, Mr. Swift."

"I've got time."

I sat down on the couch, and he sat down on a chair, with Jeremiah on his lap.

"Franklin's been laid off on and off for over a year. I've tried to be understanding and patient, but after a while it got to the point where I couldn't handle it all—I just couldn't. There never seemed to be any reward, any relief. It was too much for both of us."

"Do you still love him?"

"Yes, I do."

"Well, I'm glad to hear that. Seems like everybody's world is collapsing."

"Is something wrong?"

He said he'd tried calling, but the number had been changed. I was waiting for him to say Darlene's name, and I was holding my breath when he said it. Before he could finish telling me that she'd shot herself, all I was thinking was, Please don't let her be dead. That would do Franklin in. When I heard him say she was in the hospital, that was almost good enough. Then he gave me the details, which I truly could've done without. He said she'd done it at their house, but he wasn't home. Darlene had been drinking and had told Mrs. Swift that she wanted to talk. Naturally, Mrs. Swift didn't feel like listening, so Darlene covered the living room floor with plastic, found one of Mr. Swift's guns, and did it right there. Since she was drunk, she had only grazed her head. He said she'd even left a note, obviously meant for Mrs. Swift, that said, "I told you I wanted to talk." I swear, I sat there, watching his lips move until I didn't hear any sound coming out. I looked at him so hard that for the first time I saw how much Franklin looked like him. Then I couldn't believe that Franklin's father was really sitting in my living room with his grandson on his lap, telling me that his daughter had just shot herself in his house. What connection did I have to this man—this family? Well, they were my family in a way, weren't they? "Is there anything I can do?"

"I would like to find my son," he said.

I wished I had asked Franklin where he lived. How stupid of me. "I don't know what to tell you, Mr. Swift. I have no idea where he's living now. He didn't tell me. How is Mrs. Swift handling this?"

"She's mad as hell."

It sounded just like the bitch, but of course I couldn't say that. Jeremiah climbed down off his Grandpa's lap and went to play in the toilet. Usually, I stop him, but right now I couldn't.

"I moved out," he blurted.

"Moved out?"

"I haven't had a real marriage in twenty-four years, baby. I've despised that woman for so long that I even had myself fooled. But there's only so much scotch you can drink. That won't get me through this. She's full of hatred, and all these years I've let her unload it on our children. And look what's happened. Franklin is a good man, you know. He's just spent his whole life trying to prove to us that he's worth our love. And poor Darlene. So vulnerable. Franklin is too, really, but he's just done a better job of disguising it."

"No, he hasn't," I said, before I even realized it.

"Well, it's a shame that it took something like this for me to understand, but she'll be living with me when she gets out of the hospital. This time, I want to make sure she's cared for."

"Well, that'll help her recover, I'm sure."

He was popping his knuckles, one by one. Then he took a pen and some kind of receipt out of his jacket and wrote on it. "Well, look. If you hear from Franklin, give him this number where I can be reached." He stood up, as massive as his son. "You take care, and if there's anything you need, you use that number."

"Thank you. Maybe Jeremiah and I'll come visit you soon."

"That'd be nice," he said, and kissed me on the cheek. I walked him downstairs and watched him through the glass until I couldn't see him anymore. When I heard Jeremiah yell out "Mama," I looked up, and he was standing at the top of the stairs. I ran up three at a time and grabbed him before he was able to even think about taking another step. Lord knows I'd die if anything ever happened to my son.

34

I went back to work.

I realized that since I was good at construction, then that's what the fuck I'd have to do till I could get enough education to do something better. School was kicking my ass, but I surprised myself. I'm not as dumb as I thought I was. I was learning how to write a decent sentence, and in a few short weeks in this psychology class I realized something I already knew: that I hated my mother. But what I didn't realize was that I used every woman I ever had, trying to get them to make up for what my Moms never gave me. This was some sick shit, I thought, but I fit the bill.

I reopened my membership at the gym and started pumping iron again. Now I'm back down to 215. I look good, if I do say so myself. And even though Terri's been real cool, I knew she was starting to get attached to me and shit, so I found myself a room, which is where I been living for the past month.

I miss Zora and Jeremiah, but I ain't been back over there since that last time, and that was in February. Hell, it's June now. I did send her a two-hundred-dollar money order, but I didn't put no return address on the envelope.

All I been doing is working, studying, and doing my woodworking. I been trying not to think about either one of 'em, and sometimes I fool myself by pretending that don't neither one of 'em exist. But that ain't got me nowhere. Every time I masturbate, it's Zora who's stroking me. Every time I fucked Terri, the only way I could come was if I pretended it was Zora. And sometimes, late at night, I still walk by Zora's apartment and stand across the street behind a tree, smoking a cigarette, and stare up at her through the window. I've watched her pushing the laundry cart through the snow, with Jeremiah sitting on top. I've watched her lug groceries home in the rain, and I knew that if we could ever start all over, she wouldn't have to do so much. I know I want her back, but I still need more time. Our whole problem was about bad timing. I didn't have nothing besides a big dick to offer her when I met her, and I can't go back until I got more than that.

I wonder would it matter to her if she knew I finally got my divorce? It's probably too late now. And lately I been wondering if she coulda met somebody else, and if so, does my son call him Daddy? I was torturing myself with this question, really, and figured there was only one way to find out.

I stood outside on the steps for the longest time before ringing the buzzer. I didn't know what I was gon' say to her, really. I laid on the buzzer and waited.

She looked even better than she did last time. And my son—what a good-lookin' kid.

"How you doing?" I asked her, after I sat down.

"Just fine. And you?"

"I'm all right. You looking good," I said. I hope this didn't mean she was fucking somebody else and enjoying it.

"So do you, Franklin."

Damn, something sure smelled good. Something told me not to come over here around dinnertime all hungry and shit. I been living offa sardines and crackers. "So is everything going all right?" I asked.

"Yeah."

"How's the singing going?"

"I'm doing more writing than singing these days."

"No shit. Anything good happening?"

"I sold one," she said, so low I couldn't hardly hear her.

"Speak up, baby. Did you just mumble that you sold one?"

"Yeah."

"Shit. Well, congratulations! You don't sound too thrilled about it."

"I am, really."

"I always knew you'd make it, baby. But how come you ain't singing?"

"You want the truth?"

"I always have."

"Because I really couldn't stand the idea of being on the road and leaving Jeremiah all the time. Plus I realized that I don't have to be on a stage to make my music come alive."

"You feel good about this, then?"

"I do."

"I miss your singing, Zora." I couldn't believe I just said that, but fuck it, I want her to know. "And I miss you." I figured wasn't no sense in lying. Jeremiah was climbing on my shoulders and I was digging every minute of it. But I didn't come over here to cop no plea. I didn't come over here to beg her to take me back either. I just wanted her to know how I still felt.

"I miss you too, Franklin."

That was music to my ears. "So I see you feeding my son. Look at these little ham-hock thighs and the hands on this kid. Baseball mitts, right?"

"His doctor said he's in the ninetieth percentile for his age group. So. How've you been doing, for real?"

"I'm in school."

"What kind of school?"

"College."

"Are you serious, Franklin? That's wonderful!"

"I'm back doing construction too. Probably will be till I get my degree."

"I can't tell you how glad I am to hear this. I've known all along that you had it in you."

I could tell she was being sincere, and I knew that deep down she was probably thinking, What took you so long, motherfucker? But Zora knows what and when to say shit, and I appreciated it. Neither one of us said anything for what seemed like hours. We just kinda looked at each other like fools.

"What you thinking about?" I asked.

"You really want to know?"

"Yeah."

"What made you come over here today?"

"Because I couldn't come until I knew I wasn't mad no more. And I couldn't come until I could hold my head up like a man and not be embarrassed about what I was or what I wasn't. I couldn't come back and face you like this until I felt good about being Franklin again. And I couldn't come back here until I could tell you I'm sorry."

She looked up at me, and I saw how glassy her eyes was—I mean were. School is helping me correct this kinda shit. "I'm sorry," I said.

"And I'm sorry too," she said.

"You know, I took a lotta things for granted, and since I been by myself, all I've had time to do is think. Put some things in perspective. And you wanna know what conclusions I came to?"

She nodded.

"That you're the best thing that ever happened to me, and if I fucked up and lost you, then it's my own damn fault."

"You haven't lost me, Franklin."

"You ain't met nobody else?"

"No. What about you?"

"Naw. I been too busy anyway."

"You don't know how many nights I've prayed for this—that you'd come back to us."

"I ain't back, baby."

"You're not?"

"I need more time. I still got quite a few bricks to lay in order to make sure my foundation is solid. I'm sick of doing things half-ass. This time I wanna do it right. But are you telling me that you would want me to come back?"

"My heart does, but a lot has happened since *I* saw *you* too."

"Like what?"

"Like we're moving."

"Moving where?"

"Back to Toledo."

"Why?"

"Because I don't want to live in New York anymore."

"Why not?"

"Because I'm tired, Franklin, and I want to slow down."

"When you doing all this moving?"

"In August."

"And you was just gon' take my son and leave without telling me?"

"I didn't know where to find you. I thought you'd forgotten about us. You never come by, and I—"

"What if I asked you not to leave?" Go ahead and tell me your mind is already made up. Go ahead, make me beg.

"I have to go."

"You don't have to do nothing but die."

"I quit my job already, Franklin."

"So you can get another one."

"It's more to it than that. I want to raise our son so he'll know what it's like to play in the grass and roll in the dirt without me having to take him to a damn park to do it. I want him to grow up where he can be a child."

"You can do that in Queens," I said.

She just looked at me like I was crazy.

"And I'm going back to church and sing where it's always made me feel the best. And I'll write music. Besides, I got another teaching job."

"I thought you was tired of teaching."

"Like you said, you get to learn a lot of things when you're by yourself."

Was this room spinning, or was it just me? Was I about to lose Zora and my son forever? I felt helpless, like nothing I said was gon' get her to understand that I still wanted her, but I also wanted her to do whatever she thought was gon' be best for her and our son. You can't ask a woman to put her love on hold, though, can you? You can't ask her to wait until you finish growing up.

"Franklin?"

"Yeah."

"We're not leaving you; we're just relocating. You've already been gone long enough for me to have a change of heart, but understand this: I love you just as much now as I did three years ago. We've had some rough times, and maybe time might help us both; I don't know. But you see that little boy over there? He's ours. We made him. And if you ever get your divorce and you feel like you're ready, come get us."

I was just about to tell her about my divorce, but something told me not to. Not yet. "You can't promise me you gon' be sitting around waiting for me, baby."

"I didn't say we were going to be waiting. Our lives need to keep going, Franklin. That's been a big part of our problem. I think we both kind of disappeared somewhere along the way and just stopped moving altogether."

"You always was big on taking risks. You let that boy play in the toilet like that?" Before she could answer, I got up and lifted Jeremiah up in the air. "Do I smell something burning?"

She sniffed the air. "Nope." Then she started grinning. "Would you like to have dinner with us?"

"What you got?"

"Meat loaf, scalloped potatoes . . ."

"Yeah, since you insist. Is it ready?"

"Yes, it's ready. Jeremiah's already eaten, and I was just about to give him his bath when you got here."

"You mind if I give it to him?" I asked.

She looked surprised. "Do you know how?"

I took Jeremiah's clothes off, went upstairs, and put the boy in the bathtub. I rubbed him down with them baby bubbles, splashed water on him, dried his little ass off, wrapped a towel around him, went back downstairs, held him up in the air and said, "Where you want him?"

"In his crib," she said, and took him back upstairs. I followed her and watched her put his pajamas on.

"Where's his bottle?"

"I don't give him one at night."

"Well, won't he start crying?"

"Nope."

"No shit." I bent down and kissed him, and that was that. When we got back downstairs, I knew which plate was mine, 'cause it was a pile of food on it.

"Franklin, did you ever talk to your father?"

"About what?"

"You never called him or anything?"

"No, why should I? I ain't talked to nobody." I knew this had something to do with my sister. "It's Darlene, ain't it? Go on, tell me."

"First of all, she's okay."

"How do you know that?"

"Because I've talked to your father since he came over here to tell me what happened."

"Which was what?"

"That she tried to shoot herself. But she's okay now."

"She did *what?*"

"Back in February. But we didn't know how to find you, so your father left his number. He really wanted to see you, Franklin."

"What you mean, he left his number?"

"He moved out."

"Get the fuck outta here. You mean to tell me that *my* Pops, the chump, done left *my* Moms, the bitch?"

"Yes, he did."

I felt myself smiling. So finally you decided to be a man, huh?

"Darlene's living with him," I said.

"No shit."

"No shit."

"You still got that number handy?"

"Of course I do."

She opened a drawer and handed this piece of paper to me. I looked at it, then put it in my pocket. When we finished eating, we went back into the living room, and I sat down on the couch. Zora sat in a chair on the other side of the room.

"Why don't you come sit next to me?" I asked.

"Because I'm afraid of what I might do."

"Show me what you scared you might do," I said. She pressed both hands on the arms of the chair, pushed herself up, and pranced over to me. Then she bent down and kissed me. I closed my eyes, and just when I was getting used to her lips again, she stopped. "Is that it?"

Zora was laughing.

"What's so funny?" I asked, even though I was laughing now too. She stood up, stepped back, and unzipped her blue jeans. Then she pulled her Saratoga T-shirt over her head and took off her bra. Goddamn. Part of my problem in life is that I want everything now, so I persuaded Tarzan to chill out for the time being and decided to stretch this night out. "Can I ask you a big favor, baby?"

"It depends," she said.

"You feel like a quick game of Scrabble?"

She walked over and got the game, handed it to me, then looked me dead in the eyes. "Set 'em up," she said.